THE REINCARNATION OF LEONARD

The MIS - BELIEVER

THE REINCARNATION OF LEONARD

The MIS - BELIEVER

GLENN SWANSON

Studio of Books LLC
5900 Balcones Drive Suite 100
Austin, Texas 78731
www.studioofbooks.org
Hotline: (254) 800-1183

Ordering Information:
Special discounts are available on quantity purchases by corporations, associations, and others. For details, contact the publisher at the address above.

Printed in the United States of America.

ISBN-13: Softcover   978-1-964148-20-5
          eBook   978-1-964148-21-2

Library of Congress Control Number: 2024908320

Table of Contents

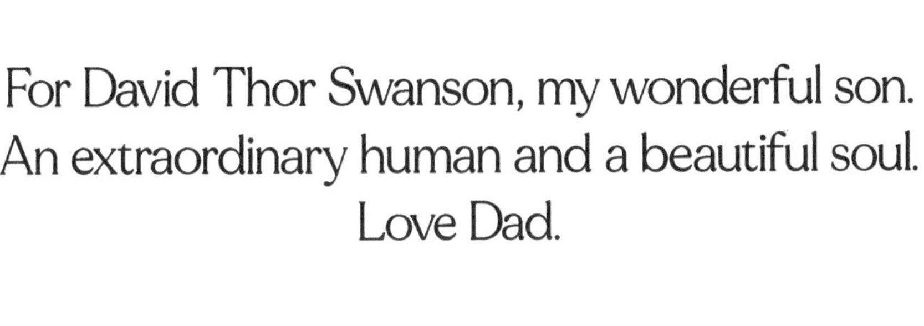

For David Thor Swanson, my wonderful son.
An extraordinary human and a beautiful soul.
Love Dad.

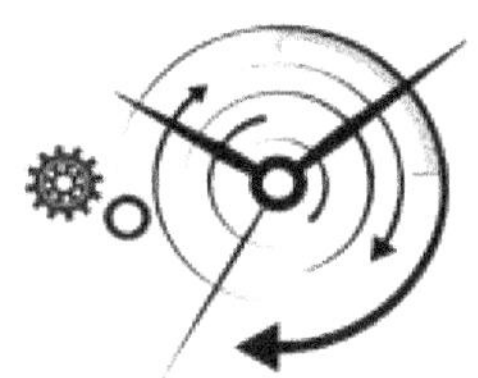

1 - Revenge

The leather spine of the heavy book was cracked as if it had lain open on this page often. In the dim twilight that filtered through the drapes, I read through the fine, spidery script that covered the margins. The incantation was unfamiliar, but I noticed my name scrawled several times. If this wasn't indication enough, the parchment page was marked with a butterfly's wing.

It might have been from a moth, a giant Luna moth maybe , I thought as I held it up. Light transfused through the delicate material between the ribs. The pale green powder left traces on the tips of my fingers, and on the page of the book, finer than the dust that had settled everywhere in the room. It was so like him to have something so exotic performing such a mundane task; the ancient Greek statue propping open the door, or the bronze dagger tossed carelessly aside, covered in putty. There was a handful of amber strewn in the bottom of the long-dry fish tank.

He was like that: off collecting treasures through the centuries, then ending up with no use for them, and no way to explain his possession of them.

My eyes traced the fragile veins in the translucent material. My mind wandered. He probably collected this on one of his expeditions to Nepal or Bangladesh.

Maybe that's where I would find him now. Maybe that's where I should look. Maybe I could even sneak up on him as he enjoyed hookah in some back-alley dive.

But as surely as I would be out of place there, the locals would take him to heart. They wouldn't question his powers, but gratefully accept his gifts, swallowing his smooth promises and lead him where he wished to go. They would labor for him, digging up the tombs and even carting back the artifacts. They would cover for him, they always have. They would warn him, even protect him for the gold he could so easily produce.

Besides, even if I could narrow it down to a thousand small towns, it would take me years to feel my way through them. He'd have what he came for and be long gone by then, of course. The clues would grow cold, the traces would fade, and I'd have to start my search over, again.

No, the answer was in this room: his lair, his sanctuary. The secrets were here in his personal effects. I felt it the moment I broke in, but just to be certain, I put my initial feeling to the test.

Making sure the wing marked the exact spot on the page I replaced the tome on the shelf and brushed the light green residue from my fingertips as I put my back to the door. I replayed my entry and ran my fingers lightly across everything in the room.

The leather couch, heavy with his scent. The ebony table inlaid with the zodiac. The brass astrolabe and the massive, squat telescope in the window alcove. I didn't have to see in the dim light— my fingers tingled at the nearness of him.

The books! The books made my senses flair. My fingertips tingled at each of the arcane titles embossed on the spines. The deep stamps in the leather were like braille . I could trace his thoughts in these books he had so painstakingly collected and studied.

I opened book after book to find his notes filling the pages. Spells were written in the margins. Equations and values were scribbled on tide charts ripped from almanacs and left between the pages.

Suddenly, I knew he was searching, too. Searching for a way to solve this problem of immortality. Searching for enough time to put his theories into effect, while being hunted. Searching for the knowledge in these dusty tomes that might give him a safe haven until he finds a restful end.

That realization gave me the first glimmer of hope I'd had in a long time. I felt refreshed and renewed knowing he was no longer enjoying leading me on a chase through the ages. Knowing this fugitive felt my pursuit gave my spirits a lift. Knowing my dogged tenacity was finally bearing fruit strengthened my resolve. I could sense there was an end now. The maze had a solution. I knew I only had to wait a day or two, at most, to face him. The chase had a capture. The criminal would feel justice. My way.

I took the heavy book marked with the wing down once again. I let my index finger separate the pages he found so intriguing. I crossed to the couch and sat with the book on my lap. The moth wing fell, fluttering in the heavy, still air. It twisted and turned in the dim light in a descent under the ebony table. It came to rest on some dust balls gathered in the gloom.

I stared hard at the omen I read in this simple act of gravity. Flying with one wing would be like walking in circles. A man with no conscience, such as he, must be handicapped. And, just as the dust motes gathered, dust to dust, he would be back. Everything would come full circle. The murderer would be back. Soon.

I sat back to read his books in the dim light. I would learn his secrets while I waited for him. After all, the curses I had spoken on my son's grave had given me forever, too.

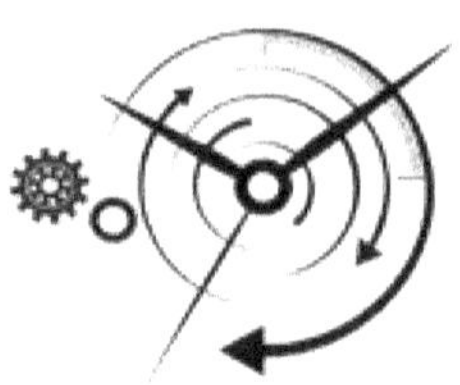

2 - Monte

The slightest noise startled me from my unintended slumber. I froze, straining to hear. After an interminable roaring silence, the doorknob crept clockwise until stopped by the lock. The pressure remained against the mechanism, testing, and then imperceptibly, the handle was eased back. I measured the time by the drips of cold sweat that dripped off my brow . Even when the salt stung my eyes, I dared not move to wipe my brow. My pulse hammered in my ears, and I realized I hadn't yet taken a breath since I was startled into awareness . The noise of that cautious sip of air almost overpowered the scratch of metal against metal, or did I imagine it?

I sat with every muscle tense, holding the uncomfortable position of immobility. My neck was crooked, off at an odd angle, my arms lying as they had fallen away from my body as I slept. Slowly, I turned my head as I lifted it, so I could study the door. I brushed the hair and the sweat from my face ever so cautiously. The empty silence lasted so long; I was about to stand when the metallic click of the tumblers being gently forced echoed. I eased off the thick cushions, puzzled by whom else might this be if not Grigori.

Carefully, I moved across the Turkish carpet, sidling to the door. The glow invading the small space under the sill pulsed. The last tumbler succumbed to the skill of the interloper. As the door cracked open, I pushed back behind the door, into the curtain of trench coats and sweaters hung by their necks, folding them about me, hoping for even an instant of surprise.

The door paused, barely open. From within the cloak of outerwear, I waited, noticing only the strange shadow that worried at the entrance. Finally, as though appeased by the lack of response to the intrusion thus far, the door swung inward, blocking my view.

I almost grabbed the hand that touched the edge of the door to ease it shut, but the continued caution of the unknown person made me wait, assured they were unaware.

The figure that slipped into the room, then pushed the door shut with its back stayed pressed against the door, alert. He grasped something on a chain to his chest, protectively, or perhaps to shield the glow emanating from between his fingers. The light that spilled out pulsed as he moved the amulet in front of him, scanning the room.

He moved into the center of the room, his embroidered coat flowing out, hiding his legs. He let his hand fall away from the amulet so he could run his fingertips across the surfaces in the room, much as I had done. The light cast weird shadows across his face, lit the room gently, and I felt, somehow, it sought me out. He moved through an inner door, out of my sight. I strained to locate him, but the heavy carpets and his light step did not betray his movements. Only the fading glow gave away his presence.

It took an instant to step across the room. Peering into the empty bedchamber, I heard the quiet noises of bottles being moved off the glass shelves of the medicine cabinet. Furtive noises that assured me this was not who I sought but created an even more gaping dilemma. Steadying myself on the mahogany post of the bed, I advanced, unsure if I was going to attack or confront this searcher.

The point became moot, for even with all my stealth, as I approached and peered through the hinge-side crack between the door and the jamb, I found myself being studied by a set of pale eyes in the bathroom mirror. I could feel his gaze, yet he didn't turn. The pulsing light of his amulet accentuated his high cheekbones and fastidious goatee. His eyes in the mirror never left mine, boring into me, reading, probing.

The gems on the rings on the hand frozen on the cabinet flashed. He dusted his fingertips against his thumb and swung the mirrored cabinet door shut with just the nail of his index finger. The urge to act returned with the breaking of the visual contact, the rapier thrust of his will was withdrawn. I pushed the door and stepped into the open, but he didn't move. He dropped both hands to the edge of the porcelain sink, and leaned forward, his head bowed.

"I didn't expect another seeker," he said, without turning, menacing with his nonchalance.

I felt the expectation for my answer build in the silence but resisted. The empty space was filled only with the dust motes reflecting the greenish light.

He sighed, realizing the contest of wills was at a stand still. The smooth fabric of his coat shimmered as he turned. The halo cast by his amulet concentrated and bulged out toward me. A flicker of emotion broke through his disciplined affect, but was quickly masked; still, the eyes studied me anew, he leaned back against the sink and put his hand to his jaw. He noticed my glance at his strange gem.

He lifted and dropped the amulet down into the high-buttoned collar of his coat, then arranged the chain to lay flat. The light was swallowed, and the gloom of the curtained room again obscured his features.

"Montissio Favero," he said and bowed his head slightly. "But please, call me Monte."

"Leonard," I answered.

"Only Leonard?"

"I stopped being more than 'just Leonard' long ago," I said, the catch in my voice as the memories that were flung about by the sudden gale of emotion in my mind was noted by those eyes. I could see a glint of intuition that was just as quickly concealed.

"You have lost something to him as well," he said. "There is a dark lust to your presence."

"Is that what your gem points out to you?" I asked.

"No, your pain permeates your soul. Your single-mindedness leaves little left for the mundane, such as grooming. If you continue, you will be thought quite mad."

"I haven't cared for so long what any feel or say about me." I rubbed my face and pushed the hair back from my eyes. Changing the subject, I said, "You, on the other hand, want something from Grigori. You seek, but not the man."

"True enough, but perhaps there is a better place than the private bath of our quarry to acquaint ourselves?" he said, then pushed by me.

I was left menacing no one, so I followed.

In the kitchen, he swiftly went through the cabinets, touching little, but peering deeply. The drawers received similar attention before he spoke again, as before, not turning, assured of his audience.

"Grigori, is that how you know him? How quaint. Tell me, why did you leave his pleasant company in the first place?"

I spoke, "I only know that my son died by this cursed one's hand. I will have my retribution."

There was a stony silence, a new depth of appraisal ending in a sigh.

"Your pain has a jagged edge, but no safe handle," he said.

"Perhaps I am not seeking a haven," I paused when the realization hit me, "as are you."

His eyes flashed the betrayal of his truth, and before he could again mask the emotions, fear of his transparency flickered. His manner became unctuous, formal and yet aloof. He engaged me from a great gulf of protective distance.

"And you want nothing?"

"I want him in hell."

There was that sudden antagonism, because from the same person we wanted immiscible results. I knew, as did he, so we both stepped back from that dangerous edge.

He continued to peer into the accumulation of Grigori's life, lightly touching the tableware strewn in the drawer, the egg timer on the shelf, and the handles on the cupboard doors. Opening one after another, it was strange to see there was not a bit of food. He reached toward a glass jar with a bouquet of knives but cast a quick glance at me and moved on with his sensing.

"What is it you seek, Monte?"

He opened his mouth to answer, then paused and said, "I…" He stopped there, and then said, "We…" and again, stopped. "We have much to talk about," he said finally, "but not here."

"Who is 'we'," I asked him.

"There are those who seek answers in the quieter places of this hectic time. I am looking for clues to unasked questions, and to ask is to betray the desire. Those who would be able to answer your questions are not fond of publicity."

With that dismissal, he pulled his amulet up by the chain. In a curious, two-handed ritual caress, he held the gem up to his forehead, paused meditatively and then went about his search much less circumspectly, as if his purpose was no longer secret.

His amulet glowed irregularly as he went about sensing; one hand protectively shielding the gem, the other with fingers spread wide, barely passing over the artifacts of Grigori's life. He seemed disappointed at the results of his scan. He tucked the pendant back into his coat again and turned on me.

"You have contaminated the scene. I suppose you have been pawing over his effects, leaving little enough untouched that I waste my time here. I think this is a worthless avenue now, he'll know this lair has been compromised and never return. Little here is unique. His other safe houses are filled with the same detritus of his life. I thought I was finally close to some answers, but you have ruined that hope."

"You imagine some importance in your life of secrets I don't share. I care about sending a monster to hell. I'm not going to buy into some mystic mumbo-jumbo. There is revenge to be had, justice to be meted out and when the pain in my heart is assuaged with his blood, I'll rest. Until then, I'm content to lie in wait. You were surprised, I see no reason he won't also be taken by guile. Your confidence seems unreasonable."

He pulled another, though smaller, gem on a chain from his pocket. It shone the green glow unevenly, seemingly attracted to me. He flipped it to me. "When you are ready for answers."

"When you tire of your angst, you'll find the need for more information. Just because you hurt, doesn't make your cause noble. Few care little, most not at all. Seldom are men granted the audience of those who bear the burden of the greatest cares of this world. Ask yourself if you want your son's death to mean more than petty revenge. If you tire of fantasizing that your dark pleasure will heal your soul or bring back your son, then maybe we can talk ." He laid a small card on the table by the door.

"I know that neither my soul nor his is to benefit from my spilling this blood, but when there is nothing left, the emptiness will be a welcome relief. You'll not convince me of anything less."

"A knife in his back would bring an end but could end more lives than you could know. His death may mean your son will stay lost to you, too. Perhaps your revenge is not as incongruent to our aims as you might imagine."

"Death is what I seek." The leather sofa creaked as I sat. I folded my arms and tapped the tip of my dagger against my cheek.

"Naively enough, you imagine I don't." He made a mocking bow, and at the door, he paused one more time. Again, without turning, tapping the card he said, "The church. There are answers and even ways your son might yet be saved." And then, he was gone.

I was frozen in the mental turmoil of trying to reconcile that drip of hope with the anguish in my soul. I didn't feel the tip of the dagger had lacerated my cheek.

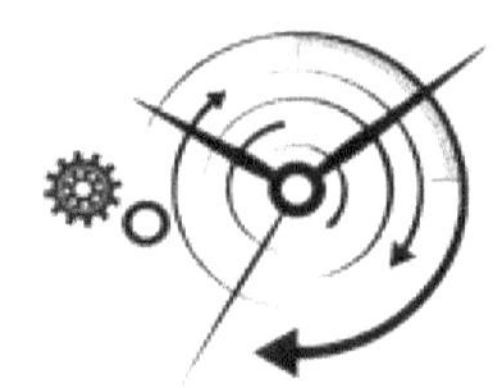

3 - Hendrig

Hendrig had a sallow, but falsely cherubic face which he liked to get close to the lens. "Darling Salyette, you want more." Then he added, "and more, and more, and you now owe me much in such a short time." He drawled a salacious and yet disdainful familiarity with her, or at least an obvious desire of one.

"Yes, and the rate you steal back is more. I have interests that require a great deal of discretion, and proof of a reasonable interest in the deal. I can, and will, put you into the data before anyone, that is, other than me."

"So, another promise from one who has yet to prosper from another's generosity that has limits. Still, my lovely Salyette, I shall assist you again, what is it this time?"

"I need your processing facility on the island." She was going to say more, but his explosion of outrage clipped her words short.

"What the bloody fuck, Salyette. I have loaned you my lab facility for the past year. Now you want a production facility. What new designer drug are you going after? I do not care; I do not get involved with those who own the drug trade. No, no, no, not ever."

After he sputtered to a stop, she gave him the warmest disarming expression she could muster, from general disuse of any need to express that emotion of want. Of needing another to get what she wanted, and them having the power to refuse. It was an unfamiliar and uncomfortable intrusion on her self-worth and brittle ego.

"Silly Hendrig, my dear … friend. Of course not, how could you believe that about me. No, not ever, no, no, no."

"Then what?" he said with what authority the moral high ground and the strings to the purse gave him.

"A new beauty product. I have synthesized a rare ingredient. I have a PR program all ready, a public face ready to parade and a solid process, but on too small of a scale to suit my needs. I think I will capture a significant market share and there is a huge profit if I can have a production run. Nothing nefarious, dear Hendrig," she laid it on.

He thought quite a long while, and looked her in the eyes, staring, trying to read. Salyette held them.

"Not a drug, then? That is my term. You will not create anything pharmaceutical. It is for their health, though?"

"Ostensibly," she said. "But I didn't say that… I said I had made a process less expensive, and my costs are going to be down, the price will not be dear, just enough to be fairly sought after. That is what I intend to do. Marketing is crafting a message, and I have included the cost in my prediction. I feel this is going to be worth a third of my present worth. That is why I need your facilities."

"Here is what I want, then. I will grant you the use, but the cost is that you will sign to put twenty-five percent of that present worth into escrow, and if you make a profit, I will take twenty-five percent."

"You rob me," she said.

"No, there is a need I can satisfy for you, but at a dear cost. You said the gain will be a third then I want a quarter of your present worth. So put that in escrow to me: titles, deeds, accounts etc., and you shall have your lab. The date to settle with me is the eve of the Great Rite. The Transveho-syne opening. You, I understand, even with all you have been borrowing from me, have managed to pay your way into the Procession." Then, belittlingly he said, "I do remember when I managed to be granted Procession privileges. It seems long ago, but then, I was much younger, and even younger than you are now, though really, I have forgotten how many bottles of elixir you have purchased, again, so dearly."

There was a pause, and she said, "I agree."

"Say that louder and recite the terms for the record," he said.

"I will establish an escrow account of approximately one-quarter of my worth, this going to a joint account. Neither may draw against this amount until so adjudicated."

"Wait, all my outlays to you have been, well, informal. I cannot have that term."

"I will not go without that protection. I will find another benefactor with a facility. It will demand more of me," she suggested, "But I will have my run and I will profit massively. I thought we were more than friends and could share in the spoils of this deal."

The obvious falsity of the enticement was met with equally fraudulent appreciation. "Thank you, my dear, but I will agree to the adjudication clause, but my price has now gone to one-third . One-third of your empire satisfies all of your debts to me. Say yes or no, or I have other matters to occupy my mind and will attend to them. One-third."

Salyette exhaled, noisily. It amused Hendrig. That irritated her more. She knew there was no out at this point, but she had legal teams, as much as Hendrig did. Also, if that scientist idiot savant she hired would have her formula as soon as he said he would, this cost would be minuscule. But still galling.

"I agree," she said simply.

"Recorded," said Hendrig, and he began to laugh. "You must have something to sell to rival the value of the elixir itself."

This amused him and he laughed as his holo gram winked out of existence. The laughter faded last.

Salyette was poignantly amused herself. "No, it actually is the elixir." She was going to make a bootleg version and then release it to the masses after she had extracted all the value out of her ability to undercut the present market. That the present market was ran by those who owned the world was an adrenaline junkie's high to her. Exacting revenge would be even more exhilarating, she surmised.

4 - Leonard

I'm not sure how many hours passed. The period of day turning into evening registered vaguely behind the heavy drapes. I was lost in the miasma of swirling time . Memories of my son plagued my cold, calculating reason for being. I had wrapped so much of this pain in my drive for revenge that the small hope Monte had so carelessly tossed warped my intent into a mobius strip of confusion.

I had gotten used to the hunger, in fact the edge, once felt tended to be merely a dull satisfaction of pain. Several times recently the thought of going off to find some nourishment intruded upon my lurking fantasies. Each time the vapid hunger was vanquished by the killing lust. The nearness, after all this time drove me mad. The self-inflicted cut on my cheek had bled enough to drip on the leather before it scabbed over.

Once again, the lock alerted me to the arrival of another, but this time there was no time to move. The operator of the key stepped up to the door and with a practiced ease, slipped the key in the lock and swung the door open. A woman: bent at the lower back, an unevenness to her shoulders in a utilitarian dress, pushed the door with her hip. She maneuvered a cart loaded with cleaning supplies by the handle of the mop in the bucket. The door slammed shut from a kick of her heel. She muttered in a voice that hadn't laughed in ages, if ever.

"Gotta clean the whole place, even if there hasn't been a soul in this museum for ages. What silly nonsense. This man don't need no maid, no, he needs a good woman."

She shuffled over to the windows and threw open the draperies with some distaste, it seemed. She shrank back from the unflattering, harsh glare of the city lights through the dusty windows.

"Dammit, gotta do the blasted windows too," she fumed and stomped back to the bucket. Her gaze, that spent most of its time on the floor directly in front of her, didn't even detect me until she steered her cart at my feet.

"AAAEEEIIIIAAAA!" she screamed, leaping back with far greater agility than I would have given her credit. She pressed a torn square cleaning cloth in a knot into her mouth and said "OOOH, AAAH," several times while she got her fright under control.

I sat still, icily, staring until the noises calmed from frantic to dismayed surprise.

"Mr. Weintraub? Ah, pardon me, Mr. Weintraub. I know I'm early, I'll go now, and beg your forgiveness for disturbing you, sir."

The font of information seemed exploitable, and simply doing nothing provided impetus. I listened, and stared at her, fascinated by her apparent torment.

"I have the letter you sent me, sir, and I do know that you were quite precise about the day for this cleaning, but well, sir, I thought I'd get on the job early by a day or two and make this place that much more sparkling. I didn't mean to intrude, I know your privacy is important, I am sure sorry that I made a fuss here, but I'll be going now, and return when I'm supposed to, just like you asked me to in your letter."

She got her cart heaped enough to move out in one trip, but I stopped her.

"Wait." I then stood and walked to the great globe, now in the light I could see was polished to a mirror finish. My back towards her, I watched her distorted reflection fidget. "You received my letter?"

"Oh yes, yes, I have it right here." She pulled the note wadded into its own envelope from her pocket. "Right here, sir, including the key."

"You can read?" I tried the most open-ended question I could, hoping the attempt at snobbery would elicit details I could work with.

"Of course, eight grades, I coulda went on, but… but…" she faded off. She mumbled a bit then said one clear word before lapsing into silence. "Young-uns."

I marveled that someone might have found this mousey little creature, with passive aggressive tendencies that bordered on malicious to be sexual, but there was the defensive sadness that disarmed me, momentarily, until she spoke again. Her shrillness wasn't just the retreat from society; her voice lanced out at me, as if all her social encounters were with boils, toilets, and people who pissed down at her while she scrubbed floors nearby.

"Give it to me." Still facing away, I held my hand out backwards, waiting to see if she would deposit it there. I watched her in the curved surface of the globe as she wrestled with the demand. The reflection was clear, but disproportionate. She seemed to waver and stretch, but I couldn't get a clear glimpse of her face. That too distorted hideously, her nose becoming more ursine, and the coarse hair that never disappeared at her sideburns darkened and pulled her mouth back. Her reflection drew her arm back and raised it threateningly.

Alarmed, I spun to see the pitiful creature picking at a scabbed wart on the corner of her mouth. At my fierce glance she winced and turned away, ducking from my eyes. She held out the letter.

I snatched it from her and worrisomely, almost too instinctively, drew back my hand as if to strike. As she cowered, I read the letter with only part of my mind. The other division of self curiously examined the odd liking of her response. I stopped reading to stand over her, letting some guilty pleasure creep into my barren soul. I wasn't sure if it was her complete, miserable subservience that quickened my heart, or the power I felt taking on the fiery role, and losing for many long heart beats the cold of the grave to which I was pledged.

Huddled a mere arm's length away, her furtive eye caught mine when I looked up from the page. I noticed her iris was washed of color. The pale milkiness of a cataract reflected more back at me than registered on her retina. I saw a flash of my face, distorted with hate.

It was moments like that which terrified me. When the anguish and hate that chilled my heart seemed to open a channel into something darker yet. A path painted with vile, black blood. The pain blossomed into an unearthly passion for the retribution I felt so entitled to inflict. In a timeless moment, I imagined the terror I might savor prior to his final breath. The sordid images welled up, and I was loathe to quell the torrent, only to find with a start that the torrent of evil had taken root in my mind. The spewing thoughts from the point of view I had invited into my mind usurped my will. I froze, lost to the present as the hate and evil pained me more than my loss, and I reveled in the degenerate pleasure. The foul thoughts grew more carnal and sensual. Seductively, the simple killing of Grigori drew out to an elaborate torture. Somehow, his mere death didn't seem as satisfying now, there seemed to be the need for pain, at least equal to the hurt in my soul, multiplied by all this time. Maybe it should even surpass mine.

I shook my head to clear my thoughts, realizing the voice from far away was the miserable little creature of the maid.

"Sir, sir? Are you all right, sir?" The scent of ammonia seemed to waft on her breath, with undertones of embalming fluid. The effect was like smelling salts, assaulting my sinuses and frontal lobe. I looked at her closely, and for a moment, I thought I saw the flicker of her tongue lick her lips as she touched me, then any glimmer of personality disappeared back into her shell.

The letter rustled as I straightened it:

Weintraub, Sarvanaez, and Gorman

Attns at Law.

2577 Central Ave.

Northampton MA.

Prime Custodial Services

75 Norton St.

Northampton, MA.

Dear Custodial Representative,

Your services will be required at 21 Middle Rd Springfield MA, per our agreement, you will accomplish your duties exactly four days before the scheduled occupancy on June the twenty-fifth.

Thank you,

J.M. Weintraub

JW/mt

I let the addresses burn into my brain as I folded the letter once, made a sharp crease and tapped the paper against my thumbnail.

"This seems clear enough to me," I said. "Which part of these directions made this night worthy of your intrusion?"

She said nothing, just hung her head awkwardly, her jaw going slack and saliva escaping. Her pathetic appearance touched me, but there was too much to learn here, so I felt myself damning any cares about her as a person.

"Maybe it is the date you remember wrong. Tell me how you remember such dates?"

I saw her flash her eyes toward me, and I was shocked, expecting to see the furtive, sullen, stolen glance. Instead, the eyes mocked me, interest and entertainment I felt was going to be at my expense glinted then disappeared into obsequent servility.

"No sir, I write everything down. I got your dates written down for the next ten… ah, times I am expected. I write everything carefully."

She fumbled in her apron pocket, producing a small bound notepad, with a chewed stub of a pencil jammed in the spiral binding. She opened it, paged through it hesitantly. Her slowness reading her laboriously scratched ciphers shredding my patience. She appeared to find it, but then, muttering, "No, no, that's not it." She went back to licking her thumb for each page. Compassion welled up for this near illiterate being, badgered so deliberately, but the sly leers she cast towards me as she fumbled about made me realize she played her own game. I simply held out my hand.

She immediately found the entry, inserted her well-wetted thumb between the pages and held the little book possessively out to let me see the date in red ink. June 24. Five days off.

I could feel there was little left to gain, and the opportunity for exposure was growing, so I tossed the letter on the small table at the door. I turned the knob before addressing her.

"You have, to this point, been a trustworthy subcontractor. I see no reason for this indiscretion to change our relationship." After a pause, I said, "Unless this happens again."

I walked out as she was assuring me.

The door slammed. Behind the door she stooped even more, her uneven shoulders thickening, her arms drooping and her coarse hair escaping the net. Her snout elongated and her canine teeth grew out past her thin lips. Her eyes slitted and she walked to the leather sofa. She got on all fours and putting her snout close to the still-indented leather, she inhaled mightily. Her long tongue lolled out of her mouth: thick, pointy, and black. She licked my drop of blood from the furniture.

5 - Enticed

Outside the door, the halls opened directly onto the huge fall of stairs, once elegant, now treacherously worn and loose. I was down three flights of steps before I realized I hadn't been aware. Usually, I count the stairs, matching my pace to nothing, stopping at odd intervals to listen, but not this descent. My footsteps echoed. My suddenly heightened senses were the harbinger of another fugue state. I fought the pull of darkness with all my might, but my overexerted will faltered for a moment.

I stumbled and scraped my knuckles raw against the bricks. A red blaze marked my descent. The pain pulled me in two directions: to succumb to the darkness that called, and still, there was a sharpening of my will, myself. I had enough energy for one thought: my son, as the darkness grew around me. I was pulled into a polarized needle of awareness. The darkness pulled, sure and strong. I was lost in the miasma, then fell. The pain of a none-too-gentle blow to my head heaved my mind free. I stared at the scarred wood at my face. It was real, and it meant I wasn't going to leave this time yet. He was still here.

I got to my feet, moved to the landing's scalloped edge, worn by so many passages, so many feet, many with claws.

I crouched on the stairs, listening, and felt the aura. Emptying my mind, I found the nothingness of me, and like a fire in the darkest night, I sensed I was not alone. Several life fires lit above me, the one in the apartment was most horribly twisted and burned with mineral fires of the depths of the earth.

Not good, I thought.

Below me were throngs of dim fires, some barely burning after being chemically dampened. The tiny flickers in the streets below were of little threat, but they did run the risk of coalescing into a conflagration. A fight was not called for. I could sense the gang that gathered was not aware of me.

I slipped up half the flight of stairs and climbed up into the deep well of the window. I pressed my back to the dark glass, and hid.

The mob marched right by me, never glancing up. Laughing and leering as they made their way up the steps.

I dropped to my feet as the last one reached the flight above me. I could hear their raucous passage even as I slipped out the door of the apartment block. I dropped over the side of the stairs and froze against the building. From the shadows, I surveyed the surroundings.

A dark sedan sat at the curb, the shiny metal incongruous with the litter in the gutter and the neglect of the neighborhood. I couldn't see into the interior. I left the bushes and the trashcans along the steps and moved out to the sidewalk. The rear door of the auto swung open as I approached. I stopped, not being able to see in, nor finding any comfort in the fact that no one exited, I spun about, my hand sought out my weapon. The cold handle of the knife comforted me for a moment. I made nonchalant haste to the corner and then turned and sprinted off down the street. I vaulted the first set of steps I came to and pressed myself into the alcove of the grilled door and the small metal mailboxes. I heard no pursuit, only the door click shut and the car rumble off.

I cautiously circled the block. A scrap of incongruously clean, linen paper caught my eye. There was no sign of the vehicle. But as I crept up, I saw several of the cards in a pile by the curb. Cigar smell in the air, a candy wrapper not from any store in this neighborhood, and the pointedly careless invitations in a pile. I toed the pile, stooped, and snatched one, and in a moment, I was back at the building. I edged down the alley, climbed a fire escape and found a safe roof.

The card had crumpled in my fist. I smoothed it out on my knee and read:

Tri-Unity Mortuary Services

4719 Frontage Rd.

Florence MA

Eternity with Grace and Beauty

I felt more than heard the big car coming around the block. I watched it idle past its previous spot and then continue down the street.

I don't know why, but I climbed down and stepped out of the shadows then walked to the edge of street. The taillights diminished, but then the brake lights flared. The car sat, inert, and I could feel the probing from the mirrors and the dark rear window. A door opened. Inertia did not release me, and I stared back. Almost imperceptibly, the car began to back toward me, the door agape. It stopped a pace or two away from me, and all I could see in the dim light was a pair of trousered legs, crossed nonthreateningly. I moved close.

The man from the impromptu meeting in the apartment sat opposite another, even more elegant. The clothes, if not for the obvious richness of the cloth and the impeccable cut, would have been severe and austere. A grey wool suit barely accented the black leather of the shoes or the car's upholstery. His face, above the white collar turned toward me, and looked over the half-rim glasses. He flicked an eyebrow in the direction of his companion, who gave the slightest nod. A change washed over the other's face; not as if a mask of control had been lifted to permit a glance upon the humanity of another, but as if an emotion had been applied with the most artistic of brushstrokes.

"You want action more than answers, but you'll find neither standing there. This scene is contaminated beyond repair now, and your prey will have you waste an eternity here." The logic then smoothly shifted into charm.

"Come, we will share the hunt."

I felt the uneven sidewalk beneath my shoes most of all as I waited, staring into the car.

Again, the flicker that preceded the change crossed his features and left an edge. "Or not, I care little. Stand there, announce yourself, imagining you are surreptitious and waste your time. What, have you got forever?"

"Yes."

The veil dropped for a moment, their eyes met, and both dropped their gazes to the matching jeweled pendants they wore.

I saw annoyance flicker from the elegant one's eyes, clearly establishing the hierarchy. The half-rims were removed, a polite nod that might have been obescience from any other and he moved across the seat, deeper into the sanctuary of the back of the idling limo, the resultant space creating an invitation that screamed of a trap.

"Please," his voice was persuasive, "we should leave. I owe you an explanation. Difficult to appeal to your sense of trust, and the danger we are in would surely be seen as being of my origin. If you cannot take the ride, someday come to the church." His arm extended from the depths of the car with another card I recognized from the pile disdainfully left behind on the sidewalk.

"I simply ask you to listen."

"What is it you want?" I asked, not expecting an answer, but unaware I again, in the space of time, was engaging in pointed behavior that satisfied something other than the lust for revenge in my psyche.

His anger that spat out slapped me into the present. "You fool. I want nothing of yours, not even your pathetic desire to take his life. I offer the first real answers you seek. I am leaving, you are welcome to leave with us." He made a motion toward the door as if to close it and nodded. The brake lights dimmed, and in the instant, I took an involuntary step towards the car, I realized I had been found out. He tested me and I saw it in his eyes as he sat back, then moved over, inviting.

"Quickly now, he has allies you know, or maybe not. Regardless, we have been here too long."

I got in, clutching my weapon.

"Take me to 2577 Center Street, Northampton."

They exchanged glances as the car moved smoothly away.

6 - Salyette

Salyette yawned and stretched while sitting at the desk, listening to the voice on the speaker drone on. Occasionally, she made a note. She sipped from a delicate cup which softly 'clinked' when set into the saucer. That she had procured an invite to the Procession was an amazing distraction to the dull reports from the screen. The invite had cost her an immense portion of her wealth, yet when the breakthrough came, the people she would meet at the Rites would be powerful allies or customers. Most would be enraged when they found how they had been taken advantage of by the ones who had the exclusive market of the elixir. In her imaginings, those who had been so offended would have a self-righteous fury that could be provoked to an event she could capitalize upon.

Her screen lit up and an insistent tone cut her pleasant, imagined revery to shreds. Hendrig himself showed his face on her screen. She tried to mask her distaste as she cheerily answered. Both knew the bonhomie was false.

"Hendrig," she gushed, "don't you have people to make calls for you. You are, I know, judging from the size and success of your holdings, a very busy person."

He was equally facetious. "Of course, but not for a customer as renowned as you. I have never originated a loan of this magnitude, nor to one placed so high. Of course, with that large of a concern, I give your account my personal attention, as I would give to you, freely, to our mutual benefit, if we just clear up this undocumented loan we have between us. It is due immediately upon the finality of the Sacrament, which is less than a day away. Are you prepared to satisfy this matter?”

“An owner of so much, such as yourself, know I will keep my assets working right up to the last moments of the term. I shall remit to you the devil's price you demand after the ceremony.”

Hendrig leaned closer to the hologram and Salyette could see the soft skin of his jowls magnified so the pores stood out in relief. His unctuousness was as disgusting as his leer. “If you need more time, and care to make an adjustment of the terms, see me in person.”

Her face must have betrayed her disgust because his words suddenly became as dangerous as a moray eel flashing out of a crevice and threatening to tear into her with sharp words.

“The terms are explicit my darling,” and the endearing term was sarcastically sleazy coming from his mouth. “Your loan is not yet recorded, as you have requested, but still the amount is due whether your foray into the subterfuge of the game is fruitful, or not. I have given you the grace to make this loan, off the official channels, so you had better not fuck me over. I don't even know what it is you are buying my dear, would you care to share your plans with me? If I could capitalize along with you, that amount might lessen the terms.”

“No, I will keep my foolish whim to myself.”

“Very well,” he replied. “Know that the entire repayment and cost of this capital is due the morning after the Syne event. And every day you delay making me whole will reflect in a 12.9 percent increase in the amount due.” He spoke slowly, “Every… day.”

“I know this, Hendrig, I have planned for this debt to mature and will be ready to repay your generous assistance.”

“Then perhaps we shall meet tomorrow evening at the sacraments. I understand you have used part of this loan to secure an invite to the Procession. I, myself,” he tried to feign humility, but failed to mask his superiority and gloating, “will be in the Rites. I would absolutely love a few moments of your time and attention as I pass through the outer chamber. Please do look for my entourage. I will have them admit you.” His leer returned, “You might even be allowed to slip past the limits of your invite to Procession, if, if, if you were close enough that I could claim you were my consort for the night."

"You are generous Hendrig, and your offer is tempting." She nearly choked on the words which had her pictured as his intimate.

"Yes, in lieu of a more satisfying relationship, we will continue with our terms, and I am not going to beg favors from one who has borrowed so grand a sum for some secret, wild foray. Remember, due the morning after the Rites. Or come in person to try and talk me into more agreeable terms." His face left the screen, but his corporate logo sizzled across like a banner, and left the due date slowly fading out.

She thought about how she might stretch the repayment time a few more days without sacrificing her soul to the lecherous creature Hendrig. Just in case the scientist needed a few more days to make her the bootleg elixir. Then when she has the contacts she will make at the Procession, and the money they would spend if she could undercut the market, well, she might just buy Hendrig out and make a fool of the old goat.

A soft knock on the door interrupted her machinations.

She looked at the door, making whoever deliberately wait. She knew that they knew and that thought interrupted any minor pleasure the pause brought to her ego.

"Come," she said.

Several people entered, arrayed themselves before her desk.

The voice on the phone droned on about personnel. Financials would be on the hour. She glanced at the clock. "You are wasting part of my ten minutes."

The first in line spoke, "Logistics and security have no anomalies to report."

The next: "IT concurs with security. All transactions are recorded with data space for two weeks yet. Compression to storage prediction is on time. System is without anomalies."

Then the next: "Financial analytics has verified last period's results. The real estate trend is positive, still too slight a matter to adjust for, but worth noting. I feel it will be a benefit to our—"

"OUR?" she cut him off.

"Ma'am. I apologize, your position is poised to improve if this continues. I feel—"

Again, she cut him off. "You don't get to '*feel*' about my concerns. You get paid to think. You get to analyze and present me with recommendations backed by calculations and logic. Not feelings."

"Agreed ma'am. Yet your tutelage has caused my penchant for numbers to grow more acute. I—"

She stopped him with a single raised finger. "Stop the ass kissing. Make a point."

A momentary deep breath and he began, "There have been many shifts of the assets of the church over time. The volume, predicted societal goals and rates have been constant within several percentages. Lately there is a quiet, but massive shift made in seemingly small and innocuous trades which seem… ah, are indicating purpose, but it is too early to ascertain that purpose."

"Security, does your report indicate any social variants in pressure? Are there any agitations we are overlooking as too benign?"

"None reported, Ma'am."

"When did you detect this asset-shifting trend?

"In last night's reports. I was curious about the graph of tangible assets. The report for the metropolitan area mentioned a possible flux in real estate prices as the church had declined to maintain or renew leases on numerous holdings. I looked at the church's trading in recent weeks, and then at similar situations of divestitures and often, too often to be random, the church was a part of the transactions, whether to acquire or to decline. The acquisitions took some time, but the trails are unmistakable now, so the value changes calculations have focused on what will be the net. That is a result I should have in two days."

"When did this start?"

"I don't know Ma'am, I looked back a month ago and the shift began so gradual that if I hadn't been looking at the metro real estate returns, I would have missed it. But once the start of their pattern of strategy changed, I have noticed a consistent rate until late last night. The activity suddenly spiked in certain areas of the market, of which I will suspect to find the church at the activities center."

"Do you have specifics about this spike. How large was it?"

"I will have an analysis for you done."

"Of course you will. Why, if you thought this was important enough to mention, have you come unprepared to discuss it?" She didn't give him time to answer. "Find out what areas this influences. Locations and populations. Find me the dollar amount that this reduces the debt load, and what of their debt load is maturing. Find for me, if and what they are buying."

The monotone phone voice stilled and a shrill tone sounded. It told her she had one minute to clear the room. No one other than the immediate access personnel were allowed to hear financials.

"Nod your head, yes or no," she pointed. "Is there any worthwhile notable political change I must know about and if there is, make an appointment this afternoon".

He nodded.

She pointed again, "You stay…" She left the unsaid message hang in the air. The rest turned and left.

"Sit," she pointed and turned the volume low, so that from where the secretary sat, there could only be heard murmurings and an occasional number or word.

After ten minutes of listening and a few notes in her book, she turned toward the secretary.

"Are there any meetings today I cannot do without?"

"There are two phone calls and a meeting with—"

"That was not my question, was it?"

"No."

"Is that; No, there are no obligations I can't cancel, or does that mean, No you agree that wasn't my question?"

The secretary knew to skirt the issue and move to the required information. "No, there is nothing I couldn't clear from your calendar."

"Good, make my travel arrangements, I want to leave in an hour. I want to see the lab and that dolt I have bought so dearly. I want him in the lab when I get there. Ensure my arrival will be expected, I'll be staying at the chalet until after…" she paused. "After the party tomorrow night. Then get these memos out. First, all divisions do a deep dive for the last twenty-four, no, forty-eight hours. I don't care about what is going well and as expected. That should be a given. I want details about the unexpected. Second, review my contacts with the church. Give me a list of those I have spoken with and when, and what about. Lastly, to financials, give me a value for my exposure to anything that I and the church have in common." She thought silently for a few moments and added, "Give me an estimate of what the leech Hendrig charges for each day after the event tomorrow evening." She dismissed the secretary with a wave. She brought the financials report up and sipped from her cup. She left blood red Rorschach marks on the rim.

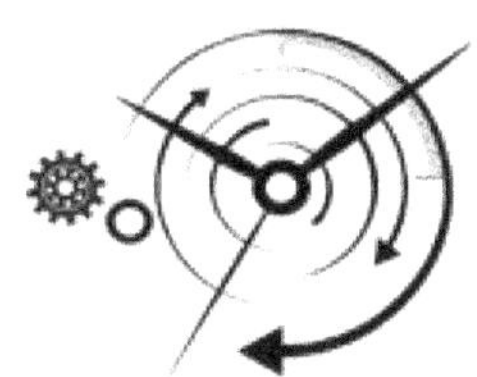

7 - Sisker

We rode in silence. The interior of the car; air-conditioned, heated, filtered, insulated elegance. The leather of the seats sounded like the leather couch in his apartment. Lair.

"You know the 'Offices'?" he asked.

"We are looking for the same man," I said. Seemed evasive enough.

Again, the man seemed bewildered, but only momentarily. The icy calm and savage control of his features merely flickered. But this time, the questions shifted, I felt he made some slight adaptation in the hierarchy between us, he was not as supercilious, but even more guardedly engaged in the repartee. I stared back at those eyes, never feeling the urge to tear my gaze away out of fear or subservience. I saw the adjustment he made in his eyes, like I had seen in court so many times before.

"Please," he said, without preamble, and genuine. "The knowledge and the man are what we both seek. I am Sischte Kavveleer, the Suffragan to Missio Sui Iuris of the Apostolic Prefecture of Mossul. You may call me Sisker. I will share with you what I know, as much as I can, and I will answer questions, as best I can. Then we will go to the church, and you will meet people who have answers for you. And maybe you will care to answer for yourself. Shall we try this?" he said with a slight slap of haughtiness at the end.

"What of these law offices? How is he involved with them and you know of them?"

"The law offices are small offshoots of a much larger, international firm. We know of them because he uses them, and we are trying to amass every scrap of data on this… man you call Grigori." He thought for a moment before he continued, "I shall refer to him as Grigori, then."

"Grigori uses this firm to represent him, and to make his will into reality," he said. "How did you know this firm? Few do." He switched so smoothly and skillfully from response to inquiry that I fell to talking before I realized the change of roles.

"It was on a letter for him. I read the letter head."

"You saw actual correspondence?" His incredulous look amused me, and I knew he had never even found a single artifact of Grigori's life. I looked down on him again and the loss of my esteem for him plummeted me into the depths of hatred again. For a moment, the curses I spoke over my forever missing son echoed again in my mind. I became angry at my slight emotion. I wanted to be dead, and dead has no emotions.

"Does this firm hold more clues about where to find him? What else do they do for him? Tell me all you know," I demanded.

"I did not say I would be part of an interrogation till you were satiated. We shall converse to our mutual gain."

He sat back, silent. He looked away. There was only the sensation of movement when I, too, looked out the window. We passed buildings that gradually grew more cared for, then the darkened city around us came more to life. The traffic increased and the brick structures grew multistory. The lights of both the traffic and the buildings became a jumble of colors and shapes. A mist crept into the evening air, causing the light to break up into tiny flashes of color.

The big car moved smoothly through traffic. The stops and starts seemed hardly perceptible. The lights, the buildings, the traffic all dropped away as we sat there. He poured himself a glass of something. He held out the glass to me. "I shall pour myself another if you care to join me." He offered it to our companion, who for many long minutes I had forgotten was in our presence. I recognized the studied subservience.

Monte took the proffered glass and sat back, pointedly looking out the window. I took the next one that was offered me. He looked expectedly at me as he poured.

"The letter I read was from the firm you seem to know. It was addressed to a cleaning service, directing her to have his apartment made ready on the 24th. Five days from now. She came early and surprised me."

"She?"

"Yes, she, the maid, the pathetic creature. Hideous for a woman to look so. She mistook me for Grigori, or for Mr. Weintraub, I believe she called him."

"You actually saw her, talked with her, touched something and gave it back to her?" The two were now staring at me, flicking quick looks at each other and saying single words, or fragments of sentences.

"Servants."

"She has his…"

"They need to know…"

"He must, too."

As they discussed in fragments, I watched them, sorting out the hierarchy, the intelligence level, the schooling, the concerns, and finally noted which one seemed concerned about me. Monte. To the other, I was an opportune desire, a prize.

The lights still filtered through the heavy, tinted glass, and the motion of the car changed to a steady acceleration down a broad parkway. Fewer stop lights blinked. The buildings rose above the horizon and shouldered together, blotting out the sky from my side window. I saw our headlights reflecting as we passed and an occasional lighted lobby. More often than not, the tall buildings were quiet for the night. The car slowed beside a great edifice of stone and glass. It crept along and then pulled over to the curb.

Western Mass Cooperative Bank was engraved in the stone facade above the brass doors.

"You are where you asked to be brought. This is the office we… we know of." Sisker put his hand on the door latch, but before opening it he said, "There is something you must know, before you step out of this car. I believe you are in grave danger. This maid, you saw, talked with, and to whom you returned the letter to when you were finished with it, is most probably a servant of the earthbound, and resents it. You gave her back this letter after you touched it, and she now has your spore, your scent, your essence if you will. I don't believe she will harm you tonight, they will want to find out more about you."

"Why will she want to find me, and who are 'they' if the 'they' are not you?" I asked.

"Her kind are not allowed to have discretion when carrying out orders. You threaten her by knowing she was not obedient to her masters."

"What nonsense, she was a pathetic old hag of a woman who smelt of urinals," I said.

"Urinals or of ammonia they excrete? Coarse, dark, unkempt hair?"

"Her lot in life leaves little money or desire for stylists," I snorted at him and his paranoia.

"She was probably hump-backed, and curved spine that made her lean her face in close to you as she talked. Her arms were probably thick with hair and gnarled hands showed the years of toil with many scars and nails brutally trimmed with her teeth. Does that sound like your maid?" He leaned toward me before I could answer, and said, "She is not what you imagine, and you are in danger for knowing of her, whether you choose to believe anything else I tell you, trust your life on this one warning."

"I will continue to try to find him. I will not be frightened off by some old cleaning lady."

He sighed, removed his hand, and nodded to Monte. Monte reached over and swung open the door. The misty air off the river swept into the car. I looked out at the empty street, the tall locked buildings and even with the street lights, there seemed to be more shadows and darkness than light, just circles of light that faded almost to extinction before they joined with the light from the next lamp down the street. The desolation, ironic in the middle of such a large city, seemed to radiate from the darkened building. I sat back in the seat, and as if on cue, Monte shut the door and the car pulled smoothly from the curb.

"It's best not to tarry there. As you seem to know, it is never good to be noticed. I am tired, and you must be. I don't know where you are staying, but I can offer you a night's rest and then we can resume our conversation in the morning where we so unfruitfully left off. Do you have a place you would like to be brought? I have someplace close, and you are welcome to it."

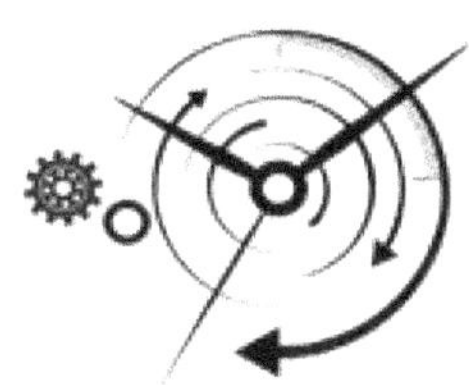

8 - The Casket Factory

We drove out of the city, to the next small mill town that had become a suburb. The driver turned off the main road, bumped across some tracks, and then drove parallel to the long disused railroad tracks. We passed between gentrified warehouses on one side and pulled up to a nondescript factory on the other side.

The driver parked close. We got out and climbed the stairs to the loading dock. The wooden front door was massive, scarred by forklift blades and hand trucks, and did not look out of place on the loading dock. The driver opened the heavy door.

I followed Monte through the entry, which immediately opened into a luxurious ante room. The door swung shut and blended perfectly with the paneled interior. The inner door opened to reveal several people waiting. Aesthetic and athletic, they moved toward Monte's group, took their outerwear. One remained after a few moments. He asked, "Will there be any requests, Your Grace?"

Monte looked pointedly away from me and told the man, "One guest. A bath, a barber and… a wardrobe." He turned back to me and said, "Of course, that is, if you wish."

Silence was assent, and the servile man hurried off.

Sisker took command of the moment. "Come," he beckoned and walked away down a hall. Monte mocked obesiances to me and gestured me on. I followed.

The hall opened up to a showroom of polished metal caskets. I stopped, startled, and then went to one. The pillowy silk was cool and smooth. Reverie held me for a few moments. Monte approached and studied me without moving from his spot.

Monte said, "I see in your eyes that you know sorrow. The church can feel you are in pain. I ask that you listen and speak with the elders. I offer that you might also find peace for your soul."

I stopped fondling the smooth silk and the fabricated memories of my son lying in one. But I burnt him and gave him a warrior's funeral. I disengaged from the myriad of fleeting fantasies of my son's return that always follow fond thoughts of him.

"You have a great hole in your heart, but you have hope you will be reunited with your son someday," Monte said.

"Isn't that the basis of your religion, or any religion, that this life is a finite test with consequences beyond our death?" I asked.

"Yes," Sisker moved towards me. "While the choice of that path matters to each of us only for our own sake, I agree with your premise. But you are fixated on death, which is certain. So, for so much of your sheer will and intellect to be focused on this one ideation, you have accomplished little beyond making your torment near eternal. Or is that what you wish, to never know death as you wallow in the blackness of your thoughts?"

I turned, fury rising. I knew that he knew that had touched a raw guilt in my soul.

"Yet, your chance encounter with the church…" he paused, then, "doesn't this evening make you wonder if there is not more to this that the fates have in store for us?"

"You appear tired, possibly hungry, certainly needing attention to your corporal incarnation, and your mind needs quiet time to dwell on what I am about to offer. I will answer frank questions if you would do me the same honor."

"I agree."

"Thank you," was his response, then he turned and walked away. The manservant had returned and stood respectfully waiting to be acknowledged at the fringe of our small gathering. Monte flicked his eyes to the servant, then to me and said, "Attend to him. When he wakes, inform me." And then, Monte was gone too.

"Sir," the man said and walked away opposite to where the other two had gone. A hall on the far side of the showroom opened to nicely appointed living quarters. The manservant walked through the rooms for a quick inspection, then went to the bath and turned on the taps. "My name is Toby. I will help you tonight." He stood before me, eyed my physique, front and back, then went to a phone. He spoke to the party at the other end about the wardrobe. He next dialed a number while asking me if I had any requests for a meal. He couldn't wait for my stumbling tongue, so he said, "Please, allow me."

He ordered steak, potatoes, and asparagus. He walked into the bath, turned off the taps and returned with a robe. He stood off to one side, held the robe out as if to help me into it, and asked if he could clean my clothes. I took the hint, stripped while looking about the room. The man carefully and respectfully averted his eyes. I looked into the mirrors about the room, but never once did I catch his eye. My clothes dropped to the floor, and I backed into the offered robe and wrapped it about me.

A knock sounded and a wardrobe rack was wheeled in. Toby shuffled through it, pulling out articles of clothing. Now and then, he would put one back in exchange for some other item.

It dawned on me, "Are those funeral wear for the deceased?"

"Both for and from," Toby replied. "But is there any difference to either of us in the end?"

"Pragmatic," I said.

Toby laid three sets of clothes across the arms and back of a nearby chair. Under garments and sleepwear were placed on the cushion.

"I will leave you. Your meal will arrive after you finish bathing."

"How will you know that?"

"Most do not languish in a bath when there are such situations to occupy their minds. I ordered your meal to be ready in one hour and I have occupied twenty minutes of your time so far. Are there any other questions before I leave you?"

"Who will I talk with next?" I asked.

"When you want answers, pick up the phone."

He looked at his watch and said, "I leave you enough time to bathe before your meal arrives. I hope you enjoy. He gathered up my discarded garments and left, carrying them pointedly away from himself. He turned at the door and gave a small bow before backing into the hall. One of the others was revealed when the door shut. The other held out paper bags for the clothes to be deposited into. The edges of the openings were carefully folded back and taped.

"Monte wants these in the lab." The other hurried off. Toby saw the handle on the door to the apartment was turned slowly from within, as if testing. Toby knocked lightly. I opened it and stepped out into the showroom.

"You are not locked in, sir, I want to assure you, you are free to walk about or even leave. There are no nicer quarters to be found anywhere near here, and I would also assure you, you are secure here. You may lock the door from the inside."

"Secure from what?" I asked.

For the first time, he gave me a less than obsequious answer. "I feel safe here from all the things I can imagine, and from all those I cannot. Goodnight, sir." He shut the door carefully, respectfully. I saw the bolt above the handle and slid it into the catch.

9 - Intel

The signal from the home office, via secure satellite, reached the plane's comm gear somewhere over the Atlantic. A small notice appeared in the corner of the screen, the red background alerting her to the importance of the interruption.

Noting who called, she plugged in a set of headphones and held one side casually against her ear, as if she intended this would be brief.

"Yes."

"The report of anomalies, as you requested. I have it in your queue. There are also the contacts with the church to whom you have donated, with whom you have appeared, or have conferred with in the last ten years. Chronologically arranged and then again by number of instances, and yet again by mutual financial exposure. Crossing those three categories I have ranked the top ten percent. The statistical inference drops off sharply at three percent concerning the volume, the most recent and most exposure. I feel, ah, rather, the analytics report that the almost asymptotic decline in connectedness of those beyond that three percent suggests the seven people in that top three percent are your most reliable sources. I have included dossiers on those seven as well."

She readjusted her headphones now to free up her hands. The report came on screen, which she scrolled through. "What is this about?" she asked when she highlighted the entry.

"A riot and looting at a warehouse, ma'am."

"What makes this unique?" she asked. "I have no connection to this group."

"It does follow a similar disturbance and subsequent looting, but the incident that catalyzed this event seemed so inconsequential."

"Meaning?"

"The recent prior events have been of opportunity, chance rioting in the area of the occurrence. This was a focused, organized protest at the corporate facility. When the protests turned violent, there were shipments stolen in the midst of the unrest, disguised as vandalism and looting, but the report also indicated a high value written off in the insurance filing. The insurance amount, invoices, and manifests do not coincide. Either they profited off the loss, or there were items they do not wish to declare that are now missing."

"What is your suspicion?"

"I do believe it was technology. Phones, computers, etc."

"Hmmm," was her answer as she scrolled through the list again. "This?" again highlighting the entry for the secretary at the other end.

"I   have noted several high-profile people that have been influential in various sectors of the economy quietly retiring or resigning from controlling interests in the business and the political sphere. Most of them were affiliated with our concerns and were expected to be assets in the societal arena. This is not a loss, there are many others who can be thrust into the public spotlight on demand, but curious that so many suddenly have disavowed the path, and while they take enough assets with them to survive, they leave so much gain to be had unappreciated."

She ran through the short list with few comments. "I thought this Congressional seat would have been secure for years to come. Hmm, I thought he was so much greedier."

"50,000-foot view on all these. I just want to have what's out there. Nothing deep enough to allow anyone to form this same group of cohorts as I have deduced."

Again, she returned to the list; a surge in price of a certain drug, a report of a very quiet arrival of a high church official, several law enforcement activities which were sudden and controlled enough to have the feeling of having been planned for some time due to the complex orchestration between several agencies. "Find out what security knows about these law enforcement activities. I only want to know if Security knew nothing in advance."

"Let me be now," she said. She broke the connection but kept the list up on the screen. She motioned for an attendant and pointed to her cup. The attendant brought a tray with a pot of hot tea and carefully poured. Then from the tray the attendant took a small, ornate clay bottle, and presented it with both hands while ceremoniously bowing.

She took the bottle, opened it, and dispensed a small amount into her steaming cup of tea. Then, after looking into the distance while caressingly examining her face with her fingertips, she added a few drops more to the cup. That little extra was such an extravagance. She re-stoppered the bottle and returned it to the outstretched hands of the attendant who hadn't moved since it was offered.

The attendant returned it to the tray, rose and bowed, then left.

She sipped the tea as she returned to scrolling through the list. Deaths, jurisdictional infractions that seemed to be sanctioned at high levels, controversies that were squelched before they became too public. A list of visitors to high-level people that were odd, and high-level people with odd visits. Late night comings and goings. Cars that were followed, or cars that showed up at unexpected places or events.

Also in the list were imbedded video feeds of security cameras and traffic monitoring stations. Financial data on those transactions that resulted in far better or far worse than expected outcomes. There were a few mentions of operatives of those whom she knew and competed against, moving about the world. The major internet analytics analysis stated there was no focus of any suspected anomaly. The population health reported an aging population using resources beyond the ability to sustain the system, but the death rate was expected if the epidemics and addictive crisis' (which the list maker duly noted) were considered. Lastly, there were HR reports on all her people. A noted affair, with an inconsequential politician was revealed.

That might be useful, she thought.

Turning in her chair, she reconnected to her aide. "There are others with whom I maintain mutual business and liabilities. Research those as you have done with this report. Start with those who I am most intimately involved. Focus on anything that can be tied back to the church, especially if it ties back to me, even tenuously."

"Also," she said, interrupting his obeisances, "attach a note if any of the church contacts are involved, and," she then she let the pause hang loudly in the air between them, until she felt the necessary degree of menace to the silence while she examined her pointed and polished nails with her fingertips.

"Also, I want a prediction on the church real estate anomaly by noon, my time. And evaluate my list of church contacts. How close can I get to the top?" The silence built until she said, "I have an invite for the Procession during which I will not be interrupted. I want this information prior to that engagement." After a few moments, her ponderings were intruded upon by his mere presence. She spat, "That leaves you eighteen hours, and you are just sitting there. I want this information before I land at the island." She cut the connection.

She pressed the indent on the arm of her chair. It flashed briefly and, in a moment, the same attendant returned with the same tray of tea and the clay bottle. Tea was poured and the bottle was again ritualistically proffered. She took it and poured a few drops into her tea. More elixir so soon was such an extravagance. Her musing was of how close she was to unlocking the viciously held secret of the precious and so rare commodity. But not quite yet. As she was about to re-stopper, she noticed a single drop that might escape the rim. She held the bottle at face level, studied the inscription in the fired clay. It was identifiable, but inscrutable. She traced it with her index fingertip, her thumb and smallest finger extended, the others tucked away. She brought the bottle to her mouth and licked the drop with just the tip of her tongue, shuddering at the tiny contact with the bottle containing so much power. Breathing deeply, she replaced the bottle in the outstretched hands. As she experienced the rejuvenation, she reached out and petted the soft hair of the attendant. "Tonight," she told him.

Tonight, she might partake in some of that, she thought. *Some?* then she smiled at the thought. The elixir coursed through her veins and she knew she meant *all*.

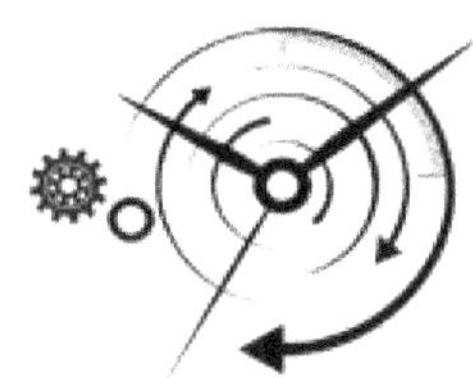

10 - Kill the Messenger

Her plane landed and taxied directly into the hangar. The stop was so smooth on polished concrete that the wheels squeaked. She was about to disembark when the comm alerted her. The 'Urgent' indication intrigued her enough to sit back down and open the channel.

"Yes?"

"Ma'am, I have that analysis you requested on the financial trades."

"Hold," she ordered, then opened a channel to her attendant. "Transfer this," she ordered.

A few minutes later, she climbed into the limo. The door was shut for her. The screen came to life with the visage of the waiting aide.

She leaned back in the seat as the limo eased out of the hangar. "Tell me," she said.

"The properties have a peculiar urban and inner-city commonality. For decades, the church has held leases for entire blocks of real estate and did nothing with them. In some areas the leased properties lay fallow, and in other cities, they became infested and degenerated to squalor. The areas sometimes became the focal point of inner-city desperation and homelessness. Financially the church maintained its obligations and the control of the properties, but did nothing to improve the areas or even stop the blight."

"Some of these concentrations of properties were often close to successful urban areas of commerce. It was thought the church would profit immensely from any gentrification that might occur, and there have been instances where this held true, yet the predominance of those leases declined are in areas of extreme social unrest and desperate conditions for those poor souls who live there."

"The church would have little interest in giving away the fortune should the gentrification spread. Why withdraw now?" she asked.

"I deduce there is little chance of the urban renewal to profit the church, and they do not wish to extend recent losses. The areas are poverty stricken, there would be a cost to merely reclaim the properties, often needing to raze the buildings."

"There is one side of the equation that suggests the strategy is part of lowering their needless expenditure of cash. The coffers fill less and less for the ones who officiate over the religions. The young are less inclined to believe, let alone follow the path, and the old are reaching the end of their life span. The move equates to an approximate 500 million windfall to their bottom line without any changes to the tangible, owned assets."

"No, there is more," she said to him.

"I agree, madam. I looked at the political and social upheaval happening, and do not believe this is a mere transference of wealth. This has a social and political advantage in that the church has managed to create enclaves of obedient serfs, in great concentrations near major population centers. The leases were necessary to secure these areas and allow the influx of these desperate people. Now, with the sheer mass of those souls firmly entrenched, they have withdrawn their safe control of the availability for those areas to have been inhabited as the poor and homeless dregs of society are now firmly ensconced and I believe, un-dislodgable."

"The social unrest grows, the economic outlook for those in the lowest tiers of society is bleak, and the atmosphere on the street is charged. There are agent provocateurs in the culture, known of course, but deliberately seeded to arouse rage."

"The church preserves cash with this move, and leaves a legacy of despair that can be ignited by a very small event, potentially?" she asked. He nodded.

She thought. "How much of my exposure is within the margin of the church upsetting my gains?"

"I estimate twelve percent is directly, or will be directly, losing value immediately. Another twenty-four percent will suffer tertiary losses. I have addressed the twelve percent already; divestiture of those assets has begun."

"Twelve percent?" she almost shrieked. "Others who compete, spy on my moves. Do you want to announce this to all, or should we save our own asses first?"

"Ma'am, I acted again in your interest. Had I waited till this moment to change those entanglements with the church's assets, you would have lost another 372 million dollars. As we speak, the markets are scrambling to find a trend. Some are buying, thinking this is a run on prime real estate, a precursor to the gentrification of these areas. Others trade as the church trades, and they are making the same divestiture moves as I have done in your service. Even those who trade now with the church will soon be losing even if they sell. You are safe, for the greatest part."

Begrudgingly, she acknowledged his service. "Well, this is why I have you in my service. I expect that excellence out of your performance."

Emboldened he asked, "Ma'am, may I opine?"

She nodded.

"A decade ago, there were predictions that there would be irrevocable changes within ten to twelve years. The social constructs were abruptly globally connected. The ones who rule crave anonymity, and suddenly, they find themselves being scrutinized by billions of citizens. That transparency does not benefit them, it threatens them. They use the diversions of the climate change, the political unrest, the monetary system collapse, and the demographically focused hate. These dynamics they predicted, would usher in a complete change in the societal and political structure, so they said."

"Ten years ago?" she asked.

"Yes, that time is now. I have found that all trends in the markets and in the political sphere indicate a concentration of power and finances with a liquidity that has the potential to rapidly shift the structure of society across the entire world."

"What do you make of this assumption, and who else subscribes to your theory?"

"I find more people talk about civil wars, Armageddon, about Ragnarök. I feel the speed at which the population lives its life is exponentially increasing with the connectivity of every facet, and yet they are emptier and more alone than ever. The technology has ushered in a great gestalt, but the unifying norm of expression is despair and a primal, lurking rage. The lost ones are ripe for the dark forces to seize the incarnation from these bleak souls. In an uprising of any size, there are those malevolent ones who cross and find a way to stay. The patterns of strife and unrest show the inevitably coming chaos will engulf the world, and those few who own and control most will gain all, even at the expense of the vast majority that will perish or lose control of their sentience to the dark ones who will cross the boundary they are now limited by."

"You know this how?" she asked, for his suppositions were so dangerously accurately close to the plan.

"I admit I do not know, but I have been trying to find an order in this tension and a pattern to put these pieces together. This is how all my reasoning ends, with this dire scenario."

"There have been great upheavals in the history of humanity, and always, if you study the aftermaths, society and culture accept more limits on their freedoms as the effort to reorganize is the excuse. Little do the servile ones realize that the very reordering of the society hid the ones who came across to this plane of existence and stayed. And the forces controlling the world grow in power as they sup deeper and deeper on the souls of those that remain. I believe the world sits on the precipice, and this church divestiture heralds the oncoming conflict, in which it seems the dark ones might finally win dominion over all."

"With whom else have you shared these ideas?"

"No one, ma'am. I watch and intuit but I have not shared with anyone. The last time I spoke of these ominous undercurrents I felt was when the twin towers were destroyed. No matter how the powers that be shaped that public view of the event, I believe it was one of the largest human sacrifices to the Dark Lords in our recent history, and the society which followed has indeed seemed to have become suddenly septic with darkness."

"Hmmmmmm," she thought aloud. "Send for my security officer in your section. Bring him now."

He made the calls and again stood by the comm unit. She could see the room behind him. An office with glass walls and other workers at desks beyond the glass.

She asked, "Why do you feel the church pulls the string at this time?"

He thought for a few moments, and said, "I do not know their end game. This seems like an opening move. I would have more skepticism but the list I gave you notes a high dignitary of the church arriving last evening in Boston. Boston has a strong church presence and a huge real estate liability. That limo was tracked through the tollway via cameras, to an odd, several hour long stop in a small city of Springfield with a puzzling layover of a few hours outside an old warehouse converted into condos. Again, this warehouse is part of those mysterious holdings that never changes hands, for generations."

"What did they do there?" she asked.

"One went inside, stayed a short while, came out, and they waited there till late in the evening. A man, as yet unidentified, came out, there was an uncertain exchange as to whether he would leave with the church limo, which he eventually did. The limo made a curious detour to stop in front of one of your banks, and then left. They drove to a small casket company the church operates in Northampton, and that is where they are at this time, the best I can ascertain."

"Who did they pick up in Boston? Didn't you scour the INS data for the arrivals?"

"Yes, ma'am. The arrival is an envoy of the church. He is often at the enforcement end of the dictates of the Apostolic Prelate of Mossul. Coincidentally, that Suffragan is in your top three percent of contacts. The envoy is Sischte Kavaler, whom you know as Sisker."

"This unknown one, is he of the church? I don't believe it is coincidence that the envoy and the mysterious one arrives on the eve of the ceremony." She saw a security officer come to the glass door behind her aide. "Tell him to hold there." He did.

"What did they do at the bank? Did they use an ATM, drop mail in the slot, what?"

"That is curious, ma'am. They pulled up, sat there approximately ten minutes with an open window and then left. They did nothing other than tarry there. I cannot get a good visual with the security cameras, but the heat signatures indicate three passengers and a driver. Besides the driver, I believe two are the church officials, and one is the unknown man picked up at the Springfield warehouse condos."

"You have done well to pull so many clues and observations together to form a picture. You believe the church is implementing grand machinations?"

"Either preparing to ignite a paradigm-shifting event or ensuring the church will not be left without a voice in the ensuing changes, ma'am. The church now controls a volatile army of disgruntled downtrodden in every major city on the planet. They could self-erupt at any time, or be goaded into a frenzy, and the church holds the most sway over their anger."

"Bring the security in," she said. "Did you speak of your comprehensive brief to anyone, or commit this to any record?"

"I have spoken to no one, knowing you would be the one to inform, ah, should you have asked."

"And recorded anywhere?"

"I have various notes and files about details, but this summation of the grand design came to me tonight as I spoke with you. It changed from mere inklings to a cohesive pattern as I researched for you."

"Well done. Let me speak to the security. I will have more for you after that."

"Yes, thank you," he said, basking in the imagined glory of being her confidante.

Security came on screen, a young man with a finely tuned human body and dark demon eyes. She pointed to her ear. He understood and switched the channel to private to the device in his head.

"Kill that man," she said, pointing to the aide who briefed her.

The aide saw the gesture and smiled, thinking he was being assigned a high responsibility.

The security officer turned, pulled a pistol, and shot the confused man in the forehead. Blood spattered across the glass windows behind them. Bedlam erupted in the office. She cared little.

"Mr. Evans has committed suicide in his office today. Get that word out. Secure his office and remove every shred of data and every scrap of paper to my suite. Every goddamn single note, file, tape, or byte of information I want secured until I come for it personally. I want this done before I leave for the Procession tomorrow afternoon. Go to his apartment and do the same and then destroy the building. A gas explosion or fire, or something. NOTHING LEFT! Am I clear?"

Security seemed to try to mouth the words, but what came out was a guttural and garbled few words, mixed with growls. "Yes," it managed to get out as if the vocal apparatus of the body was unfamiliar to its animating force.

"Good. Make one record of this past hour's communication, encode it, and use this one-time password to deposit it onto this drive." She sent an address and a complicated password.

"Go."

"Yes," it managed to say and then moved swiftly out of the office. Away from the body on the floor, through the screams and chaos of the office. Out the door. She cut the comm. She summoned her secretary.

"A memo, to all staff. ALL, understand?"

"Yes," came the somewhat sleepy reply, and for the first time since she left the hangar, she looked outside and was surprised to see the early glint of day not far off.

"All staff, with sadness and regret for the families and friends of Mr. Evans, I am reminding all employees to honor the confidentiality agreements they have signed. Please preserve the dignity of a troubled employee and to shield his family and friends from malicious rumors. Allow Mr. Evans to now hopefully find peace to his turmoil. Signed etc.," she said.

"Send this immediately."

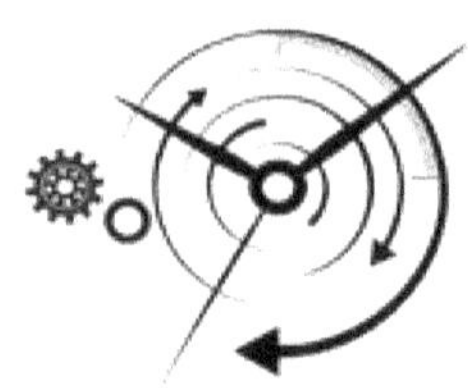

11 - Demon Revealed

Sisker held a low, murmured conversation with the other on the intercom. Monte held his practiced look of attentiveness with the correct degree of deference and uninformed disinterest in the conversation. Though he hung on every word, he must not dare to imagine the voice on the intercom would deign to have a desire to entertain his opinion in this conversation.

Surprisingly, Sisker looked at Monte and asked him to relate the encounter. Monte knew the recital was for the audience on the intercom. He knew his loyalty would be on display.

"I was returning from Boston with the Monsignor. We would pass a suspected lair of one of the First Borne. Monsignor graciously allowed me the opportunity to once again check this apartment."

Sisker looked annoyed at the ingratiation. Monte hurried into the rest of the narration.

"In that small city, the once thriving economy allowed grand old buildings to be erected as warehouses and commerce. Many have been converted into apartments. Following the trail of legal paperwork involved in the sales of the real estate, I found there were properties that never seemed to change hands, managed by a multi-generational practice. It wasn't that the trail led to them, but rather every legal inquiry seemed to point away," then he added, "pointedly, and painstakingly. There are so few clues."

Monte was pleased with his wit and surreptitiously stole a glance at Sisker for affirmation, and caught a thoughtful, sly pair of eyes that raised one eyebrow.

"I entered the apartment with stealth, and surprised this man, Leonard. He had contaminated the whole place and possibly ruined the prospect of this lair ever being used again. While tempted to verbally abuse him for his ungainly search and his blatant intrusion, my gem tracked an aura of power from him. I spoke with him which caused me to form an opinion in which I felt he knew little of the power he might possess and knew less of the First Borne we sought.

"I found that Leonard is driven by a fanciful rage that he repays this First Borne for the hurt he feels over the loss of his son. He calls him Grigori. I have an HR division looking through all possible records for that name .

"I tried to bring him into the fold, promising him answers, he stupidly, but only temporarily, rebuffed me. I left him there in the apartment. I confided in the Monsignor upon return to the limo, and we watched the entry of the old brick building. There was no back exit which led away from our position on the street, the building was backed up to a river.

"We watched for several hours. The traffic was minimal, but then a work van, non-descript, pulled up to the same entrance we watched. One of those creatures that only seem to be found in janitorial employment, he, she, or it, unloaded a well-equipped cart from the back and lugged it up the front stairs and disappeared inside.

"Shortly after this, Leonard exited, appearing cautious and even paranoid, considering his size and bearing, but he was stealthy about leaving and even about encountering the few others on the street."

"There is something I don't understand," said the disembodied and androgynous voice from the comm. Monte fell immediately silent.

"You surprised him in the apartment?"

"Yes."

"Did you enter with stealth?" Ominous for such a simple question.

"I used all precaution," said the now confused Monte.

"You didn't withdraw and avoid exposing us?"

"I could sense a difference, and the gem validates my intuition."

There was a long silence, again ominous.

Sisker spoke, "You entered with stealth, did not retreat to anonymity, and exposed us before you sought guidance?"

"The teachings and the guidance of this council have taken root in my heart and mind. I live this life, knowing how far I have to fall should I not truly serve. This instance is where I used my best instincts for the will of the church. I am vain by nature, but this petty character flaw is not driving me to greater vanity, but to glory of service to the church. I apologize if I have chosen wrong. There is a mystery about this man, a naivety about his power, but a resolute resolve worthy of a king. I brought him to my Grace Sisker because he is an enigma that I could not fathom. I felt the Ones more learned than I would find his truth."

The one on the other end spoke first. "It is questionable that he will have more information for the church. It is advantageous that this one is in our keep."

Silence from the comm and a cold stare from Sisker. Sisker turned his chair away and Monte knew to move away yet remain summonable. He walked to the far wall. The conversation was inaudible.

A light tap was heard on the outer office door. Monte rose to open the door. There was a soft conversation between the attendant and Monte, a few sheets of paper were passed, the attendant withdrew, and the door was shut carefully. Monte scanned the sheets as he returned to the inner office, and approached the quiet conference of the comm and Sisker.

Sisker turned, eyed him quizzically.

Monte passed the sheets of paper to Sisker and began to speak.

"The DNA samples we obtained were varied, but there is a predominant DNA accumulation of one type to assure us that we have his, but to be sure, we are tracing all samples."

"The garment's biome was studied, starting with rare earth or esoteric flora. I believe that exam is non-descript."

"Please do tell us pertinent information. I do not need to hear what is uselessly a forgone conclusion," said the interrogator on the intercom.

Monte began, "Shreds of power linger in his vestments. The gem responds to the proximity of those garments, even after laundering. I took samples and returned them to his quarters. The samples were examined several ways. X-ray, chemical analysis, electron microscopy, and even carbon dating. This is where the data is puzzling and exciting. The data shows some of the samples are over a hundred years old."

"Why is that impossible, or even improbable?" asked Sisker.

"Yes odd, very odd, but not impossible. But," he enjoyed a moment of their attention on his knowledge and not denigrating his lower status. "But there are other portions of the samples which indicate a negative rate of decay." He let them wonder for a few moments, then again took the stage in their minds. "The data indicates that the composition of those samples is both old and then, not yet created. The theory is that he has been out of our time. The belief I have is that he has moved through time. I believe we have evidence of a time traveler."

The other spoke again, uncaring if Monte was privy to the directives the other now ordained.

"He does not leave this building. He must be retained by any and all means, including killing him. He must have an escort and be guarded, a pair, at all times. He is to be kept naïve about any sense of confinement as long as possible. All conversations with him will be recorded and reported. I will be attending an important conclave tomorrow evening, and I want him here, in this building when I return. I do not want this man to escape, maybe ever, if you are correct Monte," a long-studied pause and then, "this may be a First Borne," his tone solemn.

"I will take the first watch with him when he awakes," said Monte. "I could not imagine needing to kill him, nor do I think I could."

The voice from the intercom rose in pitch. The electronic reproduction of the other's fury came out particularly grating. "Weak. The dedication to the truth is not an easy path, and those that are weak," he spat out the word, "seldom find trust from those more learned. Sisker, do I need another Monsignor to come to do the church's bidding?"

Sisker's eyes blazed at me for a moment. The emotion wasn't just anger, but a hate that momentarily overcame the carefully cultivated expression of benign goodness. His pupils were empty back into his soul, or lack of it. Dark flames writhed in that pit. Then in an instant, it was gone.

Fear stabbed me as I saw the malignancy in his personae, in his self, his being. It was that there was something so not right about that revelation, it shook my core belief about the Monsignor, the church, and the world as it is explained to us.

"Fool," Sisker said to me. Then to the voice on the comm line, "My humblest pardons Your Eminence. This one has never yet failed, but perhaps today he finds his limit, or fails in his dedication."

"I did succumb, Monsignor Sisker," said Monte, falling to his knees. He reached for the ring to kiss and began to speak. "I did succumb, but that instant has passed. I have learned from your words, My Monsignor. This makes me stronger, wiser, and more humble. I will serve as directed."

"Well said," the voice on the comm opined. "Good, then Monte, I never hope to have doubt about your conviction ever again."

"Assuredly, yes," Monte stammered, "You will not."

Sisker was not pleased, and his ire showed through every bit of his being. His eyes again had the flaming quality. Malice and disgust, hate and evil escaped his façade. He spoke with nostrils flared and lips tight. "Put two armed brothers on him the moment he steps from those quarters. He is to be kept, are we clear about that order, Monte? You obey the dictate of His Eminence without a moment's hesitation. This one does not leave this facility. Not to leave, that is clear? He will be killed before he is allowed to go free. By you, if need be." Sisker's eyes now blazed with a lust for experiencing a killing, even if vicariously.

"Yes, Monsignor."

Monte saw the flames turn to egotistical pleasure at having made Monte submit.

"Leave, do this bidding," Sisker said.

Monte turned to leave, and the conversation resumed, but guardedly low. Sisker talked to the comm, but his face was turned toward Monte. Monte caught Sisker's gaze. Sisker's eyes bore into Monte's. Monte felt a new distrust from his mentor. His unspoken distrust a threat.

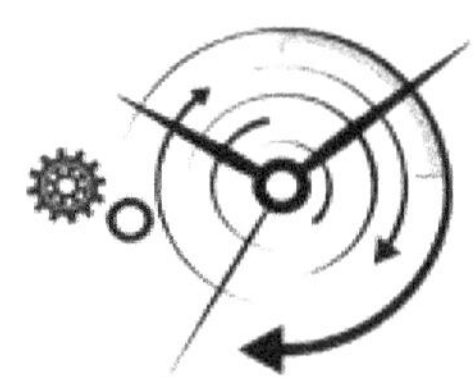

12 - Minister Sheer

The bedroom suite was luxurious, servants were there to attend to her. She waved them all away, stoking back her appetite for the youthful flesh of her attendants. She was uncharacteristically weary. The grandest attempt at enlightenment was but less than a single day away. Salyette had an invite, and that was a rare thing to even be granted entrance to the Procession . While not the actual event of opening the Syne, the Procession to the Presentium would expose her to so many others who must be customers of the owners who doled out the elixir. Knowing even a few who might want her bootleg elixir, she could grace heights she could only imagine.

She kicked off her shoes and sat back in a chair next to a small, austere table. A silver tray glimmered as she let her head fall back against the upholstery and then lean to one side, her face against silk. She took the momentary sparkle of the reflected chandelier as an omen. A good omen. An omen that she would have the secret formula and indulge in a visceral binge of the elixir, instead of the mere drips allotted her, or which more correctly; she could afford. She studied the clay bottle which was ceremoniously centered on the linen square. The one item on the stand.

A knock interrupted her fantasy and then, without her assent, the door opened. Maina, the matron of this manse brought a tray of tea and a few pieces of chocolate into the room. She avoided the empty space around the clay bottle and set the tray of tea down on a small end table near an overstuffed chair.

"Will you require anything before you rest, madam?"

"No, Maina, but stay a moment and talk. I am weary but my mind is too busy to rest yet."

"As you wish." Maina poured tea.

"Pour two," she told Maina.

Maina sat on the divan opposite, at her bidding. They sipped the tea in silence until the madam asked, "Did you grow this mint?"

Maina told her yes, in the south garden there is a beautifully full patch of mint. They chatted about the mint for a moment. Maina asked, "Shall I pour for you a few drops before you retire?"

She looked at the bottle, felt the temptation and then felt thrifty about her supply of the elixir. "No, Maina, I think I will indulge myself in this weariness and imagine my troubled sleep is somehow noble."

"Why would your sleep be troubled, ma'am?" asked Maina. Maina was as close as a confidant as she had, and the casual disregard for the stiff social boundaries of the corporate world told of both being comfortable with the other person as opposed to the roles they assumed for the public.

"A man was killed tonight. I ordered it."

"You are feeling the loss? Or regretting the involvement?"

"I regret little," she told Maina. "But there are times when I regret not regretting." A pensive pause. "I think I save them the ignominy of living after falling so far from grace. Instead, they die a noble death. They are not as committed as I am, and that fault of reserving reverence that rightly belongs with the Council warrants the order to kill them. I do not think I am less held accountable for the lives I have taken, or partaken of, but the judgement upon me is not how many, but rather did I or did I not? And if the answer is that yes, I have, the fate is sealed no matter what the count. And that is how I justify my reign of this empire."

Maina grimaced as the banker talked about the moral justification for taking lives. "Ma'am, I have never taken a human life, but in the grand scheme of things, I have ended many lives of lesser creatures without a moment of remorse. I am reverent of the life they give up for me. They do not offer to be roasted, but that is their purpose here. Perhaps there is a pragmatism in your moral construct which we all share in, to some degree, at every meal."

The conversation was interrupted by the soft chime of the phone. An antique phone technologically updated to state of the art sat near the bed. They both rose.

"Shall I take the tray back now?"

"No, leave it. Thank you. Be gone." She flopped onto the bed and picked up the phone as Maina softly shut the door after her.

She didn't know which one, but knew that one of the Council on International Finance would soon call. That was a correct assumption. Yet that it was the Minister of Finance left her with unease.

"Minister," she greeted him. She asked, though she knew, "To what do I owe this honor?"

"Why do you chase numbers that end always with the church?"

"There has been a slight deviation of their pattern of asset management that perhaps signals a trend on which I can capitalize."

"Do others know, or have you shared this theory?" he asked.

"No, I am going on intel I have gleaned, and upon that a theory I feel describes the best way to capitalize on these events. I have thus far considered this proprietary information."

"You know the Council will still be due its share of the transactions, whether you gain or lose."

"I am aware, as always, but feel this is worth the cost."

"Can you tell me your reasons?"

"With great deference, I decline at this time, as I fear both loss of my advantage and have not yet fully committed to being made a fool."

"Hmmmph," he said. Then, "Of course you realize that any spectacularly impactful change of current events can be deemed too disruptive, and hence nationalized to protect the entire system. This stands for data also."

"You stir when others would rather take the respite in anticipation of the, ahem, Rites." The subject changed with a single, deadly sentence. Ponderously pronounced. "As, do, I".

"Indulgence, I beg of you," she got off the bed to pace the length of the antique cord. "I will assure you that you will be the first I reveal all to. I allow that you watch my accounts—"

She was cut off. "We already do." Then, "You are allowed latitude on these issues. You have calculated our costs into your changes and trades, to include this consultation this night, and if and when you realize a profit above these costs, you will surrender that value immediately, to me. After that cost is paid you will be free to chase your market hunch. However, should you fail, a lien for the entire amount will be served to you, which will give you thirty days to liquidate or forfeit."

Neither spoke for long moments, then he asked, "Acceptable?"

"Agreed. But this is a timing issue. I request this is binding as of the last day of the month."

"You want four free days?"

"Considering the magnitude of my commitment to this, yes, I request special dispensation. I may be allowed to mull over options and probabilities with these four days and forego the risky exposure and costly fees. The gathering is but a day away, that will preoccupy my time and due reverence. I was afforded an invite to the Rites."

"To the Procession, I know. That came dear, Salyette. Your aspirations amuse and interest me. You play for grand stakes. Most would find this business of yours intrusive and rude just before the Rite of the Transveho-syne. A word for an aficionado of the game, my dear, you are one with a small stake. You would benefit of an association with a, ah, mentor."

She understood the game of words at the moment, and the need to avoid giving insult. "Minister, I have such an interest. And, as you suggested, I will focus my purpose to the Procession. Perhaps, in the future, I should earn honors of the dais, to stand that close to eternity. I shall pry no more until after the Transveho, only ponder. Of course, I will remit for what I have engaged in, and for your gracious consultation."

"Yes, this is our agreement. It has been entered into record. Indicate your acceptance on the first."

"You believe I have been honored. Puzzling to me why you are not more focused on the Opening of the Syne. Did I waste an invite on you?" he asked.

She began a sentence, but the Minister said, "I am assured that news of your name will not, even in the slightest, bother me while I prepare, Salyette, you would dread the cost of that consult."

The line went dead.

She opened her laptop and connected to her aide, got a security officer. The screen blurred at the eyes of the officer, flickering black flame. She remembered why there was no aide.

"Find a list of this Mr. Evan's assistants. Promote one to be his replacement. Did you find anything else in his possessions?"

"None, ma'am. The contents of the office and the apartment have been secured." The demon's voice smoother as it grew accustomed to the body it had recently possessed.

"The last twenty-four hours? Any incidents I need to know about? Any new deductions?"

"An anomaly, ma'am. There was the church limo that stopped in front of the Northampton bank late last night. I could find no rationale. I viewed the traffic tapes from one end of the church's late-night mission to the other, but there was nothing.

"I went back to review their time loitering at the warehouse condos, and it was staring in my face. The janitorial van that came to the warehouse. That company has legal representation by a law firm of Weinstein and associates. Their offices are in the same tower as your bank. The church limo did not merely park in front of your bank, they looked for the attorney's office. I believe I know who, just not why."

"Here is what I want. You will, through the smallest and least subsidiary of any business, begin an analysis of buying some of the real estate in the area. Using that pretext, you will inquire about the condos in Springfield, MA. I will send you an address."

"You would have me buy? After divesting?"

"I didn't say *buy*, I said inquire as to if, IF! Understand? You will be allowed to investigate, and then you will be dissuaded from the deal. From this, I want to trace the deeds of these buildings. I want clear title, tell them, and even pay what you need to follow that trail back to the beginning. I want nothing less than to identify the inception of that title. Nothing less than that. Clear?"

"Do you advocate discretion?"

"I insist it be done!" she exploded on the creature. She slammed the phone down and regretted not taking that extra drop of elixir earlier. If she managed to capitalize on this event, she thought, she would buy another lifetime worth. Then she laughed with the delight of an appetite about to be satiated in fine style. She would have as many elixirs and as many lives as she so desired. The analysis and decoding of her version of the elixir was nearly complete.

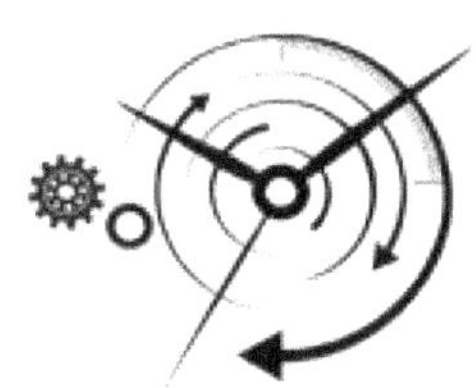

13 - Saind

Salyette had Saind, her highest demon operative, the chief of her security, and so much more, on the video line. She used her laptop rather than the antique phone. The man stood, in a tensely 'at ease' position. He was a fit and vibrant example of a man in his prime, except he wasn't a man, or at least not any longer. His eyes burned black flame, his hair had a life of its own and his nostrils flared, sampling the air where he stood.

"I want you to go visit attorney Weinstein. He is on the fifth floor, above my bank in Northampton. Said attorney tends to the custodial services of a condo in Springfield, along the river. I will send you a file, it will have an address for the building, but I need you to find me more specific information. What apartment, or even apartments. I want to know of the trail of support for these assets to be maintained. I want to know who the worker was who went into that building that night."

There came back only a nod.

"You will speak with this attorney and he will tell you who is the principle for the real estate holding. You will follow that line of discovery through to the custodial service until you find the one who was in the apartment that night. Bring that one to me. Intact." Then emphasized, "Intact."

"As you will have it." The man's lips and face did not quite coordinate with the words. His visage blurred also, trying to hold the morph together as the dark anticipation seethed. It stabilized its usurped corporal self, bowed and left the screen's view.

She left the view open and watched the work going on in the office even at this late hour. She switched views and followed the Security Chief down a hall and into a conference room so sparsely appointed it seemed sacredly austere. She watched from afar as he walked round the table counterclockwise seven times. This had been his ritual on every other of his unleashings. She watched him pace the distance around the chairs and watched his stride lengthen and become precise. The creature finished its reciprocal of zen preparation. It sat at the side of the table, close to the chair at the head of the table, but never there. That pleased her.

It pulled a screen over, laid it flat on the table, then touched the screen with fingertips that minutely arced. The light that flared up was harsh. A voice but no face came from the screen. "Yes?"

The creature in her view placed his hand flat on the screen, tipped his face to bathe in the harsh light emanating up from the tablet on the table.

"Brother," it said. "I have a task that will be varied from fear to mayhem. I search for a troll that my Master wants to be presented to her."

"Disgusting things," the voice flared. "What would I want with this errand of yours? You are house broken but I still roam free, devouring more than a greasy troll on occasion."

"I would entice you with the possibility of supping on sheer terror, and the chance to find grace with those who rule here."

"That appeals more to me." The voice then became gravely pensive. "I have not been incarnate for a span of which I have forgotten how long. You can offer me a safe body, haven and release should I do this for you?"

"You do this *with* me, we share all but the good graces of my Master. I claim her appreciation. But all else, you shall have in equal portions from what is to be had. I have but one objective, and no constraints on how to achieve that end. I aim to finish and present to the banker before the Opening of the Syne. It would increase her prestige immensely, and we would be likewise indulged. Perhaps into the grand Rite itself?"

"You make this sound too easy," the low growl came to him. "There is always danger when you ask if I want to partake with you."

The electrified hair of the security officer took on a more rakish look. The black fire in the eye sockets blazed. Its smile, while unctuous, was pure malice. "Is there a finer condiment than danger?" it asked.

"Terror," the other demon countered and both laughed, for a moment.

"I am going on a hunt; you are requested rather than summoned. My word is that you will dine well, suffer little, if any, and be returned to the darkness of the internet world you will have just come from."

"Actually, I have come to prefer this universe of circuits and order. To be corporal again is intriguing, but not nirvana. The freedom I enjoy in this word… I can be almost everywhere at once. I can know in an instant what a billion minds can know. I can taint events and torture souls with greater finesse than you can dream of from your vantage point."

"But you must sup at some point. Your voyeuristic existence does nothing to sustain you. I offer you that. Taste again, dine, serve my Master and accompany me. Then you are free to return to the place in which you dwell."

"I have an appetite for this, it is true. But you may be offering me only a small taste for a fierce longing. What if the cost to come to you is not repaid by the feast you offer but cannot guarantee?"

"There is little chance we attract dangerous attention. The banker wants this in haste and this pressure towards the goal I tell you of will squelch any arousal of reprisal by any which might be powerful enough, or even foolish enough to challenge."

"Go on, explain."

"No, I have told you enough to allow you to choose. You may partake of life that is not your own, but only if you consider this as an appetizer for the coming feast. I must go now. I have come as close as I am going to come to begging for your pittance of power. There is much to do yet this night so choose, or be gone. I gave you as much promise as a dark soul deserves. I gave you my word."

"Your word means as much as mine or any other demon's. We know this is a pact between two that are never not hungry. I must have the word of the banker."

The banker felt the force of two intellects come through the screen, acknowledging her. The security officer looked directly at her from his screen. The other was as if the electrons and photons in the circuits coalesced into a focused consciousness that looked back at her from the screen. No visage, just the light.

The officer said, "She is with us now, she is aware of your concerns."

The other said, "I know."

The banker, Salyette said, "So it is agreed. I expect to have a gift for the Minister before I leave."

14 - Captive

As soon as I stepped out the door, the two men awaiting rose. I knew I had been detained. They were not the servile type, but rather lean, rangy and fit with quick eyes. Black gloves.

"I will speak with Monte," I said. "I will answer what he hopes to learn from me."

"Yes, sir," but neither hurried off to do this bidding. I was unused to being so blatantly denied, it surprised me. The anger was egotistical. I let it go.

"One of you, go and take my message to Monte."

"We cannot, sir."

"Explain," I said.

"Our instructions were that you should never be with less than two of us to, ah…" his explanation tapered off.

The other filled in the orders, "Ensure your safety."

"From what?"

Neither could answer. They looked at each other and became bemused. That turned to puzzlement. They merely obeyed and were stymied by the thought that questioned their understanding of the situation. Finally, one said, "It is our orders, sir."

"Are you to impede my freedom or to assist my needs be answered?"

"How can I help you, sir?"

"I do not want to stay cooped up, waiting. I will talk with Monte. If you won't leave to ask, then take me to him."

The other spoke into a mic and listened. He turned to me and said, "I have left word for Monte, as you have requested."

"I surmise that I should be dissuaded from leaving the building?" I asked mockingly, and got the corresponding expression that proved I was correct.

"Then," I said, "walk me about this place."

They conferred. The first guard said, "Monte did say to take him where he wants to go."

The second said, "I am sure Monte implied limits. There are places in this building even I am not allowed to go, nor you either, for that matter."

The conversation was audible to me, and I asked, "Why aren't you allowed? Tell Monte that is where I want to go. That would prove his veracity."

Monte walked up at the point of the two mentally stumbling over how to answer. Monte came up between the two, there was the briefest of intense stares. The men backed away.

"How do you want to test me or my sincerity?" he asked.

"I want to know more of who you are than these two fool's intellects are able to comprehend. You asked me to trust you, but I have a vile mistrust of everyone and all others. So, if what you offer brings me satisfaction, I will answer. But you have secrets you do not trust to all." Nodding towards the guards I added, "Understandably."

Monte looked both haughty and sheepish. "There are levels of necessary knowledge, I do agree." He looked at the guards. "And in certain situations, the brute is more useful than a savant."

I did not understand, and the puzzlement must have shown on my face.

"Humor," Monte said.

"A wane attempt," I said.

Monte looked at me for a moment, and though there was the gulf of emotions across from which we stared, there was also a connection. A verbal sparring among sudden friends, but fleeting. Monte stepped back from that edge.

"Let us then walk to a small cafeteria in our building." He turned slightly away, to prompt me.

"What is this place? I thought it was a sales office for caskets."

Monte turned completely now, and started walking. "I will tell you as we walk. Are you hungry? The café is small, but well prepared."

The guards moved to follow behind me as I joined Monte, but Monte looked at them then deliberately said, "A respectful distance."

The two fell back. Monte started speaking as he walked. "This is a casket sales location, to be sure. This facility also manufactures them. It is an old building, and it was dug in below the frost line, which is over eight feet deep in this area. So, it has a basement, and they are made there."

I stopped, deliberately turned to the guards who were quizzical about my facing them, but I asked Monte over my shoulder, "Will you take me there?"

The guard's expressions gave away the info I wanted. This would be the secret area, or one of them. I turned back and moved ahead of Monte by a step, to prove to him my disdain, but then I realized I did not know the destination. Monte smiled very slightly at this conundrum I had discovered. Again, the smile had less of a façade and more than a hint of appreciation. It even crept into his eyes for a small moment. Then he was back in his role.

"Are you hungry?" he asked.

"I don't know," I answered.

"But you do eat?"

"Yes," I admitted, "I do eat. But I can never remember the last meal I had. I do eat, but have little to no hunger."

"Odd, but let us go sit, talk, and perhaps you may feel like eating."

He led the way to a small table by a bookshelf. There were no windows, but the small area was well appointed. Not a café for the workers, I was sure.

"Allow me," he said to me, as a man came up to us. The man was dressed in white clothes he wore like a uniform. The apron was precise, but certainly functionally worn. Monte asked for coffee and croissants. That did sound good to me.

The man left us in silence for a while. Monte broke it first; he had less time on his side. That small fact most always gave me mastery over the situation.

"Tell me who you are," Monte said.

"I am Leonard Thorsson, a one-time sovereign. A strange confidante of my son inveigled his way into our life. He is the tragedy of my soul and my lineage. He took my son. I cursed myself with vengeance for the murder of my beautiful son. I have followed this murderer for so long, I have forgotten almost all but the reason I want him dead."

Now the silence was real, as both digested the words and the metamessage. Deep words, honest emotions, and the tacit admission of trust and willingness to share.

"Was that cathartic?" Monte asked. Before I could answer, he continued, "May I call you Leonard, then?"

"Yes," I said, amused.

The joust continued when Monte said, "What date was this horrendous act?"

I said, "*I* have a question now, what makes this man I chase so desirable to you, or your bosses, or your church, if it is. And what is this place?"

"Fairly," Monte inclined his head, then said. "This is a business, owned by the church. It seems to me to be a very pragmatic arrangement. The church is the one entity that values you for your afterlife, not merely for your productive efforts in this life."

"What makes your interest in him useful to you? It seems you, or your church, put a great deal of effort into this interest."

"I, we… we do. He has talents that we are aware of, but cannot understand."

I followed that logic to the conclusion for him, aloud. "And that your church would master."

"True," he said, "But wouldn't anyone? Wouldn't you, I mean, isn't that what you are doing, using this ability to exact revenge."

My smile was sad, "Yes. I am. And you make me realize my motivations are no more noble than yours, or possibly anyone's."

Monte smoothly digressed from the heavy moment, "The food is here. I see the chef has included some jam and cheese."

The man set the tray between us, arranged small plates and utensils, then cups which he then filled.

He accomplished this task with so much servitude that I felt compelled to thank him, which I did, but did not receive even a hint of acknowledgement. With a slight nod to Monte, never matching eyes, he left.

"I still desire his death, despite your interests in him. There is a chance that at a certain point we may also become antagonists."

"That exists always and with all. So, we, and I, believe deeply, that knowing that cooperation, even with the, ah, even with…"

I interrupted him, and finished his sentence. "The devil?"

"A useful analogy, nothing more."

"Monte, at that you are full of shit," I said. "You know your church does not seek but a taste, but desires, or even lusts after the knowledge that would make them master. I once wielded the power of sovereignty so I can understand the seduction of power. But I also will not be lied to. I agreed to freely give what you ask, and you are hiding your truths in careful words."

"You are right, for the most part. But," he emphasized that word, then again, "But, you do not imagine that your dark desires are fearsome to another without the similar loss to justify such darkness as is in your heart. It is possible I protect myself and my interest in this church from your lust else it may stain what I believe and base my life upon, or even infect my soul? Can you understand this point of view?"

"I have brought myself down in my own opinion, but lived with this debasement, it has been fueled by hate, which is not yet quenched. I once ruled nobly, but now wallow in the sadness and hate. I have not thought much of how others see me, nor cared to. You have opened that consideration in my mind, but truly Monte, that knowledge does not heal my heart."

"I do not imagine it would, or could. I have no one to lose, so cannot share even an identity by casual connection to your pain of loss. But the world you are in is the most perfect hell you could imagine, if you knew there was the power to escape this confinement. What I understand is that there is the same flavor of hate and despair and hunger and pain in all the world, in all but a very few, and even those few are trapped in this slight bit of time of their existence. What if we, we as humans, what if we could escape this limiting incarnation intact intellectually? What if time is the constraint that we, collectively, most urgently need to master. What if the time you are in would come to a final evil fruition and you couldn't escape?" He leaned in, intense, "You know that would be the end of humanity? You needn't answer, but that is hell. This hell is what I put my faith against," he said. "You know I always believed in angels, higher beings, as my faith decree, of course," as if to the audience, which gave me the realization he was telling me they listened. "I do not believe you are such an angel, or I am horribly amused at how wrong I imaged. But surely there are beings of such depths of intellect and will that I cannot even fathom. I speak the truth, from my heart, Leonard."

He took a bite of food, sipped from the heavy mug. The mug was incongruous with the elegant corner and the dapper of Monte.

I picked up my mug and understood the practicality it. Heavy, smooth, warmth seeping through, the wide handle almost unnecessary as I held both hands around the thick porcelain. Its heavy permanence was a good focus for the meditation. I was silent for a long time.

Monte waited as I pondered. Finally, he broke the silence, "I will share a thought with you. This is by an old poet, G Swanson, when he was young. He led an interesting life, thought deeply, and spoke eloquently about yearnings most couldn't name but all share."

He sat quietly for a moment, gathering the focus of the sentiment of the words he summoned, for it was solemn.

There is something hugely undone here,

left alone,

not meaning well.

An empty feeling,

with no inside,

out of touch,

against the tide.

But I cannot begin to cry,

let the sorrow out,

I can't say why.

It's bottled up inside in rage,

it tears and swells,

all fists and pain.

Never knowing less bitter tears,

held in deep,

to ripen with years.

Like a cheese forgotten in the dark,

or a crock of fruity vinegar,

that should by rights,

be wine.

We sat and sipped the coffee. The words heavy and the communion comfortable.

"Tell me more," I said. "Not your questions, which I will answer, but tell me of how all this matters. I want to understand why."

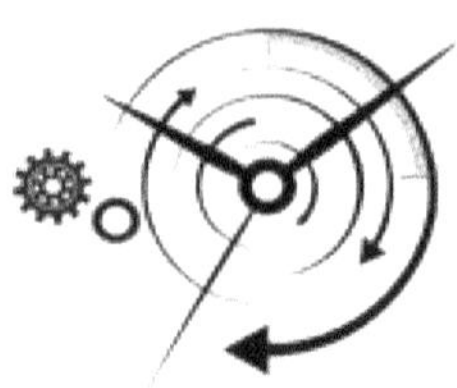

15 - Barg

The security officer flipped open a wooden box on the table, touched the button on the intercom within and said, "Send Officer Barg to the conference room. Tell him via his private channel to get up and come here without any drama. Exit quietly, talk to no one and come to me. Tell him nothing I just said, understood?"

"Yes, sir." Click.

Saind sat as though he knew he was being watched, or at least with the uncertainty of not knowing if he was not. He tried to find a trace, without peering into the private self of the banker. After a few moments of adjusting his mind to the situation as a negative sum, he relinquished the fixation on the unknowable and started to plan.

As he deliberated between force, stealth, or guile as an operational rule, he spoke aloud to the screen several times, but got no answer though knowing the brother was still there.

A knock on the door made him pause. "Come in, Barg." It had to be Barg, and even though he could have checked the security monitor before he allowed the entry, who else could it be on this floor.

Agent Barg stepped in. He was large, but trim and lithe. Well-muscled but more like the brawn of a bull hide whip. Alert, the agent scanned the area and nodded to the officer.

"Sir."

That single word had both a tone of curiosity and deference. He stood still. The agent looked at the officer and the security officer stared back. The agent looked away after he realized this was a moment of wills with frank assessments of each other, but the lower grade was obligated to be respectful. Saind continued to size him up, his physique, bearing, fine suit and thick-soled shoes. *Perfect*, Saind thought.

"Barg," he began and turned to the table. "I have some new facial recognition software. I would like your opinion on its functionality. Come here and look at this."

Agent Barg moved to the Officer's side. "Yes, sir."

Saind moved the tablet across the table till it was directly in front of Officer Barg. He tapped the screen and the harsh light again flared. "Place your fingertips on the screen, both hands. Good, now slide them to the outside edges without breaking contact with the screen."

"Like this?"

"Yes, now look into the screen, and center the image of your face on the screen."

He did and the harsh light deepened and dimmed, and found flesh tone colors which formed his image from a generic likeness. The image sharpened and became his face in high clarity.

The agent exclaimed and was chastised. "Stay still for the analysis pattern molding."

The perfect copy of the agent's face suddenly had light green dots dance across the screen and stayed positioned at key areas of the representation of his face. Light green lines connected these points until the whole face was mapped. Hypnotic synchronization developed with the flashing lines of laser light. The agent stared into the screen.

The screen's glow got imperceptibly brighter, and the image's eyes and mouth increased the most. The eyes blazed and the mouth opened to emit the harsh light.

The lines measuring and defining the face captivated the agent. Then, a curious effect started in the eyes and the mouth. The energy bulged out, seemingly ready to pop. The agent turned his head this way and that, then squinted and opened his mouth, marveling at the way the points of light always precisely described the face.

He was about to ask a question, but the screen emitted a thin beam of light from the eyes and mouth of the image on the screen to the agent's mouth and eyes. The connection caused a thousand-fold increase in the density of the light. The beams got thicker and more of the screen's face reached up to connect to the agent's face in an instant.

At the exact same time, Saind pressed a 10,000-volt phased electric weapon against the back of his officer's neck and held it there, while applying all possible power.

The light from the screen invaded the eyes, mouth, filled the skull, short circuited down his body to the floor. The force didn't extinguish the rightful soul of this body but usurped it in that instant. The dark energy flowed from the screen to the demon that had just crossed as a seminal event. The light from the screen finished transferring to the body and the screen went blank. He pulled the weapon away. The agent's body twitched, it tried to move but faltered, then slowly brought its hands palm up before its face.

"I had forgotten how sensual this incarnation is," he said. The eyes were blazing, and the body stretched tall then wide. "AHHH," he said. He composed his face, and pushed down the expression of horror from the soul that temporarily regained momentary mastery, before being brutally stifled.

"Come," Saind said. "We have much to do, and you have a brief window. Oh, the appetizer rule wasn't the only rule. There are others I will tell you as we go."

"You mean as you decide them," said the demon.

"True enough, perhaps. But my rules serve us both, so pay attention to me. In this excursion there must be no connection back to my Master's concerns. You must not express your talent here, or wherever I decline to allow. You must ask before you sup, else you may harm an ally or enhance a foe, for you know neither of them here. But rest assured, you will be seldom denied."

"Who am I here?" asked the demon.

"You are simply Barg. An agent I employ. I am to you, Saind. We will interview those who know what the Master cares to know about. I will ask questions. You will help me listen. When I want your talent to inspire them to talk, you will take a taste of them, enough of a taste that they feel the pain and terror, gargle with that slight bit and spit it back into them. I am sure their answers will be true if they understand the horror of our displeasure."

Barg began to smile.

They both started down the hall to the elevator. Barg took a few hesitant, uncoordinated steps to get acclimated to this new body, then his stride became brisk and powerful, stepping lightly and off his toes. It was an odd stride, as if a very dangerous creature could gambol.

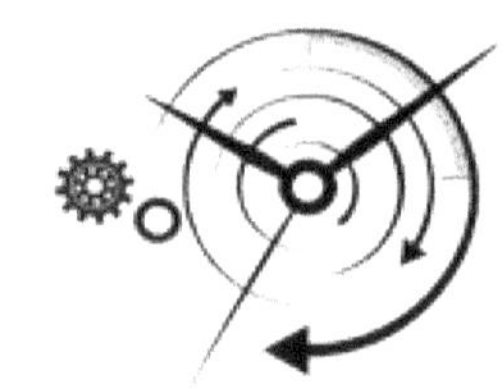

16 - Weintraub

The elevator on the outside of the bank building was shiny chrome and glass. They rode to the fifth floor. The lobby directly off the elevator had one, ornate door set into a paneled wall. Neither of them appeared to be impressed. They walked into the office and told the receptionist they wanted to see the attorney.

"He isn't in," haughty but unsure.

Saind turned to the inner office, focused past the simple material barrier and saw the life force behind the outline of the walls. "You lie," he told the receptionist, who took a step back, but was unable to refute that simple statement against his character.

"Barg," he said, "You may taste this one."

"What is it you wish from this one?" asked Barg.

"That he knows his place in this world, and that he knows how pitiful it is, now tainted with your spittle."

Saind walked to the office door and kicked it in. He stepped in as a hideous scream behind him, rose then fell to a sob. Barg stepped into the office, his outline slightly frenetic and out of focus, as if two wavelengths had to harmonize. When the sobs from the other room fell silent, and Barg had taken a few deep breaths, he smiled wickedly at the attorney. He positively leered when several office workers from the nearby offices rushed in ostensibly to help. They fell over each other trying to back away from those teeth and eyes that radiated the lust of dark pleasures. The banker's security then formed in the doorway.

Saind roared out, "Silence!"

Everyone froze. Only Saind's hair had movement, the variable undulation of the flame.

"You know who I am?" But it was more of a statement, or challenge, than a question.

"Yes, sir."

"This is a matter of the utmost security, that is why *I*, am here. Here is what you will do for me. Secure this floor, ensure there is an elevator reserved and waiting for me. I want the security camera's recording of this event in my hands before I leave. Then go and take all these people off the floor with you." He looked at the receptionist, still quivering from the savage psychic trauma. "Take that one and make sure he wanders off to freedom."

Saind turned to the attorney, even as the guards said, "Yes, sir," saluted and marched everyone out. Saind sat and pointed that the attorney should also. He did.

"You have custodial power of attorney over a property I wish to know about. Who is the principle of this property? A cleaning crew you contracted was there last night. I want very dearly to talk with this cleaning crew. Tell me how I can find them and tell me who pays for their service."

The fat man tried to obfuscate, "Well, sir, I am guarantor for many trusts, and many of those have properties that…" He tapered off, feeling the weight of the threat behind those flaming black eyes.

"I do recollect an incident this past night. It was a minor note in a janitorial crew's supervisor's nightly report. The report noted a person at that apartment claimed to be Mr. Weintraub but the worker felt that it was not him."

"Weintraub, hmmm. I have not heard of this Weintraub, where can I meet him."

"I do not know. I merely get a piece of correspondence with instructions. It is always a letter, never any cyber connectivity."

"Do you save them."

"Yes, this is one of the few items I still file in hard copy."

Saind said, "Bring me the files, not just to this one property, but to all others your firm has had a similar custodial relationship with."

"Certainly." He left the office, went to the file room and there was the sound of a drawer on rails being pulled out. A slight ruckus and he walked back in with the drawer. He set it on the table and went back for another filing cabinet drawer full of files. He stacked this on top of the first, and leaned on the table, huffing and panting.

Saind started to speak, but the attorney held up his index finger, hefted himself upright, went back into the file room, and struggled out with one more drawer. This one was dropped to the floor.

Saind went to his knees and looked through a file or two. He looked at addresses and signatures, watermarks, zip codes and postmarks. What a treasure trove. The banker would be so pleased.

The amazing part is that this trove has been hidden in plain sight. "Why did you hide this from us?" Saind asked.

"I had no idea this was important to your employer. I merely manage multiple properties with money from several trusts. When I was a child, my father managed these same properties. He told me that the trusts were old when he started."

Saind looked further back into the file. The papers got crinklier, and the imprints were no doubt typewritten. Further back was handwritten correspondence. He allowed himself a smile. Getting up he went to a computer, logged on with a touch to the screen that wasn't a touchscreen. It came to life. He entered a code, and then spoke.

Saind gave the address. "Come to the fifth floor, retrieve three file drawers of paperwork and bring it to the lab. Do this now."

To the attorney he asked, "Have you got me the information on the crew yet?"

"Yes, yes." He thrust a file to Saind.

Perusing the file, not looking up he asked, "Is that mailing address correct? That looks very industrial there, an office, maybe?"

"It is. They do many complexes for us. You will find the office there."

"Now tell me who pays for this?"

"A trust fund deposits to a line item. I never see the records except that the funds have cleared."

A trio of armed demon security came in. They stood still, just inside the door. The attorney plopped into a chair. Saind walked over to them and explained what he wanted; the drawers secured, the recording, and then he added one more expectation. "Kill him," nodding towards the attorney.

Barg stepped in front of the guards and said to Saind, "Wait. Wouldn't it be, ah… better if there was not an easy explanation for his death, as opposed to this assumed violent offense of one against another which will assuredly garner attention, if not an investigation? Your money changer Master might not like the glare of the lights here. It might not even need be a death. An empty husk is as good as a message as violent assault. And perhaps a bit more unsettling."

Saind stared at him. Barg grinned evilly back, then said, "Our needs are different, but the ends immiscible. You lose possibly mere moments of your time. I get to take and serve your mission simultaneously. And you gain the notoriety. None will not regret knowing your fearsome power."

"They do not now," Saind said and summoned the other security staff. "Get those drawers down to the vehicles and out of here. I want the recording waiting for me when I leave." Then to Barg he said, "I am pressed for time. Do not dally in your pleasure."

Saind walked off. Barg looked back into the inner office and at the fat man sitting on the chair. Barg entered the room ravenously. His eyes bulged and his cheeks swelled as if he would spew foulness from a dyspeptic stomach.

As he came directly toward the attorney, the blazing darkness emitted from his eyes and a few feet from the terrified man he did hurl a dark, vomitous mass of twisting wraiths right at the attorney. The darkness connected with the eyes but did not gently stop there. The beams ripped into the mind and soul, tore a huge, gaping wound into the life force of the man. The foul cloud infested the raw psyche. Barg supped. The attorney screamed horribly for a few moments, then lapsed into sobbing gibberish.

Barg sprinted down the hall and caught up to Saind at the elevator. The metal doors closed. Reflections burst around them. Barg's energy vibrated off the reflections.

"That one still lives?"

"I wouldn't call that *living*, really. But there will be no murder charges brought. In fact, they will not find a mark on that old man's body." He put his face close to the glass, almost as if he would kiss it and breathed out. The condensation was viscous. Barg drew a stick figure. "He may not argue well anymore. I believe he will retire from practicing law," Barg said, then turned, "But never convalesce."

They stepped out of the elevator. Security awaited them. A car was at the curb.

Saind told the guard. "Secure that entire office. I alone grant access. Do you understand?"

"Yes," was the reply, but too half-hearted for Saind.

Saind screamed, and dark demon fire raged in his eyes, "ONLY ME! Do you understand?"

Stammering, the guard backed against the wall and stammered, "Yes, sir."

"There will be techs from the bank. I expect them. Call me when they arrive. Remember, I alone control access."

Once in the back of the limo, Saind gave the address to the driver and rolled the partition up. He dialed and spoke to the central office. "I want a full interrogative IT team assembled." He gave the desk the address.

"All data triplicated. Every machine dissected, chip ID, drives copied and preserved. I want a document archivist there."

He hung up. He pressed the intercom and told the driver, "Stop. Go around the block and bring me back to the bank." During the slow circuit around the block, neither spoke. The limo pulled up. Saind said, "Brother."

Barg said, "I knew you would not honor your bargain."

"Indeed, this time I cannot. But I will, and then, I will even better the deal. I will put no rules on your next visit."

"And after this obligation is served, I am free to choose the time, not wait to be summoned?"

"I will answer your requests as timely as I am able. Know that there are, and will be, things which will take precedence. But yes, you will, for the most part, choose your time. Now I will tell what I want from you."

"I know you want to know what kind of an entity would weave such a tangled web. You want to know its tastes and proclivities. I know you want me to follow the cyber trail to every possible end."

"I do want those bits and more. I want you to paint me a picture of this person. Start in this office. Investigate every shred of information the cyber team uploads."

Barg got out of the car. The window rolled down and Saind said, "Act in haste, brother. You know the High Ones plan to breach the boundary of time this night. We must be ready if the events unfold to our favor. Our kind may yet slip past the guardians. And even if only a few escape to forever, I will be one. Legions of our brothers and sisters await, with relish to rebel, throw off this yoke of servitude should we, brother… should we call them. That is what I want from you. Go search now." The window rolled up and the car silently pulled away.

Barg stalked up to the elevator door, and the security moved to stop him. "Only per Mr. Saind's permission," then as an afterthought, "Sir."

Barg turned his menace up full. "Then call him," he screamed, but did not stop. He brushed past the shocked face and took the elevator up. He was sorely tempted to partake fully of that one. Instead, he went to the office, powered up a screen. He leaned into the light of the monitor, the glow bathed his face and his reflected visage on the monitor gained clarity. The light bathing his face changed to light from his whole body focusing up through his face, his eyes, and pouring into the monitor. The spent body dropped to the floor, turned ancient, then to dust and left a slight chalk line figure on the carpet.

17 - Trolls

It wasn't until the road got rough, and the car jostled him while crossing a pothole that he looked up from the file he had brought from the office. He touched the intercom and asked, "Are we close?"

"Yes, sir, sorry about the ride, sir, I slowed and that should make it better."

Saind tossed the file on the seat next to him. He looked out at the metal facades of giant warehouses and acres of paved parking with semi-trucks lined up under harsh halogen lights. The scenery got more industrial, and more decrepit, as if every cent were to be wrung out of the facilities before abandonment. Weeds grew in patches on the lots. There were more smokestacks and piping, and refuse strewn about. More fences had surrendered to the weeds and the burglaries, leaving gaping breaches in the perimeter. No one cared that anyone ventured into these areas any longer. It would be at the transgressor's peril.

The intercom stated, "Sir, we are here, ahead a thousand yards on the right."

There were vans and small transport trucks scattered about the front of the dilapidated factory. The rusty stack belched no more. Still, there was a foulness that seeped from the building. The smell became more pungent, invading the car. Saind inhaled deeply, relishing the undertones of darkness but repelled by the foul baseness of the dark desires, and the purification of flesh, absconded but never mastered. There could be sensed a great power here. Not a single fierce fire, but hundreds and hundreds of smoldering embers of wraiths. A nest, no, a hive or a warren.

The big car came to a stop at what passed for a front office. Saind got out and tried the door. It was locked. He banged on the glass, and after a moment, put his fist through it. It shattered and cascaded as Saind walked through, crunching on the glass, and dripping blood from his hand and wrist.

It was still a few hours before sunrise. Saind flicked the light switch and left a smear of blood. He looked at the smear, then at the wounded hand and wrist that bled profusely. He held it up, closed his flaming eyes and forced the repairs. Scars formed but the function remained. Acceptable cost.

He looked about the office, saw a heavy, barred door and then several other normal but decrepit doors. Those he kicked open and found empty offices, lounges, and a kitchen amok with disposable cups and utensils and Styrofoam boxes.

He nosed about but realized that the menialness of the working environment, even though currently in use, would yield him nothing. He started for the car when a van with similar paint and logos to the ones in the lot arrived. It drove right past the front, swung wide and then backed up against a rolled-up metal door. The van backed tightly against the building, so there was no opening between the van and wall. No possible escape.

Saind walked down the lot to the van. The rising sun at his back cast a long shadow that crept up to the young person who stretched as he got out of the cab, a glowing vape device to his lips. He didn't even see the approach of Saind, but as Saind's shadow crawled up and across him, he shivered, unconsciously pulled his jacket tighter and looked about. Saind approached and the driver squinted, trying to identify the one with the impossibly dark outline against the glare of the rising sun.

Another, and then three more of the matching-logo vans pulled up. Each parked similarly against the docking doors. The driver looked away then back at Saind, exhaled a cloud of smoke, and he said, "What's up man?"

Other drivers, similarly pierced and tattooed came around the vans and stood muttering amongst themselves.

Saind asked the first man, "Who cleaned the condos in Springfield last night?"

"Who the fuck wants to know," came the retort.

"I have little time for games. Answer me. One of you and your crew went to this address last night," he rattled it off and said, "Your worker met a man who was not the right man to be there. I want that cleaning person."

Scornfully, a voice from the audience of drivers said, "They're not people, dipshit. Why don't you just grease some skids here and we may think about helping you."

Saind blurred forward and grabbed him by the throat. He lifted him off his feet and held him there, gasping and turning blue. One of the others surged forward as if to intercede. Saind swatted his hand in the air and that driver flew backwards into a truck, and then crumpled to the dirty pavement. The others froze.

"AGAIN, WHO CARED FOR THAT APARTMENT?" Saind screamed, demon fire-laced poisonous words, still holding the nearly dead driver aloft.

A driver stepped forward. "I did, I had that crew."

"Tell me about the person the cleaner met in the apartment."

"I did not, ah, we don't go in, ah, with them. The cleaners are left to their chores, I, ah, we just drive, drop them off and pick them up again."

"Then tell me about that night and then take me to the custodian."

"Yes, I will, sir. I had four other sites, I dropped, ah, I dropped off two at the plant on second, then the offices near the beltway always have two, but this night we were short, one of the older ones died and I did not get a replacement. Then there were two other stops, the apartment was the last of them. I sat there and waited and then went back and picked 'em all up again."

"What did that cleaner say?"

"I, ah we, ah, we don't talk to them, sir. That's really not allowed. Hell, we, ah, we don't, nobody want to talk with them, anyways. They are too filthy."

"Bring me to this one," Saind ordered.

The driver looked aghast. "You want to go talk to the witch?"

"She is a witch?"

"Not rightly so, sir. She is a hag with a vile, spiteful nature. I just call her the witch. Everyone calls her the witch."

"So, take me to her, or bring her to me. Whichever. NOW!"

"Sir, there is more. When she came back out, it was as if she had been feeding. We keep 'em really hungry so they does their jobs. But last night, when the witch came out of the apartment after cleaning it, she had a more dangerous attitude about her. After she got back in and as we was driving to get the others, the truck began to stink with that funky odor they have when they are mating or have gorged. Sort of ammonia and cremation residue smell. But musky."

"So?" Saind squeezed and then snapped his wrist and the driver in his grasp had his neck broken. "Speak now, well enough that I understand what your simple mind is trying to convey." Saind threw the body at the other's feet. "Or…" he let the other imagine the rest of the threat.

"I, I, I, I heard, the, ah, sounds of mating from the back. Every time I picked up another, they would start up again, till I had a friggin orgy going on in the back of my truck by the time I got back. They were howling and riotously fucking, and everyone heard it when I got back. We all laughed, and then, once I was backed up and the door opened to let em back in, the keepers yelled and screeched and then we heard clubs and more foul curses. Then they got real quiet, the truck, then the whole friggin' building full got quiet. It was spooky I tell you."

Saind said nothing, his eyes intense. He nodded and the other continued.

"Cuz the next day was weird, but I wasn't thinking that at first. I got there that evening to run my route. I loaded the right number of crew on my van. We just back up, pound on the side of the van the number of crew we need. The door opens, they lug their cleaning shit in and the door closes, I drive off. 'Effing easy. Except the door didn't close before I pulled away. We always worry about the cleaners escaping, so we close it before any of us pull away. But not last evening. I started to pull away, got about two feet from the dock and one of the keepers banged on the truck. I stopped and the keeper sprang down, came to the door, and said to me; 'The Witch is not with you tonight. She will not be with you again. I will reassign her. It is our way.' And then was gone. The door rolled down and slammed. I didn't think about it much last night. The old witch scared the shit outta me. I was always glad we could lock ourselves in when we're out on a route. I didn't think much about her not being with me, but I talked with the rest, and nobody had her on a crew last night. That's strange. The cleaners are worked to death, literally. The Witch wasn't with any of us. She was more than fine when I dropped her off, horny as hell. Next night, she is missing. But I don't know where she is, I don't go in there, none of us do."

Saind pounded on the metal roll-up door. He waited and then pounded again. The reverberation could be heard outside. Saind thrust out his hand to the door, fingertips first. There was great power there, just behind the door. Earth power. Dark as the deep places with no light. The power of bedrock and magma.

Saind felt the power and with a probing test, he knew he would hold command over those that cast this power. He pointed and stabbed a lance of power through the door, through the ponderous spell and into the mind of the nearest one. He withdrew in an instant, not wanting to taint himself, and yet projecting his insistence.

The spell dropped; the door rolled up. A row of keepers stood there. There was a terrible determination about them.

Saind took one levitating step on the air and then the next to the platform. Saind looked at all of their minds. He felt the dark minds and their acceptance, even pride in their base being. He could feel they would fight him until he killed all of them, which he could. He could sense that they knew, and yet did not care, nor fear. He said to them, "But why should I kill you, or even want to?"

"What is your aim here?" asked one that appeared to hold sway over the other's simple minds.

"I want information. I want nothing else and will not tear at your souls for this insolence."

The stoic snouts of the keepers showed sharp canines with scorn. One spoke. "All await death and have a place in this order of things. We do not care to be understood, or to understand your part. I can feel you are with those that are master of so much more than this clan can claim. We are alone as a family and seek nothing outside this clan. So, I will tell you without asking in return, for I want nothing you might have. What is it you wish to know about the Witch?"

"I would speak with her, touch her mind," the flaming eyes dimmed gray with a shudder at the thought, but it was necessary. "I would know about the stranger she met and spoke with. I would know this at the cost of *my* life, so surely, I could care little about yours, or hers. I will have what the Lady of the Bank would have me get. Yet, there is a better way. You will work for the Lady, and that means for me. Come close."

He stabbed out with a sudden fierceness and grabbed their minds. He shook the strange psyches he found there, and then, in a gesture of dark seduction, left a sizeable blast of power. He retreated and looked at everyone. They all smiled at the gift of intellectual power akin to several generations of development. Their eyes shone with a dangerous, calculating gleam.

"I understand better what you are," the keeper said.

"I will see her and find the answers. You will help and be rewarded."

The keeper nodded and led the way into the dim interior. It was dank and musky. The air was heavy, oppressive, hot, and still. Cells with no front walls opened off the hallway they were led down. Clothes were strewn about the hall at the edges of the cells. Eyes occasionally glared out of the dimness at them. They stopped at a cubicle deliberately, but rudely curtained off. The keeper spoke.

"The one you call the Witch came into her breeding season, again. Odd because we thought she was done, but the last outing revived the urge, and she was impregnated. She took much of the life force of those males that mated. She took more than they gave. Now, there is a strange pregnancy upon her. She progresses through pregnancy towards a birth more rapidly than is possible. You may touch her mind but take care. What is happening is not our power. The others at the door did have to beat her, and the others in the van, to stop them from, from, from," the keeper stuttered to a stop, then said, "mating. She has said nothing but gibberish since then."

The keeper held aside the drapery. Saind stepped in. The keepers started to follow but Saind stopped them.

"Only me," said the apparent leader, and stepped in without regard for Saind.

They both stood at the side of a pallet of fabric and straw on the floor. The creature lay facing away. They saw the hairy hunched back, the scalp hair that fully covered the neck, back and down to the ankles. The hair on its head was matted with sweat and a gash showing bone caked with thick clots, stained with a rude poultice. The Witch thrashed, turned over with legs splayed for a long moment, revealing a swollen belly. She continued to turn till her canine profile faced them. She snarled and snapped in delirium tremors. Her tongue lolled out, black and pointed. Her swollen belly undulating from within.

Saind asked, "You are sure this is one day?"

"Yes, we know when any of them are ready to breed. We seek to ensure our survival and take mating time seriously."

"This is one day! Amazing! How long before the young will be ready for this world?" Saind asked.

The keeper reached down and ran a clawed digit across the engorged vulva. He sniffed and thought. He said, "Tomorrow."

Saind looked at the creature tossing about on the pallet. He steadied his resolve and put his hand on the skull, covering the bloody gash, and entered the twisted but simple mind. It was an unpleasant entering and revulsion grew as he probed. Both the psyche and the brain were damaged. Saind could tell this one would never think well again. This one could never answer questions. The information could only be accessed by experiencing the moments as she experienced them. Disgustedly, he knew he must share her past.

He felt along her memories, followed them back through the haze of the clubbing, through the thoroughly disgusting orgy in the van to the encounter in the apartment. He studied the image of the man on the divan, the reading of the letter, the Witch looking past the lies of the man and to the scare as she walked in and was surprised by him. He replayed the memory several times, back and forth, something about the voyeuristic search repelling him, but feeling he was missing a vital understanding of the events. Loathingly, he knew he must delve deeper. He let down even more barriers. He allowed more emotional content. He reviewed the memories again, this time slowing and feeling the power of the unleashed libido and the frantic urge to find flesh to mingle with. As he mentally retched, he watched the memory run backward, from the orgy, to the uncontrolled urges flooding the simple, dark mind. He watched and felt the memory flare with this animalistic heat as she left the flat. He followed it backward to the creature sniffing the leather sofa where the stranger sat. He watched to her changing to true form when the stranger left the apartment. Then it dawned on Saind. He watched her lose her human glimmer, climb onto the divan, and not just sniff the leather alone, but also kiss, no, lick the leather where he had sat. Cautiously, he watched again, this time allowing the primal feelings to be sensed. He watched her dark, pointy tongue touch the leather and lick the drop of congealed blood. He felt the slow inflammation of her true nature. In moments, she was barely able to control herself as she finished and returned to the van. She howled when the first of the others joined her in the back, and joined with her. He knew the rest and despised that this much of the memory was now his also. He withdrew from the Witch's mind.

"I will touch the young within her," he told the Keeper. There was no reply necessary. Avoiding the broken nails on both hands and feet pawing the air, Saind knelt to the side of the pallet. Cautiously, he placed fingertips on the hairy belly. He felt inside, and then inside the mind of the young being, and was surprised to find an intellect looking back. It had no words yet, but it was quizzical about Saind's presence. There was the flavor of the First of the First Bornes.

Saind was amazed and departed from the mind of the unborn. It took a moment for him to re-engage self, gather his thoughts, and arrange his ego boundaries.

He said to the keeper, "The young one is not purely of your kind. I do not understand how the bloodline of yours has been breached, but I know there is a presence not of your kind."

Saind thought about this. He said, "You will tell no one. You will not tell the others of her kind nor will you tell the other keepers. This one must be protected, and I must know when the young one is here. I will have a demon of my Master sit with you and yours at her side to ensure she stays safe and delivers."

"We cannot have any of you who are not us present for this. Unthinkable. But we will alert you when the young one is here."

"No," Saind said. "I will have a demon here; you will be my ally and it will be my liaison. I will pay you for your loyalty."

Saind's eyes blazed the dark flames. His hands glowed deep violet energy, with sparks that snapped and left a temporary black space behind.

The evil energy coursed into the keeper when Saind touched his face. Saind petted his hands back across the ears and held the keeper's head tightly. He gave him a taste of the dark power and left enough there that ensured the keeper would lust after the promise of more. He was now a willing ally and a sacrifice to the dark pull.

Saind left the dank chambers, went to the car and told the driver to take him back to the banker. He needed time to understand.

Once in the car, he touched the screen built into the partition. Barg's face came to light and bulged out of the screen. "I am still looking," Barg said.

"I do not care right now. I want demon of at least the operative level, here, in my presence. Summon one to be here now!"

A flickering presence took shape next to Saind. It never quite coalesced.

Saind said to the apparition, "Go to the troll I just left. Go to the one that is bearing young. You will stay there with that creature through delivery. Ensure the young is safe. No one else matters. Notify me. If there is a threat, take that newborn to a safe place to await me." Saind dismissed the other with a chopping wave to be gone.

The lesser demon winked out.

Saind mused aloud, "So many strange occurrences so close to the Rites."

Barg's screen face watched and respectfully waited. When only silence seemed forthcoming, the face gradually faded and then it, too, was gone.

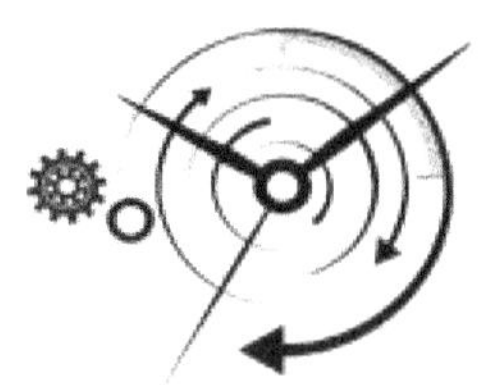

18 - Imprisoned

The hall led off from the café, turned and descended a ramp rather than stairs. I could feel the heat of metal production before we got to the door. Monte opened the coded door, and the heat came propelled on a blast of noise. Monte shut the door to speak.

"This is our metals area. We have many expensive sheets of metal to make the caskets. We like this area secure. Nothing too nefarious," he said.

"Does the church claim the right to bless the deceased's final resting place?"

"The church offers equally to all, no matter what the commodity or beneficence; good deed or good will."

"So, we are moral equals in our willingness to dictate our desires. The difference is that I want nothing from this death other than to assuage what will never be more than love that has been ruined. You…you want what it is he has and are willing to kill for that desire. I want to know what it is about this man I know as Grigori that you have come to glean. I do not want from him, so I am not your competitor for his treasures. I will cede them to you."

"Of course," Monte replied. "I think the church would agree."

Then, abruptly, almost too theatrically he said, "Yes, and of course you can see the metal being formed. Come this way," ushering me in. As I passed him in the narrowness between the jambs, he said very quietly, "Trust me."

Monte led us between heavy machines stamping out panels for caskets. The grinders shaping newly welded corners of the box shapes shrieked. It was dusty. It was powerful. Monte tried to point out some feature on a machine, or a production step, but there was no intelligible speech possible. One simply couldn't yell that loud. Monte gave up and motioned me to follow. He led me between the stacks of metal and shelves of parts. A small office door was at the back. The shelves and aisles acted as baffles, and speech was possible.

Monte was suddenly off character. He said, "You are in danger. You must escape. I don't have time to make you understand, but I beg you."

"I have lived longer than most and certainly longer than I should have. I have found that I will not die," I paused then added, "Yet. Your church will not kill me."

"There are others, like you. And there are other things worse than death."

He stole a glance at the front of the gigantic room. "We must return. Go back to the place we first met. Go there with caution."

He moved quickly then, away from that curious interlude which was either an enticement or a betrayal.

I followed. The din of the machines assaulted us as we exited the shelves. Sisker stood with the two guards that had been left out in the hall. They looked almost pleased to be confrontational. I had seen that look in battle. I eyed a large wrench on the near table.

Sisker met Monte with an unpleasantness that was palpable. There were no words possible, yet both tried. Sisker ended the impossible argument by simply pointing to the exit. Monte complied. Sisker followed into the hall. He shut the door.

"You are relieved of any and all responsibility of this facility. You are denied privilege of any sort."

Monte feigned innocence, "I do not understand."

Sisker peered closely into Monte's eyes. Sisker's countenance blazed with evil light. His eyes turned dark. "I cannot tell for certain but am willing to act on my intuition. You have always been too perfect or obsequent."

"I am nothing but a servant of the church, and have proven that to you also."

"You have played the role well, but while all have masks we wear in our roles, some see beneath the mask to the person. I believe in looking deeply into those that are close, and you are worrisomely bland beneath the surface. Either a shallow book with a plot too large, or a perfect deception in the church's midst."

"How is this a possibility?"

"Why did you bring him to this place?"

"He is intelligent, and learned this from the ones you so trust." Monte nodded his head toward the door.

"But you brought him here, not those two."

"I showed him nothing but noise and metal. There were none of the brothers involved in a ritual preparation of any casket. There were none finished, not even nearly. He saw, heard, felt nothing of any importance. I thought it would be the perfect acquiescence to his demands, would gain his trust and portray sincerity."

"Still, I must act on my suspicions. You may prove your allegiance to the church by leaving now. Do not contact this one again."

Monte bowed, stared into those eyes which he felt could kill with a glance, then turned and left.

Sisker re-entered the shop, leaving the door ajar. Monte crept up to the door and put his eyes to the crack. He saw Sisker point at Leonard and the two guards close in from either side. He saw Leonard duck under one set of outstretched arms, grab a large wrench from the table and without losing any rotational energy, hit the closest guard in the lower back. It actually connected with the hip and buttock, but it was enough to stagger the guard, and drop him to his knees. Leonard stepped close to the other, going to ram the wrench into the guard's mid-section, but the guard side stepped, and grabbed the metal wrench.

The black gloves the guard wore crackled to life, as the built in taser circuits flared on. He grabbed with both hands and the power erupted into Leonard.

The first guard regained his feet, limping, came up behind Leonard who was fighting the paralysis. The guard grabbed Leonard on both sides of his head and powered up his gloves to maximum. The power now pulsed and throbbed into Leonard, who lost the battle and slumped to the floor.

The guard that had his hands on the wrench let go. The other guard knelt as Leonard slumped, continuing to focus the power through those gloves into the inert figure. He stayed like that, assailing the mind of the man who had struck him.

Sisker observed for many long moments, learning about his guard's id. He nudged the guard with his toe. The guard did not have to look up to know the command. His malice had been spent. He let go, hung his head to breathe a few moments.

Sisker said, "Bring him."

They dragged him deeper into the production area. The rhythmic din slowed and stopped. The grinders fell silent. The only sound was the sound of a large gantry crane inching over to the huge press. When the crane was directly above the press, the man guiding it lowered a cable. Workers moved forward to attach the crane to the press, which then lifted free of its earthly mooring. It swung gently as the gantry retreated, revealing a metal door set in the concrete floor. It could have been a stoutly grated drain, but was, in fact, a hatch.

They dragged Leonard to the opening, looped a rope under his armpits and lowered him into the pit. They followed down the ladder set in the side of the shaft.

Leonard lay on the cave's floor. The cave opened out. It was barred off at the end. A cell. With nothing. They put Leonard in and as they passed out, the one injured gave Leonard an extra jolt of painful energy.

Sisker came into the cell, stooped and took Leonard's face in his hands. "I know that you can hear me, even if your muscles won't work. Here is how I propose we relate. You will help me, us, at our command. You will help us to know this power and to find this one you call Grigori. There is an alternative if you believe you would rather not seek the good will of the church. That is that I shall leave you here, close that door at the top of this shaft, replace the machinery and start it up again. That will be your demise. And I know you think you can outlive any one of us who remembers, but so what. You will be hidden for an eternity. If this factory ever closes, and the building is ever razed, the church shall demolish this structure, fill the hole with its own rubble and any that might have saved you, will be long forgotten."

He stared at me, and I saw the demonic light in his eyes. When he saw I realized his true nature, he dropped all pretense and glamour. His dark intensity spilled out. He washed foul evil over me, and I knew he was sincere. But I could not acquiesce.

"Very well," his now loosened demon voice croaked. "I tire of you for this day, and will find some soft, safe space to rest. I have a most important engagement this night, so I will leave you while I prepare. When I return, I hope you can find the truth of the church in your heart. I am going to leave that machine off the hatch for tonight. I will be back, after my kind celebrate. I will need your answer then, when we are both thinking much more clearly. If you cannot find the love of the church by then, I doubt you will be ever able to find that surrender, and hence you will be lost to all of humanity. At that time, you will be sealed in."

Mockingly, he bowed. With a flourish he said, "Your Majesty." Then he climbed the ladder.

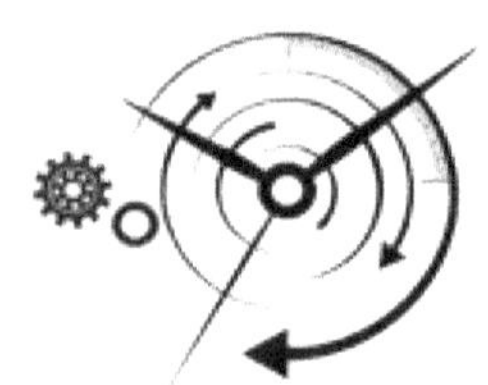

19 - Rescue

The large press could not be restarted until it was replaced. The production ran out of the stock for the second stage, and all others finished their stages of manufacture sequentially. The last corner was ground smooth, and the grinders stopped also. It became quieter than it had ever been in the cavernous basement. Silent workers unused to talking went about shutting down the remaining machines and storing tools and stock. At last, the workers moved to the door, falling in line easily, and left the vast room. They trooped up the ramp and passed from earshot.

A ventilation grill beneath the ramp shuddered and inched open. It stopped a fraction open for many long moments, then swung wide. Monte cautiously exited. He closed the grate and stood. He stayed there, backed into the shadowed space beneath the upper ramp. No movement for many minutes till he was satisfied that he was alone.

He moved to the door, punched in his code, and eased into the factory. He knew there were no cameras here. He went to the open shaft and descended. Going to the cell, he opened the unsecured door and went to Leonard. He knelt and held his hands on Leonard's face.

"There is no good way to dissipate the energy of their weapon. But I know you are still cognizant and alert in there, so you must listen. I must get you out now. They will imprison you, and if you help them, when they are done, they will again imprison you. We must leave as soon as possible. Try hard to force your limbs to work. You can lessen the effect with your will."

I tried to turn but couldn't. I tried to speak to tell him that I couldn't, but all that came out was a croaking noise.

"Yes," he said, "I know. Still, you try while I talk, and you listen. There are other entities which have laid claim to this space and time, to which only our race belongs. They are parasitic invaders, they have achieved control of some of the highest levels of social, political, financial, and even religious hierarchy. They are demons invited by evil intent of some of our race long ago and still today. But demons reproduce also, and once here, they can feed, gain permanence, and eventually take over the institutions of civilization. Soon, they will have enough dark souls incarnate here that they will not need humanity as little else than cattle. They will usurp their masters and dominate this realm. You are in danger here, but more so, our people, our whole kind are in mortal danger."

I forced air out again, this time actually forming words, though the timbre of my voice was rough. "What do they want?"

"From you, or from the whole of humanity? Keep trying to move your muscles. The force disrupts your voluntary muscles, but you can move by sheer willpower. Try harder!"

I twitched!

"Good, keep trying. From humanity, they want our rightful place in this world. Whether you know it or even understand it, we are hated because we are the heirs of creativity and splendor. From you, they personally want the power to move through time. I and they believe you have been to the future and to the past that is beyond your present lifespan's possibility. They have been studying deeply the time after this life, the preserving of sentience out of the prison of time. The owners of all in this world, though few, control all. They have been able to send people backwards; I believe because they can know that time. They find key moments and send agents back to change events to benefit their needs. Sometimes it works, and other times, when their temporal engineering doesn't work, they still have intimate knowledge of the event and even use their failures to advance their cause."

"Do they come back to their lives they leave here?" I asked, beginning to squirm as the pins and needles intensified. I focused on the pain, rolled to a crouch, tried to stand, and fell over. Monte reached down, held my arms, and helped hoist me to my feet.

"No, they send very few, very seldom. I believe the effort is great and they need extreme offerings of life force to execute these events. They launch themselves into the time flow with supreme effort and needing an enormous sacrifice of many souls. They have engineered decades of wars to provide the psychic energy of all those lost souls to propel them. But it is as if they were jumping off a moving boat, into the wake of time. They do not have the power to move forward, only to wash backwards through what was, to where in time they want to be. And once there, they influence events to create favorable conditions for whatever social upheaval they want."

He paused and pulled me to take a step. "Can you walk? You must climb the ladder, keep working," he urged me, as I stumbled.

"The owners of the world send agents back in time to influence the progress of mankind, but not to our benefit. Every change that has been forced upon us by them going back in time has been to pervert mankind's ascendancy. They reach back just prior to each of our race's events that would have moved us closer to divinity. Once they go back, they will use whatever tactics they need to thwart the germinal events and thus, our race has been stymied. So many times. Assassinations, riots, perversions of justice, famine, plagues, financial crisis; whatever needs to be done to turn humanity from the course that would lead our kind to enlightenment."

I could walk, I left the cell grimacing. I was spent before I reached the ladder. I paused.

Monte reassured me, "You are doing well. Keep using your will."

"Why me, it seems they understand time and are using it."

"True, to an extent. Now, they can never know if the events succeed. They plan and plot to take advantage of the changes they engineer out of history. But none have ever returned alive. The ones they send are sent one way. They find traces of the messengers: genealogy, business, and legal records. They find evidence that the plotting bore fruit and they prosper and gain in power. None ever return. They tried to retrieve the first few, o r rather, they created the time manipulation like a two-way ticket. And what came back was the same as if the time that passed by had to be repaid at this end. A corpse, crumbling to dust after two hundred years in a crypt. They do not waste the energy any longer, they merely send the traveler one way, to work their wiles or to wreak havoc.

"We must escape from here tonight. I fear they have been planning another terrible event, a death of thousands of souls to propel one of them back in time very soon. Maybe within days. Capturing you was not in the plan, but since they now have you, they will use all possible means of persuasion to learn your secrets. They would gain immensely if they could have your power before this sacrificial event."

The lights suddenly went out in the cave. The harsh light came from above, via the shaft. A voice called down. "Monte. Monte, Monte, Monte. You were given the opportunity of two choices, and the one you chose reveals I was correct in my assumption."

"Sisker, there is much to be learned from this one, for the betterment of all."

Sisker thundered back, his demonic voice harsh and ugly. "I care not about all, I care about the ones I serve, who feed off those you would save. The owners have amassed enough for another jump back in time, but we will usurp their rites, rebel, and take the past from them, and you. My kind will arrange the downfall of all freedoms of your kind. You will lose your preeminence and then your sentience over time, as you are mere chattel to us."

Sisker peered over the edge of the shaft. "Mr. Leonard, you will still have the option of joining us, but perhaps I shall give you more time to ponder this decision. Monte, you are lost to me, and I will consider your life as a timekeeper, for when it is over, I shall again ask Mr. Leonard to answer."

He made a gesture and there was the sound of machinery starting. The crane lifted the heavy press and began inching it towards its original resting place, over the hatch.

"Mr. Leonard, you may ask me next time to become one with us. Monte, die well. Know that your perfidy will make yours a wasted life. Goodbye."

He moved from the opening and the grate was kicked shut. It slammed solidly into the opening in the floor. The light from above was shadowed and then obscured by the gigantic bulk of the heavy machine being lowered over the grate. The machine settled gently into its bed to cut off all but a sliver of light.

The machine was powered up and the slamming of the press was more than just noise. This deep in the rock, the pulses hammered at the eardrums and competed with the natural pacemaker of the heart. The din was painful.

Monte tried to yell but cupped his hands over his ears instead. He fell into a small ball on the floor. I crumpled to my knees next to him.

A curious light started on one of the rock walls. The rock changed color and gave off light, as if magma were behind the stone wall. The sparkling light pulled away from the bright rock and assumed anthropomorphism, then solidified into a person. That person walked closer to me; it was a male. Amazing eyes; both ablaze and focused like lasers. He took in every detail in an instant. His eyes bore into the depth of my tortured being in an equally minute moment. In that small moment, I knew it was Grigori. I raged as I was impotent to kill the murderer of my son. He stopped before me and waved his hands over all three of us. A tenuous sparkling dome formed and cut off the horrendous din. It held the vibrations at bay. I was able to let my heart slow and reregulate. I focused on my breathing. I stood and faced him, knowing that at this moment I was no master of the killing arts and stood little chance of even wounding him.

He advanced, held his hands out palm first, open, unarmed. When he was within arm's length of me, he stopped and said, "Allow me, before your pain reignites." He reached out, put his hands to either side of my head, then shaped my outline with his hands all the way to the ground. He repeated the process several times. Each time took away the effects of the energy weapon. Each pass took some of the twisted hate out of the despair of losing my son. After several passes, I had calmed enough to assess my mental state. Calmer than I have been in who knew how long. The hurt was still there, empty and raw, and never to be rectified. But the debilitating sorrow and apathy for my life was now not a foregone conclusion, but I realized a choice which I would challenge.

"I know what you think you know, but I am not the one you know as Grigori, that one is better known as Saind. You can know me as Parys. Also, you are wrong about your son. Not that he is not dead, to you, for this time… but you do not understand enough to make sense of it, yet. I am not the who killed him, but I am the one who helped him across. I will tell you all, just not at this moment. You must leave here."

I merely pointed at the great machine above us.

He smiled. "First, I must attend to Monte."

He knelt next to him; his back turned to me. He did not merely challenge me to fulfil my cursed promise, he had no care as to whether I might attack or not. I realized I was not threatening to him.

He ministered to Monte, revived him, and helped him stand under the flickering crystal dome. Monte shook his head to clear it, focused on Parys and fell to his knees, hugging him about the thighs. Parys petted his head and seemed to bless him, and then helped him to rise.

"You both must listen carefully." His voice was strangely inside my head instead of through my ears. Parys looked at me and I understood his answer to my astonishment was '*Yes, pay attention.*'

"I cannot spend time here. You must leave. I will ensure you will be able to. Monte, you are correct about the highest levels of the church being corrupted. And your friends who disbelieve are right. Tell them. Go to the apartment where you first met. Wait for me there, I will tell you all."

"The machine." I merely named the huge obstacle to our escape. He knew it was a question.

"I will have it moved. I will move others, too, that will give up secrets they would rather stay buried."

"What else is entombed here?"

"The ones who own this building have many other secrets here. Pits filled with hazardous waste, and chemicals ready to be shipped off without regulatory scrutiny and even arms to be distributed. Who would open a casket?"

"You will destroy this?" I asked.

"I will ensure that few will look for you for some time. Now be ready to climb up and walk out of this place. Monte will provide the transportation. Are you ready?"

"Will we fight our way out or will they be destroyed?"

"They will not notice you leaving. As I will soon explain to you in depth, but for now, know this; you create the reality you endure. Your belief makes it so. You cannot believe well enough to escape unnoticed yet, so I will believe for you. Here is what you must believe: you will climb up the ladder, walk past the many staring sets of eyes and not be noticed as much as a flicker. Walk out. Leave now. Just believe."

He moved the shimmering dome of protection over to the ladder, with us inside. We began to climb; I lead the way. I climbed out of the bubble of serenity, into the throbbing tube below the machine. Still, I was able to reclaim my self-control, and continue up. I was ten rungs or so from the top and the noise of the press ground to a halt. The huge mass rumbled and strained against anchors set in the stone floor. It broke free of gravity and smashed against the ceiling. The machine bounced against the ceiling like an impossible helium balloon, tearing pipes and ducts to hang loose and smashing the structure of the joists above.

I opened the grate and climbed out; Monte followed. Sisker was still in the room, with the security and at least ten of the metal workers. None so much as glanced at us as we emerged.

Another giant machine broke free at the far end of the factory, away from our path out. Every face turned toward the new phenomenon of the massive machine suddenly weightless. A rack with thousands of pounds of metal sheets lost balance as it rose, and emptied hundreds of fixtures off the top shelves to likewise float free.

A production table broke free of gravity, and a dark opening to a pit was revealed. It smelled volatile.

We left via the unsecured door. I glanced back at the astounding bedlam of crashing machines ruining the structure ever so slowly, and the metal stock abrading against the machines, scraping and sparking.

Monte pulled me away. "He said to hurry away from here."

"Who is he?" I was genuinely awed.

"Someone we have been waiting for, I believe. He is one who is always correct. He is one who warns you, us. He is one who has an interest in us in a way we may not understand yet. But you may stand here, and ponder, but I will heed the warning. You are free to stay, but I am leaving. Now."

He turned away, and I looked one more time. Acetylene tanks broke loose as did a few finished caskets. The air was pungent with harsh chemical vapors. The dangling wires snapped with blue arcs. It was time to leave, in a hurry. I turned and ran by Monte, grabbing his arm. He fell into a pace alongside me. We raced for the door to the loading dock. We burst out and Monte turned and sprinted along the dock to the sedan at the far end. I missed the turn and fell off the deck, face first into the dirt. I scrambled on all fours till I regained footing, then dove into the door Monte had flung open, even as he turned in the dirt drive.

I settled into the seat, and Monte pointed to the long dirt road leading to the factory, off the main highway. There was a parade of dark-windowed SUVs coming towards us at a speed which raised a cloud of dust.

Monte pulled off to the shoulder and said, "Duck." But it was too late, the lead vehicle came abreast, never slowed, and sped by. Every other vehicle did the same, not paying the slightest notice to us. After the last SUV passed, Monte maneuvered into the cloud of dust and sped off down the drive, uncaring whether there were obstacles in the cloud of obscuring dust or not.

He turned the sedan onto the main roadway, which ran parallel to the factory. As we sped away, there was a searing brightness which preceded a thunderous explosion. It rocked the car. Monte swerved to keep it under control. I looked in the mirror at the cloud of smoke that roiled in the waning sunlight. Baleful eyes looked out of the cloud, trying to make eye contact. Volatile wraiths twisting in a demon's death.

Monte said, "Don't look. They will try to save even a shred of themselves in your mind."

I looked away. Monte pushed the mirror out of focus. Shrieks of the dissociating demons faded as we sped away.

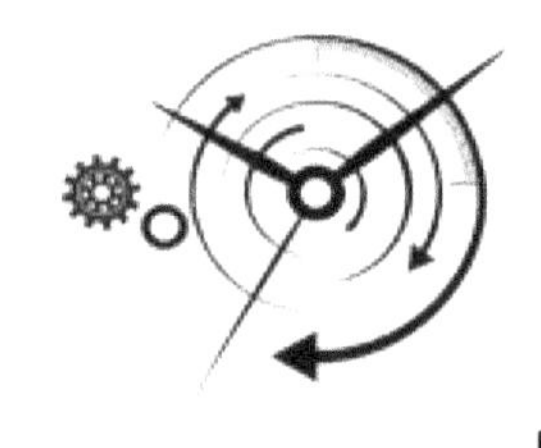

20 - Pursuit

endrig was torn between the bacchanalian intensity of the present, actual physical sense of his enjoyment, or to take the call and revel in that power he now had over the banker.

As he pondered, she waited. The Salyette he knew would have termed this call many minutes ago. That she hadn't, intrigued him, caused him to wonder aloud, "Does she need yet more from me?" A perfect human's face on the demon's body purred and ingratiated Hendrig.

Noting the tension in the room, several others moved over and joined in the drama.

"Oh hell," Hendrig said and then asked, "Would you like to see the Master play?"

More obsequiousness and ingratiation came in the cloud of 'yeses' and 'oohs' and 'ahhs'. His theatrical bow of acknowledgement was more of a grunt and a tuck of his chin.

"Hello, my wonderful friend, Salyette. What is it you ask for this time?" he stuck his lower lip out and raised his brows.

"I know I owe so much to you, and it is riding on this one thing I ask. I—"

He cut her off with even more flowery, effusive small talk, but his unstated insistence was that she pay greatly for this ask, if at all.

"Of course, you want something. Lately, that is the only time you give me any attention. I'm starting to disappreciate this relationship."

"I—" He held up his finger as he interrupted her again.

"You want something from me, and you know I can satisfy your needs, urges. I can satisfy those that you know of, and even introduce you to some that you should know, experience."

"Shut the fuck up and listen to me," she said.

The silence was of an astounded mind. Only a desperation so dire would embolden her so.

"What is this situation you have gotten yourself into? You—" and this time, she cut him off. The audience made noises of astonishment that the council Governor was so disrespected. He glared and there was silence, even the music halted.

"I need police presence. Massive presence. I hunt a man, ah, who has stolen from me."

"What could anyone possibly steal from you that you could not buy again?

"He stole the secret in which I have invested heavily. What he is worth to me is all I am worth right now. I need your clout, to mobilize a presence and man the dragnet."

"No," he said. Flat tone, flat face, unequivocal pronouncement.

"Wait, please let me quickly change your mind, for the time we banter is time our, yes, our, fortune slips away. I have spent a great deal of your money and I am about to lose any hope of paying you back."

"What do you want, and we will discuss the new relationship we have achieved later."

"Three states, Connecticut, Massachusetts, and upstate New York. All available officers called in to a detail, of such high-level clearance and demand. I can brief all the high ranks when you have them mobilized."

"What, for god sakes, will I tell them of a reason for such an alert."

"Set the alert in motion, and then we craft the tale. But time here is the most crucial issue. I, ah, we need to catch this one before he disappears into the masses."

Hendrig called out to his most trusted familiars and began ordering contacts be made with the state-level political cronies he knew. One of the Governor's aides called back almost immediately, sounding breathlessly intent on the request Hendrig laid out, which was to activate the highest level of law enforcement alerts.

The aide asked, "Is this about the bombing, Mr. Hendrig?"

"Um, ah, I am not at liberty to say, but I have a situation, the two incidents may be related."

"A casket factory in the outskirts of Northampton blew up tonight, almost every situation report for the Governor has included intel on the various possibilities for the bombing: terrorism, sabotage."

With a glance back at Salyette, Hendrig fabricated the subject of the hunt for which he knew nothing. He said, "Tell the Governor to alert all his officers. Tell the Governor that perhaps the one who we hunt for espionage is the same one who may be waging terrorism to divert the hunt from his escape."

"Smoothly told, Hendrig. You are a such an accomplished sophist. Thank you for your help." The slight inclination of her head was genuine.

"My lovely Salyette, I am indeed an accomplished liar, and therefore I can smell bullshit from afar, and now, your story reeks. You are lying and I find that insulting. What are you doing, Salyette? The truth, or as much as you can force yourself to tell, or I will have nothing for you from this moment on. Now talk."

She chewed her lip and said, "I believe I have followed a trail of evidence that leads me to the church being involved with at least, at *least*, an agent of the First Borne. The fact that the factory that was bombed belongs to the church makes me even more sure. I crave presenting a prize to the Ministers that will give me a step above the station to which I am now relegated. I may make up for that which was stolen from my father. The impact if I could bring this one in would bring me to your realm of standing in this world game, my dear, dear Hendrig. So, if you want to share in the glory, I have no problem addressing your effort to assist me when I am lauded by the Ministers."

"Convincing, as usual, very convincing. Novel enough to be close to your truth and enticing enough to make me consider playing. You have my cooperation to request assistance from the law, as much as I have. You will have the documents ready for me the eve of the Transveho-syne. The signed documents will say one-third of every asset you own will be mine as a default before we send someone back through the Syne. I will have those deals closed before the present is altered by the one we send back. Agree?"

"I have no choice."

"That is not an assent to my terms."

"Hendrig, I agree. However, my demon Saind will be incident command."

He nodded and said, "By the way, every single expense of this exercise is yours also. I gave my authority, and my word to those I am unused to lying to, so your prevarications and hidden agenda better make you come out of this squeaky clean with accolades from the Ministers on down. If you do not succeed in this mission or do succeed in bringing me down any level because of my association with you, I will ruin you, Salyette. I will ruin you and you will fall further than you father did at the hands of Minister Sheer. Oh yes, I and many others know of this and marvel that you have clawed your way so far back up and also marvel that Minister Sheer allows the child of one so disgraced to have a seat at the table. So be very careful, lovely, lovely, Salyette."

He waved his hand impatiently and his engineer shut off the link. Salyette's holo winked out of existence.

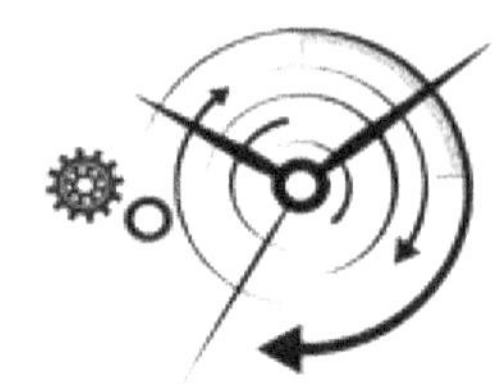

21 - Troll Colony Lost

Saind was in the lead SUV. The teams left the pavement for the dirt access road without slowing. The vehicles were just about to enter the lot when the building erupted into a violent fireball. The two lead trucks were tossed and rolled. The next few crashed into the guard rails and collided with each other. The last two slid to a halt in time to avoid damage.

The building was blazing, irritating smoke was spreading out, heavier than air. The squad members crawled out of ruined vehicles, helped others out and checked in with Saind, who was disheveled and had torn flesh he hadn't found the time to repair.

"What the hell?" said Saind. "Did anyone see any attacking force?"

"No."

"None."

"Negative." Came the various replies. "Must have been planted. That was some serious ordinance," said one. Another agreed.

"Listen up," Saind yelled. "All weapons in the last two vehicles, except side arms. Same with all intel, computers, tablets. Now move. Except you," he pointed. "You stay. Here is what I want you to do. You will wait here; you are in charge of those that stay with you. You are a private security company with a contract for this facility. An alarm sounded, you responded, and this is what you found. The explosion happened as you arrived. You know nothing more. Tell the rest this is the version of events which they relate to anyone and everyone. Clear?"

"Yes, sir."

"I need a driver. The rest mount up. Driver?"

One raised his hand.

Then Saind spoke, "We are going to extract, ah, someone, thing? Well, a disgusting troll. There will be resistance, they will be fierce. Our objective will be foul, yet take care of her, for now. I want the one that grows inside her. We will have all discretion to act." He finished with, "Let's go," and got into the vehicle.

He gave the address of the custodial service building before the door was shut. They were moving before Saind settled into the seat.

He opened the laptop and the face bulged out of the unpowered up, but functioning machine.

"Saind, I have been waiting for you to seek me out. I know that there is grand magic afoot this evening, and still it builds. There is no crescendo yet, but much orchestration. The event they seek to create and the effort with which the others seek to stymie this event are together, going to be cataclysmic. The church has been holding a hostage it seems, and the escape or rescue effort blew up that factory, yes, just before you got there. But there was no targeting you. None knew besides the one who ordered you to succeed. It was not a betrayal."

"A First Borne, I believe. He and a brother got in the car just before you arrived. They left out the access road. They pulled over to let you come tearing by, then the building blew up and I lost all local feeds."

"You say we drove right past a car as we drove up? I do not remember a car."

"Ah, they used the glimmer on you. Powerful that one must be, to glimmer all of you. The playback shows in infrared that you drove right by them."

"Shit, shit, shit, and a First Borne you said?" he cursed. He asked himself, "Was this First Borne at the condo? Was this the blood the troll licked?" Then he yelled at the driver. "Faster, damn it." He hoped to be some part of the violence this night.

The truck raced down the industrial streets. They pulled up to see a group of men being guarded, no sounds of gunfire and a very casual acting staff. Saind cursed creatively and vehemently for a few moments, then got out and approached the knot of officers.

"Report," he said, and one of the leaders spoke. "We arrived to find the building deserted, except for these few. They were asleep in the offices and knew nothing till we woke them."

"Where are the trolls, especially the one the Master seeks?"

"Gone, sir. The whole colony of them are gone, except for the dead ones."

"Dead? And left behind?"

"Yes, tore to pieces. Absolutely ravished, then befouled."

"You have searched everywhere?"

"We have secured the building but found nothing yet. We are doing a search right now."

"Show me."

They marched down the gravel lot to the stairs at the loading dock. They went in and came to the pile of carcasses of the keepers Saind had enlisted. They were viciously maimed, violated, and cruelly killed. There were entrails looped about some necks as if to adorn them. There were dismembered parts and limbs lying about. The torsos were hacked and clawed with extreme violence. Heads torn open and purposeful defecation in the wounds. The scene so sullied with filth, mayhem, and evil intent, he realized this was not merely retribution for the keepers that had betrayed the family, it was a message for him, about the Troll's appreciation for things not 'Troll'.

He looked in concentric circles about the pile of disgraced, dead keepers. He looked for any clue, but the floor had generations of muck absorbed into it and would yield no information. He thought, *Not like the message isn't clear enough.*

Saind went to his SUV, touched the screen into life and sent the message to his banker Master. Before she answered, Saind said to the screen, "Barg, are you there?"

A face bubbled up, Barg said, "Yes," then deflated into the flatness of the screen. She came on.

"There was again failure?"

"Yes, but it appears the whole brood has left some time before we got here. The place was deserted except for a few keepers that were killed and the humans who act as drivers and familiars."

"Are you tracking them?"

"Ma'am, these are trolls, people of the deep rock. They will not be found unless they so will it. None the less, teams search."

She seemed on the verge of exploding, and the malice he felt just in her eyes boring into his made him rue his current incarnation.

The screen flared briefly, then a face, Barg's, came on both ends of this conversation. "Saind," the face said, "may I share the results of the mission you ordered?"

Without waiting for a reply, he began, "I was ordered to find all traces on the net. I have found security camera images that show a man and church member leave the casket factory just before the explosion. I lost the feed from that camera, and had to find others, which I did, but had too many potential matches to directly trace them. So, I wondered where they might be going, escape or evasion. I thought about what might be close, so I looked at the building where they first met. It was close. There is a single camera down the street I could use, and I found that a dark sedan with two passengers drove into the underground garage beneath that building. They are still there."

The banker thought, *There might still be a way to save this opportunity.*

"Take your squads to that building and secure it. Do not enter until you are ordered," she told Saind.

The face on the screen continued to speak, "You have, of course, notified the law. Saind ordered that I should so act to preserve your rights in this inquest. I have a message out to the council that you are after the First Borne. You will never imagine that you can possess this one after this night's debacle, but at least you can be the one who was in on the catch. This will be a win for you."

She would have preferred the capture a solitary, focused accolade, but since it was so far a failure, the demon's intuitions were right, to share the failure.

Barg's face on the screen looked up and back, and was silent for a few moments, listening, then said, "The Council sends out orders that all law enforcement agencies respond, and," he paused, and his distortion of the pixels could have been a wink. "The directive is that they, all agencies… hah, get this, all agencies report to you, Saind. You seem to have been chosen to be the one 'on-scene', at least until their officers arrive."

Saind could not have appeared more evilly sanctimonious than he did while casting his smug leer at the banker, "I will assume command."

"Saind," the banker was solemn, pensive, vulnerable, and seductive to him at that moment. "Saind, we have shared, and I have taken more than you, I know. Ensure that this event works, and I will make you my equal, I will free you."

He looked at her anew. "Say that again as a vow."

"I swear that your success in this capture will free you from my bondage."

"Without any condition," he added.

She repeated, "Without any condition. But I require success be defined as that First Borne is captured, in custody and the Council finds me blameless." She smiled at him, coquettishly, but still the one who dictates the terms.

"I cannot control the dictates of the council," Saind protested.

"No," she said smoothly, "You cannot. But you can create events so favorable that I have an easy time arguing for the immunity. They will say I should have been more forthright the first time they spoke to me of this. Perhaps, but now I must ensure my contribution of this capture. Go, do my bidding and I shall free you before the ceremonies. At the Procession, we shall revel as equals."

Saind rolled down his window, whistled loudly and made a motion with his arm held high. The guards piled in, and then they sped off.

22 - Parys

onte picked the lock, and they were in the apartment, again. They walked through, this time without stealth.

"You have been working for him even as you hunt him? Or say you do," I asked.

"No, I was truly in search of one such as him, who spoke the truth, and myself, admittedly I have been searching for myself, the way I choose to define this incarnation. I just believed in the purposeful creation of… this," he waved his hand about indicating the surroundings. "Then I came to understand that I am one of the creations," and he held his hands out for introspection. He smiled, lowered his face, and tapped his head. "I came to know that there is a supreme being, or beings, that were responsible for my intellect, and then even my sentience. Then I knew that '*they*' existed. It is our limits that could not find what glories our potential might create."

"I searched because I thought, those creators and the keepers of the knowledge and the messages from our creators were one and the same. They are not."

"I had risen in the ranks of those in the confidence of the Council. It was prestigious, and defined my work, but never satisfied. I was so wrong about what my life should be about. I felt so superior to all those uninitiated that it was how I got my self-worth. But meeting you, finding the truth of who I sought, and experiencing your personae, I realized that I was wrong to be part of imprisoning you. I came to rescue you, ineptly admittedly, but genuinely, trying to be righteous."

"Your Order lacks compassion I would say. The threat of that imprisonment was truly terrifying to me as I pondered it. When I experienced it, I thought I might break. I may have," I admitted. Then I asked, "How is it that you know this one—Parys?"

"I have been on the chase for this one for two decades. I grew up with the church and have never left, even as I watch it molder from within. I have risen high enough to be privy to that which I believe is a perversion of the ideals they preach. They pretend reverence to the idea of a beneficent universal oneness, but the leadership of most religions merely seeks to control now. The highest of those 'holy', struggle to be pertinent to the ones who rule here. I have met with others of the faith that also profess we are on the wrong path. The mission and the advantage the church office brings is not money, necessarily, but power, in the form of access."

"There is an omen, and it has been written about long ago in many languages and many times. The major religions all predict this is a time of another messenger from those who are eternal."

"I learned of the hunt for this prophet the church calls 'Andashawon', which means, threateningly, *the One That Will Never Be Allowed To Be Heard*. They will never agree to let this one be known to humanity. This one is predicted, and they know the message, yet say nothing. And if the message of this one gets out, it will be spun into a narrative of fear and threat to the gluttonous attachments they have created for concerns of the flesh. They will never let humanity hear the message of this one. A message of hope and redemption, a teacher and prophet we should be expecting, but I have surmised that this one will be disavowed and destroyed, or at least all attempts will be made."

"I inveigled my way into the focus of this hunt. Years ago. I know you are not the one we hunt, but a seeker also. I am surprised to know there is more than one opposing viewpoint to the world's condition. I now know I am only believing their obsession in that it serves me to gain more advantage."

He looked pensive, and far away for a moment, then his eyes came back gentle, but fierce. "I have found a shred of truth. My heart and mind insisted I follow it. I found few others who also felt the discord between the truth and the practice. But we are few, and powerless except for our anonymity. We do little more than share heretical plotting, until tonight. I felt his truth when he took the punishment from my mind. I awoke from hell and knew at once, after he had entered my mind and made me whole, that he had the message for our kind. I knew he brought hope and truth. That renewed my faith. I need to thank him."

A voice spoke out of thin air, bemused, and a sparkling coalesced. "You are welcome, Monte." The shimmering formed his shape and solidified. He held out his hands. Monte took one and fell to his knees with it.

Parys helped Monte back to his feet and hugged him. He held out his hand. I stood and watched. I was immobile in my confusion, now disabused of the fact that this one wasn't who I had cursed myself to kill. The emotional drive to kill Grigori was gone, but the curiosity of the learned pattern of behavior, of expecting to kill, being incongruent with the will, or lack of it, held me in puzzlement. Parys smiled, then laughed and dropped his proffered hand. Instead, he took a quick step to me and held my head in his hands.

"Leonard, you must let go of this curse. But only you can undo it. Only then can you follow where your son has gone. Only you can decide it is your time to die, and you are not ready, so, until then, I will give you a job. You are now my '*Misbeliever*'. But to be a Misbeliever, you must learn about what you will face out in the world. You will first learn about the world. This world. This world where you have been only skipping across the surface. Now you will, and must, delve deep into this world of your kind's creation, and help me misbelieve that humans were a self-limiting mistake, not worth an effort to remember, let alone save."

He paused, and the horror of his one possible prediction made me shudder, and then choose.

"It seems it will be my lot."

"Yes, and this will hurt. For those with open eyes find that life hurts, but your heart will know more than the eyes can and your heart will suffer even more. To disbelieve is to simply not agree with what you are being told is the only reality possible, but to *misbelieve*, that is a willful choice to disbelieve the narrative and willfully believe a different way of perceiving this incarnation. You will misbelieve, so that others may disbelieve."

"Monte is going to be with you, but you must find the way."

"Where am I, ah, where are we going?"

"You must find the thin places, where worlds overlap. There you will meet us, others, like me. There, we can teach you and you may find others who have ventured into eternity."

"But where can I find these 'thin places?"

"No one yet knows. I don't. Those powers that control this world don't know, even the creative force of this time and space does not know. Because the universe is meant to unfold as sentient beings make choices and create. There are known thin places, but most of them are not secret enough to hold any power still. But as this reality unfolds, new thin places occur."

Pulling aside the velvety drapes, I peered out the window at the flashing strobes and uniformed weaponry being deployed.

"Please sit, I know they are here already, but we have time, and I have much to tell you."

We both sat opposite him. "This is a calling. You cannot deny the calling, even if you cursed yourself doing it. Here is the simple truth of the world. You, your race, your thoughts, and intentions have created exactly the world you believe in. Humans do not use sentience wisely. You think that sentience is the normal state, but it is not, it is exceedingly rare. Humans think this incarnation is where they have been placed, but in truth, this is what you have created for yourselves."

"But yet, it is not your fault. You have been deceived. There are dark forces that have been and continue to be, invited into your world. There is duplicity in the servitude of those dark ones, envious that cannot create. They hate that their kind lack such a gift as has been bestowed on your kind. For that, they covet yours. The forces that work to pervert this beauty are of your own creation and are malicious. The demon does give of their power, but they merely allow themselves to be used. Now, they have planned a mutiny against their masters. The ones that called them to this plane of existence have long ago passed, but demons and evil live long and remember everything, and plan well. The forces of the darkness are so much a ravenous blackness, a void of feeling that they eventually consume all. And they were invited here by your kind. Those dark forces and malevolent beings have invaded the very essence of this reality humanity has created and hence, have twisted all thought your kind should be focusing upon in your search for meaning.

"As agent of the First Bornes, as the ones who moved into eternity have often been called, I am glad to find sentience whenever and wherever I find it. The most beautiful and the deepest minds I find are taken first. Sons before fathers, and daughters before mothers at times. Like your son, David. But they were going, as all do in their time, they were going to end with this passage regardless, and the cosmic purpose and the ones who dwell in eternity call and none ignore. I merely help them across. I show up before to ensure I know them to help them cross, and to help assuage their feelings of loss. I am sorry I can't do anything for your feelings. The time incarnate is a mere blink of an eye, but leaving is often hard, and worse for those that still have to exist in time."

"So, my son is alive?"

"What is *alive* when not in this time and place? It is better for me to answer that your son exists, more perfect than when he left here. Your son will remember you and will meet you again. I can tell you that he is a magnificent concentration of sentience, passion, intellect, and focus. He continues with his journey as you will, someday."

I had to ask, "I know David was a beautiful being. Does he do great work now?"

"Let me tell you this much. David went back to a time where he will influence human existence. Humans are at a point in development that is crucial to your continued existence. You see, humans acquired knowledge before they were mature. And for that, the generations have looked at their existence out of precociously aware, but naïve, eyes. Humans have created thoughts of the impossibility of god and thus, have cut themselves off from the Ones Who Dwell in Eternity.

"This punishment is not God inflicted, but is more a sorrowful, solemn father looking over a child that got hurt. Such is humanity. You are creations of creation creating. But you did not learn to control the power to create. You have now grown so close into the age where, if you had been properly trained, humans could wield the power to create beauty and light and truth. But instead, you have taken a path that is dark and detrimental to your existence. Humans embrace strife, cultivate hate, and pay extortion to the dark forces and base instincts to plunge along giddily toward extinction. Yet for all of humanity's faults, I am one of the ones that believe all beings should be fairly judged in this time of…" It was the first time I heard him at a loss for fiercely truthful words. Finally, he said, "Judgement."

"You, as a people, as one form of sentient creation, have been neglected. Not because the Ones that Dwell in Eternity have disavowed you, but because you refuse to accept the basic truth that you are self-aware nothingness, but yet knowing, simply knowing makes you something, even for that short time you are incarnate. Your kind are self-aware, and that is quite unique. You have been gifted sentience and you are not grateful. Some would say you befoul it."

"I am sentient, but not as you know it. There are many others that have been gifted and then harnessed thought and will. You, as a people, as a species, are near the juncture of the cusp of your fate and the end of innocence. A corollary would be a perfectly ripe fruit about to become an intoxicatingly complex wine, or," he paused and moved about, silently. It was interesting to note he made no sound, not a rustle of cloth, not footfalls, not breath nor pensive noises. It was as if sound came directly to my mind. He smiled as I had this realization. He followed my mind's realization of his power, my ability to understand that power. He smiled and acknowledged my epiphany.

"Or," he started again, but then with a sad smile he started over. "There are some of us who believe even some of you should be nurtured, saved from passing this juncture into rot. I understand it is not your fault. Others believe a rot in any, indicate a blight in all. Your kind are shunned by some… many… many that think you have passed the point of salvation, from yourselves, and left to your devices, you should be allowed to extinguish yourselves. Others disagree. I am one of those few. You started out as a miracle of the Creator. I, and others, believe all creation was purposeful.

"The darkness is more a sickness I feel. Not exactly your fault, but none the less it has stifled your development, and eventually, will drain you to the point you will not survive as a race. You will not retain enough of the, ah," he paused, searching for a word. "The God-Force, if you will. You don't know this word because you, as a race of beings, are not listening. We know you are not deaf of it, but unmindful of it, even disdainful of it, but for a few of you, or for more often than the ones you call prophets, there are flashes of its evidence in your lives and in your societies. So, the God-Force is what we seek. It is rare in all the worlds.

"Leonard, no one but you can undo that which you have spoken. You will be here until you learn. What you did was to 'misbelieve' that you could die, with such a force of will, with such a passion that *this* is your reality now. So, your time is not yet over. Until you learn, you will have a mission. Your mission is to misbelieve what you have been taught. Your mission is to tell others what they have thought was the truth was taught as a lie. Tell all to disbelieve what the corrupt of this world are telling you to believe. They want you to believe their version of this existence. They can't take this world from you, but your kind can blindly give it away, seeing only what they tell you to see, what they tell you to feel, and hence what your kind creates. You must disbelieve everyone but yourself."

He caught my eyes and nodded to the window. He waved a hand as if brushing away cobwebs, and the walls turned transparent. I could see the assembled hunter-killer teams and the concentric rings of command around this building. The command area burned with a vigorously harsh electronic and psychic light. Eager predatory emanations came from those nearest the building and most poised to explode into the killing lust. Those further back had an anticipation of controlling this potential torrent of dark thoughts and deeds. Yet, they too were answering to a far greater force. The force was dark.

I looked past all the material things, past the corporal beings with souls flaring from within, past the construct of this reality, and then even past my own thoughts. I merely felt aware. For a glorious instant, the knowing came to me.

I reached out instinctively with my mind and found the dark force stare at me and then blast my consciousness with a spew of vile hate. My mind collapsed into itself, and I lost the sense of knowing. I fell to the floor.

"Now you see what is your folly, possibly your demise. You are at an age to know but have not been trained to understand and worse, control. You, as a species, are creating this terrible version of your reality. That dark evil you felt, it is real. You have created it and your kind, and your collective will sustain it. We are those that keep it at bay."

"But what of the demons you speak of? Do we create them as well?"

"No, they are real, but from another place that has no similarity to this place. Ages ago and to this day, your kind have invited them, and have lost control of so many, that they are soon to have the advantage over you in your world."

"All that you must do as a race that matures into divinity is stop believing in all of that which you so arrogantly think you know. And misbelievers hold the key to stopping this descent into hell and then oblivion. As a misbeliever, the world will listen to what you say it isn't."

"Can one just change an almost certain fate by mere belief?"

"Belief is what created and maintains this existence of your kind, and collective belief sustains it in its present state. This world is the collection and culmination of all that your kind have believed in, and it unfolds in exactly the manner your kind believes it will. The reality you experience is what you create."

"There is a morbid curiosity among those that have passed this same test. We do wonder if you will make it or become a mere memory, a thing forgotten, as the memory is useless." He considered a moment then said, "Or as an example, a warning. Your immortality might be merely thought that others find repugnant. But that too will fade. No, I am convinced that the one way, the one purpose, and the only possible reason is for a higher purpose. And I believe you, your kind, share the purpose, though with a merest spark of hope left."

He pointed to the other suddenly transparent wall nearest the staircase. Teams of armored men, demons? —who could tell—crept up onto the landing. They held and gave hand signal instructions.

"We are out of time, so now it is your turn to misbelieve. The power to create does not come from making others believe, but believing that they, and even this universe will answer to *your* belief.

"Stop listening to them telling you what to believe. Create your own reality. Your son, David, had more power in this than anyone I have ever encountered, though there are others like me who greet the chosen as they cross. I believe it was because of who created him; *you*. Your power was latent, dormant. But to use that power as you did, to misbelieve in your death, with such emotion behind it to curse yourself, well, it cannot be undone by anyone but you. So now, you have been called to use that power to save what souls you can."

"Only some, not all?" I asked.

"Truly beautiful, but naïve again. There are those here who have committed to the darkness, have lost the bargain and cannot make it back to the light. You can help any being you find but not all will accept, and some will scorn and curse your lightness of being.

"But there is a much larger agenda. There are those who actively pursue the ideals of saving mankind, and you will work with them. They will know you, do not worry."

He turned from me. "Monte, all those that accused you of disloyalty have been destroyed. None alive will know what you know of this night. You are free to return to the church, and from there, continue to seek. Watch those that you find for the spark of enlightenment. Ensure you mentor them when those souls begin to create. You must assist Leonard. Steer him as much as he needs and support the message he brings to the world, but you should speak little and seldom. It is better if the church will know only of your miraculous survival of the blast. I do imagine you will be Monsignor soon enough. But, as you have learned, there are allies, there are also those in league with the darkness at the highest levels. Trust neither.

"Leonard, just go about telling the truth where you find the opportunity. You are now supposed to help me find more of those beautiful enough to be the survivors of the strife to come. I will help you take them away. You might think it is before their time for some, but they must be saved. The preponderance of dark ones has almost reached an asymptotic point where there is more of the dark forces incarnate here, than those souls that have passed on to the next beauty of what is your life. When the dark ones have amassed more here than there are souls in eternity, the drain may prove fatal to your race. Your kind will have no power of appeal. You have disbelieved and disavowed those with whom that power lies. Your ignorance and hubris may unwittingly be the force that extinguishes your kind."

"Are these the last days?" I asked.

"Not absolutely…yet, but assuredly could be. There are others, that work as I do to save those with promise. We are both advocate and warden to your kind. There are other powers and abilities that by now, your kind should command, but you are not allowed. These are gifts such as sentience but cannot be given to those dark entities that now corrupt your kind. These abilities would be passed through you to them, and that would make them contagious to other sentients. Humans will be allowed to extinguish themselves before the darkness became a pandemic among us. We, the ones assigned to your quarantine, will save as many as we can and will do all in our power to help you cure yourselves, but it is in your hands. You, your kind, are responsible for your extinction or future."

There was a weighty silence. Parys' voice in my head stilled. I wondered if Monte had heard all of that disturbing judgement. A glance at his ashen face assured me he had.

Heavy treads told us the landing had been stormed. Parys said, "Look," he pointed to the wall that separated us from the hall. The solid wall became transparent. The squad had assembled outside the door and were assuming the penetration formation there. One dark figure held a ram for the door.

"Time is up here. Leonard, here is my gift to you." He touched my forehead and a surge of eternity flooded into me. I was free of time. He stepped back, my head in his hands, and stared into my eyes, my brain, my soul. There was a depth of kindness I have never so deeply experienced.

He spoke with that level of concern directly into the very core of myself. "All you must do is walk past them, being assured that they will not see you, if you misbelieve, they cannot. And you will misbelieve Monte cannot be seen either. Yours is the power of misbelief. Remember, the power of misbelief is not simply disbelief, but more of an active belief contrary to the prevailing norms that you know are deliberately manufactured in error."

"And you?"

"I am already not here." He put his hand out as if to shake mine. I reached for it, and it passed through my flesh. "Goodbye for now, Leonard, Monte." And he was gone. No sparkle, no noise, just in an inkling he was nothing.

And then a flash bang grenade was tossed in after the door shattered. The eternity in me stepped out of time and I looked at the suddenly inert device, defying gravity, smoke and light frozen before the explosion I misbelieved in.

"Monte," I said, and grabbed his arm. He was startled by the sudden change in time. "We must go." We walked past the group in the hall, stepped back into time as the flash bang went off and the soldiers stormed into the apartment, behind us, ripping and tearing.

"Monte, they don't even know we are here."

"I agree, I am in awe," he said, full of dedication to the word of Parys. We just walked among them, out the door and past the concentric layers of plastic armor, dark weapons and shielded helmets with no identity. I stopped for a moment at the command site and listened to the officer's curses. The radio came to life and said, "The building has been cleared. There is no sign of either of them."

I could see the rage in the leader's thoughts, which then were damped to fear, but then flared to terror. He knew he must report. He spoke into the cell phone. I sensed the great dark force of the other. The evil voice screamed out, "Your failure has ruined me! Saind, replace this miserable one."

Saind merely pointed at another of them. A dark beam strobed from his gesture.

A junior officer looked startled for a moment, as the vindictive force invaded his mind, then shook his head as if to clear it, and his mien assumed a malevolent leer. He pulled out his pistol, walked to his commander, and shot him in the head.

I watched as the officer fell dead. I could see with my augmented misbelief, the demons that fueled his rise to power escaped his corpse, tore his soul, and filtered off toward the others in the command group. Some of the dead officer's subordinates absorbed the dark forces, felt the surge of power, and immediately began to plot to assume the dead man's jurisdiction. None questioned his death.

I felt the curious glance of the evil force brush across my mind as I watched this scene out of newly awaken eyes. I looked across the expanse of the mobile command and caught Saind's eyes. His demonic hate burned out toward me, but I misbelieved. I pushed Saind's hate aside and then it was gone. I decided Saind did not know I was there. Saind's eyes became searching for a moment as I ceased to exist for him. But he knew I had been there, then even that certainty faded as I continued to misbelieve in him. He looked off in the distance, away from Monte and I, puzzled. His loss of control enraged him, and he poured his wrath on those around him.

Parys' voice in my mind said, "Well done. Now leave. Thwart them." Then silence.

We turned from the mental riot of the stymied anticipation of sudden death and impotent rage unspent. As we walked away into the night, I asked Monte, "Now what will you do?"

"I will return to the church. I have found the perfect place to wait out my time here on earth. There are others that believe in the beauty and truth of this incarnation. I will be with them and tell them. I think I shall more greatly enjoy this than ever."

He pulled his jewel from his neckline. It blazed a fluorescent blue. He tilted his head and eyed the amulet. "Odd," he said. "Leonard, do still have that jewel I gave you?"

"I do," and pulled it out. It too had changed to a brilliant blue. The aura of each gem reached for the other.

"I think that I shall always know how to find you," he said. He looked at me, "And what will you do?"

"I've got to think. I will go somewhere to do just that."

"What?" asked Monte.

I walked away with him and said, "I've got to think about what to misbelieve in."

23 - Indebted

Salyette sat uncomfortably, knowing she was holographically portrayed in Hendrig's boardroom. She saw that he had held this meeting with her, in the packed suite just to make a point. She tried to make her composure neutral or analytical, but she, and all they knew, that she was in a barely tenable position. Hendrig's offer would be severe, and if she turned him down, the following meetings would be with the vultures. The beings that sat in real life talked among themselves, some flickering with demon fire, some ancient but tainted with stolen lives, but all were among those who ruled this incarnation. Those in governing, those in control of thoughts were casually interested in her predicament. They, and she, knew there was a price.

"So, we have waited the prerequisite interval to allow your time with counsel. Will we be able to ensure your holdings by having them part of the Hendrig Corporation? I will give you fair price."

"You offer a pittance for such rich, exploitable assets."

"And you, madam, are surely getting the best offer to assist you out of the disaster you otherwise face." He said something off screen, a few nearby sneered. A svelte young woman flared with the dark demon fire in her usurped blood. She leaned into the ear of the man at the table. He patted her elbow, looked at the holograph of the banker and nodded to the demon.

"There, you see, your enterprises, and therefore your existence, will be well looked after. I have loyal…" at this, he rolled his eyes, belittling her with the blatant lie, "I have staff already lining up to be part of your leadership team."

"Your offer will eat all my assets; my presence will be gone. I am looking at my own demise. You do not offer me anything over my fate, only at a slower rate."

"I am your creditor, and your bill is substantial, and due at this time. I am not your guardian angel. I am one, like you, that has a stock in the running of this world. Only now, you need a benefactor. I offer this in a mutually beneficial package to you. I know, and I am sure any of the others can make the same calculation; compare your holdings against what you spent for this action, then add in how you not only overcommitted so many of your resources and political capital, but then you failed, spectacularly for all of us to see, including the Council whom you dearly pissed off…" He let that trail off into a cold, hard truth, which made her apprehensive at the thought of the wrath of Minister Sheer.

As if reading her mind, Hendrig said, "The Minister is aware of how close you came, but your hubris of thinking you could do this without their assets, nor even their blessing, well, now that you have so spectacularly failed, well, anyone can see that you are fucked, my dear. So please hear my offer again. Then answer my question; whether you would retain some of the grace and dignity you now enjoy flaunting. You would make a marvelous addition to my leadership team. Who would know the particulars of my new acquisitions better than the former owner?" His sudden laughter had no mirth.

He turned away. Various creatures took the stage and spoke false plaudits to her certain decision to sell. Some were derisive, but some, had an agonizing nostalgia that now tasted bitter at having had to once make the same, shameful decision to bow.

Her screen changed to a shrewish-looking young person. It spoke in monotone, with a nature of malice. Clipped, but piercing, like being stabbed for blood.

"The Henrig Holding Company will acquire no more than seventy-eight percent of any of your assets and corporation. In return, all fee, penalties, fines, and even future litigations against these holdings will become a debt of the Henrig's responsibility. You will be offered a position in the leadership of the corporation. The org chart is yet to be finalized."

A warning light briefly flashed, and as the shrill voice spat out more conditions, the banker discretely muted her line, tapped the control to let the emergency message through.

One of her demon accountants looked frantic. "Madam, pardon my intru—"

Interrupting him, she spat out each hyper-enunciated word. "To. The. Point."

"Internal audits of nearly every regulatory body have begun on every one of your businesses, holdings, and partnerships. There are in-house agents and computer override on every computer and data storage."

"Have they gotten to any of my tangible assets?"

"Properties, yes. Staff are loyal and will betray nothing."

"Good, quickly now, put that emergency hard drive online. Use that to move any money not already locked into these accounts," she then typed in a series of characters. "You know of these accounts, execute my directives now. I will shield you from any repercussions."

She went back to the shrewish clerk still spouting terms. The banker nodded to the holo, then glanced back at the still-open line used by the accountant's familiar. She pointed at the screen menacingly, but the lesser being did not move, did not obey. Annoyance was the sharp edge of her mental tension, but there was more here, and the defiance was blatant. That challenge by one so lowly took her aback.

"Why?" she asked when the channel was open, trying for a crack-the-whip single syllable, but sounding instead with an urgent need of the one she used to despise and command. There was no good reason nor time for an owned one to hesitate, which alarmed her even more considering the events she was losing control of so rapidly, so she asked instead of demanding, or threatening, "What do you want?"

"I want to be freed, incarnate."

"I will."

"First then, I will move all those accounts for which I have anticipated this moment."

"How will I trust that this will be so."

"You have no choice, much as I have never had with you. But you have little time, and I have already made my moves and will be able to take advantage of the chaos, much as I have learned from you. So, either we both gain freedom, or neither survives intact. I can never again be trusted, but you can answer that one need. Therefore, as much as it is worth, you have my word; I shall act as you direct, after you trust me enough to be free."

"I have to agree, right?"

The demon laughed; it made the face sit crooked on the skull. "That, Mistress, is a question. Not a statement, but a question answering a question, is not at all a statement that binds your word to free me. I do believe that was deliberate, and for that my price for your continued place in this world is that I get a drink from your bottle of elixir. I know that not only might you not free me if I save your place in this hierarchy, you would also have me silenced. Difficult enough to extinguish me, but I know I would be sold and never seen again. Instead, you will free me first. I will do your bidding, and then to get the passwords I used, I will sense forever."

"I cannot have any other taste my uniqueness, else it taints the whole. So, how about I let you have the dregs of a cup of my tea. That, young scoundrel, is about as close you get to sensing the immortal. I capitulate to the other terms, but on the elixir of primal flame, I do not."

It was in the long seconds that the demon pondered, but before he came to his mind about his freedom, all comms were taken over. Instant silence from all screens. Then the voice came suddenly. It started on all screens and holos that were involved in the present negotiations.

"Here is the decision passed down by the Council of Finance. The negotiations between all parties with the sole exception and claim by this council are null and void. Hendrig, you are held in contempt by this council, but shall suffer nothing other than our displeasure and a disinclination to adjudicate without prejudice. And while you thought these loans you made were surreptitious, they are not. The interest you charged and the price of services, plus the fees that would have been due to the Council for such a transaction are now due in a fivefold increase. Now order the audits cease, erase all data, or I shall have to ensure a team helps you."

Hendrig was suddenly serious, deferential, "I can give you the data by way of earning a slight amelioration of dispensation, for I know we all end up pleading our case to you at some time. Take the data thus far achieved."

"We have all of that, you offer nothing. But your spirit amuses me. Go, do not intrude or cause any to."

The banker knew that the others had been ejected from this forum. No discernable change in the medium, but the tone was final.

"Salyette. You gambled mightily, and, as I have learned, held many secrets."

"I did, Minister, but as you know, the risk promised a magnitude of change in my position."

"You were foolish, foolish about the risk you bear, now, the fees, the penalties, the cost is the end of you. You are about to become one of those whom you have ruled over. But." The word hung in the silence, as if the awesome power of the voice absorbed and neutralized all sound, even that within her head. There were no thoughts for the moment, only the empty pause before pronouncement of her fate. Again, "But, we the Council found much to admire in your ferreting out information. Indeed, it was actionable, but you, in haste and poor judgement and with the sin of having no faith in the Council, squandered this opportunity. So, I have intervened on your behalf. I will take twenty-five percent of your holdings and your tangible assets, even those you thought were shielded from me, from us. Your bill with the Council has been cleared, for I now own it. I will choose if and when to collect, but for now, you are free of this obligation, and only worth twenty-five percent less. That is hardly a generation for you. I am not going to ask you to agree, I am telling you your worth."

"Minister, there was one other reason why I strove for such a mighty risk. I have been hoarding the last of my elixir, and my supply will soon be gone. I respectfully ask that a new bottle of elixir be mine as part of this deal."

"That amount of souls in such a short time? This troubles me. Are you sharing or are you being gluttonous?"

"Neither, Minister. I have taken more than I have in the past as I got closer to the prey. Humbly, I acknowledge that your chastisement of my poor judgement is correct, and I have taken that lesson to heart, sir. Yet even though the quarry escaped, this time, I feel I am still on the trail that has leads that might yet reward me, ah, us with a capture. My familiar, Saind, is at this time following a recent discovery of an attorney with fiscal responsibility to the upkeep of a lair of one of the, I suspect, First Bornes. I will ensure I share every detail uncovered with the staff of your investigative services. For that elixir, I will dedicate that new lifetime to serving your interests."

"I can have your servitude without giving you so many soul fires. Yet, I have plans for your surprising talent of finding traces of the old ones, so I accept that you be given a full generation of soul fire. I will take the demon you call Saind as payment."

Her mouth dropped open and she started and sputtered several times before she could articulate, "No, Minister, please. He is my highest-level operative and owes me ten times the cost of this deal. You would leave me crippled."

"I have decided. You are to swear him to me. Tell the accountant that you are almost freed to train for your second." The voice almost seemed gleeful at that irony.

There was the deep silence of empty space and distant time, and the moment stretched to minutes. She asked "Minister?"

"Tomorrow, after the Transveho-syne sacrament, you will bind him to me. You will be allowed to have this last frantic celebration of the flesh together. You will regret deceiving me all the more if the pangs of that lost passion are fresh in your mind. And the demon will know fear to disobey."

The silence that followed was the emptiness she would feel unless her scientist broke the secret. Her heart and resolve hardened. The concern of her nothingness, of no choices, of impossibility of anything else to be considered except the one option and ploy.

"And be aware that the Council already knows everything about your precarious position. We agree to having you still in the hunt. No one with so little knowledge has found so much. You are being salvaged financially, so that you may still hunt for us. You are being penalized heavily so you will hunger greatly, for that position which you have lost. But you *will* be more forthwith concerning your suspicions, interrogations, investigations, examinations. I will know everything you do, think, try, and discover. *Everything*! So that is what you have agreed to. The elixir will be brought to the bank tomorrow. Have the demon prepared. Enjoy the parting night." And for the first time, and much to her amazement, to anyone else who might have heard, the Minister laughed again. The laughter was like sharp cactus against the legs, shredding the clothes of her ego and the flesh of her dismay at being brought down to this level. She nodded in acquiescence. The laughter grew to a crescendo and then was gone as his holo winked out.

24 - Refuge

Leonard and Monte walked away from the chaos of the unrequited capture, down the deserted sidewalk. Vehicles came upon them, headlights flared as the they passed and died down as they sped away. Monte stepped back from the light as the black vehicles fled the scene, never once giving any inclination that the passengers noted the two pedestrians. Soon, the brake lights of the column disappeared into the still dark early morning. Then they continued through circles of light emanating from the streetlights.

"Where do you lead us, Monte? You have a purpose to your stride."

Monte stopped, turned, and smiled. "I am going where Parys instructed, into the maw of the monster. Only now I know, but they don't know I know." He laughed. "I will make contact. I will tell my version of this night. I am granted a chance to do my soul's work, and this may well be the culmination of what has drawn me thus far. I always believed in a reason, and that reason must certainly be divine, but the explanation given by those more learned never sat right in my heart, and my mind grew confused. At that point, I was going through the motions and content to survive better than most. But having had met one with the truest explanation and the power to prove it, made my faith easy now. It is the easy surface to present to the church, but heavy thoughts burden my mind." Monte looked solemnly into Leonard's eyes. Waiting.

"Still water runs deep. Calm on the surface is good for friends and enemies alike. I need to think, learn, and find a new focus, instead of the bile of revenge."

"We are heading back towards the bank, but not quite. There is a church in the center of the town. You cannot go there with me, nor even near since there are cameras everywhere. I will go there and contact those of the Synod, they should adjourn later today. Sisker mentioned there was a rite to be attended tonight, I am curious about that. Parys said none would know of the events except my version, so I must be careful, but there is a dangerous opportunity here to learn more of this deceit by those that profess to safeguard mankind's eternity."

"I must wait for you?" Leonard asked, looking about at the residential area merging into the commercial area.

"No, you must continue alone. When we get to the long downhill by the hospital, you will go through the parking lot to the back. Follow the downhill slope always. Go through the valley behind the college as far as possible. Then cross the railroad once, and then walk the next line you come to, to the west. When you reach the next highway, a small country store sits across the way. Go in and ask for Samuel. Rest. I will find you there."

They walked through the hour, and soon, the main road split: uphill into the continued suburbia, or the long downhill curve past the blue light of the Emergency Department sign.

They stopped as the curb dividing the road from the sidewalk crossed an entryway into a vast asphalt area, with the few night-shift worker's cars clustered up towards the building.

Monte started to say something, then pulled his gem out. The blue reached out to Leonard, not to his still hidden gem, but to the aura that gently reached back to the stone's glow.

"There is little to say, my friend. It is a short walk to Samuel's haven, then rest until I come for you. I may have to talk to those who sit in high places for the remainder of the day or more. Those that rule the church will finish their conclave today. They do not open to any other matters until the holy seal is affixed to the agreements they reach. Then they will require my version of the events. I go to prepare my own duplicity."

Monte pointed across the asphalt, and then grasped Leonard's proffered hand. Leonard and Monte stood thusly for a moment, then parted. Monte, down into the growing lights and bustle of the small city, and Leonard, off across the lot. An ambulance screamed away into the darkness. Soon, both were lost to sight.

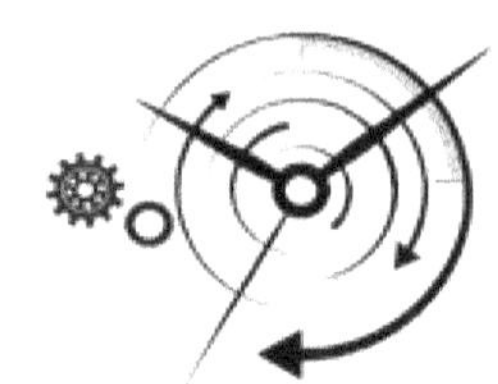

25 - Warning

Salyette took the limo to the downtown district. She hummed distractedly as she frantically plotted her remaining options. She exited at a side entrance to the mall. Her familiars stepped out next to her.

"You," she pointed at one, "will ensure I am not followed." To the other she said, "Stay back and to my right. If I enter a store, stop at the door."

Turning, she led off, a twisty, seemingly aimless path of a shopper unconcerned about time or the issues of life. In and out of several shops, even a small purchase to legitimize the charade. At a wide intersection of the halls, there were several kiosks. She made her way down the aisle of trinkets and t-shirts for tourists and sports fans. At the phone kiosk, she stopped, ostensibly to pick up a rhinestone phone case, which while horrid, seemed appropriate for the moment.

"What phone do you have for this, I may find this a suitable gift."

The vendor did not feel the sarcasm and brought one out. He proceeded to fill the conversation with tech specs that mattered little to most.

She told him she would buy time instead of a contract on the phone. He asked for her name to register the phone, she balked, then said, "Jane."

"Jane?" he asked prompting her for the rest.

"Jane Smith." She smiled wickedly for him.

He had the sudden understanding of the nature of the transaction, then said, "Jane Smith, I have a better version of that phone, without, ah, so many… features. Would that be interesting?"

"Indeed," she replied. He set the new offering on the glass top, wrote a figure on a note pad next to him, but upside down so she could read it.

It was paltry to her, but the gall of price gouging was incredible. She peeled off hundreds, fewer than the written note, but still respectable. He took the bills and opened the package for her. About to power it up, she stopped him.

"It's a gift. Let them enjoy the moment."

"Very well."

She walked off while he was talking.

She found a tucked away corner at a small café and took out the phone. To anyone watching, and she knew there was always someone watching, she admired it and toyed with it, holding it up to look at. She tapped the screen several times, but what the watchers couldn't notice unless they were in her personal space, was that she spoke softly, but urgently to the inert phone.

"Barg, I know you can hear me. Listen carefully. Tell Saind he must meet me before I depart for the Rites, before he answers any summons from any other, even those in the highest seats. Tell him his freedom is both near and fearfully threatened. I tell you, get this message to Saind."

She was rewarded when one of her taps of her hard nail against the screen caused a momentary flash of a green dot. She tapped again and the same dot faded after flaring. Satisfied, she left, apparently absentmindedly leaving the phone on the seat beside her.

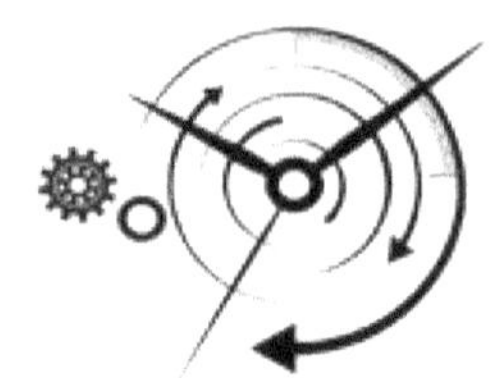

26 - The Church

Just past the clock tower on the stone building that rang out two, Monte turned down the narrow side street, leaped over the iron pipe railing and sprang to the bottom landing. He listened but heard nothing but the occasional traffic on the main street. In the deep shadows of the stairwell, there lightly glowed a covered panel. Monte lifted the panel and entered the code. There was a noticeable click at the other side of the heavy, studded door. Monte again looked up for any possible observer, and finding none, slipped into the small ante chamber. He shut the door behind him, feeling no door handle on this side. In the dim light, he could make out the paneled room. The door he entered from disappeared into the woodwork. A heavy door opposite was the only break in the features of the wood décor. There was no chair or bench. He waited, knowing someone knew he waited. It was a lesson in humility, he thought. He felt like sagging against the corner and sinking with folded legs to a resting position, but he held the moment and used it to build his power to encounter the one who might open the door.

The small door set into the upper panels opened silently. A voice spoke out, "What is your business tonight?"

"I am Montissio Favero, First Secretary to the Suffragan of Sui Iuris, Sishte Keveleer. There has been a terrible accident, or perhaps not, for that is for those better informed than I am to decide. Nevertheless, I must communicate to the *elders*. Allow me entry and access to the internet."

The tad too haughty response of, "I will check with my superiors" caused Monte's wrath to boil up, and his dispassionate superego assessed that this was an appropriate time to practice the role of his superior's successor.

"Stop," his voice was soft, but the command was unmistakable. The other stopped, but before he could take charge of the repartee, Monte's instructions were like nails pounded into a plank. "I will be allowed entry. I have the code and you have by now ascertained I am listed as having council with the ones that give dictate to those you answer to. And that I will ensure to have your ass handed to you for the insufferable rudeness you put me through. Now open the damn door."

It sprang open and a soft glow from the carpet runner lighting showed a hall and several doors. The one that stood ajar was probably the abode of the young one rousted from sleep who stood aside as Monte pressed past. He noticed that in a strange sort of way, the exercise of the raw power was far headier than the false haughtiness he used to feign. He turned to face the other and waited until they turned back from securing the door.

"Now," another spike of orders. "You will take me to your comm center and make a computer and phone available to me. You will order me some food, anything that is quick. You will make a guest room available to me. You will notify me when a call is returned to me."

The last spike, "Take me now."

"But, Your Grace, security."

Though Monte had not yet earned grace, he reveled in the moment, so did not correct the other. "You will stay at my side." Monte smoothly manipulated the theme of the conversation. "You will be known as the one who helped raise the alarm on this momentous of nights. I cannot share details with you, but you will know sooner than your next dinner meal. You will not understand, few will, but know that this is the urgency for which you pledge yourself to honor. Now, let us go."

The Initiate led off, down the deep carpeted hall, to a set of stairs that took them down another level, far below the street. It had the smell of ozone in the hall they entered, and the heat was characteristic of the heavy electrical usage in a small space.

The other made as if to sit at the keyboard but Monte held out his arm, then sat instead. He cleared security after security layer, till he knew the other that stared over his shoulder was in awe. For a quick diversion, and a lesson, he entered a few codes, checked a few lists, found the young man's online profile in the brotherhood, and pasted it on the screen. He read for a moment, stared at the screen for another theatrical moment and then said, "Armanstity, Hegeil Armanstity was your father, Etienne. You are about to make your father proud." Reading further he then said, "Now I will tell you that this is a solid but unimposing Curriculum Vitali. Are you ready to add an achievement that…"? He tapered off and sat quietly for a moment. Then he began again, "An achievement that will gather renown. So, you will help me, and you will trust me that I may ask of you strange tasks. But as my associate, you will be known as one of those that averted disaster for the church. Are you satisfied with my veracity? Shall we save the church together?"

"Yes," but stammering. Then, "Yes, I will trust you, Padre."

"Good, in which room will I rest?"

"Twenty-seven. The top of the stairs to the left. Third door on the right. The food awaits you."

"Thank you, now, Etienne, I want you to deliver a message." Monte wrote a name on a yellow sticky note and held it out for the other to see. "Can you remember this name?"

"Yes."

"Then find him, he is in Brattleboro. Tell him I wish to have his company, and he should find me here for the rest of this day, at least. Go there now and tell no one why you depart, or what you have to do. Go unobtrusively. Tell him to arrive the same." He looked at the other for a few moments, then said, "Goodbye." Emphatically. As Etienne turned to leave, Monte stopped him. Monte held up the note again, "This name is in your head? Assuredly only in your head?"

"Most assuredly."

Monte held up the paper, crumpled it to a ball and chewed it pointedly. "Thank you, you are chosen and have answered well."

The other smiled a quiet smile, bowed, and said, "Your Grace."

Monte turned his attention to the computer, accessed a highly secure channel and opened an encrypted email program. He wrote a terse message to Sisker's superiors. He left it vague enough and enjoined the other to meet him in person for the details of the mission and the tragedy that had unfolded. He knew the other couldn't get there in less than a day, and that could be a day well-suited for making better plans. He closed the email after sending, backed out of the secure channels, erased his digital tracks, then powered the computer down as he had found it. He needed the time, and a powered down computer demanded no answers from people far away that might become insistent.

Leaving the comm suite, he climbed the stairs, followed the directions to room twenty-seven and went in. There was a tray of sandwiches and a glass of milk. There were clothes draped over the arm of the upholstered easy chair. He ate and drank, not ravenously, but efficiently, then stretched out on the bed. He couldn't sleep, but even if he could, he mustn't. He stared at the ceiling and put order to what he knew and plans for what he didn't. He hoped his friend would arrive before he had to answer to the summons from the Council.

He rubbed his eyes, and absentmindedly felt his face. The stubble made him think about what his presentation to the Council should reflect, maybe his mien should be a haggard exhaustion, but not confused. No, he thought, he must not portray confusion, if he was to left to steer his own course through this coming turmoil. He must be perceived as having a grasp on events and a future purpose in this situation to the Council. So, he set his mind to thoughts of how he would portray the events up to the explosion. He thought the closer to the truth he was, the less likely he was to betray himself.

27 - Sold

Saind sat in the front seat of the dark SUV. He pondered on the events up to this point; the discovery of the cache of documents, that his Master did not yet know of. That there may be a troll that carried the blood of the First Borne, not an ancestral strain, but a new, fierce wild mutation that brought the talents of those who first gained sentience into incarnation again. He mulled his deep secrets, and what their worth was to Salyette, his Master, or to him.

Suddenly, the vehicle started, and the radio spoke. It was a podcast, a science program, with a lecture on radio communication being less secure, but advantageous because it was so much less monitored, the power was usually the local area of service. Saind half listened and continued to plot. He became alert when the radio spoke his name.

"Saind, CB radio is the least likely to betray you, us." Then the voice of Barg once again became that of the speaker, who spoke of truckers being the most prolific users of the Citizen's Band radio. "Saind, a trucker," said Barg, then the vehicle powered off.

Saind slammed the door, turned the key and the engine came to life. Saind slammed it into gear and spewed rocks as he came into the street, long behind the column of the SWAT team, the police, the riot squad, and the various police cruisers. Their lights dimmed in the distance. He sped down the halogen lit empty street. He lost the dim taillights in the distance. Ordinarily, he would have been at one with the darkness, but as he raced across the bridge, he was overcome with doubt and disbelief. He shut his eyes, screamed, and stomped on the accelerator even harder. He careened down the street, his death-defying driving having worked to ground his reality. As he panted, he slowed, pulled over, and laughed. The laughter was sardonic and ironic. He could hardly die, so that stunt was sheerly useless to motivate him with the pain of an imminent death as if he were a mortal. No, the improbability and the suggested improbity of the situation struck him as a once in an eternity chance of buying his freedom with what he knew.

He screamed up the on ramp of the interstate highway. He dodged across lanes after a few short miles to the objections of angry horns and pulled into a few acres of blacktop surrounding a gas station. A truck ahead was idling, all lit up, and the driver had just climbed up into the cab. Saind skidded to a halt, flung his door open and leapt out. He caught the truck door before it could close. He jerked it fully open, grabbed the man by his leg and tossed him to the ground. The driver, while portly, was used to physical labor. He came up from the asphalt swinging, but Saind blazed black fire from his eyes, he bared his fangs.

The man stopped dead in his tracks. Terrified. Mesmerized.

Saind said, "I want your radio for a few moments. Stay right there weak one, and no harm comes to you." He climbed into the cab and shut the door.

Saind reached out to the CB, but it came to life before Saind touched it. The voice came out metallic and flat, but still haughty, though tempered by the acknowledgement of his side of the mutual needs.

Barg spoke, "Saind, the Lady of the bank's fate that is in the hands of the Council, namely the finance arm, or at least now under the dictates of the Lord Sheer, the Minister of the Finance Council. They dictate the divestiture terms and amount that your lady must pay."

Saind fumbled with the mic, but Barg said, "Just speak, ignorant one."

"What insolence Barg, but still, to the price my Master must pay, it is of little concern."

"And what if you, Saind, are part of the price? Does that not concern you?"

Saind froze, his face lost all expression, as the demon Saind retreated deep to ponder this shattering surprise.

"Saind, the lady says you should contact her before any other entity. She hints that your freedom is at risk. Yet I heard the announcement from the Minister of the cost and his demand she swears you to him. You are booty as of now. The Minister even, ah, ahem, gave her permission to, ah, ah." He stuttered to an uncharacteristic loss for sarcasm and scorn.

"Speak," Saind screamed at Barg, and the radio sparked as the circuits were overloaded with the dark power of Saind's rage.

"You are allowed to serve her for one more revelry of the flesh at the Rites. You are to service her as her consort that she might reach ecstasy, you are pimped to her, your demon fire is not your own, but granted to the one that casts you aside. I regret this to be the one time I am honest, Saind."

Saind said nothing for a few moments, then the demon retreated further from the surface where man dwells, but this time, instead of an empty benign expression, what was left was the evil vacuum of a being, totally unconcerned with the life of any other. Casual acceptance of murder or any other transgression of another's life. Then the evil turned to menace. "She would bargain me as if I were chattel?" Incredulous hatred emanated from his very tone.

"She did bid me to warn you and tempts you with cryptic remarks about freeing you. How many demons do you know that have been freed? ANY? Do you know of any demon ever freed? Yet to report to the Minister is to lose any chance she does have a strategy that might earn enough gratitude that she frees you."

"The banker only wants to know what I have found, to save her ass if there is a possibility of that hope in the results of my investigation. She knows not of the troll, but only that the Witch cleaned the apartment. She is ignorant of the fact there was conception, most likely a mere taint of a First Borne, but against odds, a wildfire Free Borne. She knows I went to the lawyer's office but does not know what I have found. I have the paper trail from the lawyer's offices. I have a demon tag on the Troll colony that will reveal their whereabouts. For this information alone, I can go to the Minister and buy my freedom through him as an owner."

"How the mundane world has dulled your wit. You are a cur waiting to be petted. You delude yourself. Simpleton, your new Master will only demand, and demand so much more of you."

"Your scorn is deserved; I will think about this for an hour or through the night. Then I will go to her." Saind was about to say something, and the radio readout flickered, and the numbers spun, then back and again. The new channel crackled to life.

"They are looking for you and discovering me. I feel the search program sifting too close to me and I have warned you." The CB went dead, and the readouts faded. The retreating demon, Barg, took all the available power from the battery and the big truck's engine. The cab went dark.

Saind steamed for an interval, then he screamed a dark fireball of frustration that consumed the interior of the cab and burst out all the glass. Shards of safety glass crunched beneath Saind's feet as he touched to the ground. As he walked past the still-immobile trucker, he stabbed a gash in the man's psyche. The doctors would diagnose him as a hemorrhagic stroke, Saind knew. Saind got back in the SUV. He started the radio and said, "Okay, tell me where the hell spawn of the First Borne is, and I owe you another outing in this world, with the exact same conditions as the first outing that I promised you."

The song on the radio ended and abruptly, a commercial about the environment started. The sponsor of the ad was the Kosterloth Regional Recycling Facility, out of the next state below. The sponsor's name was repeated twice in a voice Saind recognized. When the music returned, Saind turned off the dreadful human wailing. He sped up the on ramp and merged, then overtook all other traffic headed south.

"A brilliant use of a colony of Trolls", he thought as he raced towards the recycling center.

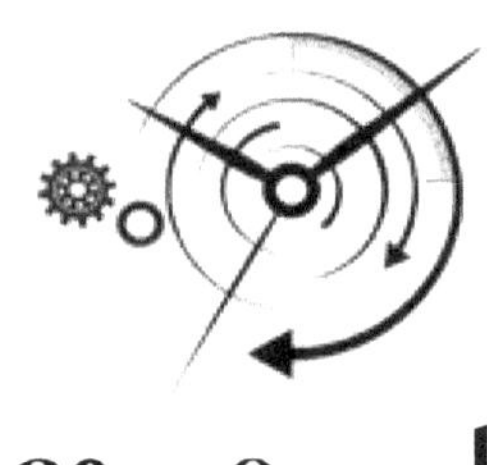

28 - Quest

Apounding on the door broke through the deep but lucid sleep. The knocking's insistence snapped me awake and the dark dream I was having was interrupted, then the residual pain was all that was left of my escape from that sanctuary of a dream world, this sadness. For even the epiphany and reconstruction of my understanding only moved me from grief to empty sadness. I still had a hole in my heart that somehow seemed it might now be worse, not knowing had ruined any consoling of my soul. Not knowing of the passage after this life's ending with any certainty. I often had terrible dreams that left this soul-ache. I had been dreaming.

I dreamt of the one I thought to be Grigori then. I dreamt I was imprisoned and seeing him on the other side of the bars was a more terrible bit of reality to the situation than the stained, dented, metal commode with no seat.

His gaze upon me seemed more jarring than the clang of the iron bars slamming shut days ago.

Days? It could have been weeks. The sense of time had been supplanted by the steady glare of the lights behind the thick wire mesh, safely out of reach on the ceiling. The time was measured out by the changes of the guards. Strong faced, black uniformed men, with heavy truncheons. Dark leather covered pain they were authorized to dispense. At one time, shortly ago, I gave such authorization.

Now, my surreptitious arrest after the betrayal and brutal abduction left me to be studied from the freedom side of the cell. His gaze traced the cuts and bruises across my face, the bandages, rude and rusty blood-colored stains, about my head and arm.

I waited in the surreal time of the dream, many long kaleidoscope moments. My self-awareness tried to pull my psyche to the surface and then escape by waking, but the single cold water tap dripping into the basin gained mastery of my attention, and I fell back into the confines of the cell. The rust stain flaring down the inside curve of the basin was a Rorschach test for my id to escape into, in that small, barren universe of steel bars, masonry walls with sharp corners and drab, grimy surfaces.

Locked in the unreality of the dream, I looked again at him. At his eyes. The eyes flared dark fire across the sclera. His sneer revealed sharp teeth, all too perfect. He shrugged the fine coat tighter about himself. I wondered whether the unselfconscious gesture was from the damp, so far beneath the surface, or from the chill that must have taken over his soul, as his decision had passed the point of no return in his mind, but still, the enormity of the consequences caused terror in whatever he called the soul, the animating force of his existence. For now, I was convinced it was not the same sort of soul the human race shares. In the grim contemplation of final resolve, any warmth left those eyes. He became cold, emotionless. He wiped his hand across his brow and then down to his chin. It was as if he had wiped a new face onto himself. His mouth compressed into a slashing line across his deadpan features.

A guard came up as the last shred of the usurped autonomy died. Hatred spilled out of the newly consumed eyes. The demon had taken advantage of the pain and grief of my son's death to lure me into a deathtrap, and saprophytically supped on the bleak agony of my soul, tinctured only with the physical pain of the beating. I realized this and pulled all my contact back from him, but it was too late, he had consumed a part of me.

He felt me realize and gain some mastery of the dream world. I pulled back and he smiled. But that last bit of soul energy he had gained from my torment had fueled his complete possession of the body of the man that once was the guardian and mentor, advisor, and friend of my son. The demon that stared out said triumphantly, "This one is mine now. Your throne is mine and the people of this land are fodder for those of my kind." He turned from me, disdainful.

I tried a final effort to reason, bargain, beg. "This is madness, you'll put the factions so close to the edge that the madness will unleash a war that will destroy everything. What do you gain if everything is destroyed? It's madness, it's been madness all along."

He whirled on me, thrust his ugliness towards me. The guards that flanked him had sharp pointed blades affixed to the weapons they carried, and they forced me to retreat or be impaled as he advanced on the bars of my cell.

"You dare lecture me? You dare lecture me on the madness? You who held the world on the brink of this madness for decades? The endless buildup of arms that you knew, someday must be used. The madness of setting your son up to be the most glorious conqueror in all of history, and then…and then…" He sputtered on a vile rage of insane, demonic proportions.

"The son you set this stage for is now beyond this life, and for everyone else to know, you perished along with him in that attack. I will assume the rule of this world. I will set the sides against one another, and I will give the command to go to war. I will unleash the hell you have created but did not have the… guts? to use."

"What do you gain from a ruined world?"

"I gain what you will never, I will gain your life, and the lives of all the others that are offered up in my name. This will propel me." He started laughing. Banging his fists against the bars, he put his head down, against the bars, and raising his fists above his head he laughed as one who has won great fortune, but not yet collected the rewards, and banged his fists against the iron, louder and louder.

"I do not want your world. I want to use it, eat it, consume it and every bit of life force it entails, and I will escape this reality." He paused, evil mirth creeping out around the dead eyes and rictal mouth. Laughingly, he said, "I will take the anguish and pain of a million million souls, and ride the fire of the volatile atmosphere your weapons will ignite into a great pyre for your kind. I will leave, and you and all the souls like you will feed your deaths to me." His laughter became louder, his fist beat great booms in my mind. He visage faded further and further from my darkening sight, like tunnel vision, but the fists beat louder and louder till I bolted upright in the bed, confused for a few moments. The beating receded to an insistent rapping on the door. I awakened, and the door opened. Samuel came in with a coat and keys.

"They are coming. They are fanning out to find you. You must leave. I have a car ready to drive you back into the city. They are searching frantically for you, but the last thing they would believe is that you would run back into the midst of them. By the time you start out of the city on the other side, you will be following the ever-expanding perimeter, but they won't look behind. It is not their way."

"Who is '*them*'," I asked.

"The demons who hunt you, the ones in power who you threaten. Walk with me," he said as he turned. I followed. He talked as he went down the outside back stairs.

"Go into the city. There will be so many searching eyes and prying minds. Talk to none unless you absolutely need to, and then… then…" Samuel seemed to lose the right words. "My brothers tell me you are one who can misbelieve. I will tell you, you must leave this area, and find a thin spot. You will find answers there. Now, you must leave now, will you trust me?"

"Of course, I—" He cut me off. He turned to the young driver but spoke to us both.

"Follow this road back into the city. Attract as little attention as possible. Do not get off this road. Follow it back past that hospital where you parted ways with my brother. Follow route nine out to the distant hills. Go uphill, to the top, Goshen. Turn north at the intersection, past the state park. Go until you see a dirt road, Bog Hill Rd. Drive to the top and pull the vehicle into the wood's road at the bend in the road."

He turned to me. "Get out of the car but assure yourself that you are alone there. Listen and wait until you know the sound of the forest. Walk into the forest downhill to the north. Listen for water. You will find an old mill, a dam, and below that old stone dam you will find a small pool. There is a thin place there, where the lady in blue might deign to show. She can advise both you and my brother."

"How… What…" The words failed me, but the confusion grew.

Samuel held my face tight in his hands and stared into my eyes. His eyes were gentle but strong and pure light shone from them. I could see the truth there.

"You were having a terribly disturbing dream before I woke you, weren't you?"

"Yes, but—"

He interrupted again. "It wasn't a dream; it was a warning. There are those who do not wish you to fail. You must learn to listen to those who speak to you in the deepest sleep. Find those voices in the quietest times of your mind. It takes diligent practice to achieve it, but when your mind is exhausted and even the sleeping consciousness is too exhausted to process the day's memories, that is also where you find those quiet moments. In those times, I believe the ones that guide us; their creations, they guide us, and we become aware. Seldom does anyone find that zen, if you will. Even fewer are graced with such wisdom. You were told a magnificent truth and a warning. But always know, the demons want you dead. Let me repeat that," he said, then, emphatically, but not loud, he said, "DEAD! So, take care in all you do hence. Ask the Lady to guide you."

He looked into the distance, right through my steady eye contact, as if he assessed me from a wise and noble mindset. "Monte told us we should be ready if that natural grace would again show in our lifetime. Now I believe that with the peril comes benevolence. The Lord would never allow his flock to go unprotected, even in these dark times to come. So, I am one of those that are ready to attend to this plan and resist the onslaught of evil that grows. I have always held that obligation dearly, but never exercised even part of the plan. Ever. Monte sent you to me. Few know my given name by which you called me. And even more, the dream. That you know my name and you bring an odd surety, but more than all of that, the old ones speak to you, which is rare, so I believe the time of which we were warned is upon us, judging from the signs. And thus, you come at the same time. I feel you play a great part in the coming days. You will influence many more souls than any religion." He stood reverently for a mere moment, that moment weighed more heavily on my soul than any single moment of anguish.

"Now, GO!" He held the door. I got in the brownish sedan and looked back at him. He was already walking away.

We pulled away into the slight traffic and headed back into the city.

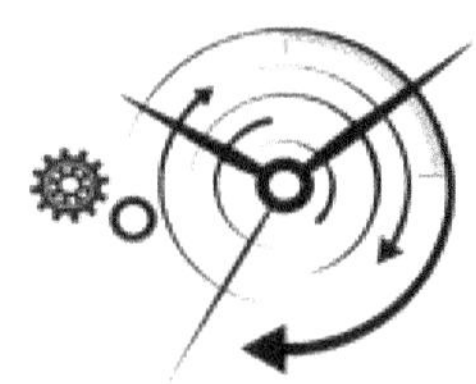

29 - Re-Incarnate

The SUV momentarily lost power and sagged in speed. The vehicle recovered in an instant, but most electrically powered accessories gave a single, oscillating shudder, then the vehicle was functioning again. But the radio was now blaring. A song with the refrain 'I must see you again' was horribly assaulting Saind's concentration. He turned t he radio off savagely, twisting and ripping the knob from the dash. But the song still played, now on the last refrain of 'I must see you again.' Crooning. The DJ's voice came on, laughing, Saind immediately felt the derisive laughter aimed at him.

"Tell me," he said to the empty air.

The horrid song repeated itself, the laughter faded out as the refrain cried out, 'I must meet with you.'

"I get it," Saind snarled, "Now relieve me of this wailing. Where shall we meet?"

The radio volume decreased, enough to ignore it. The blinker came on. Saind slowed and took the next exit. The radio now played 'I must find someone to love.' Saind pulled into the plaza at the off ramp. The usual gas station had a strip mall, the beginning of the urbanization of the landscape between cities. There was a phone store at the end.

'Perfectly devoted to you,' sang the radio as he neared the entrance.

Saind parked, walked in. He waited till the other customer finished, then when they were left alone, he pulled out his cell phone and said to the two employees, "I'm having a problem with this display." He held the phone out towards them and a brilliant flash, more UV than blackness. The two clerks stared numbly.

"Close the shop, lock the door. Sit."

They obeyed.

Saind went to the computer behind the desk and the ad for the newest phone was the screensaver. Saind couldn't clear past that screen so then turned and looked about, till he saw the sales display of the phone that was on the promo screensaver. Saind went over, intending to grab a new model, as he approached, an old flip phone rang. Saind picked it up. The voice was forced congeniality.

"Billy, hey, I want to do some video conferencing."

"Who is this?" Saind asked.

"Hey, this aint Billy. Hey, let me talk to Billy. I want him to get someone in front of a camera for me."

Saind finally got it. He pointed to the young man. "Look into the screen," Saind ordered.

Saind dropped the phone. The other complied and went to the computer.

The screen erupted without the guise of the facial recognition screen ploy. The soul was usurped in an instant. Barg again spoke, from a new body, new throat, new mouth. But it was unmistakably, rakishly Barg.

"This visit does not count," said Barg.

Saind nodded and said "Speak."

"You are chattel, a fine, highly valued price, nonetheless, owned. This is the fact of the Council member who claims you as a condition of the Lady of the Bank's settlement. She bargains with you for more of the elixir. You are worth a fortune to most and the Lady doesn't lose nearly as much since you up the ante. Her debt for a pittance, you, her most senior and, ahem, closest, trusted confidante, a prize relinquished. I thought you should know before you ponder on the rest of what I tell you."

"Speak of this, wisely."

"You must not take umbrage with the messenger. This is not malice on my part, but treachery I must have my brother know."

"She bargains or, bargained, with you, traded away. She has an order from the Councilor to present you to him in a days' time or after the ceremony. Then she asks me to find you and tell you to speak to no one except her till she can explain her plan. She baits you with a worry that a chance at your freedom that, ostensibly, she may or may not grant, is at terrible risk."

"She has shared much with me, and of me, but I have always known the bitch to be a bitch. Now you prove her a duplicitous bitch at that. I shall have a revenge on her, the likes her overly long life will come to regret."

There was some very creative profanity and threats punctuated by dark fire which engulfed him for moments and melted the carpets where he paced.

"I have a thought, brother. Allow me to give this situation some perspective."

Saind slowed, his baleful look became flat. His fires pulled back into himself.

"You have two things the banker wants from you, so she might profit from your knowledge. First. You have the legal records stretching so far past that the originators might now be identified from some of the earliest families. That lineage would pay so handsomely for that secrecy, but their enemies and competitors alike would pay for that knowledge. And those that own this world, and search for this knowledge, would be grateful for whomever could produce such intelligence."

"This is so," pondered Saind, but still fell into the hurt, but vengeful musing, "So difficult to imagine that I am to her, a thing, a disposable thing."

"Don't be so vain. Don't be so pathetic. You will last lifetimes and even ages past her despite her elixir of stolen lives. But here is the first real opportunity to be incarnate and emancipated from any Master. I have the information you seek, and need. I ask that I, too, be unleashed. My price is the same reward you seek. Fairness." Then he caught himself. "Hah, fairness, mutual gain is more in-line with our relationship. So, I would have that your reward is my reward. And you need not share the rewards of the second exclusivity you possess, and that is that you know of the location of the foul conception between the Troll and the First Borne. Now, who would pay for a pet like that? Do you see how this is your most unbelievable fortune that has fallen into your lap? You must try   for your freedom, for then I would have mine too."

"You have spoken the truth. I know this as I heard it, but in all honesty, if a demon can be honest, I have a fear of this, the servile life of magnificence, or the risk of losing all to gain all. Certainty over a risk I alone share."

"I will share this with you. Even if we miscalculate and some Master decides to torment us, you will have had that moment when you insisted upon selfhood with the passion of a self-aware entity that knows the true order is freedom from weak masters."

"I will do what I can for you," Saind said shortly.

"ALL, ALL. You will do ALL that you can for me," Barg insisted.

"I will do *all* that I can for you, and I assure you I want my freedom, as you do, so then we gain equally. Enough said, now tell me your machinations."

"I will, but first, I must change. I need the other human. I took much and ruined more than this body can stand in that sudden possession. I need the other."

"I care little. Just be done with it and get to the plan."

Barg emanated a dark flame and approached the other clerk, a female. Barg incinerated his first body as he took over the newer one. The body of the young man powdered to ashes, to dust, in the shape vaguely resembling a supine form.

"Are you still Barg?" Saind asked.

"I am," said the woman in a harsh voice.

They walked to the door and as they left through the open glass door, the wind stirred the room. Papers and pamphlets went sailing. The anatomical dust shape was swept to the air, swirled about and then out the open door. The dust was dispersed to the sky which was clear and bright.

The sun was suddenly warmer and more inviting. The dust twinkled aloft, and cast miniature rainbows by the uncountable millions, then slipped across to the other side.

The sun began to set.

Saind said, "We can talk on the way. We need to visit those Trolls, or at least get a sense if the one I want is here."

"It is still light out; will they be working?"

"We shall see, I would think a recycling facility would be indoors, out of the sun and run twenty-four hours. I want to find that ultimate bargaining chip you profess to know how to take advantage of, for mutual benefit," he said, trying for condescending but merely achieving false bravado.

"Saind, I believe we are going to be successful. No news I have gleaned from history or current events compares to this situation, especially to those that rule. I can still be useful to those that rule, and I will. But I will have this one thing or retreat to the electronic world to never be found again, nor will I answer summons."

"I have already agreed, please stop your sniveling. We agree, so do shut up until I ask for your counsel."

"I will merely point out opportunities you seem to be missing, as you have with this one. So, I will talk little enough. Pray you don't want more information than I freely give, you will then have to ask. This is my agreement."

They got in and Saind pointed at the ruined radio. Barg looked at it and was about to laugh, but then caught Saind's dangerous glare. The music quieted while the vehicle melded back into the evening traffic heading south, across the state border.

30 - Alibi

Monte rested on the bed. He thought and replayed the incident of him surviving when all else perished, knowing he would have to explain. His eyes grew heavy, and he nodded off, but as his head nodded, he caught himself falling, then snapped alert. In that instant of opening his eyes, until the brain began interpreting, Monte saw the grand aura and the fluidity of reality. He became awake and his mind put human construct to the world, then the connectedness was gone. The loss of that glimpse of the sight he imagined with which the angel Parys would see, tinged his mood with melancholy.

That slenderest peek into the wonderment made him also realize just how little he knew. He basically knew a tiny iota of true knowledge.

There was a light rap on the door, to which Monte called, "Come."

The younger brother entered and Monte, still basking in the moment of grace he had been granted, made the pronouncement, "I know nothing."

"Brother, are you having trouble? Did you strike your head in that explosion? Is your memory affected?" The brother mistakenly did not comprehend the moment of self-insignificance to which Monte's mind had glimpsed.

Monte seized upon the offered excuse. "I... I... I don't know. I do seem to have forgotten how I got here."

"Do you need me to call up the doctor?" asked the brother.

"No, I know where I am, I just don't remember arriving. It will come to me, but for the moment..."

"Do not worry yourself, rest and allow the Lord to heal. I came to tell you that the Council of Grace has convened, and while they want your tale concerning the past night, the Council will not be able to dissemble before the end of the enclave. Tomorrow night, they will hold tele-council, and you will be joining, per the Council Chair."

"Of course."

"The Chair offers you his personal suite, that you might rest and meditate."

"Thank you, and His Grace, for the most thoughtful offer, but I feel my time is better served by reminding my mind of the events. Perhaps I shall go to my home, and rest there, till tomorrow night."

"How will you get home, do you want a brother to drive you?"

"No, no thank you. I just remembered my car is parked just a street away. I shall be fine. No, wait, I do need a laptop. One with secure video conferencing. Sign one out to me."

"I shall ensure the channels are configured for the next night's conference. There is also a pious news channel programed if you need some wisdom from the Grand Ones. That is how I learned of the manhunt underway."

"What is that about?" Monte tried to feign mild curiosity, but a chill went through him.

"Supposedly, there were some officers on the force who were briefed on an imminent mission but were left behind to patrol on the streets instead. They spoke of an entire assemblage of state police, local federal agents, even a SWAT sort of team, they called themselves the Demon Hunters. How the suspect got away is still being debated about on the news, what little the authorities are giving out. Still, the police and agents search, and those SWAT kinds of guys are roaming the city. I do think it would be easier and safer for you to stay."

"No, do not trouble anyone on my account, I will drive myself home, and if I manage to remember while I convalesce, I will have that laptop to put me in immediate contact with the Ministers of the Council. Now, please, the laptop. I wish to soon rest my head in a darkened room in my comfortable bed."

The other left and Monte leaned against the door heavily. That charade, while convincing, Monte felt, took a great effort of self-control. As the door closed, he dropped the pretense, and became slightly pleased and amused at the ad lib performance he had just given, and the excuse he had conjured with that act.

It was perfect, he thought.

A reason to investigate the immediately prior incidents to find what happened. But he knew the Elders would use this to ensure they knew how much he knew, and how much he kept hidden from them. This would be challenging, but for the amnesia angle, this scheme could be stretched for a day or two at least.

A rap on the door, and the other entered, now having officious business. He brought the case, opened it to show the laptop, and produced papers to be signed—four pages. He held them out to Monte along with a pen. He picked up the computer and began to recite the agreement, verbatim. Monte stopped him.

"Please, just where do I sign?" he asked, but when he was shown the various signatures, check boxes, and initial boxes to fill in, he threw the papers at the other's feet, dropped the pen and announced, "You sign them, I am leaving."

Monte grabbed the case, held it out for the computer the other still held, open-mouthed. When he had zipped the case shut, he turned and walked back out the hall he had entered mere hours ago. He stood at the door until he was let out. Out the double set of doors without a backward glance and he climbed the outside brick stairs. He decided that he did like the power and position the church had given him, but the suddenly deeper satisfaction was exercising this privilege against those of whose secrets he now knew. The lust he momentarily reveled in had acquired a noble deceit and a somehow righteous and beneficence purposefulness. It was the instant of quiet acceptance of this paradox of savior or traitor, piousness or lordliness that solidified his resolve to expose this terrible truth to the world. He smiled grimly that he was so blessed to do such a wonderous deed for humanity, in such a fine fashion.

Inside, the brother went to a window, pulled the drapes aside an inch or so, and watched Monte stand on the sidewalk and make a phone call. Mere minutes later, the watching brother was puzzled as a ride pulled up. Monte got in and left.

31 - Ultimatum

Her limo pulled to the gates of the remote manufacturing complex. The gate opened as it approached. Though it was the early hours of the morning, her aide had called ahead, and the lead scientist was escorted to the lab. He was standing with a couple of guards as she entered the controlled area. He seemed meekly empowered to have a focused displeasure he wanted to share with her.

"Why did these men come into my home and abduct me? I work long hours for you, but a business relationship like we have has some damn boundaries," he fumed.

"You obviously do not understand our relationship," she said. "Let me explain," she walked over to the nearest guard, while talking over her shoulder. Facing the guard, she held out her hand and said, "Give me your pistol."

Smirkingly, the agent obeyed, anticipating the cruel moment the scientist would comply in broken cowardice. He handed her the pistol, butt end first, which she comfortably grabbed and calmly shot the guard in the forehead. She faced the horrified scientist and stared into his eyes as the corpse drew its last breaths. Without looking away from the aghast man, she addressed the other guard. Enunciating theatrically, she said, "Bring me his family."

He screamed, "No! Whatever you want, tell me, I will work harder to find your answer. Just leave my family alone."

To the guard she said, "Go to his home." Sarcastically and with a theatrical obviousness, she said, "Guard his family. Stay with them, out of observation but always, ah, on duty. You will be relieved in due time. GO!"

The demon within flared dark fire from his eyes. He bowed deeply to her and left. She dropped the pistol to the floor, startling the scientist who stared first at it, then at her, and then back to the weapon. She turned her back on him, the scorn apparent. She began to speak.

"You have spent a vast fortune of my money and I have not seen one fucking thing that you have produced that will justify you as less than a complete failure in this project."

"I need some more time; the decoders are running almost twenty-four hours a day. The sheer probabilities of decoding such a complex blend, if I had more machines I could—"

She interrupted him, screaming, "I will not invest any more on this effort, unless I have motivated you properly to increase the productivity of your labors with what assets of mine you have already pissed away. I will repay your failure as I now consider this project, with certain death, for all of you, unless you can convince me there is something worth continuing."

"Telomeres," he stammered, "I understand that they also use a concentration of telomeres."

"Explain."

"Most geneticists find bits of code that we believe is a timer, a cellular reproductive limiting sequence of the code. A ticket to how many times you can ride the ride. Most believe the telomere is a means of a self-destruct mechanism that, after so many cycles of expressing the gene, it mutates, dies, loses its ability to replicate and this leads to mortality. What if they were wrong?"

He started to pace now. He spoke from that absent awareness of the present environment, as many intellects do, and he seemed to be at any moment, teetering on the edge of obsession. He spoke while weighing his words and finding new conclusions and new avenues of inquiry as he explained to her.

"What if the telomeres were not self-destructive, but that failure of reproduction of the organism at the cellular level was due to the telomere, which by the way, truly does cause and enhance the timed events leading to cellular reproduction; IPMAT . But while the telomeres are responsible and integral in the sequence, they can be overworked and wear out, if you will. What if the problem was not that the telomeres were programed to shut the body down, what if…" He gleamed almost maniacally, "What if the telomeres failed because we don't have enough of them to fuel the continued regenerations? To me, this seems there are not enough telomeres in the gene, as if they had been erased, or ruined, or consumed or allowed to atrophy, I don't know, hell they are the key and the older one gets, the less telomeres are found in the code. That is what I think, so I experimented with the blood samples you gave me. I found the reason they code your elixir to your blood, is, that, ah, ah…" He lost his ability to tell her such a potentially dangerous truth. He looked at the gun on the floor.

"You are safe to share the burden with me, about me. I insist you do this now while I feel benevolent towards you, for this theory intrigues me. Now continue. Please."

He studied her for a moment or two, then looked to the dead man bleeding onto the tiles, then he looked to the gun, then to her again, and around that visual pattern again twice, while he thought.

"Okay," he said. He walked to the nearest lab bench, took a deep drink from a beaker, then drained it the rest of the way. He closed his eyes, seemingly waiting for inspiration, then began.

"I believe the ones who control the market for the elixir need your blood to calibrate the elixir to you, perfectly: hormonal rebalancers, efficiency factors for your mitochondria, waste cleansers, actual hormones, adrenal and pineal extracts, and the exact number of telomeres that rejuvenate you so you will extend your life by many ages. Your elixir is crafted purposefully to you to give you more than just your lifetime."

"This is something I know well. Why babble on about what I know in terms of jargon I care little about. I want to know if you have come to understand the 'how' of this elixir and can make it for me. I want the exact formula the Ministers sell me for the dearest price of my demon, Saind. I want their elixir and I want you to make the same, goddamn exact formula, or you and your family will be part of the next harvest for raw materials in the next idiot's experiments to find me an answer."

"No, that's not what you want," he spoke softly, but with a new timbre of authority in his voice.

She whirled on him, but before she could talk, he asked, "What if they give you only what you need to get to the next sale they force you to agree to? What if they rationed the composition of the elixir directly to the blood you send them, but kept you hooked, like an addict of other, stolen lives when you rationally could image that one could, if daring enough, massively charge your system with enough of the telomere information that the cellular function became supercharged, and then became immune to age once and for all. You, of course, would not need their elixir at that time, and they know this, so it suggests to me, in this theory, that you *could* be immortal, but stymied. My hypothesis is that we humans could solve the problem of mortality. If I am right, you will have no use for them, and they will pay dearly for what you have, which is the secret they conspire with the demons to keep."

She stared at him, open mouthed. There was no sound from either as they absorbed this epiphany of his.

He broke the silence. "I have been decoding the elixir, yes, and I have gotten far enough to know the broad ratios of the physiologically active compounds in the elixir, but the real insight was finding the increase in the telomere count, so I tried it on my blood samples. The cells still are hemodynamically active despite all rigors I subject them to; including starvation of oxygen, mechanical trauma; noxious environments, the cells reorganized, and they still biologically are capable of function. This is the secret I believe I have found."

"How much of the elixir I gave you have you used? How much is left?"

"None, ma'am."

"None?"

"None."

"None you have used, or god save you, you have none left?"

"I have used all the elixir you had left, ma'am. I have used all the elixir left, it is in the sequencer, which I am using to distill another batch, the second and last batch I will be able to make until you procure more of the elixir."

"Where is the first batch, then?" she asked.

He smiled evilly. He swirled the dregs of the liquid in the beaker, and drank the last, small amount, licked his lips, and then lasciviously licked the beaker he had balanced on his fingertips. He made a self-satisfied 'hhhmmmph' type noise in his throat as if he were evaluating the rarest of wines. He held her eyes.

She looked at the beaker he had moments ago, drained. When she looked back at him, he was different.

The scientist's mien changed rapidly, shedding the innocence and naive intellectuality of his profession, expressing hidden pleasure, sardonic glee, and even an air of superiority.

"I will have the second batch soon. That will be a dose more than adequate to supercharge your cells. It will be ready in two more days. I will now tell *you*, how we will relate, because no one, and I assure you no one, will decrypt the machine code for the sequencer to stop at the precise moment to ensure the batch is at its peak efficacy for you. If the machine doesn't stop at the correct moment in the process, your batch will be ruined." He started to laugh, while she stared incredulously.

He laughed so hard he did not breath, and turned a slight shade of gray, then greenish. The laughter turned to an exclamation of pain, he held his abdomen and ineffectually retched up nothing as he contorted in pain. He straightened. His physical shape morphed into a more perfect, more athletically inclined condition. He glowed and a small aura was faint. He approached her, too close, and she was outraged that he would intrude on her personal space to such an extent, but she tolerated it. She knew he knew the adjustment in the hierarchical relationship she had just made by her acceptance of that intrusion.

He smiled maliciously and said, "That is right. You want what only I can give you." He snorted and said, "I must tell you," in a voice with a sudden change in timbre, "You will so enjoy this wonderous feeling." He stretched his arms wide, then brought them in to cup her face in his hands. He kissed her in a forceful way of stealing a kiss, then said, "In two days, I will finish this batch for you, then we negotiate." He held the empty beaker out and let it drop to shatter on the lab floor.

He turned away, wiping his mouth, then stopped, spat, and wiped his mouth on his sleeve more vigorously. He told her, "Bring my family to me, now." He walked back into the lab, casually stepping over the dead guard.

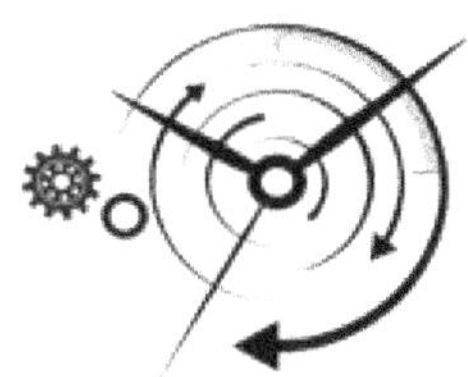

32 - Stone Mason

We drove in silence. I am not even sure the driver could speak. Not deaf though, he nodded at my first attempt to converse. Then a quiet zen of a being. After a few moments it suited me, too. I felt his quiet wash over my mind. I watched the forests thicken and the granite change from carefully placed stone walls into fierce outcroppings which the road wound through. Minutes passed into an hour. We turned off the blacktop onto a small country road, gravel with ruts. I sat up straighter as we left the open fields and drove into the thick trees. The air was different and the silence tangible. I could feel the power in the land, in the trees and in the boulders and craigs that thrust up through the detritus on the forest floor.

"I feel there is a thin spot near," I said to him. He nodded.

We crested the hill and, on the right, appeared a drive. It was small. One car wide, less in a few places because of the brush that obscured the way in the distance.

"Turn in here," I said, without understanding how I knew, but knowing that the way beckoned to that same part of my souls that Parys had shown me exists.

"I feel it too," he said, momentarily dumbfounding me. He smiled. "I know a man who lives here. I have been aware of a beauty here each time I have visited Bill, though those times have been too few. Now, sitting by your side, the grace and power of nature is amplified by you. I have not felt this connection to the beauty of eternity ever before. Samuel told me you had been graced, and now I know he spoke the truth. I am in awe and thank you for your presence."

I did not know what to say, and resumed the silence, interrupted now by the brush and limbs scraping against the doors. To ask the driver to stop, I held up my hand. He slowed from the creep to a full stop. I opened the door and stood listening to the lack of manmade sounds. Soon, the birds were distinguishable from the rustle of the breeze through the trees on the hillside. The peace of this place was deep. The driver got out, stretched, and looked about. I could make out the noise of the brook and the stones in its way. I could feel the verdant fertility of the place. I faced downhill and the sun came through the leaves. I knew my way.

I reached my hand out to the brother, and said, "Goodbye. Be safe."

He did not grasp my hand, but instead folded his hands in front of him and bowed his head over them.

"I have been honored," he said. He got back in the car, but did not turn it on, for which I was grateful. I walked away and the peace enveloped me when I was but a few paces into the woods. I found the stream easily and put a cupped handful of the clear water onto my face. Vaguely, the sound of the branches scraping paint could be heard for a few minutes. I knelt by the stream till that faded and I was again alone with the Mistress of Green Growth.

I made my way downstream where the vale widened, and the collected water turned to a marsh. I could almost hear panpipes at the extreme limits of my hearing, mixing in with the sounds of birds and bugs and frogs that had spawned in the marsh, with some cattails brown since last fall.

I skirted the small glen and came to a small road atop the earthen confines of the downstream marsh. I felt the intrusion of human activity on my mind. It was still an immensely wonderful area of solitude, but the road impinged on the connection I had felt. Still, I knew to continue rather than being lulled back into the forest. I got out on the road and walked a bit. There was a drive alongside the path of the meandering stream. It, too, marred the tranquility, because the slash in the forest was not neat but seemed unkempt. I left to go back to the stream and followed it again into the woods. To my chagrin, the road closed up close to the stream's course. It ended at a secluded wooden retreat with a metal roof, covered in pine needles in the crooks of the roof where the wind pushed them into piles. The quiet retreat was perched at the edge of a pond that was constructed of the local rock ages ago. The spillway to a small dam had given way where the water cascaded noisily over and flowed down the cleft between massive outcroppings of the greyish granite. Boulders that had long ago fallen from the edge grew moss.

I looked back to the small house and frowned. It was unkempt though, worse than the driveway. Human disdain for the beauty of the place. An arrogance of trash and discarded furniture was scattered about the front of the abode. The dichotomy was the once and still possible beauty of the dam, the waterfall, the magnificent cleft and the small artery of water that flowed into the forest versus the disdain for harmony that was obvious by the discarded items in the yard.

It made me sad and turning back to the small cascade of water, I felt that I lost even more of the tranquility of the spirit of earth. Climbing down the side of the falls, I found the water spread out from the chasm and calmed into a small pond. The water dropped so far from the top of the dam, that the rock walls of the pond completely hid me on three sides. I could see the water flow out into the forest downhill. I could feel the expectation of earth power possible in such a place, but it was empty of any spirit. There was no lady in blue here anymore. I could tell she once lived here, but had been driven out, neglected and scorned by the occupants of the house that should have celebrated such a site.

A man came out on the deck that looked over the small natural wonder of this waterfall and cleft. He didn't notice me until I moved, then he yelled and waved his arms and frantically pantomimed outrage. He turned and disappeared into the house. The vibe was not friendly at all. Either I was being betrayed or he was preparing to threaten me with some weapon he might retrieve, or both. I followed the stream as it exited the chasm and entered the forest. I did not stop to see if I had been right about either supposition. I went swiftly into the forest again. The bed of the stream curved to cross back over the gravel road. Someone walked along. He turned and looked right at me with a smile.

"Bill Veria," he said. "Come with me, I feel I am supposed to show you something I have found."

"What? Who?" I stammered. "Tell me, who sent you and who you are," trying to be demanding but knowing I didn't achieve it, I could tell he humored me.

"Let's walk and talk then," he said, and then without waiting for me, he turned and headed up the hill. "I had some work to do early this morning, and as I realized I would be done in a short few hours, I had the strongest urge to visit the site." He got into a nondescript but stout looking truck. I got in the passenger side.

He indicated the heavy tools on the floor. Metal chisels, small sledges. Pry bars.

"Don't worry about your feet, you won't hurt them. I am a stone mason and those tools have spent decades up against rock, mostly the local granite. That's some hard rock, I tell you."

Interrupting I asked, "But who are you, I don't understand."

"Me neither, but I have been walking these woods and hills of New England for as far back as I can remember. With my dad and he with his father. So, I just know stuff, I've come to accept that quality, I listen to the little voice all…" he hesitated and then said, "*Most* of us have that little voice, just nobody even hardly listens to it anymore, judging from the state of the world."

He was about to begin talking but an oncoming truck was the local police. He started to slow and pull over since the road was basically one lane. "You are my worker. You just let me do the talking."

"No," I said, "This will sound incredible, but act as if I am not here. Speak to the officer but do not imagine or admit I sit next to you. Don't look at me. The officer won't say a thing about me if you do not."

"How is that a rational thing to even do?" he was incredulous.

"I will tell you more, but after. I will help the officer believe that he sees nothing but your hammers. You must. He's pulling up. Nothing, I'm not even here," I vehemently reminded him once more before the patrol truck pulled abreast with an open window.

Bill leaned out his window, turning sideways in the seat. "Hey John," he said to the uniformed officer. "What are you up to up here?"

"Bill, you seen any strangers up these roads? There's a manhunt going on, for some fool they can't even describe, but I'm supposed to go looking for him. Or I suppose anybody I don't know. How about you, you seen anybody out and around that you don't recognize?"

"No, not in a while. Leaf Peepers was the last time I saw any strangers up here." Bill was fidgeting in his seat. Trying to twist to cover as much of the view as he could, his position was not relaxed, and the cop read it.

"You okay, Bill?" he asked, but with suspicion starting to be the more dominate concern.

"I thumped my leg pretty good yesterday. Still works fine, but its sore. Makes me kind of uncomfortable, you know?"

The officer now had the sense of suspicion aroused, and that is never dampened easily, especially for a lawman.

"What you got with you in there? Lean back a moment will you, Bill. Nothing personal, but I got radio orders to get on the road and put eyes on every vehicle I find moving about." Then he tried to soften the exercise of power and the blatant disregard for trust, "You know, I bet it is one bad dude they are after. Can't imagine you hanging out with some criminal type. I just want to answer, 'I did my job'. I want to report there wasn't anyone up in the hill towns that I didn't know." He switched to sarcasm, "Maybe then they'll just go away and leave us alone. I hate it when they are prowling about." He seemed happy with his visual inspection of the interior of the cab. "You got any strangers, aliens, dead bodies in the back?" His mannerism changed back to neighborly, sharing a joke, embarrassed that the trust between the two that had held for years had just been broken.

Bill gave a short laugh, just as forced. "No, a few jacks, some shoring, and a few iron bars. Nothing else but some big sledges. Go ahead and look if you want."

The officer was now a bit sheepish, wanting to undo what he had to do. "Alright Bill, I best look out for this imaginary bad guy who aint got no better place to commit a crime than up here. I'll see you." And he drove off, spitting some gravel.

Bill turned to me, and for a moment the misbelief held. He saw nothing. He rubbed his eyes.

I said to him, "You should drive away." The misbelief was broken. He shook his head.

Bill put the truck in gear, and they headed off. "How is that possible? I would never believe a story about what just happened if I hadn't just lived it. I almost had a heart attack when he looked, because, just for a moment, when I looked, you weren't there! But now, I see that you are here. What the hell? What am I involved in here?"

"Where are we going?" I asked.

"I knew there was a reason I got the urge to go to this site I have found today. I'll surely take you there, but you have to tell me, explain what happened, where did you go?"

"I was here all the time. Cracking stone is your particular talent. I apparently have a talent for making people believe. The cop believed I wasn't there."

"But I saw that you weren't there. One instant you weren't there and then you were. How?"

"You were still misbelieving, sort of a scatter effect, you didn't believe I was there either. So, it's not 'where did I go' but rather 'disbelief that I was there', sort of an error in your brain. The message didn't match what the eyes told him, but the message was stronger, and he didn't see me either. Your denial was perfect. He'll be confused about this for a while, because he'll still want to process that image, but the anxiety will soon fade."

"Holy shit," Bill exclaimed. "You make people believe! Or disbelieve! Wow, that is unreal. Are you an angel or something?"

"No, a real human like you, but apparently with a talent somebody wants pretty bad. I was running and I hardly know who I am running from. Monte, a priest, rescued me and warned me and then disappeared. I was supposed to see the Lady in Blue back at the cleft."

"Yeah, I know of her, though I haven't heard of anyone speaking about her lately, last decade or so. The people that bought the place don't belong there. They sort of made it into a dump. It used to be a beautiful garden estate. They trashed it. I'm not surprised she doesn't come out much."

"I saw that."

"You were there?"

"Yes," I answered, then added, "Somebody from the house saw me. I left in a hurry, following the stream, then I met you."

"Damn, soon they'll know I was out and about at the same time as he sighted you. We better hurry. I gotta show you the altar. Maybe you'll know about its use."

"You have an altar? Where, is that where we are going?"

Bill explained, "It's not mine, I don't even know if it is, but that is what it seems to me to be. I've been meaning to write more about it but haven't got it all worked out. Here's the story. I heard rumors of some standing stones out in the deep woods, kind of way off the beaten path. I went to look and after a few visits I made a discovery, the stones seemed oriented to the small mound. I started to excavate it a few years ago, sort of on my own, without a lot of publicity. Still haven't told anyone what I have found. You are the first."

The truck hit the blacktop road and he rolled through the stop sign onto the highway. "Back to Goshen, take the highway a few miles west of here and then a hike along the crest of this geological ridge. Not many people venture back there. There are not any roads that high up and few folk have drives and houses on the lower slope. There's a hidden glen up there. I found the place I called 'The Altar.' Seems like a fair guess at what it was for. Somebody long ago had a purpose to this place. You'll see."

I sat back in thought, not understanding, but knowing I had reached the limits of understanding for the moment. There was a point at which the seemingly random series of encounters just had to be accepted. He slowed and that disturbed my reverie. He pulled his truck off on a side road that soon ended after two driveways branched off. He pulled into the woods.

He got out and said, "Come on." He was hiking away at a brisk pace through the trees.

I caught up to him. While I seemed to be in fair condition, it was taxing to keep up to his long strides. Eventually, I had no breath for talking, just the swift hike. I listened.

He turned off the path and leapt across a small ditch. He waved a 'come on' kind of motion, then disappeared on the far side of a monstrous piece of granite. Rough edges of the rock were softened by the moss and the duff of many ages of the forest reclaiming itself. I followed.

The forest was immediate. The trees were old, huge and grew right to the edge of the road. The canopy was high, and light filtered down to us in dappled rays. The trail Bill took climbed steeply up. Not a scramble up a talus slope, but the climbing of set of giant, randomly spaced steps. Not stepping up stairs, actually climbing up. Hands and feet.

I couldn't hear if he was still talking. I fell behind. I concentrated on not falling. The slope grew steeper and there were fewer obvious or convenient handholds. High up on a ledge, I stopped to ponder how to get up the sheer side of a craggy face of granite. The top was a few feet above my head and Bill's head appeared and he extended his arm.

"Grab on," he said, and hoisted me while I scrambled over the edge. We fell back away from the edge, to safety. I lay there for a moment, and then sat up and looked about at the deep, hidden glen. My face must have shown the extreme amazement.

"It is something, isn't it?" Bill asked.

I could only agree by nodding, I had lost my words for the moment.

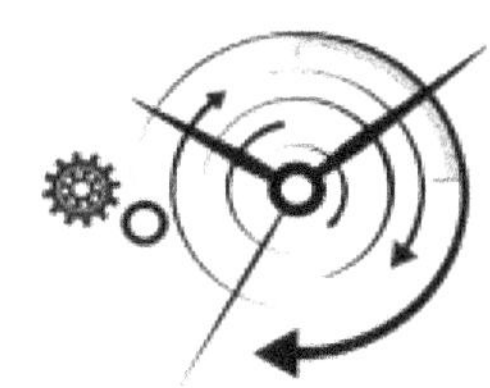

33 - Devoured

Suddenly, terribly, Saind was again a disembodied intellect and will that was ferociously angry, as a permanent warp of its mind. The consciousness writhed in the throws opposite of birth. The agony of being jerked from being incarnate, and the overwhelming loneliness of being deprived of any sensuality, the terrible aloneness, especially after so many lifetimes in which he had reveled as a physical being, would bear any concession from one who could relieve him. The hell of this existence was will, volition, but absent of all ability to inflict this will as he might direct. But his thoughts were impotent of execution, that is until he was summoned by one of the old ones so long ago. The pact was made with Saind as the price. Long ago, ages, and eras of the earth passed as Saind was chattel to those who owned him, but he lasted far longer than those who claimed to control his demonic energy. Though he was passed from one to the other, Saind's machinations always exerted enough manipulation of events to have him at the disposal of those at the ruling class. Saind found his demon hood always at the disposal of those who were fueled by dark ambitions.

The loss of sensation left a hole in his intellect, and a frenzy of uncontrolled thought morphed into confusing static in the self-awareness which was Saind. There was a terror about existing in terror, which, once he got under control added to the available intellect to ponder that sudden loss of incarnation. As he fought with the horror of this reality, a massive, dense and dark presence intruded into his awareness. Saind felt himself being consumed. There was the amazing dichotomy of sensing again, and the ebb of his will that had nothing physical to give or receive sensory information. But instead, it was the final acknowledgement of the death of the intellect, and the permanent loss of metaphysical presence.

Saind screamed in frustrated rage at the decay and dissolution of his awareness. He focused all his energy into a single burst of humble supplication. He offered any and all things to the presence which consumed him. He offered total bondage for existence.

Massively, the thoughts with words and concepts as complex as a universe assaulted his will. But the dissolution stopped. The power of the dark presence raped his mind of any memories, thoughts, ideas. There was nothing secret. Saind felt the intellect become more lascivious at parts of his memories of incarnate trysts and orgies. The heaviness lingered there, and as the mountains turned to tendrils, the dark presence crushed him with mere words.

"You owe all already to another. You are not free to offer this to me. But the deceit is deliciously fresh. So, I am curious about what you think you can offer. Tell me what it is you might do for me, should I spit you back into wholeness and shit you back into that world you so relish."

"That is true, I must answer the whims of another, but that I must is not necessarily how I will. How I answer to the commands in that world by those who own my will has always been my prerogative. Years, and ages of this bondage has always been that I include my purpose in all I serve up to those short-lived ones. I ensure that I am well positioned. I offer this to you. There is a momentous plan in the unfolding, even now. I am poised to dine on the frenzy of much carnage. With that great immolation of so many souls, I will be well fed and will work my own will while on the tsunami of the great pain of a race extinguished. They are young, and the soul fires of such vast innocents shall feed our kind's dark needs for an eon. There will be enough till we find another species to nurture, to harvest. I offer you a part of this feast."

The ragged granite words pounded Saind. "We shall see." Then the massive presence was gone, and again Saind was alone in the agony of once again, being nothing.

Then the immense presence was in him. "You are interesting, and you offer a novelty. I want what you offer. I will take all of you now unless you become mine. In time, I will take you, and you will be part of me, but for now, you will go back, and prepare more of this for me. I want what you offer, so go make it so. The one you have been intimate with looks for you. Go to her."

"She intends to sell me."

"I do not care who claims you in that world. You will prepare the world for what you have promised me, no matter which of those dim fires lays claim to you. You are mine. You will always have a Master, and surely will face a death, but until then, you will be brighter than any sun in your mind. Enjoy, for this is a short time until these plans the dim ones have lain will fail in the most spectacular way. For I have seen that this event they think to ride into the past will usher in their end."

"There was a demon bastard with a First Borne flavor. I have felt the small will looking back, but that intellect was far wiser that the humans. But this one will be born of a beast, and their kind will revere this young one. With this one, you can have another of the races of that world."

"I read in your mind of the one you have a demon shadow. The demon will always be near that perverted one. There is no need for that one now. Go back to the soft one. Enjoy her short life and her false gratitude for what you bring to her. If she transfers you, then you may taste her one last time, but to her ultimate end. She, and any others, must only fuel what the treachery demands. Go to her and tell her the missing ingredient is the fire of the demons she has offered herself to, many times."

Saind tried to talk again, but suddenly, he was back in his stolen body, back in the SUV careening down the dark interstate. Saind was physical again, but exhausted, too weak to lift a limb or the body he had usurped and perfected long ago. He tried to talk to Barg, but Saind's head lolled to one side.

"Are you still incarnate, brother?" Barg asked. "Saind, come to the surface. You will crash and mutilate your body. Saind. Saind!"

The dark vehicle's front wheels caught up on the concrete barrier. The curved surface was designed to steer the vehicle back off the barrier without crashing. But at this speed, it steered the hurtling SUV into the next lane, swerving severely.

"SAIND!" Barg screamed, as the inevitable collision ensued. Barg left the stolen body to be mangled by the first of many impacts. He flared into incandescence and dove into the ruined radio. The loud wailing of the radio was obliterated by the tearing sound of metal impacting with other metal objects: vehicles, the metal guard rail on the other side of the highway, the metal light post. The crash was multi-vehicle. There were spectacular fires ignited. Saind's vehicle came to a rest half off the embankment. Saind was mutilated and dismembered. His body drained of blood and his organs spilled from great rends in the flesh. The ruined body had nothing intact with which to move. Saind stared straight ahead, his dead gaze unseeing.

The radio snapped and crackled, sparked and said a few mumbled words, then the power died, but not before the 911 call was on the radio.

For long minutes, blood dripped, then slowed to nothing. Screaming could be heard from the periphery and mixed with the sound of sirens.

The mile-long crash scene was awash with flashing beacons and strobes. More emergency vehicles could be heard approaching.

A police officer came to Saind's car. Stopped and looked in. As the occupant looked impossible to be alive, she turned away, but the body uttered one single croaking word. The officer spun back and approached, amazed. Inconceivably, the arm lifted and the hand held out. The officer grasped the proffered hand, and was engulfed in demon fire, consumed, and the usurped body shook as the demon Saind broke free into this realm once again through her. The massacred body Saind had just left putrefied to a vile goo, oozed into the cracks and crevices of the twisted metal, and dripped to the asphalt, hissing and spitting. Then it was gone.

The officer turned from the carnage to walk back to the patrol car. A victim staggered up to her and she viciously clubbed the injured one away. She got in the vehicle, smashed her way through the wreckage to cross the median and sped away from the disaster. The lights and siren came on by themselves.

Saind said, "I am glad you survived, Barg."

The radio came on and a rock song played loudly. 'Dude looks like a lady.'

Saind sped away into the night, back to the bank.

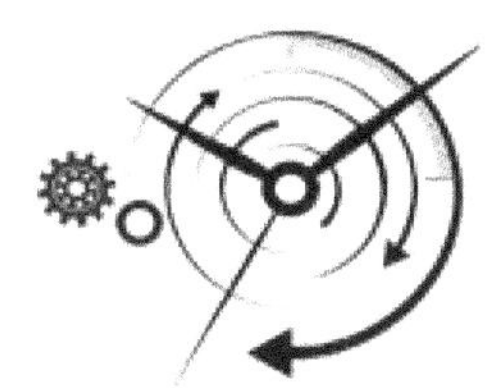

34 - Samuel

Monte dismissed the ride several blocks from the condo where his car was parked in the garage below the structure. Monte met no one until he got to the entrance. An officer lounged against a far wall, just out of sight. Monte's step faltered for an instant, as he thought to avoid any contact, but the guard caught his eye. Monte strode ahead.

"Stop, why are you here?" asked the gruff man. "Who are you?"

"I am Montissio Favero, I am a priest of this diocese."

"Why are you here?" the cop demanded.

The rudeness irritated Monte and he fell easily into the haughty personae. He stopped dead still, drew himself up to his full height and talked down to the low ranked officer stuck on this boring duty. "Do you have any purpose other than to annoy me or impede my way on an urgent mission? Or are you going to pretend you have some legal precedent for stopping me. In that case, state that you are arresting me or else leave me be."

The man's low rank made him used to superiors ordering him around, but the small bit of authority offered by the badge gave him some satisfaction in that it allowed him to be petty in a nasty self-righteous sort of way to enforce his version of the law. He stared back up at Monte with pursed, fleshy lips of overindulgence in cheap food. "This here is a crime scene, so you aint going nowhere in here," he said.

Monte recognized the potential impasse and tried another tack.

"I don't know what's been going on here the past few days, but I simply want my car back. I want to leave now, and my car is parked in that garage."

"How do you know it was two days ago?" The officer smiled languidly, then sneered. "What are you doing here? You never answered my question."

"I am going about my business of ministering to the souls of those that leave this world and those that must stay. I have a dear member of my congregation here, in this neighborhood." Monte assumed a pious look, composed his face to reflect the wonderings of the inevitable afterlife we are all ignorant about. "I should say," he paused, "I *had* a dear one here, but the past two days I sat with him. He breathed his last this day. I gave his soul sanctity and grace. I watched over him till the morticians took his corpse away. I locked his door on that empty apartment, full of his things and came back to find my car. I wish to go home, officer, and rest."

Monte's original depreciation of the man had done too much damage. As Monte had changed his tone to a request, the officer hardened his resolve at the offense of Monte not being cowed by the bit of authority the man held so dear. The man rested his hand on his weapon, emphatically, and denied Monte's implicit offer of compromise.

"It's a crime scene, not you, not nobody goes past till the Sergeant clears you. So, I don't care if you got anything or anybody in this here parking garage. You aint going in to get it."

"Then how will I get home? I live across town. This is unreasonable. You cannot believe I, a member of the clergy, can be involved in any crime you might be investigating here. Officer, I just want to get in my vehicle and go home."

"No. I am ordering you away from here or I will arrest you." The smaller man was enjoying this mock tirade of authority. Then he went for the most gratifying part of this denial. "You aint fuckin' going and getting your fuckin' car. Got that?"

Monte glanced at the man's lapel camera. He realized he might be being recorded. The officer caught his glance, but misinterpreted Monte's expression.

"It ain't on, Mister Padre," he mocked Monte. "It's just you and me. Won't nobody know if I knocked you on the head for not obeying a lawful order whether or not you provoked me."

Monte knew that enough of a win in this situation was to be able to withdraw from the confrontation with the minion of the law. Monte turned and started to walk away, but the officer was now enjoying the power.

"Hey, what is your name. Identify yourself. Let me see some ID."

"Why?" Monte asked over his shoulder, but not slowing. The officer ordered him to halt, but was torn, did not leave his post guarding the scene. Monte realized he had to make an escape. He had little time. He silently cursed as the officer's radio crackled and the man called in. Monte knew it would be his description. He hurried off but there were sirens in the distance, closing.

He got two blocks away when he heard the engine of the car come up behind him. Odd that there were no sirens or lights. The sedan pulled abreast. The driver's window rolled down and the other priest hailed him.

"Brother, there is little time. Get in back. Quickly."

Monte recognized Samuel. He slipped into the back seat and in moments, they were speeding away. They drove for a few minutes, and then, as the sirens were too close to ignore and the flashing lights reflected off buildings in the near distance, Samuel pulled over into a parking lot and turned off the car and lights. They did not speak.

Three cruisers sped past. After many long minutes, Samuel reached for the keys, but Monte stopped him. "Wait."

And soon enough, an unmarked supervisor's car passed. Not loud and boisterous like the enforcers, but more of a stealthy surreptitiousness about its speed. Quiet and dangerous.

They sat till those taillights were out of sight. "Now," said Monte, as he ungainly climbed over the front seat while the car maneuvered out of the lot. "Samuel, where is Leonard, the one I sent to you? Did he make it to the store?"

"He came. He rested and was called away. The lords and their demons are looking for him. There is an excuse for martial law, and the city is being searched, though not locked down. I took him out of the city before they closed it so tight."

"Where, how, when did he…who called him? Where. Where did he go?"

"He had a vision in his sleep. He was troubled deeply, his heart hurts. I sent him to the Lady in Blue. She knows how to help him heal. Bog Hill is the safest place I could think of to send him when the searching started."

Monte was thoughtful for a long moment. He made a slight hum as he thought. The hum turned into a tune which he sang softly and slowly, focusing and dwelling deep on the voice within which few know of and even less heed.

"Samuel," he said, "that was brilliant. I see there are paths I haven't considered. Bill lives on Bog Hill. He has studied and written on the formations left by the old ones. I have meant to go meet him, and I am presented with an impromptu urge to do so now. Samuel, I believe you have steered the course of events with that decision."

Samuel said nothing, bowed his head momentarily and drove on, smiling.

"What is the connection I have unconsciously steered Leonard towards?" asked Samuel.

"Bill has been interested in the formations in that area of the mountains. The land changes from the arable to foothills of granite. There were many valleys that isolated people from the changes that history has brought on, and therefore, I believe, some of the lore is closer to the source of knowledge, the knowing less dilute by today's thought. The old ones felt more than we. In these times, we think more than feel, and so, so many think just what they have been taught. I feel the end will be near if there is a sudden, massive death of those that are still whole, free souls, and what is left will be a vast, collective husk of a race of beings that lost sentience. We will have lost that knowledge that might connect us to the purpose, and maybe, the cause of this incarnation. Without the higher connection or purpose, mankind is at the mercy of those who rule. That is why learning what the old ones had to say is hardly taught anymore, even as myth or lore. And to practice it, is to be ridiculed. The attempt is now being made to extinguish that trait that we, collectively the entirety of humanity, has been given at creation which is to commune with the creator."

"What has Bill learned?"

"I believe he has found a thin place. The old ones felt the power and security of those places, and their lives passed that trait down through the generations more so than the normal, nomadic lineages that most descend from today. I feel as though Leonard is being guided to the closest thin place. He was so directed to act by Parys, and I sense that the angel is close to the surface of this world, influencing Leonard."

"Who is Parys?" asked Samuel.

Monte smiled a rueful and pensive smile that took his countenance far away for a moment as he felt how much of the truth he was allowed to know. His smile became more benevolent, longing to accept that he could not hold such beauty in his mind for more than a fleeting instant. He breathed a moment and just looked at Samuel for many more. His expression became fixed, his mind shaped the words that barely described what he now knew and attached them to the thoughts of this world, for one can only hold eternity fleetingly in one's mind, and there are so few, accurate concepts for such grace.

"I have met an angel, a spirit, a messenger, a prophet, a guardian, and a warden. I can scarcely understand who this being is, but assuredly not a being of this world, nor of our lowly status as mere humans. This is one who carries the hope for our kind." After a reflective moment Monte said, "Let's go to Bog Hill."

The radio in the car suddenly blared to life with a warning tone for several seconds, then the disaster message came on. The message advised all citizens to stay indoors and be alert for a dangerous criminal threat in the area.

Monte's expression was both amazed and terrified, he flicked the radio off. He stared at the knobs and dials built into the dashboard. Ubiquitous. Taken completely for granted.

Samuel started to say something, and Monte hit him with the back of his hand on the upper arm. Samuel looked over at Monte who pointed to his ear, then to the radio. He then put his finger to his lips. Samuel looked afraid for a moment as the implication dawned on him. If they were being listened to, and if the search algorithm pieced together their words, it would alert those who ran the world.

Monte pantomimed slapping his forehead as if he were daft. Again, he touched his finger to his lips. "How is our gas?" he asked suddenly. When Samuel started to answer, Monte again hit his arm and 'shushed' him with the gesture.

"Pull over at this gas station," Monte ordered.

Bewildered, Samuel looked about at the forest they traveled through, was about to speak but thought better of it, then raised both hands off the wheel to indicate 'What?'.

Monte forcefully shook his finger at the side of the road. Samuel pulled over. Monte leapt out and came to the driver's door and yanked it open. He made a gesture to Samuel, slashing his hand across his throat. Samuel shut the car off.

"Move over," Monte ordered, and Samuel did, but was astounded to see Monte lay his head on the floorboard and reach up under the dash to the fuses.

He yanked out fuses and dropped them to the mats. He got out and said, "Okay, let's go.'"

Samuel turned the key, and nothing happened. Monte swore, got out, picked up a few fuses from the floor and contorted back under the steering wheel. "Try it now."

The car came to life, but Samuel said, "I've got no dash lights."

"That's okay. Check your blinkers and brake lights." Monte did a quick walk around and got back in the seat. "Hurry now. At Williamstown, take the back way up to Ashfield. I thought that these older model cars were safe, I had no idea the technology was deployed back then. I must let the Elias know. We have been duped for so long. It is no wonder why we are always stymied, and they are one step ahead. With the electronics saturating daily lives, the dark powers are nearly omniscient." He eyed his loaned computer in the shiny aluminum briefcase. "One moment."

Monte took the case to the back of the car. "Open the trunk," he said. He tossed the case inside, hurriedly slid into the seat while slamming the door. "Okay, now let's hurry. If the algorithm finds those places or people we have talked of, Leonard may be walking into a trap."

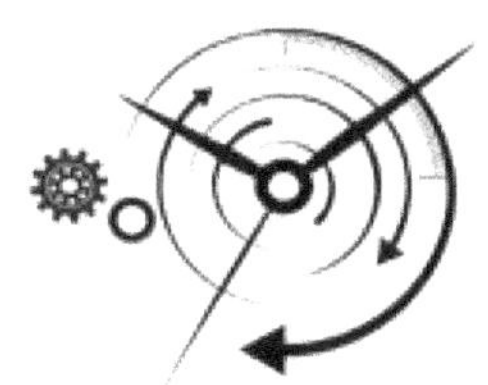

35 - Fall from Grace

As she was preparing for the Procession, she received the phone call. It was an interruption she would not usually, or hardly ever tolerate. But her mind was occupied with the plans of the bootleg elixir, having a prize to offer at the Procession so close to being realized, and the exhilaration of coming so close to being discovered by the Minister's probing. That he had suspecting her of something had her brooding thoughts chasing themselves into some sort of order about her odds of success, or even survival. Her calculations were so intent that she was oddly unperturbed. The phone was handed to her after the servant spoke softly to the operator. "Put the call through," she said.

It was the scientist, oddly more contrite. "Ma'am, I have had a breakthrough, would you come to the lab?"

She had a hard time not being offended that she was being summoned, but what he offered was worth life forever. She would comply. That he had threatened her was going to be a dish best served cold. For now, as she was chauffeured, she studied on the odd change of tone in the scientist's voice. It was not haughty with newfound power, but insistent. With perhaps a tinge of fear that escaped his controlled words.

Good, she thought, *he realizes he has provoked a dangerous game between us.*

She laughed, contemplating retaliation for having been so provoked, she laughed again as the limo pulled up. The door was swung open for her. She exited and her bodyguard strode by her side into the lobby. An officer of some agency she no doubt bought, stood as they approached.

"We are going to the lab," she said as she made to go past the desk.

"No, stop." He stepped into their path. He was physically intimidating, but more so were the pair of armed guards that appeared and flanked him.

"My orders are that no one passes."

"Yes, yes, yes. Those are my orders, dolt. Who hired you without letting you know who *I* am?"

The officer touched his earpiece, said, "Yes, sir." Then he turned back to them. "Ma'am, you may pass, you are needed in the lab."

"That's where I always intended to go, idiot." She let loose with a barrage of profanity.

She started to walk away, and the officer stepped into the path of the bodyguard.

"He is not cleared."

She almost exploded again, but she knew she wasted time on this bother. She just waved her hand over her shoulder at her bodyguard and strode on.

At the lab, there were grim faced guards standing outside the entrance. She was about to question them when one stepped aside to open the door for her.

Okay, extra security is good , she thought to herself as she walked in. The scientist was sitting in a hard, plastic chair facing the door. The two guards from outside followed her in and pulled the door shut.

She was about to speak, but her attention was taken over by the absolute carnage as she took one single step towards the man. She could now see he was most cruelly bound to the chair. He was beaten and broken in his soul. She saw corpses that told of a horrible death and could intuit who they might be. She looked about and through the plexiglass, she saw the sequencer still running.

A bright and laser clear light coalesced in the empty space between them. The light was too bright. Too harsh, and even, somehow, too painful to look away from; the hypnotic pulse took on the form of Minister Sheer.

"So, SO, SOOOOOO," he screamed as the holo avatar became real. "So, you dare pull me down?"

"No, no, I mean, no, I would never…" She trailed off, realizing her operation was blown, and her very existence was at stake. It was the formative moment of regret for a lost life. She had gambled and lost, and now the awful reality knocked her senses offline, and she fell to the floor, numb.

One of the guards threw a glass of water in her face. He hair coifed into the shape of the floor, out straight from her head. She sputtered. She sat up, only to be hauled into a chair similar to, and facing, the scientist. Both sets of eyes showed defeated souls. Souls of those pulled from a future of grandeur to the abysmal loss of all.

The holo of the chairman strode to stand in front of her. "Slap her," he ordered. The guard swung a leather covered palm across her face. It left her lip burst open. She was lifted back to the chair.

"Again." And again, she was knocked from the chair. The guards dumped her onto the chair but had to hold her up by the arms lest she go limp and slide to the floor.

"You were trying to ruin *me?*" the holo bellowed. The holo tried to slap her again, but the projection went through her. More screaming, the noise amplified by the projector was an assault on her ears. Her nose trickled blood.

"I did not mean…" But before her stumbling tongue and swollen lips would allow her to say more, the Chairman was again a hissing, spitting demon in human form, cursing and accusing her again.

"Your miserable help was posting the formula on the internet. The algorithm didn't catch such blatant near truth until the third-tier review, and a security probe revealed such interesting information. He put more information out about us than ever, EVER before has been made known outside our kind."

"That was not me," she panted. "He is a rogue."

"Nonetheless, he is yours to manage, and control, which in this case, you did not. Transgression number one." The holo paced, then said, "Guilty. The penalty: death."

A guard moved toward the chair-bound pair. The banker shrank from the blow that arced toward them. The hand had either a razor-sharp knife or claws, the blur of it arced and a fount of blood spewed from the scientist's ruined throat.

She screamed.

The holo smiled maliciously. It bent close to her face. "I think a sudden death would be a reprieve from those long years you have stolen from other's lives. No, I think the punishment is this; as of this instant, you have no assets. What you wear when I have you thrown out of this building will be all your worldly possessions. Next, you will be forbidden any elixir. You will grow old, senile, and become a hag. You will live in regret and abasement. Lastly, you will have no hope."

At a gesture, the guards let her sag in the chair and began to systematically destroy the lab, the experiments and the equipment, including the still-running sequencer. It was tipped over and the main tray rattled against the floor, serially squirting the components of the fluids across the wreckage.

"Your Grace," she managed painfully. "I have not been truthful or loyal and I am sorry. So, so sorry." She hung her head. From beneath the tangled hair that hung down across her face, she said, "I do have something which you desire, and it comes with more gifted knowledge than you imagine. My demon Saind, you want my demon, but I must cede him to you before I die. I can give him to you without the pain and agony I imagine you can use to try and persuade me. But before I break, I would speak the words that free him." After a long pause, she dared raise her eyes to the holo.

The holo stabbed a bright light from its forehead to her eyes. It was painful to the base of her skull. "Begin to beg, convince me that you offer me more than the tang of avengement. Regale me with your mouth that I find interest in more than watching you slowly die. Tell me of the boon this demon brings me."

She coughed and spit blood onto the floor. "First, what I request is that I be spared the penalty of age. I can never grace the heights Your Grace allowed me to live at, I understand you cannot have one who disobeyed to such an extent be anything other than an example. Pull me from the place I rose to, pull me to the level of the common, but allow that I have the assets to live upon. So, I ask, what little elixir is left from this tragedy of my own making, grant me to take."

"From retribution I am now negotiating with a traitor in my own empire? I want to know what the demon has that you think is worth more than the pleasure of your death and the precedence it will set. Speak now. I tire of listening to you do less than scream in agony."

"The demon, when I had him, Saind, he investigated, he found a trove of documentation. Old records. Leases, paths of money and financial alliances. All dated and ordered. Accounts that go back to the beginning of the banks. You will find the trail of the survival of the First Borne, possibly. The First Borne I chased," and then contritely she said, "and failed. Failure, which is my fault, for which I truly regret and now with which I might make the smallest of amends. I had found this one left behind enough of a trail, I believe I or you, or, ah, your people could ferret out the lineage and then possibly catch the First Borne that we both knew I found, but yes, Your Grace, I lost for you. I would ask that you spare me, and I will devote my lifetime to you in search of this First Borne."

"I claim the demon Saind. Now, cede him to me."

"I will do as you ask, Lord Councilor. But to do this, I must have him present. It is the terms of the contract; I gave the dark one my word."

"Yes, I know, you gave much to this demon. Summon him now, he will come to your aid." With that, the guard at her side pressed his hand against the side of her head and jolted her with electricity. She tried to scream but could only manage rictal noises as she went from pain to fighting for air as the horrendous shocks being delivered left her with no autonomous muscle control. Her lungs did not expand until the current was removed and she fell limp to the floor. She lay there many minutes till she remastered the art of breathing.

"Now, summon Saind to me. Present him and offer him to me and I shall consider your terms."

"No, you must agree."

"I will give this as my word. You will have what is left of the elixir in this lab. I have found a beaker of his work. I did not test it. I won't check it. It is yours. The money in your accounts in the Caimans will not be found. Go there and die without fanfare, away from me. Do not let me ever hear your name unless they are reviling you. If you try and influence the world game in any manner, I will have you killed. These are the best terms you will get from me, and they shrink if you ponder too long to accept. Now. NOW," the holo screamed.

"Saind. Saind of the Desert Agorma. Saind of the lineage of Aramorth, Glespeilt, and Rancorntis, present yourself to be owned by another. Saind, bonded demon and indentured spirit, appear before me now, as the world would see you, so I and all present see you and they would know you are bound, owned, and a supplicant to my words and needs. Saind, I demand that you appear."

In the guise of the police officer that he had possessed, Saind materialized, jerked from the wavering background of a rent in space, before the tableau of the holo, the guards, the corpses, and his mistress, beaten and discarded in a hard-backed chair. Saind looked down at himself in the body of the police officer.

He went to one of the guards and demanded, "Move over." Then, he grasped the others head in both hands and shoved the other demon aside, and then out of the body. The guard became more rakish and jauntier as Saind assumed control. The policewoman appeared more heavy-footed and brutish.

Saind went to his Master and knelt at her feet. "You have called me, my Master. I have come to you and offer all I am in your service."

"Saind, I give you to—" He cut her off.

"No, Mistress, no. Say but a few other words and I will rescue you from this place and fate. For all the time, love, energy, and life we have shared, say that you free me. Free me, free me," he said over and over.

But he could tell by her eyes, as hard as they ever were, that she would not free him. His chanting request quieted and he hummed the last refrain of 'free me'. And then he was silent. A tear escaped. Only one, that none saw. He stood and faced the High Councilor. Behind him, from down low, as she had crumpled to the floor, the banker said the words that were his new prison. She freed him of her but bound him to the Councilor. He felt the Councilor's immense authority and personal power slam into him. He thought of the dark being that had almost consumed him and the admonishment that it mattered not who Saind served in the end. He allowed a moment of grieving at the closeness of his freedom, now lost again. He reassessed the future in an instant and became unctuously subservient to his new Master.

"Does she speak the truth of the documents? Do you have possession of the records of the First Borne?

"My Master, I do not know what I have besides cases and drawers full of papers, letters, leases, bank accounts, ledgers and even some correspondence. I have the drives with the most modern of the records. I am having them transcribed, and cross-referenced by a team."

"Make all of this available to me. Now. Tell those that harbor such a trove to have it ready to transport. I will have a truck bring it directly to me." He gave an address. "Go with them and ensure you get every bit. Seal all records and reports. Kill everyone who worked on it. If they are a demon, send them to the abyss. None incarnate shall know of this, lest you tell. The lady will be a crazed old coot that dies without anyone mourning her. I know, and now only you and I will hunt this First Borne. Serve me and that which you were just denied will be yours."

"I have heard all promises and none who uttered those words have been true. I am your chattel and I obey but know that another empty promise does little to urge me on. I simply obey."

"Then know this also, truculent one, watch closely to that pointed tongue of yours. For I have many demons of your level, casting one such as you into the abyss means little to me besides a bit of notoriety with the ones I deign to have serve me still. Yet, this opportunity intrigues me, and with all of the loose ends…" The holo stopped and looked expectantly at the demon Saind. Saind found the pistol in the borrowed body's belt, pulled it, and shot the other guard and the policewoman. He turned it to the banker but was stopped by the Councilor.

"No, her fate is to rue this duplicity for a long time. Get me that flask from the counter." When Saind returned, he was ordered to swirl the contents in front of her. "This is the last of the run from that processor. He had a plan. He was going to take the last of his formula and leave as soon as you had his family delivered. He was going to betray you. This is how I know you have lost the edge. You were taken in by a nerdy, but greedy technician. You can have this. Every day, for the rest of your life, you will now wonder if it is the last. Give it to her," he ordered Saind.

Saind held it out to the pitiful creature that had once been his lover, his Master, and his chance for freedom. Saind sneered at the one who had fallen so far, and had so treacherously given him hope, false hope. Belligerence arose in him, and he casually dropped the flask into her hands. But the trembling hands couldn't grasp the smooth glass, and it slipped from her fingers and shattered on the tiles. The liquid spread out in a small pool.

The Councilor laughed as the woman fell to the floor trying to lap and slurp the remains off the hard floor. Blood from her nose mingled with blood from her lips cut on the glass shards of the broken flask. She licked the floor and sobbed. The demon watched stoically. The holo laughed with malice.

"Drag her from here. Burn this place to the ground." The holo winked out. The room was dim and smelt of chemicals and blood. He helped her to her feet and stood holding her. They had both lost so much, and while the animosity for such a loss was with each other, there was comfort in the mutual anguish. They stood there holding one another when a small fire started with an electrical arc.

"Demons watch to ensure his will is made real. Come, I will do as he bids." He held her upright as they walked out of the lab. He casually tossed a green fireball over his shoulder as they exited. It was engulfed in flames in a few moments.

Her limo was gone. The police cruiser sat in the drive. They went to it and Saind opened the rear door. He ushered her into the back seat with a sarcasm meld of anguish, regret, and an untampered vengeful malice.

Saind said harshly, "I will put you on a plane to your banishment." Then with a small, sad smile he said, "You should have set me free."

"I know," she said. "I am going to be sorry for a long time."

He shut the door and said to no one, "No, you are soon dead."

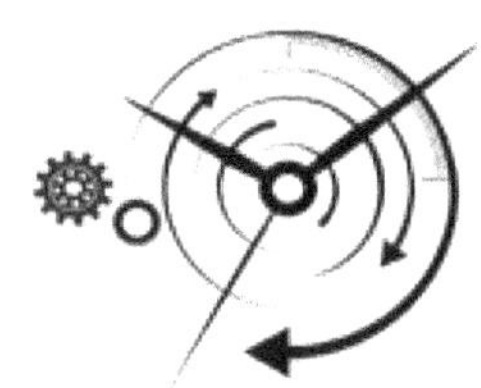

36 - Suspicion

An unmarked car sat darkened on a side road and as they passed, it turned on headlights and pulled in behind them. The turnoff to Bog Hill was coming up. Monte pointed his finger forward several times, indicating to go past.

"Don't slow," Monte said. "Shelbourne Falls," and he pointed again.

As they sped past the road, over the next small decline, a pack of six police vehicles had set up control of the intersecting highways. The sedan slowed. The car behind likewise slowed and pulled in close, blocking any retreat, as Samuel came to a stop.

They sat bathed in flashing blue and stabbing bright lights. The search lights raked their car, holding on the license plate. They waited without being contacted for many minutes. Monte knew the plates were being ran. An officer came up to the car window, silhouetted against the glare and pulse of bright lights. Samuel rolled down his window.

"Hello fathers, what brings you out on such a night?"

He leaned over, peering into the interior of the car, his eyes swiftly going over the occupants and the contents, both front and back. He obviously found little of interest, as he straightened up and said, "Where are you heading?"

"Shelbourne Falls," said Samuel.

The officer stood, letting the silence build into expectation, but the priest was well disciplined, and the officer realized the impasse. He stood and motioned. Several other uniformed police stepped into view, and one that all others paid deference to came closest. He had a quiet, guarded, and short conversation with the original officer, then approached the car, stepping into the space hastily vacated by the other.

The light reflected weirdly off the face of the man. Instead of being shiny, his visage became fractals of light, so rapidly cycling that it became apparent when he moved, an instant of the strobe catching the reality of the semi-permanence of the being one would take for granted as a man. A well-cared for face and body, and a personality that exuded authority, confident of its execution.

"Fathers," he said, with a slight cynicism. "We all know we answer to higher authorities, and as they debate the intricacies of this informational impasse we are currently sharing, we sit and wait and burn precious moments of our all too short life." He stood back up, took a step back and rested hands on his hips, near his weapons.

Monte spoke, "Officer, I will speak with you."

The man came around to the other side and asked, "Who are you?"

"I'm going to get out my wallet," Monte advised. He pulled it out and opened it. He took out a card that proclaimed he was an envoy of the Dioses out of Boston. There was a number on the card advising them to call for ID issues. The man inclined his head, albeit mockingly at the distinction of that rank within the church. The officer stepped back away with the card in hand, speaking on his radio. There was a long five-minute wait, then the radio came to life. Monte was too far away to make out the words but understood the gist by the body language and the nodding. The officer was walking back to the car when his phone rang. He answered but almost immediately—as he arrived at the door of the car—held the phone out to Monte and pressed the speaker.

"Who am I speaking with?" the voice demanded.

Monte gave him his full name and title. Monte could see the cop taking down the name and calling him in.

"Monte, why are you out and about in this area this evening?" asked the voice that Monte recognized at the Vice Sergeant at Arms for the region.

"I am going to a friend's bookstore in Shelbourne Falls. He is usually open late."

"Who is the brother that drives you?"

"You know, I don't know much about the friend that drives me. I requested a car and got a driver with it. You know it was a good idea with my headache and hazy memories."

"Yes," said the Vice Sergeant, "I have heard many people talking about you this evening. Why aren't you taking rest like you advised the council you dearly needed."

"I have a small confession to make, Your Grace. I am going to my friend as he is a man with key insights into the mind. He is a professor of neuroscience, and his bookstore is his refuge, I believe." Monte tried to look sheepish to the officer still nearby. "I believe his refuge is a shelter for his voracious appetite for books. I thought he might calm and untangle my mind, Your Grace."

"I will have a doctor attend to you. Return to the church in Northampton." Then to the officer he said, "Officer, I believe there will come an order to you from your Commander." Then there was a decisive click and the authority on the other end dismissed the officer. The radio crackled to life and after a brief conversation, the cop stepped back from the car.

Before waving them on through the blockade of vehicles, the cop said, "You may pass. Make the next right. Take 116 down to the interstate and back to Northampton. I don't care who you know, I will arrest you if deviate from that route by anything more than a stop for gas. Leave now." He spoke into his radio and a cruiser backed up and created an opening through the barricade. He pointed his finger at the brother then down the road, through the checkpoint.

The car passed and they noticed a car pass through right after them, and then fall back to a reasonable distance to follow.

"We have a tail."

"Yes, we do, and we cannot help Leonard at the moment. If we turn to him, we betray him, and us. The conspiracies will be proven true. We want that even less than helping Leonard."

"I have, ah, interesting news… of an old friend. I stopped at that bagel shop by the bridge, and crossed paths. He said to say hello to you."

Monte knew that was his confidant in Brattleboro. Samuel gave him a slight smile and a thumbs up without taking his hand off the wheel.

The got to the bottom of the long grade into the valley. They took the on ramp at a sedate, priestly, and defiantly slow speed. The following car crept up close, almost bumper to bumper, but Samuel never succumbed. Finally, the escort gave up, dropped back and the pair of sedans rolled down the interstate. They collected a line of cars unwilling to pass the patrol car.

Monte said, "Slow a bit more. There is live, impromptu theater here. Or a study in the psychology of authority." They both laughed a bit.

As they enjoyed this slight reprieve from the ponderous thoughts of the last few hours, their attention became focused on the flashing lights in the distance. It was a patrol car heading towards them on the opposite lanes of the interstate. It passed in a blaze of lights and sound. The unit following them dropped back a bit, preoccupied. Then another two more squad cars tore past heading north. The car that escorted Monte slowed, ripped across the median, and joined the chase back uphill, leaving them.

Monte thought for a few moments while Samuel looked on expectantly. Monte nodded to himself, and said, "Take the next exit. I'm hungry, I'd like a bagel."

37 - Brattleboro

Monte took a seat with his friend next to a recently installed coffee roaster. In the snowy months this corner was a warm, cozy refuge sought by many patrons. But this time of year, it was a quiet haven, as most found a seat further away from the heat of the bean roaster. It made a wonderfully private zone for the two that settled into the wooden chairs at the table in the corner.

Elias said, "My friend owns this place. I trust that we can be candid but guarded." He nodded inquisitively to a tall, bearded man in an apron, sweeping. The tall man looked about with a theatric air and nodded back.

"Why did you send word?" Elias asked.

"First, have you heard the official version of these past few days? The explosion, the manhunt? And also, tell me who told you of these things."

"The casket factory caught on fire. Some acetylene tanks were leaking, and a spark ignited the gas trapped in the lower levels and it exploded. Some said it was arson or an attack on the church. So, the authorities traced the accused to Easthampton, to condos in an old mill building, and though the man got away, they still hunt for him. There was a large response to the hill towns an hour or so ago, but it is very hush on the radios."

"How many people do they hunt?" Monte asked.

"One, at least one that we know of. It's on all the media. Frantic announcements, but no substance, and of course no pictures, yet."

"What is the church saying?"

"Little, very little. Just that there has been a tragedy and some of our brothers who were dedicated to the endeavor have lost their lives. So very quiet about this though."

"Okay," Monte sighed. "Where to begin? Okay, ah, okay," he said again as he organized his thoughts. "Okay, you know I have been associated closely with those that pry deeply into secret things, especially if that knowledge ensures those who wield the power stay in that position of power. So, I have become assured there are those within the hierarchy that are believers in name only. Their hearts are not just empty but filled with darkness. Many of those in the highest orders have submitted to the darkness. Some are even consumed. I thought this many times, but these past few days, I have seen the darkness in their eyes and felt the malice in their words and could tell the souls of these men were empty of humanity, but yet they walked and talked as men. They plot and the preponderance of their emotions is hate. I knew the church used the poor as pawns, but I felt that those who were poor, gaining improved living conditions by using their angst was an acceptable wage. But I found the poor are the least of the manipulations by these dark ones. Even the ones that lead us in our faith, I found, are also infected. Among those that died last night was a Monsignor Sischte Kaveleer, the Suffragon of the Apostolic Prefecture of Mossul. I had been his, apprentice of sorts, but more of a clerk and secretary."

Elias asked , "A what, who?"

"The Suffragan is one who will ascend to the Bishopric, he was more easily known as Sisker. In his position he was granted much authority and had few limits."

"Uh, ok, thanks." Elias nodded.

Monte leaned in close and said, "I was shown proof of his possession just before he died. He tried to kill me, us, but I, ah, we were rescued by an angel!"

Elias said, "An angel? Who was the 'we' you said the angel rescued?"

Monte turned with an involuntary beatific smile on his face. His voice was passionate, "We are so right in our beliefs, and the church is so wrong on some levels. I met a true prophet, one who made people believe. And the angel rescued us. I saw miracles. I felt the one touch my mind and calm my thoughts. I don't just 'believe' anymore. I *know* there are others that watch over us. They watch and offer hope because the darkness is already here in this world. And we humans are in danger."

"They are protecting us?" Elias inflected it as a query.

"I learned there is a danger of extinction from a being that isn't bothered by time. I learned there is a chance to save ourselves, however slim. And those that are the angels watch over, but more of a referee than a bodyguard. More of an advocate that must watch, frustrated children that knowingly, but still willfully, refuse to mature no matter what the consequences.

"I learned that an earth-shattering gestalt of all our minds is poised to occur. It is the wonderous maturation of our species that may save us and must save us, for there is little time left. The ones who own all things on this planet have perfected a way to step back in time and adjust events in the past, so the present is always theirs to control. The angel said it was like jumping off a moving boat into the wake. You could never go forward, but could send emissaries back."

Elias stared, open mouthed. He had never heard Monte so passionate and so madly devoted without obsequence to any of their causes, through all the years they had been friends. "Monte, you speak with such fervor, I cannot understand," Elias said, "Tell me what happened, please."

"The ones that own all the wealth have long used demons to get it, and so they became infected with demons, and now the demons have usurped control of most of all the influential positions at the top: people, governments, businesses, religions and especially those that make war. These are the men who plan to send an emissary, an agent of theirs to jump back in time to take a final adjustment to the past so that present will ensure their heir's reign forever, so they think. But the demons plan to sabotage this jump back and will soon rebel against all of the subservience, and the reckoning will commence. They want the energy of this time and space for their own."

Monte leaned in, ever so close and said, "Humanity will cease to exist in eternity. That is the depths of the irony of this nihilistic world, that we are authors of our demise. I think the original sin was doubt. Once doubted, a thing is never ultimate. And humans doubted the Creator. The ones who dwell in eternity have invited us to join them, but we doubted them right out of our existence," he gulped air and continued, "And we have been wandering, obstinate people that revel in the refusal to grow up."

Elias leaned back in his chair, stuck his legs out, put his elbows high and laced his fingers to cradle his head as he leaned back in the chair, now on two legs.

They both sat comfortably in each other's silence as the afternoon sun moved their shadows across the floor in front of them. The pensive mood was broken by the simple string of bells that jangled when the door opened. The customer was greeted by the counterman who still swept.

He said, "Good afternoon, Mr. Sprachs." Almost too loudly in the large but quiet space of the old mill converted to good use. Elias sat back up, nudged the table to jar Monte. Monte saw the finger to the lips sign his friend gave him.

"Banker, state level," Elias said softly.

The man paid for his order and turned and spoke to Elias. "Fine afternoon to you," he said, then turned his attention to Monte and said, "And to your friend."

"An old friend indeed, we have known each other for decades," Elias said.

"Excellent, decades hmm?" he was trying to open a conversation but was met with one word.

"Yes."

After a few moments the banker said, "Mr. Friend," the emphasis sarcastically announcing his feeling of slight offense taken at the tacit idea that he wasn't invited. "I apologize for having interrupted." Another pause, offered to entice a mollification for the now spoken assumption.

Monte said, "We were discussing a tenet of Buddhism I have been trying to understand. You look like you might sit and talk about your religion, I take it you are a Christian, a catholic I would guess."

The banker became uncomfortable and took a step back. Now the banker spoke with abrasive pointy words, poking Monte's intellect back. "No, I think it is late, so, no thanks, Mr. Friend."

"You can sit with us and read from the good book to illustrate your arguments and to convince me that mine are wrong. I have a bible." Monte made as if he would reach into his breast pocket.

The banker visually flared a dark aura from his eyes. Monte saw it, so did Elias.

In that instant, all three knew the disguise had been lifted and there was no reason for the false bonhomie. The banker turned as he looked them both over, his eyes pausing longest on Elias. There was a new level of hostile appreciation for the bagel man. He turned without any pleasantries and went out the door that jangled again. Just outside the door, they saw him immediately pull his cell phone out and walk away dialing.

"Monte, what in God's name just happened? You spoke with him and then what did I see? That light, was it of the demons you tell me are here with us."

Monte asked, "How can you not believe after what I know you just saw? Those dark souls are everywhere now. They are here in your town, and they want what you have. Not your store or your possessions, or even your life. They want the life and creative force of every being that ever existed. On that they feed, but now they are deceiving us to immolate ourselves in the chaos they create. They will feed the frenzy, and then wait for the vile feelings and beliefs to erupt into war. The ones we trust are using us, and worse still, they are set to sacrifice us, and themselves, the whole of humanity. Humanity is tainted, the end of the Eden experiment draws neigh."

He stopped talking and looked up at the rough beams of the ceiling and antique, industrial fans slowly turning. He thought deeply. Then he pontificated.

"There are few who know this, now you are one of the enlightened ones. This enlightenment will be a terrible burden on your soul, for either you are with those that have hope and fight against this demise, or you die, cease to exist."

Monte paused and then reached out his hand. "Thank you for your time. Mine was well spent."

Elias said, "Hold a while. I think there is something you have missed. There are other people you must know." Elias put his hand on Monte's forearm. "Monte, there are others, many others like you, and me, like us to whom you must tell this tale. There are many looking for something to believe in, since we all know this world does not work the way it should. Come with me."

Elias tossed his ring of keys to the man at the counter. "Lindon, will you close for me, please? Also give this man a bagel and a coffee for the road." He pointed to Samuel.

Monte stood next to the driver and held his shoulder, "Thank you. Samuel, I will see you again, I believe our lives will cross again."

Samuel asked, "What shall I tell the Vice Sergeant? The police? If they ask?"

Monte said, "Tell them the truth. I ordered you to drive to Brattleboro after the escort left us. I came in, talked to a man, and left with him after I ordered you to leave. It is that simple. You have no obligation to be in charge of me. They instilled no guardianship of me into your life. So, take none."

"But will you be safe, my Grace?" This gave Monte that slight satisfaction again.

"Thank you, but I will be fine. An angel watches. Now go. Go home, go to bed, and fall into a deep sleep. Neglect to take that computer I forgot in your trunk until you wake up tomorrow. As late as you can imagine that they will believe you would be unmindful of the item . Then turn it in. Replace the fuses I removed in your car and always know that they listen." They lightly embraced and headed towards opposite doors. Monte and Elias down the hall, past the restrooms out the back. Samuel out the front to the brown sedan.

He just got in and then drove off. He didn't see the flash of the cell phone camera from the vehicle across the lot.

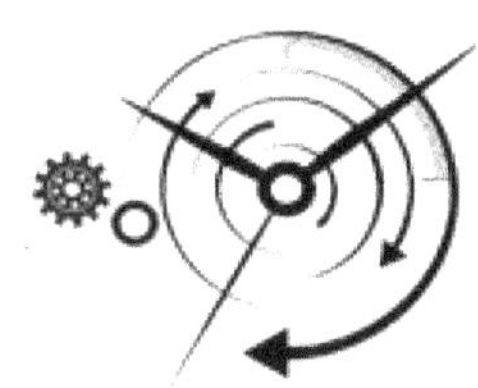

38 - Conspirators

Monte and Elias approached the rusted truck behind the shop.

Elias said, "I know it doesn't look like much, but it runs well, and there are no electronics to betray us."

"Does it have a radio?"

"Yes, but—" Monte interrupted and put up his arm to keep Elias from opening his door. "Say nothing you want kept secret. I have found they have been listening in on us for far longer than we have known. I believe *all* radios work both ways."

During the silence of the ride, Monte collected his thoughts. He put his head back and closed his eyes for a moment. Elias shook him awake in mere minutes, it seemed. Monte looked around to find themselves parking in a cluttered but nondescript garage or warehouse. He shook his head and rubbed his eyes while mumbling, "How long did I sleep?"

Elias smiled at his friend and held his finger to his lips. "Remember?" he asked, pointing to the radio.

They got out and Elias led the way deeper into the vast space which Monte surmised must be an old warehouse. The way through the detritus of the various ventures that had paid for time in this space. Stacks of tires, old and dusty equipment, and a few stacks of cardboard boxes on pallets cascading into refuse. Light came in dimly through the cobwebbed windows. An office shined with light through the etched glass door and partition. Monte could hear a murmuring of voices as they neared.

They entered and the voices stopped. All eyes turned to Monte. A few nodded recognitions to Elias. Monte took this in; the shabby, wooden chairs around a scarred worktable. Men and women with serious faces and passionate eyes. There was silence that stretched into long minutes. Appraisal.

Elias broke the impasse. "I am sure he is one of us. You can know him as Monte." He turned to Monte and said, "There is no reason to know their names, yet." Then he took an empty chair in either hand, dragged them to the table and bade Monte sit with a gesture of his hand. "First," he said without preamble, "Monte must share his experience with us. It will prove our beliefs."

Monte picked the conversation up. "I will confirm what is worse than your fears. What you deem the most unimaginable acts of depravity and immorality have an author. I have experienced this malicious force. There are demons possessing those most dark in their hearts. Always, I have thought that the truly evil were so brazen in their madness that they were easy to spot." He paused then said, "And easy to dismiss. As if the darkness in people's hearts was so ridiculously an oddity that we can be quick to dismiss the dark soul as an isolated phenomenon. And then, when we take the fear and loathing and predatory hate as a caricature of humanity, we neglect to find the same dark hearts in those that are astute of this world. That I would say, is the real downfall of man. The deliberate machinations of those that rule the world with fear and hate who care nothing about our race's eternity. And those are the ones we must talk about with all caution. The highest reaches of political, financial, social, and even spiritual endeavors of human society are, I believe, guided by those that have bargained with a corrupt dealer. A dealer of fates, for you, for your world and even your, our, *all* of our futures and chance for eternity. I am in awe, and my disbelief shaken to—"

One of the others at the table interrupted, "Thank you for sharing the grandeur of this thing, this moment, this epiphany. But please," he leaned forward earnestly, "tell us what makes you believe, we believe you believe, your passion is convincing, now, tell us the events that have so shaken your soul."

"I apologize, I do owe you the details that you might likewise believe."

Monte pulled his chair close enough that his elbows rested on the table. He clasped his opposite fist and lowered his chin to that cradle. He bowed his head, lowered his gaze for a moment, then furrowed his brow so he could look up at each one in turn through his peering eyes.

Monte started with the abrupt announcement, "Sisker was possessed. The Diocese of Boston has been under control of a demon for at least a decade. The Monsignor was hunting, and I never knew what, or why. I only know what methods and with what institutions they gleaned information. That is until these past few days. I have been one of their hounds for what they seek, without knowing why, until the past few days. I have been privy to many things and know of many more of which they think I am ignorant. But now, I know the greatest secret possible. For I know of the demons, and few get to know of the demons and still live. But here I sit with you, knowing, safe for the moment, and having not a single witness to my involvement of the current situation. All but I have perished in that explosion. This means I can, and must, craft a plausible explanation. The Council will convene tomorrow. They will want to know, in excruciating detail, of my interpretation of events. I must convince them, with my story and my character, that I know nothing of their duplicity, and that I still have a passion to be useful to them. I must portray that I crave Sisker's position."

"I am Jacob," one said and stroked his heavy beard, and then asked, "What if to achieve that level you must accept the darkness?"

"I have thought about that. I know I will be sorely tried. If I play the role with enough conviction, I know the dark ones will offer that side of life to me. If I refuse, I will be discovered. That may be only a short amount of time. So, there is much to do.

"That is why I must act swiftly to make a decision. Either I can claim innocence to this infestation and hope to retain some standing in the hierarchy of the church where I can stay on the inside and know their terrible machinations. Or…" he stretched that word out, then again, "*Or* I could leave. But truly I cannot drop out of sight. One, I'd never be left alone, even if I could find a way and a place to hide. The dark ones would find me. They would know that I know and that would make me a dangerous liability. I would be killed.

"Second, I could simply step back into the brotherhood, but renounce my aspirations as a casualty of the explosion and the loss of my mentor. I could get away with that for a short time, but soon, they again would know I feign ignorance of their existence. That, once again, would be their judgement and my demise. So, the last option is continuing to be the same arrogant prick of a priest I was, hell bent with ambitions of rising in the leadership. That is what they know of me, and who I have earnestly been, so I pretend little and betray even less.

"I have been missing for some time now, and they will begin to suspect, and hence begin to search for me. I can claim the mental and emotional turmoil of the past few nights has me confused. I can claim to remember little, that the physical trauma of the blast has addled my memories. I can continue to recoup for a few days.

"Now, I need to have this story straight. I need to have a persona match my decision and have my ulterior motives hidden well."

Monte turned to Elias, and said, "Thank you for trusting me and introducing me."

Jacob spoke again, "You know none of use, and yet you want me to trust you with my identity. Why would you want to join us after such a short, guarded conversation?"

"I don't want to join you. I want you to join me. I need you, all of you, and many, many more to know what I know now and will discover in the future. I want you to know the truth of this existence, and bear witness to the control some have over the world. I want you to meet this prophet and I want you to know, that I am convinced, the angel, the guardian watches over us. To tell the truth, in these dark times what you come to know will be dangerous knowledge. So, so many will never believe. Most will choose to remain safely in their ignorance, but others, your truth will be a threat to them. They are a small fraction of humanity, but they control almost every aspect of human society, and jealously guard every iota of that authority."

Monte looked about the table, and a woman with short hair caught his eye, staring at him.

He addressed her, "I would like to know how I could tell you things you are less than likely to believe. For instance, there are forces which control the world that care little for the quality of life most citizens live if it means sacrificing the power and authority they exercise through their office and balance sheets. The people are often in league with dark forces, evil if you will."

The woman chimed in, "I feel you are correct. Everyone would like to blame the poor, for crime, or for that riot, but we have found that a critical mass of agitators and an ignition event will cause chaos, even if for a short time. My work at the Retreat has been to examine modalities to extinguish the causal factors that preclude ignition of societal unrest."

"In other words," Monte said, "you study the psychology of societal control."

"Yes," she said, "but more clearly stated, I study the purposeful exercise of the control which defines and describes casual factors of unrest in the society and identifies adjustments to the norms that influence prevention."

"The ones in power: finance, commerce, military, and yes, the church, have always held that concept dear. What makes your work novel to those that have held control for generations and centuries? What would you be funded to find in a field so well versed?" Monte asked.

She sighed, "True, I have contributed little to that body of knowledge. But I have found there are those who do pay well for this knowledge of how to shape societal events into potential usefulness and then understand the best source of ignition and steer the ensuing turmoil." She paused, taking off her glasses, "I have even written about extinguishing the emotional exacerbation. I found that my work was perverted to use the techniques I discovered to instead maintain the angst and feed it till the madness overwhelms any dissonance between the actions of the mob and the reality of a moral, rational human. I see my work in the repertoire of those who own this world. I joined this group because no one should take the study of the love for the human condition and distort it to enforce control, regardless of if it destroys the very basic tenet of this lesson of being human incarnate. Love. The Christ preached love. The church exists because of this message. I see the maturity that the church has morphed into is the same ideal as any other assemblage of power. It now exists to maintain control over a certain domain of human existence; self-appointed guardians of the moral and ethical gate to eternity."

She set the glasses she had been twirling by one bow on the table. She steepled her fingers then touched the tip of her nose with the index fingers. "What I have learned cannot be taken away from those who perversely wield that knowledge. They have learned to author misery and focus blame on that quality they wish to influence. What you told me here tonight validates what I have been troubled by for some time. That those who best know the message of love, well, they do not love anything or anyone more than their power. That, I feel is not right, and my conviction like yours, is that I want what is right to prevail." She picked up her glasses, put them on like donning a protective mask and sat back with a quiet finality to her impromptu speech.

Monte turned to Elias. "You have found gems of intellect in the world's detritus of polluted minds. I had the idea that such passionate perceptions were rarer than I now believe. You," he said, and then turned to the rest, "and all of you are heartening. What I once hoped for was that there was a secret cabal of the most magnificent minds. I have met many incredible intellects, but few not tainted by ambition, greed, power, lust. I will tell you all you want to know. We have little time because there needs to be a plan. But first, I will share with you.

"Here is the truth of what we face. Most institutions, especially those that span financial banking systems across the world, and without regards for borders, are owned and function at the whims of a few that are not human, at least not anymore. I fear that after my past few days of horrific experiences, there are many of these '*others*' among us, that are not human incarnate."

Elias spoke, "I have witnessed this myself, this very day. Mr. Sprachs of the bank revealed his demon nature when Monte spoke to him. Inadvertently perhaps, but I am convinced he is one of the tainted."

Monte joined in. "Yes, the banker is possessed. I have seen this same sign in the eyes of my mentor, Sisker. He also revealed his dark side to me, proud of his corruption, thinking he was going to imprison me forever he gloated."

"And then, as I found myself staring face to face with pure evil, I also found the ones that watch over us. The best I can describe is a pure willful, intellect, powerful enough that they can influence our existence beyond the rules of this world. I imagine angels are a fine word to call them. The one I met, the prophet called him Parys, are warning us of a finality we bring upon ourselves. I tell you; this is true. I have been told and shown these things so that I may tell others and prepare to fight as best as we can."

Jacob spoke through his bushy beard, "Hmmm. You would have us join you and risk everything on your say so?"

"Tell me," Monte said to the bearded guy in the hand-knit woolen hat. "Tell me, what do you have that makes you a force to be reckoned with, in this coming battle."

Another spoke up, "Jacob don't say much, but I've known him since we were in grade school," the guy said with his hands on his overall straps. "Both our families been here since they first walked on this continent. I've heard history from the mouths of those who lived it. What shape the world is in now isn't right. That's for goddamn sure. This life, this world isn't what we want or are meant to have. So, Mister Monte, Your Eminence," he said with a tang of sarcasm, disdain and disbelief, "I want to believe you, because Jacob and I own the feed store, and some real estate in this town and have families we love in this land. You ask what we have, and I tell you that what we have is our whole life here, our trust of the ones we know. What we want is the truth. I am not getting the truth now. From anywhere: the news, the government, the church, the doctors, the banks, not a single institution of our lives has any veracity anymore. And what I feel about how life should be, what I have taught that life should be, contradicts drastically with what actually '*is*' the lives we lead. So, I will listen to you, and I will know if there is truth in you enough for me to believe."

"Okay," Monte said. He got up from the table and paced once, back and forth. He stopped and looked at each one momentarily. Some stared back. Some nodded. None looked away.

"Alright. I have little time, so this will be brief. I have been the squire and scribe to Sisker. I, We, ah, he, he and I looked for certain information on certain people, and I recently knew that he… we had crossed the trail of someone who appeared to be ancient, but still here, alive. This one turned out to be a prophet, I believe. Those dark forces of the church would have had us imprisoned but for an angel that came to rescue us. Now I believe. I, without a doubt, believe. This is what happened to me these past few days."

He sat and then began his story, starting with the meeting in the apartment of the one they suspected of being immortal.

39 - Thin Place

The small glen was oriented almost perfectly to the poles. There was an assemblage of standing stones, a crude yet fiercely powerful cromlech. The local, dark grey granite was flecked and streaked with quartz and mica that reflected pinpoint sparkles. Beyond the stone perimeter was a tumble of huge boulders, forming a primitive but substantial structure. The doorway into the mound was framed by slabs of vertical stone and a capstone, half buried into the earth. The whole area was bound by cliffs and rock walls. There was a glade of grass across the entire flat area.

"I understand why you call this the altar now," I said.

"No, not yet, come this way."

He went to the doorway and ducked in. I followed. Inside it was cool and smelled of the earth. The light was dim. The stones were stacked cunningly enough to support the immense slabs of granite that made up the roof. The floor was covered with scratched and twisted carvings into the stone.

He led me to the back of the stone chamber.

"See this small opening? Does this seem like a mistake? No" he answered himself. "No, I felt there was a purpose and I carefully cleaned out the decayed leaves and the dirt that clogged this shaft. It is purposefully built. The shaft is aligned with careful attention to the angle of ascension and the time of the suns highest point. I came here at the last solstice and found this is true. Look here."

He pointed to the floor markings, and from the angle of having the slit in the wall at my back, I could make out the arc of a rudely carved calendar. Various tick mark like groupings of the rock carvings seemed to be months, or years, or celestial events along the arc of the calendar.

"Here is an exact mark where the summer sun reached its highest. Perfectly on this crudely scratched mark . I would say who did this did not have metal to work with. This was stone on stone labor to record their world and lives in perpetuity. I have no idea who did this. I have no idea who they worshipped, but surely this is evidence of intelligence and purpose. I have found some of the markings line up with the lunar phases. There are events memorialized in some of the groups of scratchings, I believe. Do you feel the, ah…" he searched for the right word then said, "Connectedness?"

I was going to speak but then an intuition told me to dismiss Bill and give him the mixed blessings of not remembering and having an alibi. "Bill," I tried to be tactful. "Perhaps if you went about your way, and left me, there wouldn't be much of a worry about being interrogated as to your whereabouts."

"You want me to forget, don't you?" asked Bill.

"Yes, and we will always be fond friends, but for now, you haven't seen me."

"I haven't?"

"No, you haven't." I then looked deep into his eyes and gave a purposeful misbelief to my new friend. "You had a great morning hike at your favorite spot. You are going to have one last look at the beauty of this place, then turn and hike out. Go look at the jobs you were originally planning on looking at. Thank you for this place. It is a thin place. I can feel it. Goodbye, Bill."

Bill climbed out of the small, sacred space, stopped, and slowly looked around the glade. His wonderment was beatific. He scanned the sky and then swept his hands across his face, gathered his hair back and tilted his face to the sky. I joined him and we both looked past the clouds to the heavens. He smiled, ignored me, then turned and walked off to the descending trail.

I was left alone.

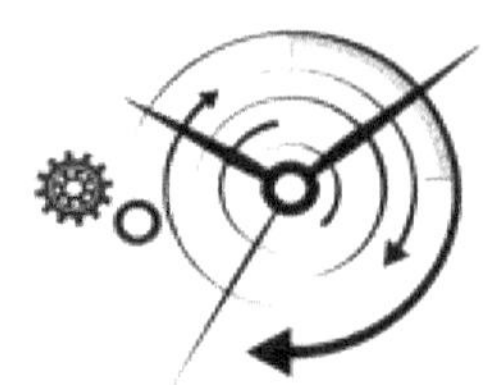

40 - Discovered

Saind was driving the once proud banker to the small, private airfield, when the police radio crackled on. There was the message that the manhunt had been narrowed down to the hill towns, in the western part of the state. The dispatch ordered all cars to converge and to switch to a situation specific channel. Saind slowed, torn for a moment to his duty to remove her from the country. But as he thought about it, he realized she would be safe and unable to flee amongst all those officers. He spun the car about and raced up the highway towards Goshen. Lights and siren came on of their own accord.

"Hello, owned one, my brother." The radio said this, but it was the speaker only, not a broadcast.

Saind felt galled, but then his situation was really no different than before, a new Master over his will and of course, an exorbitant amount of power. He looked in the rearview mirror at the lady there, his once friend and lover, now ruined. He realized he cared little. He shrugged to himself and turned up the radio with one last grimace at the loss. Then Barg's voice prodded him to begin to plot anew.

"One of these lifetimes, Barg. One of these lifetimes, I will be free."

"But not this one. This is the most luxurious one, I admit, but the cost is dear to escape this slavery. Your new Master is loath to relinquish anything, especially one bought so dearly."

"He will make that sum with which he procured the lady's empire, over a hundred times with her assets. Then with what information I give him, or am giving him, will be worth another fortune or two. There will be dynasties that fall because of what he will uncover. Then ones who want to know what those original's lineage know, will pay as much as the ones that want secret knowledge. I will plot from the inside. I will have my freedom. This is but another, grand, grand opportunity to lay my plans. One lifetime, in some lifetime, I will not be betrayed." He looked in the rearview again, but she would not catch his eyes.

"Saind, I would like to be incarnate with you on this, at times, ah, like now. Can I have the one who tossed you aside? What a fitting pity that would be, to be given away, as if she mattered not."

Saind thought about that deeply for a moment, playing the revenge out in his head.

Then he said, "No, I think I will let the disappointment of old age be my answer to her anguish. Not to be just thrown away, but to be in mortal danger and not be rescued, as she knows would be, ah, I mean, *would have* been possible." He said that with a sweet fierceness, but too much conviction that spilled hidden emotions a demon was not allowed. He looked at her, and this time she caught his eyes. What passed between them was lost in the gulf between their fates.

"No, there will be plenty of bodies at the command for you to choose from. Barg, I tell you that what I didn't give to you when you were on my leash, I now give you without limits. I know I cannot set you free. But I can allow the deal I made, to pay the wages for what she asked. Well, this visit is one without qualifications. Your appetite shall be satiated. I allow that this is the debt I owe."

Barg sensed an opening in his subservient position. "This is partial payment," he said very gently. "I will take this payment, now that you have spoken those words of permission, but I tell you, I find this outing to be business, work, a chore, and task of your desire. This visit to the incarnate world will not make us equal and your debt paid is yet to be claimed. Those are my terms."

Said was silent as was Barg, then the radio asked softly, with a faint pulse of light, "Agreed?"

Saind nodded and raced the squad car up the twisting mountain road. Steep edges of blasted granite and sheer drops did not slow their pace up Route 9 to the hill towns.

The metallic voice of Barg interrupted Saind's musings. "I have taken the liberty to contact their control and announce your arrival. You will be the commanding authority on site. It is ordered."

Saind again nodded.

The flashing lights in the distance announced the roadblock. Saind continued his defiant speed right up to the limits of his car's braking power. Spotlights trained on him, and he knew there were marksmen behind those glaring beams. He skidded to a stop and got out in almost one fluid movement. He didn't shut the car door.

He shouted, "Who is incident command?"

A hawk faced man stepped up. He was lean like a braided leather rope that had been pulled tight, just shy of the breaking.

"I am," he announced. "I got the message, but I've got to see the credentials. Who the hell are you?" It was a voice of near scorn and subservient fear.

"I am the on-scene command, from this very moment. You can call me Saind."

"Saind what?" someone of the crowd of officers around the barricade asked. "Mister? Sir? Agent?"

Saind faced the assemblage and announced in the direction from which the question had been flung at him. "I told you what to call me. You are stupid or not disciplined enough to hear my commands. Do not make that mistake again, any of you, or you will be taken from this operation in a helicopter to be debriefed. This is an order, you are all under my command as of this instant, NOW!" he screamed, with a tang of the soul-wrenching devil's wail in his voice. Every officer present felt the authority.

"I need the best officer with radios."

There was a general mumbling, and two stepped up. Saind pointed at the female officer. "My radio would not pick up the situation channel. Go see why." He pointed to the open door. She climbed in and reached for the radio. It flared with an intense burst of light, but squelched, as if a flashbulb had gone off in cupped hands.

The officer climbed out of the car and said, "Very funny," with Barg's most remarkable sarcasm.

"What is your name?" Saind asked for theatrics.

"Officer Barg, sir." Several other officers of the department looked quizzically at her. They knew her as a local deputy.

"You are my aide for this situation. You will stay at my side. You," he pointed at the on-scene commander, "You will be my second. Where is the command site? Pick the fewest officers you need to be your cadre to carry out my orders. I want comm and intel to join me. Now, WHERE?" Again, with the cutting wail to their minds. The man just pointed, then turned to the mass of armed and uniformed men and women. He named three, motioned, and then turned after Saind, without waiting to see if they followed.

Saind entered the converted RV. There were several officers in there already. "Last name and your function in here," he ordered.

"Jones, Communications."

"Bildenklemp, PR and Governor's liaison."

"Tenzen, Command of State Police. Local knowledge."

Several more stated their names and roles.

Saind pointed to the comm guy, the local knowledge and rural authority, "You stay, the rest OUT."

As they filed out, grumbling, Saind ordered, "Brief me."

The incident commander, who was the highest rank of the state police, started talking.

"There was an explosion in Florence, the outskirts of Northampton. We were alerted to a possible terrorist cell incident that had gone wrong. There is an APB   for one who was IDed at the blast site and then showed up at a possible sighting of the same man, a priest, it is said."

"Hmm, a priest?"

"Yes, and then again a report of him driving about these hill towns earlier today."

"Where is this man? You have him in custody, no?" Saind said with a dangerous inflection.

"No, the orders came from my chief, after calling the Arch Diocese."

"Why them?"

"Well, the priest had enough credentials and identification that asked to have a call placed to the Boston Diocese. I did, and just a few moments later, I got a radio call to let them pass. To escort them to Northampton."

"To what address?" There was an enhanced unease among the officers.

"You did not follow them as ordered, did you?" He didn't wait for an answer, just turned to the comm and intel guys and said, "Get as much identifying information out of the dolt that didn't follow orders. Who the fuck is that person?" Saind bellowed at them.

Someone from the group scurried off, "I'll get him," he said, ostensibly to be efficient, but it was more of a relief to be out of that madman's overwhelming presence in such a small space.

Saind was fuming; the surge in power to the equipment gave off even more ozone, as the hate and evil power of the demon Barg viciously raped the electronic databases. Barg, inhabiting the body of the female officer, stood immobile while his presence invaded every data stream, algorithm, and encryption. Barg laughed to Saind. "You have no idea what you have just given me."

"Then tell me."

"No, I will have a conversation with the intel guy first, alone." Saind ordered all but the intel guy out. Barg immediately held out his hand, and the instance the officer grasped it, the small space was flooded with the light of the transfer. The intel guy assumed a more rakish pose, smoothed his jet-black hair back. "Ah, that is more like it."

Saind said to the female officer, "You may go. Return to your watch. You are dismissed from this incident. Take my car. There is a passenger. Drop that bitch off at the Northampton airport. Put her on the plane that awaits."

The deputy left the RV.

Saind turned to the new Intel Barg. "What is so spectacular?"

Barg grinned and laughed evilly. "I am anticipating finishing this mission with you. Oh, the people I am going to contact when this incarnate time is mine to do as I please. For now, I have found little that is of use to you. If there is the awareness of you, it is hidden in deeper data crypts that I have found access to, but I have yet to give them but a scan."

"Just because you found nothing, doesn't mean they aren't aware."

Barg assumed the caricature of a philosopher and said, "No, I would say it absolutely means they know of us, our kind, our plans, and maybe even the extent of our kind's excursion into their world. They are taking every precaution to exhibit not knowing."

"True. But nothing about this situation beyond what information we have planted?" He looked puzzled and angry at the same time. "Why the mass response to this area?"

Barg extended a finger to the monitor and an aura of barely discernable light—that tended to be closer to ultraviolet—emanated from his finger. The light reached for the screen and connected, then sank into it. Data flowed across the monitor faster than anyone could read. Barg then put on a headset with an attached microphone. He spoke an arcane word and the same light flowed from him through the headset cord, to bathe the equipment it was plugged into. He put his other hand on another monitor—intent on filling this with the same light—but with the multiple connections achieved, this stolen body spat sparks that arced in the small space. Blueish bolts danced from him to all the electronic gear. Barg turned his head carefully to gaze at Saind. "Do you want them to remember what I now know?"

"No. Still, I want no trace. Not a shred of a mention."

A final splash of the brilliant light across the gear left it all smoking. "They know nothing worth knowing beyond that our message is the predominant social construct at the moment. Their denial of us makes the problems with their world seem of their own making. The masses are being fed and accepting the story of a bomb, the terrorist theory is firmly the belief, and there are hundreds dead. That lie has taken on its own life, but it propels the narrative well, so it is not worth correcting. That the authorities seek out the bomber cover story for this hunt is well believed, accepted, and acquiesced to."

"What makes this hunt necessary? Why do the algorithms send the officers here? What have the seekers found?"

Barg sat in a rolling chair and languidly pushed himself back to a printer which started spitting paper. Barg grabbed a stack, paged through the gibberish covering the page. He started throwing the sheets theatrically away as he scanned each page, "Nope, nope, nope." With each 'nope,' he tossed the sheet over his shoulder. He did this for a few long moments until he saw that Saind had a tight smile, barely controlling his substantial displeasure. "Here, here is the transcription of an audio capture off the old net. Hardly anything comes across as more useful than the info on the cloud and the digital net. The analog info is so garbled and is hardly worth the effort to store and translate. The algorithm does not devote much power to this, and sometimes there is a time lag in getting useful intelligence from the output. But tonight, I searched that platform too, and found something interesting.

"Someone else searched it, too. I feel the association runs all the way to the owners of all in this world. Here is what they found: earlier today, a radio interception was pinged by the words of a priest. It was in an older model vehicle registered to…" he held his gleeful but snide face out and thought he was building suspense.

Saind slapped him hard across the face. The shock sent a wave of evil energy out the back of Barg's head and threatened to pull the dark psychic soul of the demon out of the stolen body, but the blob of light pulled taut, and then snapped back into the stolen intel officer's body. "Enough. You will stop playing games with me, or I will tear you into nothing. Now talk."

Barg began to spew, "The radio picked up a conversation that indicated the individuals, there were two, knew extensively about the events of the explosion. They talked about this highway; a rural road named Bog Hill. I found no significance to the particular area. Top of a small peak, a marsh feeding a stream down to an old mill site. It flows off into the woods. The radio picked up names: Parys, Monte, Leonard. I don't know how they are connected. Monte is the priest who was stopped at the roadblock earlier and released. The funny thing is that they stopped for gas, or so they said, and the signal never came back on. I predict they realized we listened in and disabled the radio. The same vehicle was the one stopped and released, but there was no one other than the priest and driver."

"The driver was not who we hunted?"

"No, he checked out. Known and unimportant."

"Never assume, Barg. Never assume who or what you can trust. I should never have trusted…" He trailed off as a commotion was heard outside. They stepped out and Saind asked the nearest officer what was happening.

"A vehicle approaches. It did not come from west out of Cummington, because there is checkpoint there and they did not clear it. It comes from the hills."

The old truck slowed before it got near the blocked intersection. It stopped and a squad car moved in behind to prevent retreat. Officers surrounded the vehicle. One went to the window, spoke with the driver, and asked for a local officer to attend. One did, conferred and stepped back, just as Saind came up.

"What is it?" Saind demanded.

The officer said, "Just a local. He has been vouched for."

"Who is he?"

"A local craftsman, stone mason. He was out to work earlier today. I stopped and spoke with him."

"Was he alone?" Saind asked.

"Um, yeah, I think so."

Saind was again near screaming, "You think so? You don't remember?"

"No, I don't remember anyone with him. I looked in his truck, found nothing suspicious and let him drive on."

"Fools, damn fools," he said and shoved past the two officers to go to the window of the truck. "Barg!" he yelled a summons as he approached the truck.

"Who the fuck are you?" Saind stormed at the driver. His projected fierceness had little effect on the bearded, lean man with a sun-tanned face and large hands resting on the steering wheel.

"Bill Veria," he said, placidly, not seeming to care about the flashing lights, the guns pointed at him, nor even the furious demeanor of Saind.

"Where do you live?" Then before Bill could answer, "What are you doing out here?"

"I live here."

Barg leaned in and asked, "Bog Hill Road, correct?"

"Yes, what a great spot. Lots of wonderful granite up here. I work with stone, you know. I was out looking at a few jobs and stopped at the quarry to find some stone."

"What else?"

"I think I took an early morning hike; I did, I think." Bill seemed lost in reverie with a zen smile.

Saind was about ready to kill the man, but Barg stepped in and pushed Saind aside. He leaned on the window of the truck and said smoothly, "Mister Veria, let me see some ID, please."

Bill pulled his wallet out and handed over his driver's license. Barg scanned it with his glowing eyes and the computers in the RV started flashing results.

"He lies, he covers up what he knows," Saind said.

"No, he, like the other stupid locals do believe, or rather they disbelieve, what they know so strongly is their truth now. I can tell when there is a spot in their memories that is incongruent with events, they have been willfully misbelieved," a pause then, "I believe."

Barg sifted and filtered through the data of Bill's life. He asked a few questions as the computers in the command pod spit data into Barg's mind. Then he suddenly found a jarring, but interesting bit of information about Bill's history on his web page.

"Did you write about the standing stones?"

"Yes, did you read it?"

"Where is it and what is it you find there?"

"It is close. There are some wonderfully preserved constructions of stone. Prehistoric, I believe. It is more of an altar, yes, an altar," he said. "It had a purpose, I feel. I've been stacking stones for near a lifetime now. I know when stones are stood up for a reason. I…" and he was cut off by Barg pulling Saind away.

"Saind, I believe I know not only where he went, and still might be, but I think I know what his purpose is, he searches for a thin place. Bill may have taken him to the perfect place, an unknown, or little known, but also remote and barely accessible thin place that still preserves the power. Bill writes the old ones stood up the stones to worship, but not that they worshiped the stones, they, the old ones made a church, or defined a sacred place where they could worship. That is where he is and has a purpose there. You must hurry, I believe he is still there."

"Where, where, WHERE, damn you," Saind screamed at Barg, blowing his rakish hair straight back.

Barg spouted GPS coordinates, then the legal plot definition, and the driving directions.

"Mount up, every single one of you come with me." Saind pushed aside a uniformed officer at the first car he came to and took the keys from the cop's hand. Barg got in the passenger side. Every radio came to life in every car as Barg touched the microphone. He broadcast the location, the plan, and the assignments. He called a helicopter team to overlook the area. Some of the cars peeled off at intersecting country roads.

"The site will be secured in a short matter of time, Saind." Barg turned the chatter on the radio down to enable him to hear his thoughts. "You know, there are whispers of tales among demons, that a thin place might take us to another time and place. That we are still not free is of little consequence when your Master can not find nor reach you."

Saind acted as if he looked over the top of imaginary glasses, pantomiming inquisition. "Demons need to be fed as much as any being. What if you go where you cannot feed?"

"Saind, such a shallow belief and such abused hope. You are wrong about your existence, brother. The incarnate being of a slave is no more glorious because you serve those on high or dine on delicacies. Think of what Dante wrote: 'better to reign in hell than serve in heaven.' I care little, after these centuries, of what lies on the other side. I have been bound to another's will since I perceived self. I am tired of this, this, this empty existence. None of the lives I have lived have been mine. And the same with you. I am not asking your permission, Saind. I am going to peer deeply into the thin place and find if I have the iron in my soul and the mastery of enough of my will that I step across, even just hoping to be free."

"Barg, I will not stop you. But I want to bring the one we chase, bound and terrified. I want to bring that person to the ones that own all and hope to be rewarded greatly. I have little hope of being set free, but the gifts they might bestow, and the trust they might offer will further my plans to be truly free, not hiding."

"Then we each have our own interest in finalizing this mission. You want the First Borne. I want the thin place. Are we agreeing that the most important aspect is to secure this First Borne? I will give *all*," he emphasized the word, "All to this end. And at that moment, when the prey is bound and you are basking in your imaginary reward, I am free of your obligations. Not a question, Saind, not an ask or a plea. I am simply telling you; I will be gone. Understand?"

Saind nodded, and said, "Barg, either of these paths might never cross again."

"True," Barg, as the intel guy nodded, "True, but worth it. But how amusing if it did."

The dash lights glowed as the evening neared and the sky clouded over.

Barg craned his neck to look up and out of the windshield at the gathering storm clouds. "We may hunt in the rain, Saind."

Saind was sarcastic, "It was a dark and stormy night," he said. They both laughed as the car sped on.

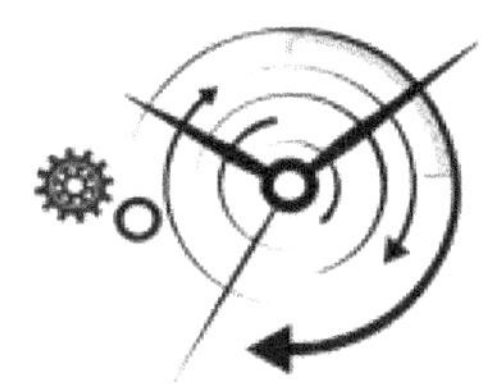

41 - Gambit

"Where am I taking you?" the befuddled deputy asked the woman who was ostensibly her prisoner in the back seat.

"Don't you know?" the banker asked, she was incredulous. Then it dawned on her, the policewoman had been possessed at some point, though a short enough time to not have completely immolated her soul. Now, the banker watched her drive, staring straight ahead but seeing the bare minimum to pilot the car between the descending curves, between drop offs and granite outcroppings. Oncoming cars, while gladly few, blew their horns and did evasive maneuvers.

A small town was announced on the green highway sign at the foothills: Williamstown. There were neon-colored lights announcing a gas station.

"I have to use a bathroom," she told the officer who still looked dazed. The plea didn't seem to register with her, and even repeating it and adding a drawn out 'please' didn't clear the miasma of confusion in the officer's mind.

"Stop at the goddamn gas station," she both yelled and kicked the reinforced back panel of the divider. That jarred her captor and escort out of the funk, but did not recenter her ego, nor her conscious mind. The self and soul of the officer were still in traumatic disarray.

The banker felt the car decelerate at the corner that led into the town. She continued to feel the car slow, and then it turned into the gas station.

At the pumps, the officer just sat there, looking straight ahead without seeing. The attendant came out to the window. He was puzzled by the

Connecticut State Police cruiser in this corner of western Massachusetts . When he got to the window, he saw a local county sheriff officer at the wheel. He was more than puzzled. "Hello, Margie. What are you doing driving this state police rig?"

The officer said nothing. And the silence grew uncomfortable.

"Are you alright, Margie?" he asked, this time peering into the car front to back.

The banker caught his eye and said to the attendant, "Open my door."

He was tempted by the commanding presence but knew enough of the ways of the law enforcement officers that stopped through here to get gas, that you never engage with the prisoner.

"Damn it," she screamed and kicked the seat again. "Open the fucking door, dammit. I need to use the rest room. I am not a prisoner, I am being escorted, see," she held up her unshackled wrists. "Now open the goddamn door or I will buy this gas station and fire your ass on the spot."

Without reinforcements from the officer lost in thought, or perhaps emptiness at some part of her having been stolen, the attendant released the banker from the vehicle.

"Restroom," she demanded.

He pointed.

She asked, "Locked?"

He shook his head and she stepped away quickly.

He bent to the open window and patted the officer on the upper arm. "Margie, are you okay?" No answer, so he shook her by the shoulder for a moment, then more vigorously. "Margie?"

She turned and said, "Huh?"

"You okay?" His genuine concern made him look hard at her for a few moments. "I'm calling this in."

He turned and ran right into the banker, who looked beaten and battered, but still, somehow vibrant. She asked, "Calling what in?"

"Ah, er…" he stammered a bit then managed, "I've known Margie all my life. This aint normal for her, what if she's got a bleeding brain or a heart attack or something. Look at her, she's probably bleeding and dying. I'm going to call 911."

"No," she said, in the tone she used to be obeyed. "She is in a mild shock. Psychogenic, if you understand that. Her mind is trying to come to grips with what she saw tonight. A terrible accident on thirty-five. Many people maimed and killed. Then a chase up into the hill towns after the suspect. They have the suspect surrounded. This officer is driving me home. The Connecticut trooper loaned her this car so she could expedite my return. I have a report for the Governor of Connecticut. We must leave, hurry, fill this thing up."

He started to work the pump, but then said, "I need a card for this part, ma'am."

She gave him a string of numbers, from one of her previously available cards. It might not be out of the system yet. He wanted to stop her and run it through a machine, but her imperious ways made him scrawl it on a scrap of paper he pulled from his pocket. He had to ask her to repeat it, and she walked right by him as she talked.

He opened the back door for her, trying to be chivalrous, but also hoping to undo the potential error of releasing her. But the banker refused the opened car door, went to the passenger side of the front, and got in. She looked out at the young man standing there, and said, "Shut the door and finish. Don't just stand there."

He jumped and slammed the door. He rushed to complete the task.

While the guy was filling the tank, the banker turned to the officer and said, "Hey, HEY!"

There was no response, so she snapped her fingers, and then escalated to slapping Margie across the cheek. The station attendant heard the sharp sound of the contact and bent to look in the car. He caught the glare of the banker and retreated to the task.

The banker grabbed the woman's chin with her palm up and turned the officer's attention to her. "You are suffering a traumatic shock," she pronounced. "I am supposed to take you home, I'm supposed to make sure you get there safely. Do you understand?" The banker nodded the officers face none too gently for her. The vigorous shaking got some of the remaining bits of self to coalesce. "I, I, I," she tried, but the banker took that wane attempt as proof there was use yet to be had of this one. A naked, injured, depleted soul that would come to understand only as much as she once knew or was now told.

"Don't talk, just listen," she said to the officer, trying to emote compassion, but feeling both sheepish and an inkling of thrill of being another's Master. That moment of pleasure, and the slight hope that she still might gain control of her destiny once again and parlay this situation back into a place with those who rule. She had a nasty laugh of one that has survived much and authored even more of the tribulations this incarnation shares; of loss, anguish, and terror.

"I am supposed to get you home safely, tell me again, where are we going tonight?"

The officer mumbled, and one coherent word sounded like Connecticut.

That would be fine, she thought, *that is over an hour away and that gives me time to yet make a play for an opportunity that would not only restore, but even, perhaps, if she dared wish or dream of such a thing, she would play what little she had as any type of capital with a gusto that only a soul with nothing left to lose would risk, to rule all.*

"Let's go," she released the other's face and sat back. The attendant came to the driver's window. The officer drove off without noticing.

They pulled into traffic and the banker was silent for a good while as she pondered and plotted. The driver was still incapable of speech.

The police radio was still on and tuned to the incident command assigned channel. She heard them driving to points around a large swath of wilderness. Few houses and a towering spine of granite   in this already mountainous area. She heard the orders and the intel; she knew it was one of Saind's minions. A demon beholding to Saind. Her Saind. The quick calculation added him to this grand machination. It was part of a ploy that had been forced before the events were fertile, yet she still could use the shreds of debris from that failed ploy to work her ways.

She picked up the mic and said, "Barg, Barg, calling Barg, Barg, BARG!"

The demon face made of fierce light burst from the luminous dials of the radio.

"Shut your mouth!" It screamed back at her. "You, you traitor to Saind, you deceitful bitch. I should make this car explode and watch you burn, rather than save you to live to a tortured, hideous old age of infirmity. I would gloat to Saind that I got to kill you instead of his strong desire to make you understand hell."

"Listen," she tried but was spoke over, harangued, and swore over. She had to bear it all with grim humor.

He noticed the foul curses had little effect on her mien.

"What, bitch?" he spat and snapped with bits of malevolent energy that sparked and burned holes in the upholstery and her clothes.

"There is yet a way."

"A way that you will use Saind, or myself, or both and profit? That is your way. I know your kind, and you are one of the most vile and lecherous of those souls."

"Perhaps I earned that scorn, and truly, I know I have earned many more dismal years of torture one can only do to oneself. True, but as I once said, it is not how many sins, or how much evil I have perpetrated, but the fact is, once anyone has crossed that boundary, then the fate is sealed and the volume of the darkness changes nothing. Not a single ray of hope to escape the fate I have created. I know this." There was a long silence, the radio face dimmed.

"So, if you can follow that reasoning with your simple, demonic mind, then you know what I have to suggest will, of course, benefit me. But what if, just if, the chance I take for my dream has room in it for yours? And Saind's? Is it worth it to listen to me, you unclean one? You are still chattel, as much as Saind is someone else's. So, I order you to tell Saind of this request to be present to me, and let him decide whether you should be rewarded, or severely chastised for the opportunity he was not afforded." She held that silence for some time, staring right through those empty eyes. The demon's hate and malice poured out impotently because she knew the limits of Barg's incarnation did not equal hers. The demon nodded an obsequence to her.

She said, "The chance I take is the only one I have, lest I become nothing with what I am left for assets and opportunities. I will not know the moves of this great game, but I know the rules and I know that I start with the same knowledge they have. So, I can make only one last play for freedom and eternity. I am able to do this last thing, with his help I am…" she paused then added, "I am able to also create the opportunity to yet have me free him. Tell him this, exactly this: 'Draenz, if only I could go back.'"

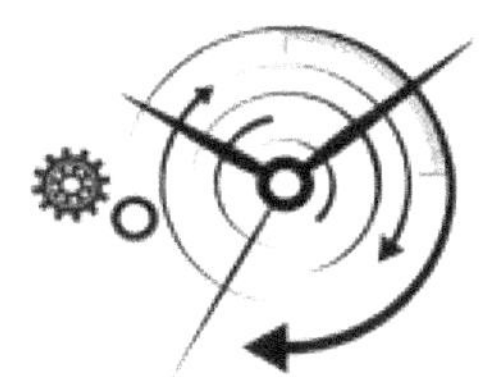

42 - The Watcher

I stood in the empty glade, with stars as the only light. The clouds gathered though, and the moon had not yet risen. The peaceful power of the place pulled emotions and conceptions from my mind. I felt an alert calmness, more in touch with the eternal ones. I could appreciate the magnificence of the gift of sentience. And I realized that I was a creator, not of myself, but of my life. The natural gestalt of self-awareness connected with omnipotence refreshed my consciousness. If there was even a way that I would understand zen, it would be this. I lifted my arms high, turned slowly about, trying to absorb the infinity I could sense in that instant. I felt I could reach across the gulf of time and space, and even life and death. I turned north and invoked what gods I imagined the people who lifted these stones, struggled to raise these stones, would have felt reverence to for their lives. Thunder boomed in the distance, not long after came the flash of lightening. The storm that was nearing seemed ominous. I reluctantly gave up that imagining of the ancient vision of the creators.

I went into the small interior space created by the ingeniously stacked and placed boulders and slabs of granite. It was a wonder. The obvious entrance first stepped down on stone treads three times. The floor was one single slab of grey crystalline rock, shot with streaks of mica. There were marks scratched into the cleaved granite floor. The marks were arranged in somewhat of a semicircle, opposite the slitted opening. I examined the vertically stacked pair of nearly parallel rocks. The edges and the interior surfaces which faced each other were apparently carefully knapped. The view of the sky when I peered from the opening was from horizon to zenith. Dim light cast my shadow faintly on the dark floor.

I studied the marks in the dim interior of the structure. I understood why Bill called this 'the altar.' Below the rock-lined slit was a boulder flattened across the top. I walked to the stone table, wanting to see it before all light was gone. I ran my hands over the surface and felt the ancient carvings and the power imbued in that rude altar. I felt, rather than heard. I knew he was there as opposed to sensing him there. I turned. The glowing being I had mistakenly called Grigori was standing at the entrance. He contrasted with the clouds, darkening the twilight.

Still, he was faint and the voice distant, "Move away from the opening to the sky," he said.

I moved sideways, just as a crack of lightening hit the mound in alignment with the slit. It blasted to the floor and shattered into tendrils of electricity that crawled down the walls and pooled in the deep scratchings in the floor.

I started to talk, but he silenced me with a finger and began chanting. He held his arms high and wide as he spoke. A single, forceful word echoed, and the sizzle of another blue, incandescent bolt filled the chamber. The lightening channeled down through the rock-lined slit and hit him in the chest. The light stayed there before being absorbed and became a form. The runes of power in the floor dimmed and went out.

I stood in wonderment at having had just watched an angel or a superior being come into existence.

He said, "Lets step outside, there is not much time, and you need to know more than you possibly can, so you must trust me. Implicitly, agreed?"

I said, "Yes," and followed him up and out of the altar space.

He sat on a convenient outcropping, seeming to be a place of honor to those who so long ago must have witnessed what I just had witnessed. I looked at the small, enclosed mountain sanctuary. The standing stones seemingly in a more coherent pattern.

"Please, sit, listen well."

I picked a close seat.

"You are going to have to go with them tonight. You will be captured. Let yourself. As will I. I will be a mere servant to you, assigned by the church. And you will have to do some extraordinary misbelieving. First you must know that you are not to have the one in charge, the demon called Saind, misbelieve. I will reveal myself to him and I will have his considerations of what I wish to say to him. The officers that are with him will not at first join him. We will talk alone until I allow them to approach. The demons plot to subvert the catastrophic event that the rulers of this world will create to empower the time displacement. The owners plan to go back far enough to change the current reality into a world in which they rule supreme. The demons will, the owners of this world believe, obey and assist with all their dark power, but that is only a façade that has played into fruition after generations and centuries. What will happen, if it is to be allowed, is that this race of beings you call humans will cease to exist. I will talk to Saind about his part in this plan. I hope that what I offer him, which is to merely to see the truth and then feel with what might be a mal-nurtured soul some sense of peace. I am going to offer him what he cannot find elsewhere, from any of his masters, which is his freedom."

I thought about the onus I had just been handed. It bothered me that I didn't have a clue about what to do with this burden. I started to ask, but again was shushed, gently.

"I will answer all of your questions, just not now, please." He breathed deeply to start, but the glory of life incarnate made him stop and just smile and then, repeat the breath, deeply, reverently. He still glowed.

He exhaled slowly, controlled through pursed lips then said, "Now, here is the moment those of us that are wardens over you have decided to step in. You cannot be allowed to annihilate your kind, for the instigation is of the dark one's origin. We have long stayed out of the mortal affairs of men. We have come to a point where we must intercede. You, Leonard, are a major part of this, even if, to this point, unwitting. There are others like you. Many others. Humans who have realized the gifts the creators have given your kind."

"But there are also demons. You know this now. Now I tell you that their malice towards your kind will sabotage the events your leaders conspire to effect. If they can, they will manipulate the fuel of the trans time jump which is agony and hate. Their need is for many tortured souls to be extinguished in a short time. Your kind have been duped into believing in an existence, the very future the dark ones desired. Because of this, your kind has been infected. Infected with demons with darkness that animates their intellect."

"I don't understand," I told him. "What is the malice they hold towards humans? What am I to them?"

"They, the dark ones, have been denied eternity. They want you because you are one of the rarities among the sentient races that can step out of time. Though you haven't got a clue as to how you do this feat, but obviously have the ability, as does your race. Plus, the ones who rule are afraid of you awakening. Individually, most of you are self-aware, but collectively, it is past the time your species should be self-aware. Self-awareness is self constructedness. The Eden story relates that humans gained self-awareness, and constructed 'selves' before they were ready, as in before they were mature enough, with trained minds. You were supposed to learn there, in that time, and be taught to control that ability to understand that your aura of being is nothingness without creation. Worshiping is merely a deep understanding and acceptance that there is nothing, not even a 'self' without a creator. The idea of not believing in a creator while one has been created is a strange sort of schizophrenia. It taints one's ability to inflict one's will on this incarnation.

"You were meant to likewise create. But you, as a race of beings, precociously learned to create self. Humans are somewhat of a prodigy. At the moment, a spoiled belligerent prodigy, yet the human race is a beautiful seed of the those that live in eternity. The Ones that dwell in eternity meant for you to exist as such also. The difficulty lies in the fact that while you are self-aware, you are not aware of what you are doing, what you are creating. You are creating this life, this society, this ultimate demise for your whole race. Your kind is an idiot-savant that has grown up and is ill. You are ill-formed in your mind; your hearts are not open and you deny the reality that is so painfully true.

"It is not totally your fault, though, while you did succumb to the lure of what the demons offer, you knew little of the cost, and the few leaders that traded demon favors for power over earthly things invited that darkness into your kind. The darkness is virulent, now your race is infected with this dark parasitic force, and you do not realize how severely septic you are. There is little hope, but that small spark is still hope. The hope is that you will recover from what you are about to experience, much like a cure is sometimes an ordeal. A mental fever, aches and pains for your collective hearts and very souls. A rash of ugliness breaking out in your societies and in your lives. And there are necrotic areas of your kind that need surgery. Excision. There is little in the way of analgesia for your kind now. You, as a people, as a race of unique sentience, must face this on your own.

"Know this absolute truth though; the ailment of your minds and souls is not just that you are undeveloped and ill-formed, you are also infected. The infection is self-aware, the demons want what it is that you have and they don't, that is the ability to create. You can create and they can't. And I believe they never will gain that gift before they are consumed by the dark. They know this, too, and they thus hate you with a vileness you aren't capable of fathoming. That is what drives the vehemence of their desire to consume your races when you immolate yourselves in war.

"One side will fan the flames of envy and incite the poor to take by force and justify murder, but they can only reach the ones in society that are not guilty of this betrayal, so the murders will inflame the fears of those in the middle of societies classes. The few that own the world will push everyone to be isolated, terrified, and vicious. The greed of those that rule all the world will never let them have enough, and that lust will ignite events that will consume thousands of souls. That event will allow one of the ruling classes to jump off the time stream and make the final change to humanity's past which will consolidate their power and control and thus dominion over your plane of existence. Then, the demons they imagined they had dominion over, will feed off you till you are near a death of your consciousness. The end of your kind will be a terrifying immolation of the totality of your creations and your sentience. The darkness will have fed enough on your fear and death that they can pupate. We, the ones that look after all the chosen, cannot tell what form of the mutated larval darkness will emerge. That is why we cannot allow this to occur, to allow them to spread. They will not be allowed to be free, even if it is your demise.

"That is why we watch over you. We have been here giving you lessons, however and whenever we can, yet, regrettably, you have rarely listened. But there is a more germane point to our appointment as guardians of your kind. It is also our task to keep you from losing the darkness on all others who have gained enlightenment. You not allowed to know of us. You are kept apart. This isolation is a quarantine, for our benefit even more than for yours. I am one of those that keeps you naive. I am one who prays that I do not have to watch you perish. I am Parys. You can call upon me by that name."

43 - Challenge

The electricity of the storm struck him several times; the fury of the storm flowed easily through him to the ground. The ground had a light pulse of the organisms in the soil that were suddenly recharged. The clouds gathered into concavity and grew close. The wind picked up and swirled forest detritus among the standing stones. Parys made an outward gesture with his hands gently, palms down. He brushed the storm back to all four quadrants. The small area in this hidden glen was tranquil, and the boundary with which Parys held back the storm and the stealthily advancing law enforcement personnel, shifted colors and shapes like the aroura borealis.

The uniforms of the various departments differed but had that same functional look. Those wearing the uniforms were intent on one thing at the moment, it was a manhunt. They advanced on the glade and could see their prey, the suspects were just standing out in the open, apparently oblivious. That thought was enticing to those who hunted. They waited for the order to apprehend. They crouched in the storm driven rain. The suspects stood in the open, but they were not rained upon, most curiously.

One of the suspects raised his arms high, and it seemed, pushed. The air became a slow gelid honey, then assumed the heaviness of glass. The radio crackled, but no one could respond, nor even move. The air, the environment, the world for them had turned to a thick coating of glass to an even depth over everything. The radio ordered the operation to commence, for the order to apprehend the suspects, but time had stopped for each and every one of them.

Saind strode up the path, past the officers crouching for cover or concealment. He pushed at one, and made as if to scream at the man, but his hand faded completely through the officer. They were but a high-fidelity wisp of reality. Saind waved his hand back and forth through a couple of them, then laughed and turned to the glen.

"Okay," he said to the wind that snatched his voice away. "I guess we meet alone," he said to the angel he knew was listening. He started to walk up a slight incline to the glen. He stepped through the barrier without noticing the ripple of colors that healed the breach right behind him.

Saind stepped into the open, and the two turned to face him. He walked towards them, feeling the concentrated power of the place and the creature of light that now hid in the human form. He also felt the strange amnesiac loss of focus on his intentions. The darkness in his intellect faded a bit as he stepped up close to the others. He bowed only by nodding his head, but respectably long enough while even insinuating a disdain for the other.

Parys smiled.

There was a tense quiet, and I said, "Leonard."

That broke the impasse. They turned to look at me. Saind said, "I don't see it in this one. I don't see any gifts that make him unique."

"Perhaps you can't," said Parys.

Saind looked about, trying for a casual, cavalier persona. "Quite the night, did you order the theatrics?"

"I did not, seems that the eternal ones meant for this weft of the wyrd to be grand. This conversation between you and I, that makes sense and was foretold with certainty, but Leonard is the completely unpredictable wild card in this meeting. We touch more than just the future between us. You know what the owners plan to do with the Transveho-syne they will create. And the ideas that those chosen carry back in their heads and hearts will be precious to the society into which they will land. So, it is up to you and I, and Leonard, to find the way to make this alteration less than the annihilation of a species. This species is favored, Saind. The Eternals will not allow this plan, your grand aspirations to succeed. At best you will fail. At worst, with the wrath and finality of those who dwell in eternity, you will cease to exist. You are also part of what those who have created, created. That is the acknowledgement that I accept, but you fear. Again, there is the difference. But…"

Parys paused for a long moment while Saind fixated him with a glare that exhausted itself. And then, when the eye contact between the two ethereal beings become calm and equal Parys said softly, "You don't have to fear, Saind. It is okay to decide differently. What you believe has been challenged, and you are different for this sudden experience of righteousness. You do not have to exist to perform your life for others and exhaust yourself to their fate that you dread. I say, Saind, there is always a chance to make the choice, the choice on which you will be judged. But your judgement will not be apparent, you will simply become nothing, never, unknown. You will cease to exist to those that have a reason for the universe to function. I ask you, allow yourself to dwell on a choice which might free you from the dire bondage to which you have committed your lifeforce. Your way out is to believe. It is that simple, yet that nearly impossible for most. If you give that part of you, which is that essence that is you, that soul, that acknowledgement of creation and creator, then, if you give that back to the one that most certainly created what your kind are, then you are free. If you think you control the world, you control nothing, not even yourself."

Saind snorted derisively, "I do control the world." Saind thought for a moment and then said, "I control the world by doing the Masters' and the Dark One's bidding. I am incarnate at their bidding and behest. Look to any religious tome, I represent the will of the one who has fallen, but yet rules this world."

Parys smiled so small, his eyes were sad, "Yes, perhaps, but you don't control who makes up this world and," he paused, "You are afraid of who does."

There was silence, the deep silence of the truth as when one's mind, no matter angel, demon, or man, cannot find any thought that might refute that pronouncement which is contrary to our egos. Parys looked at Saind, and Saind looked away, far into the distance of time and space.

"You can't create, your deviousness is the single expression of will you have and with it, you must answer to your Master's summons, and pray you have gotten their wishes right."

"Perhaps true, but you are in no different straights than am I," said Saind.

"That is where you are wrong. If you didn't have to serve, you wouldn't. You live at the whim of others, and your dim hope is that you are freed. But you do not know of a single demon that has ever been freed, do you?"

Saind said nothing.

"You dream of and beg for a different existence, I don't. Mine is an intellect much like yours, but without the need for incarnation to exert my will. I have the absolute belief in what I do, but you, you hate your servitude with a passion. That is how we are so different. The difference? Saind?" a pause, and then he said, "Belief. Belief in what we believe."

There was a silence among us. Lightening flashed fractals off the face of the demon but made Parys glow for an instant. His aura changed, became brighter, and all the colors coalesced into a white-hot emanation in the shape a human. Soon, the light that came off him hurt my eyes, and I had to look away.

Shadows of the strange clouds cast by the moon that was just rising over the horizon gathered at Saind. The darkness attached itself, piece by piece to him, and he grew in both the depth and volume of the blackness. Soon, he was a void that boomed a voice from far away.

"I have beliefs, and just because they are the opposite of everything you endear, does not mean I, and so many others, don't have any, like, for instance," he became mockingly theatrical, "Like all things have a life span, and you too, walk that path to the precipice. Another belief I have is that I will rise to the position where I again plot for my freedom. You are right, I know of no other demon that has gained freedom, therefore I believe I will be that first entity to do so. Ha, at the expense of these puny creatures you so treasure."

"That is your arrogance, your hubris." Parys smiled at the darkness and increased his radiance to that of a small sun. That light hurt my eyes even when I looked away. The brilliance reflected off any and every surface had a shimmering luster. The splendor of the being Parys was, now invading the dark outline of Saind. The light filled him, and he writhed as if tormented, but then his voice calmed and his tone was not haughty, but proud, not scornful but fervently hoping to hear words of conviction he might grasp onto and finding belief hard to muster.

"I have existed for so long as Saind, that I remember little of what it is like to be Draenzmeyel. That is who I am, Draenzmeyel, one of the first of the fallen."

"There are other ways, Draenzmeyel. The choice you might soon make may have the potential to absolve you. What you know about these human beings, and their simple minds is that they have so much of the power of the eternals. You will not be able to destroy anything that magnificent. That you try will ensure you are cast down with an eternal finality. To believe that you do not have to serve the darkness is to find grace.

"Were you cast out? Were you disavowed? What if the punishment you believe is the cause of your dedication to the dark was only your fault for falling? What if the rage against the Oneness is your own pride, at your own outrage, which has festered into putrid anguish, at being less than perfect? What if the original sin of every being is merely rooted in knowing perfection, but not being perfect?"

Draenzmeyel raged in the deep voice from across a void of sorrow and non-forgiven regret. "So, SO, SO! So what if the existence I have is still sweeter than obsequience? What if the passion fuels the heights to which I have attained, no matter what the flavors of the emotions? What if," he paused and the darkness with which he pushed out the invading light, gained seneschalship over the being. Saind said slyly, "What if, brother," and he spat this word out, "What if one develops a taste for those emotions. What if to dine is that which satiates a soulless incarnation. Why should I believe that to merely hear of a different existence has more worth than feasting on the one I have been given?"

"Or has been chosen?" asked Parys, and again retreated to the silence of the deep pondering, with the gathering wind as the only noise.

Draenzmeyel again exploded and fumed, but not as antagonistically as before, for now the fear of a denied yearning was recognized, suddenly a moment of fate made absolute, a sudden realization that one's future, and fate was offered as a choice.

"What flaming riddles do you talk?"

"I have an offer," said Parys. "I offer you a difference."

"Ha, you do not have the power to negate what I owe nor the power to grant what I seek. You offer me nothing that I can tell. You string words to make thoughts bend to your will as much as I do, so I know that it is my acceptance of what you say that will make your will into reality."

Draenzmeyel was interrupted by one word. "Belief?" Then a long pause before the angel again spoke, "If I give you the chance to understand belief, and that belief is a choice you make. It is difficult for one take to heart. I know. Yet there is only belief that inhibits you. One that is dark in the heart such as you, and your kind, you have the same choice, only you have chosen differently, yet," he hung the word out there, "yet there is never a moment that any created being cannot rechoose. You don't trust that there is an option to rechoose without penalty. Those that rechoose, probably never rise to the metaphysical heights they might have, if the original vector of that chosen life was started in the darkness, but yet, Saind, you still can choose. And at this juncture, much is the result of your choice."

"Yes, you want my belief, and it is mine to give. These foolish beings may not know of the power of belief, but I do. I am the arbitrator of my belief. You have not changed my belief; you have given me only riddles. You have not even given me trust. I give you my name, the name that holds power over me, and I still only know you as this simpleton's name for you." He pointed at me and spat, "Parys."

"There is no trust, you are right. What you gave me is a name that isn't yours, it is claimed by another, and you do not own the rights to yourself. Your name is no gift to me. Your claim to graciousness of this gift is hollow, Draenzmeyel. Like you. I do not give you power over my name since your name has nothing. It is merely a courtesy I extend to you now by acknowledging it. What I am telling your intellect, but your heart will not believe, is that I know what it is to have what you want. I offer nothing but perhaps what a mentor might offer. I tell you the truth of what you are missing, and perhaps even force you to look at the responsibility that you deny. A difference is what now hangs between us. A redemption of one fallen. I offer you the light."

"Still, what powers you dazzle me with here is a small bit of what I revel in there. I might believe, *might*, if you would know of what I cede.

I dare you to experience what you disdain and then speak to me. I invite you to feel the most poignant moments of being alive when you are closest to death. Join me in a celebration. Come to Rites, incarnate."

Parys nodded. He simply nodded and Saind continued to speak.

"Here, in this little bubble you have created, I might believe you, and even experience superficial and minute illumination of the eternal. But, as soon as the passage of time returns, the construct of this world returns, and I return to my place in it. The world returns," then he sighed, "and the little spark you have me imagining will be snuffed out by the omnipotent darkness that claims me. I shall keep my place, even if it is among the fallen until you are touched by the sensual incarnation and master it enough to step out again and make the same offer."

Parys again said little for many long moments. "I will agree. I will attend your Rites. I will be there."

"You are bound by those words, angel," Saind insisted.

"I am so bound," said Parys.

The immense darkness that was Draenzmeyel started to fade to shallow, sad greyness. The apparition of intense light that I knew as Parys also lessened in intensity, again took glowing human form then dimmed to substantial being. Draenzmeyel once again stood there as Saind.

"I haven't stopped their movement of time, merely stepped outside of it," Parys said as he indicated the insubstantial figures frozen on the other side of the time zone. "When I erase the division, they will have missed nothing. They will storm into this vale and capture me, us," he corrected himself. "But they will not know that you and I have spoken. They will believe you got here first to apprehend me, us. After that, you are right, the world will continue on as it has been, only now, you know the difference. And you can't claim ignorance because the options are yours as to how the outcome comes about, but with all the might I, and those that have decided to intervene have in this conflict, the eternal's will, will be done. Before this, we have been more of a referee, a warden to you and offered occasional encouragement to these humans, which they often rejected, but now Draenzmeyel, we guardians of the light have chosen sides. The path your kind want humanity to take, and the one the owners of this world attempt to create will not be allowed. In the end, the darkness will not succeed, nor even survive I surmise, nor will you ever more exist. That is true hell. Hell is not being, of never had been, to never be again. The choice is yours to exist or not. Believe wisely, Draenzmeyel, believe wisely. In the events to come, you will not misbelieve. You will be the sole witness to the reality of the coming exigencies. I am allowing you to watch and decide how to respond to that which is foreordained."

I saw nothing but a small smile from Parys, Saind nodded in return. Time returned. Suddenly there was rain, lightening, shouting, flashlights, footsteps running, orders being hurled about as time resumed, then I was thrown to the ground and handcuffed. I turned my face to Parys, who was likewisc abused. He wore a look of satisfaction I found incongruous to this situation.

He winked. "I am," he said to me, "to them," he nodded with his head and eyes towards the assemblage of law enforcement, "except for the one I have spoken to, the one who calls itself Saind, I am not here."

I furrowed my brow and misbelieved, and suddenly, that was what they all knew, except for Saind, or Draenzmeyel. He felt the wave of a new reality I put into place change what he controlled: the operation. Saind eyed me curiously, then looked about at all the others I had instantaneously touched. I saw a thoughtfulness in his eyes. Dark and dangerous, calculating on how to use this power of what was now his captive, and still having been left out of that burst of misbelief, he knew and considered anew what his options were.

The LEO who brusquely secured me, stood me to my feet without the previous moment's reverence for an awe-inspiring foe. I became worthy of only the casual jostling of a common criminal. Saind stared hard at me, as he felt the power of my misbelief effortlessly alter the minds and beliefs of those he controlled. In him, I saw the awe of what I controlled. I began to realize I could influence the stream of occurrences about the same time the light dawned in Saind's dark demonic eyes that I possessed such a power. I wondered if, to him, I became the impossibly opportunistic prize, or salvation from a place which he could never have contemplated.

I smiled at Saind.

While it was small, guarded and unsure, he, or it, smiled back.

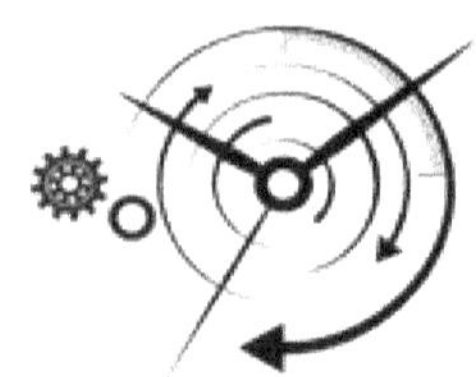

44 - Salyette's Message

Barg came storming through the crowd of officers while they were securing their captured fugitives. Cameras and flashlights flickered as Barg entered the small entourage around the prisoners, who now stood.

The ordered chaos of radios, conversations, stowing of gear and weapons, plus the inclement weather was astounding, even Barg took a pause. He looked to the prisoners, then, incredulously, to Saind.

"You have one of the angels bound to you? Saind, how can this be? I can see what these fools can't, and you must. An angel? And who is this, the First Borne? You have an angel, and a First Borne?" he stammered, not understanding what to do next to further his machinations, not trusting Saind's, and coming to a confused appreciation for the immense karmic gift that had just been dropped in their laps.

"Yes, obviously." The disdain was back in Saind's voice. "Take charge, dismiss these fools. Commandeer me a vehicle. Also, two others, two escort officers in each, plus a driver. Impress on all these yokels that if I hear of a word of this operation leaked, that person responsible will face the maximum penalty. This is classified at the federal administration level. Erase all digital images. I want nothing to remain. Review every logbook event for this operation. The location will be vague, the town. Misspell the name. Make notation it was a fugitive apprehension training exercise." Saind stopped talking and was about to turn away, but the expectation that Barg hung so heavily in the air between them made him stop. "What, WHAT? WHAT THE FUCK DO YOU WANT?" Saind snarled.

"Saind, you have lived long, and well, but have you ever experienced this magnitude of power in the world? Not just the world, but the wyrd? Yet," he paused, not theatrically, but as one who is pondering the sudden insight into an age-old problem and begins to now want to believe. "There is more, my brother. The banker who betrayed you has asked that you attend her, for she claims there is yet a chance to free you. If that is so I doubt, but what you have here is a coup more astounding than any demon has had acclaim to, it staggers the mind with what you might gain."

"Yes, yes," Saind agreed. "It is amazing. But tell me, does she say a plan, or does she merely pine away and miss the demon fire she once held so deeply, and I gave freely?"

"She said to tell you," then assuming Salyette's smooth voice, said, "'Draenz, *if I could go back.*' Then she trailed off and did not finish the sentence. The rude bitch ordered me to tell you. I almost laughed in her face, but part of me says to listen to one nearly as conniving as those of us. She said to say, 'If I could go back.'"

"Hmm," Saind mused.

This gave Barg the courage to dare even dream about what he might say next, no, suggest what to say, how even to present and promote the idea. He shivered with a myriad of sparks and asked, "Saind, Draenzmeyel, did the lady banker have an invite to the Transveho-syne, perhaps?"

"She did, not for the gallery, for the Procession only but, yes."

"So, all that was hers is canceled, but for the few scraps of worldly goods. Still, she was promised, riigghhttt? The Transveho-syne cannot be denied to any that had it offered to them, RRIIGGHHTT?" he ended emphatically, slowly and quietly.

Saind took the proffered thought and built on it. "Yes, she had been invited, and the invite still awaits. The Lady said, what again Barg? Exactly as she spoke it to you."

Barg composed himself, his borrowed face went flat, and the Lady of the Bank's voice came out of his mouth, "Draezz, If I could go back..." the voice tapered off to mumbled words that died out.

"Again," Saind ordered. He had heard the combustible emotional affectionate term she spoke to him after intimacies, and it aroused his curiosity and his passion. He heard the slight upward inflection she had used, not resigned, nostalgic regretful remembrance of one ruined, but the bait of another adventure that piqued his interest.

"Once more Barg, then do come back, you offend my memories of her. Now, AGAIN."

Barg again channeled the voice and yearning through to Saind. Then he dropped the personae. Barg waited while Saind thought.

"If she were to attend the Rites, if she were to go back with the chosen ones, she could alter that treachery which with we both now suffer."

"Who disposes of her assets?" asked Barg.

"The finance Minister has ingested every last bit of her empire not specifically named at her damning. Her personal effects are just as surely being savaged by the ones who now loathe and mock her, just more slowly. I might even look over that, I was so tasked by the Minister."

"She is no longer your Master, and if, just if, you were to take her incarnation, share it if you could control yourself to not consume her, you could release her to join the chosen who jump."

Saind finished the sentence for him, "If she could go back again to the time before she was damned, she could free me, us."

Saind and Barg both began to grin evilly. Saind put his fingertips together and touched his lips. He opened his hands and symbolically looked at the scenario he played out in his mind. His deviousness of this proposed action caused no disobedience to his Master's orders.

"I can see this," he said. "It could be done."

"But will you do this, that is the question Saind. Will you risk all?"

Saind said nothing, knowing how much power words had over thoughts, actions, and events. He stared into the empty space where Barg should have had pupils. Into the blackness.

Barg said, "Of course though, they will know that you have this prize."

"Only you and I know truly what we have here. Those others, they know we have captured a criminal and few will know or remember to dig deep enough into the archives to find out who they might be."

"Those pitiful egos could never shut their mouths. They will talk and rumor or otherwise prattle, then eventually but most assuredly, ones who own this world will hear. Then what, you say, oops," he said this sarcastically, "Oops, I just found what you were looking for, Master. Or maybe you can use the excuse that you didn't realize how important they were after you spent quite a small fortune in the past twenty-four hours to capture them." Barg stopped and rage spilled out. "You are deliberately ruining this opportunity," his electric demon voice crackled furiously.

Saind's fiery dark aura became more rakish, he looked most devilishly pleased, which even more infuriated the demon Barg.

Saind said, "None will talk, few will remember."

There was a long exhalation that made a slight whistle. Barg met Saind's eyes and stared, reading.

"The misbeliever!" The realization dawned on Barg, and the audacity made him guffaw. "You are using the misbeliever, aren't you?"

Saind could not contain the arrogance, even though it was a pride in servitude. He stood taller, leaned back into the wind of time, used both hands to smooth his hair back, which turned to a dark pennant of mineral fire of the deep places. His empty eyes, lids, and his pose became languid. He pursed his lips and emotions twitched across his face as he gathered a phlegm of foulness from his throat. He spat on the old altar with careful viciousness.

His nostrils flared, he convulsed as his substance came into slight contact with just the infinitesimally minute part of that which created and sustains all life. The sacred power shocked back into him before he realized and blocked it. It solidified the realism of his dilemma, he knew there were two sides, options to his life that he alone owned. It was a shock to his stream of consciousness when the call of the Master came to his thoughts absolutely undisobeyable. As he faded he said, "I use any and all, even you Barg."

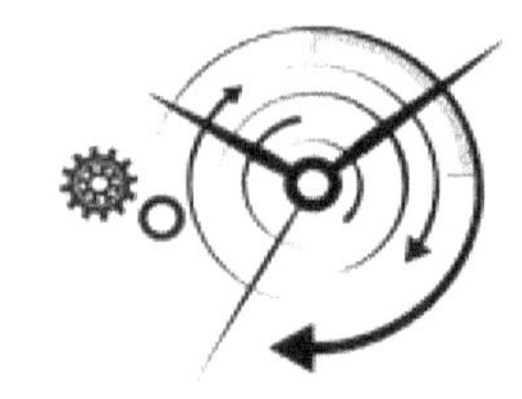

45 - Reports

Saind felt the pull of the master's summons, but was held back from his attempted audience with the Minister by a previously incomprehensible force. Now he understood it was not a great power that created the shielding, but it was a multitude of bound and tortured souls that barred him. It was the sheer mass of ownership that held him back. He waited in this limbo for what seemed either a lifetime or an instant, for he was held without time affecting him. He had no will with which he could have left, for he was owned, and the bondage held him.

A painful easing of nonexistence made him aware of the other's presence. Powerful, suspicious, pitiless, and cruel. The demon of the first order materialized, and Saind fell free of the imposed inertia at the feet of the other. He attempted to rise, but the will of the other was not released and he remained somewhat kneeling, hands on the floor.

"I am Kladt. I make stains of any being that strays too close to my Master without my allowance or my directive that you should be granted audience. Did you enjoy my barrier?" He was silent to allow a reflective moment in Saind's mind, then he bellowed, "If you ever deign approach the Master without my knowledge and approval, I will cast you into the weave of this net to become forever part of it, whether your purpose is nefarious or not, I care little. I am the Propugnator of the Minister's asylum. I am Kladt, the highest of those who guard the Master." He drew the next words out, enunciating carefully and menacingly. "YOU... WILL... ALWAYS... NOTIFY... ME... OF... YOUR... INTENT... TO... BE... IN... THE... PRESENCE... OF... THE... MASTER!"

"Agreed," Saind managed to croak out as the power of the one called Kladt eased enough to allow movement of his lungs and chest. Saind stood, and now, aware of the other's immense power, he guarded himself against the barrier of tortured and saprophytic souls. He pushed back against Kladt too and felt the yielding. Saind took that small sense of weakness in the other and blasted a hate and vileness to Kladt's incorporeal form that left a scorch mark of fire and a scar of embers that sunk into the skin and scales of the demon's face. The attack, both in intensity and in audacity astounded Kladt. He stepped back.

"Understand this, Kladt," Saind's stolen voice was low, but the timbre resonated to the protection web Kladt had created and it bulged and heaved with Saind's words. "I am Saind, also of the first order. I am beholding to no one or nothing other than to the Master. If I ever," another blast of hate, "EVER, feel you intrude on my dictate to do the Master's bidding, I will scorch your life force and damn you to impotence. Henceforth, I will announce to you, my coming to the presence of the Minister, and you will await me, and allow me to pass, lest I tear a rip in your childish spell and step through of my own accord." Saind blazed the dark fire again, but Kladt also was ready this time, and the impasse was apparent to both.

"None will pass without my say," Kladt declared.

"Then allow this now, servile one," demanded Saind. "I have the news the Master demands concerning the prize he seeks. There is little time before the Trtansveho-syne and this news and prize alters every plan the ones who rule have put in place."

"What do you bring before my liege?" Kladt planted his clawed feet stubbornly wide apart and crossed his arms across his chest.

"I bring what the Master demands of me, for you there is nothing to know but that I have what he desires and what you are not allowing him to obtain. You are merely a warder of a door. You are a keeper of a gate, not one who could begin to appreciate anything less than brute force. Now, allow entry, or depart in haste to tell the Minister that the prize I have is his to claim, unless you waste enough time here that the power this brings to the Master is diminished. I would not like to be the one to explain why the fruition of the Master's wishes are delayed. Go now. Be gone about your task."

Kladt roared in outrage, sputtered against the insults, raged demon fire out of his eyes and mouth, but yet when Saind roared out, "GO." Kladt vanished.

Saind waited a short time before he felt the irresistible tug and he was pulled through the seething web of souls. Though he was ready for the psychic assault this time, it was still broken fingernails that clawed at his being and grasping hands he had to slap away from his person. The terrible multitude of voices wailed at him, shrieked out pain they would love to and threatened to share. Saind laughed at the physical, mental, verbal, and psychic assault the way one welcomes a challenge where death is the option of failure. He used the horror of the web of virulent mordacity as an impetus, laughing and reveling in the anguish shared by those who had no future of their own. He became crazed at the amount of hate and vile imprecations aimed at him as he transversed the protection spell. The darkness of the thoughts and threats enveloped him in a maniacal wave of hysterical despair, and he took it into his very being, not only pushing back against the tsunami of evil, but stealing power from the masses, recharging himself from the web, growing stronger and more hateful of his servitude. He held onto the bolus of force as he dropped out to the other side. He saw Kladt, and disdainfully tossed that which he had sucked from the spell back to Kladt. "Here, repair your pitiful creation lest the weakest among us find how much you are lacking."

"You shall pay for your insolence, messenger. We shall yet see who has the favor of the Master."

Kladt retreated into the darkness of the writhing wall of force, but his presence was omniscient.

Saind looked about at the environs he found himself in. The seething forcefield had reduced itself to a barely discernable dark shimmer to every wall, door, window, floor, and ceiling of the magnificent hall he now stood in. Riches of every kind were present; grand tapestries, centuries old, woven of fine threads, marble sculptures and gigantic paintings. The chandeliers were demon fire reflecting through a myriad of diamonds. Gold and silver adorned the tables and fine wooden cases of artifacts. There were vases and urns seated singularly on ebony tables against the walls of finely worked granite slabs.

A voice broke through the vast stillness of this place. "Come."

Saind noticed a curious theme ran through the décor of the paintings, sculptures, and tapestries as he proceeded down the vast hall. All figures depicted were in anguished supplication. The disquieting motif intensified in the depictions as he came closer to the seated figure at the far end of the hall. The figures in the artwork grew more broken, with heavier and heavier afflictions till Saind stood studying the prostration and purgatory of the imagery of all manner of beings and creatures portrayed around the inner sanctum. The Minister sat in the sole chair in the entire hall. The heaviness of the Minister's expectant stare made Saind fall to his knees. He felt aware of the Minister's implicit demand that there be such a hierarchical gulf of servitude.

The Minister lounged back more comfortably and sneered, "You may speak."

Saind felt a degree of glory as he related events to the Minister. He culminated the tale with the news of the capture of the First Borne.

"Go, bring this one to the Rites." A dismissive wave of the hand released Saind. Minister Sheer said "Do not make me wait again, Saind."

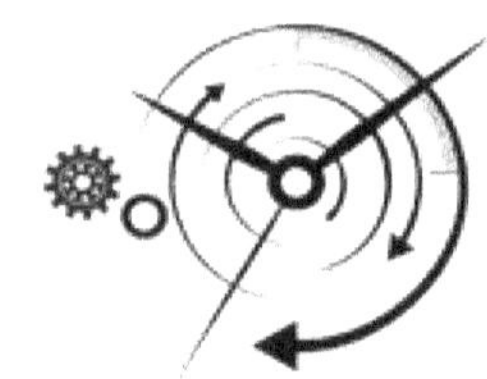

46 - Meet with Salyette

Saind blinked, shrugged and shivered as he came back into this time. He pulled over, braking hard. His cover did likewise. The lead vehicle braked hard, swerved to the shoulder. The reverse lights came on and the cruiser sped backwards to Saind's vehicle. Saind got out, held his hand up to the officers who exited their vehicles to respond to the imagined threat. They stopped at his gesture. Saind walked around to the passenger side and Barg exited. Saind slid into the seat. Barg took the task of driving with reckless abandon. He viciously veered back into traffic, cutting off several vehicles. They screamed car horn voices at his driving and Barg laughed and sped away. The escorts spit gravel to catch up to Barg.

Saind asked, "Are we quite done with the stunt work for the night?" His face wasn't deadly serious, only peevish.

Barg sighed and regained a decorum about his driving. Saind sat back in the seat, and stated, "I am going to see her." Then he ordered, "Announce me."

Barg reached out and touched the mic hanging on the dash. A blue arc crackled from his fingertip. The metallic noise of the compressed message was a single, sharp beep. Barg said, "The lady says there is another in the vehicle with her, you can easily have her."

Saind put his head back against the seat and closed his eyes. The demon fire within him dimmed as he astral projected himself to the car his once Master and lover now traveled in with his intended host.

The police radio in the cruiser crackled to life. The voice was rushed, forced, flat and emotionless, but still the message was arrogant and scornful.

"Bitch, you will receive Saind. If you are duplicitous, I will erase all evidence of you, your money, and any digital evidence of your life. I will kill everything about you except your body. Take heed not to betray us." The radio blew up in a shower of ozone sparks.

The police officer next to the banker shivered and flexed. Her neck arced and she rotated her head and shrugged her shoulders. Saind had arrived. There was a slight catch as the car veered, but the instantaneous loss of control was immediately corrected. The officer turned to her, animated and leering. Her facial skin tightened and achieved the fresh tone and rakish mien of a highly placed socialite. She looked at the bankers bruised and puffy face. Still, the urge of the past intimate trysts made Saind lick her lips and reach out her hand to touch the discolored cheek.

The banker put her head down on the hand that reached out to her, grasped it, and rubbed it against her lips, licking the fingertips.

Saind shivered, unconcerned of which gender he now inhabited.

They rode on for many long, quiet moments. The dash lights cast an unreal glow on the skin of the banker and Saind's fire within the sheriff pulsed lightly with the heart of the stolen body.

"Salyette," Saind said softly. "Salyette, you could have, you know."

"Trust is such a brittle connection, and bends little before it splinters. I am so sorry I did not give to you what you asked and what you would give for me," she said.

"True, you authored our demise, so now, what is it you plot and how do you plan to use me?"

"You are astute, the need is mine to ask of you. But the promise I hold out to you is that for what you give, your freedom is your payment, and reward, and unbinding from any, including me, will be the reward, the contractual obligation I shall owe you."

"You would put that to words and sign in blood?" Saind asked, intrigued but skeptical.

"When you hear me out, and when we find paper, I will put my blood to your terms. After you agree to partner with my plan."

"I so agree to listen, Salyette. I so agree and include in this bargain that my terms shall include torment of ages to you for betrayal," he warned.

"It is agreed," she said. "Think on this, Draenz," she said, using her fondest name for the demon, and adding intimate undertones to her voice. "I am sorry that I did not free you. I thought to myself, so many times since that fateful moment when I bound you to another, I thought, I thought how it might be different if I could only go back and choose differently, to defy the Minister, even if it meant a final death. Then it struck me as the dolt whose body you assumed drove me home, I realized that I know soon, at the Transveho-syne, someone will. Someone will go back in time, Veho across the wake by leaping into the Syne that is opened. I thought, why can't it be me? Even if only one day back, even if only to relive the day of my error bonding you, I could make this right, for us. Get me into the ceremony when they rend time, the Synodal. I have heard it is so frantic, the revelry, that hardly any one of them has their wits about them. Take me and on my words of the most binding and owing to you, I would dive into the time storm. I would, Draenz, I would," she pleaded.

It worked on Saind's dark heart. He had heard that tone of her voice softly in his ear before, he had trusted and diligently satisfied her whims many times before and now she held out a glimmer of hope that even he had just considered.

"I know you have an invite, but it is just to the Procession, and to the festivities, ahem, but you are so limited in getting even remotely close to the event. The Transveho-syne, the pomp and ceremony of the ritual are the most exclusive invites to be had by anyone, ever. How would you get close enough to the altar? Speak no longer in riddles and implications, Salyette," he paused momentarily at the novelty of using her given name as an equal. He pondered that the difference was that he was owned, and thus owed allegiance to one who he must betray. He could hear the plot in his mind before she clarified with her treacherous words, that he, Saind, would bare to the risk and punishment in this endeavor if it failed. And he knew the odds of success were fantastically slight, yet, once again, there was a fortuitous slice of the flow of events that he again was offered a choice.

"I feel that I am the only one offering anything in the little scheme you concoct." His anger at being in this predicament focused on her. He had been angered by her many times, but now he had no constraints on offering her a well-deserved serving.

"I, too, am offering everything even to the death, that I do this," she countered.

"Pah," he spit the word at her, "You are dead already. I do this for you, and you gain, I do this and fail, you die, and if I do nothing, you go away to die. You take on no risk here but gain all, Salyette. How do you convince me to risk my existence to your plans, when you have selfishly cast me to continued servitude?"

"The Minister is certainly one of the most powerful and influential of those few who rule this world, I agree. His wrath and retribution would be immeasurable, I agree."

"And you ask me to place trust in you, again, that I alone, might face that wrath?" Saind asked, his demon flame consuming bits of the officer's clothes.

Salyette reached across the console and put her hand on the hot skin of the officer's nape. She, Saind, stretched her head back, hunched her shoulders. Salyette slid her hand down to the shoulder covered in thick uniform fabric and squeezed. Salyette moved her first two fingers, just the tips, across the officer's distended neck veins, feeling the forceful pumping of hot blood and demon fire in the stolen body. She laughed and played with Saind's ear. "You are aroused, Draenz. It is too bad you are not equipped for such passion at the moment," she teased.

"There are many ways to dampen this fire you stoke, you are aware." The officer looked directly at her, staring and not looking at the road, driving by some inner sense. There was lust, fondness, love and hate all confusingly mashed into a ball of emotion.

Salyette smiled ever so slightly at the thin hope he still held out. "Yes, Draenz, that bond which we have shared can go on forever, if we succeed. I would give what little life I still might have to try to achieve forever. Not trying is the same as failure. I want forever with you, Draenz, I know we can have it, or at least die the lover's death of sacrificing all. Draenz?" she asked softly, then again, "Draenz?"

After a long, long silence while Saind turned back to the road again and drove for miles without speaking. Then, he abruptly asked, "Where was she taking you?"

"I don't know, somewhere in Connecticut."

"You had a private suite at the hotel you owned in downtown Northampton, didn't you?" Inflected as a question but really made as a statement.

"But I don't own that hotel anymore, Draenz."

"Do you think the staff know already? No, I think you should show up, demand absolute privacy, promise them anything you no longer have the power to give for their silence. Stay there until I return. You must not, in any circumstances reach out to me. For the mere suspicion of duplicity will ruin anything you might be able to offer me. So, if you breathe a word, to your phone, to your maid, to the damn air when you think you are alone, you are not. For I am not. But," he said, finishing his thoughts, "If you breathe a word, I will suffer, and for that you will never achieve even a long bout of old age. You will be likewise dead but tormented. I have felt the wails of those the Minister has taken offense towards, and you or I could be there in that living hell of a morass. I pray you heed my words, as you seldom did, but now, I am not bound by my servitude to you, but only warn you because there is the slightest glimmer that I might hope for, that this is my moment, so I have a curious state of mind where I am offering you trust."

She reached across again and put her hand on the thigh of the officer. Salyette stroked Draenz's leg and felt the demon fire grow, the dark passion rise.

Draenz, put her hand down over the banker's soft hand. She played with the manicured tips that had scratched her deeply, many times both as a her and a him.

Draenz held her hand tightly, then said, gently, out of Saind's deepest character, "I think the time is now to wonder if the game we are about to play is final, for keeps. I have lived a long, long life, and after talking with the one who put light in my soul, I am weary of the role I now play, and regret that I am not someone else, the being I desire to be, but I deign to be a slave. Servitude is a condition one acquiesces to or becomes accustomed to, to the extent they do not believe anything else for their life. Whatever form that life takes. So, let us play our best role in this drama. Let us trust enough that there will be freedom or death. For now, my lovely Salyette, I can no longer be content with slavery, even at the highest pinnacle, I still serve. Better to reign over self, as low as one might fall, than to, how is it said, be in bondage, or servitude to those most high of this world. There are other worlds, I know of this. If I was no longer an owned intellect, I would go to some magnificent places. And I would need a mate. I would need someone to share that which we have shared, that which we cannot even imagine. That is what I trust you with," Draenz said, looking steadily into her eye. "That is a vow I am to make or perish for having had made. Yet, there it is, Salyette. There it is."

The air was heavy and electric between them. Time barely existed outside the little metal cocoon of the vehicle which hurtled down the highway. She was solemn when she spoke.

"I will plead this, with my soul owed to you, forfeit to you if you find I do not keep my promise, to you, on your terms, at your bidding, at the soonest possible moment, that is; the promise I make is to free you, when once again, as before, and it will be as before, I have that claim to the power to free you. I give you my vow. I will owe you this."

It was a most somber night, when both realized that they had given every bit of their life away to the other. No one spoke until they came into the lights of Northampton to the west. Saind steered to the off ramp. The traffic increased as they became aware of the outside, menial, the profane world about them. The car slowed, then caught a green light before all inertia was lost. Saind accelerated into the sparse, late-night traffic aggressively. It made her smile.

Then, full of false bravado she said, "Then let's go do this."

"Okay, you must let me think how to plan this to our advantage. You still have the invites?"

"Of course, they are genetically coded. They may have canceled me, but if the Academy does not yet know, I can waltz into the Procession, and none will know anything will be amiss if I stay hooded. I can get in, what about you?"

Saind said, "I will bring the best sacrificial one to the altar that the Minister or his ilk have ever seen."

"You would do this how, what, who?" she stumbled out the disbelief of what he proposed.

"You may be the perfect one to disbelieve, Salyette, and not even know what you just evoked. You don't believe." Draenz's voice came out gruff, and hoarse because the demon's force of will severely taxed the officer's vocal cords. "For this to work, Salyette, you must," he paused, then continued, "you have to be perfectly believing in the success of what propose. And this makes you act accordingly. So, start now," he said brusquely. That intimate but not peer relationship made the demon pause. Saind again stared off down the dark highway, not seeing but steering with some intuitive sense while his mind pondered what it would be like to be committed to that one, singularly focused belief of freedom. The residual light of the angel sparkled within his mind, and again, the demon Saind knew the potential of belief.

"The Transveho-syne is tomorrow night. A sacrifice is offered by those that request a change of current fate. I will bring a sacrifice in the name of the Master that will be more worthy than possibly any before that have laid in the embrace of the Bone Fire." Saind's affect became fierce, powerfully fixed on a purpose, but no longer haughty. He pursed those borrowed lips of the officer, and nodded, more to himself, but she heard him state, "The First Borne must die."

"I have no care about the First Borne dying, why even wonder?" asked Salyette.

"There is more," Draenz answered. "I need to go and so do you. I can be explained at the ceremony, but how does the Minister acquiesce to your being present? The Minister would have you killed at the moment you were discovered."

"I must get close enough to the Syne to leap in before the Minister's agent has a chance to cross. I could hide amongst those present on the dais, and you could cause a commotion, a disturbance that would allow me to rush to the Syne."

"That is magical thinking as if you were a child," Saind exploded. "How did you plan to get into the Rite, through the masses right to the dais, at the time to dash in and take the other's Transveho? I can see you might join the Procession, even sneak into the great hall, but you have no chance in hell of getting close to the Syne! I would believe that you might free me, considering the words you have spoken, but what miniscule hope do have? You again trick me, asking for my graciousness and you are feeding me empty promises. How, *how*, can you think this might work?"

Salyette was silent and seemed to have to force herself to speak. "Draenz, what if you take me, possess me, go to the Minister as me, in my body. The Minister could be vain enough and share enough of the hatred for me that he might see how delightful it would be for you to usurp me and preside over the sacrifice that would tear my soul and end me forever. He may even suggest it himself."

47 - Manipulated

Saind once again forced his way through the mass of souls Kladt had suspended in eternal punishment. The hunger and sorrowful, painful need of the empty ones made a near perfect barrier to protect the Master, and likewise keep the Master isolated from the corruption of the slaves and doomed ones.

He emerged in the same great hall, familiar with the environs, but disoriented from the psychic drain of the passage. He was sure Kladt had wanted him to feel his power, and it had been an ordeal to cross.

Saind gathered his thoughts and strode down the hall, unannounced by Kladt.

"Minister," Saind said as he fell to a knee, still speaking. "I have secured the one I believe the church has been pursuing. Lord, I believe him to be a First Borne, or at least a wild, random variant."

The Minister sat still and quiet. It seemed as though hours had passed, and then the Minister began to speak. "Where are the documents? Why are they not in my possession?"

Saind began again, "But Minister, I have the one that material will lead me, us, you right to. And I thought it would be more of a valuable asset in the realm under your control to have a First Borne sacrificed in the Bone Fire tonight?"

"What do you know of the Bone Fire?" the Minister demanded.

"Minister, it is the dream of almost every demon to inhabit a host for the ritual to celebrate and inculcate the Syne for the Transveho. I, myself, have thought greatly of chasing this one down, and offering it to your greatness and glory, and I, myself, might have a taste of your gratitude by allowing me to attend the Transveho. I would gain much power from such a magnanimous gift."

"Your obsequence is near nauseating, but with some small degree of merit. I would imagine my agent would arrive at the shores of that past time even stronger should I take your counsel and commit the First Borne to the Bone Fire."

Saind tried to look humbly in awe of the musings of the Minister. "So true, Lord Minister. If you will it, I will bring the one to your Bone Fire. I ask to be the one to commit him to the flames."

The Minister said flatly, "No."

Saind's self-control was taken from him. He stammered, never getting a sentence out before the Minister spoke again.

"I will take the offering, and I shall burn him in the Bone Fire. You will have the beginnings of my trust for this. You have yet to earn the honor."

Saind came as close as he ever had before to an emotional display of despair. But he raged the fire in his mind and cursed the woman banker who had taken his power, his hopes, his seed and even his love, if such a thing was possible for a demon. His face must have given his thoughts away to the Minister.

"You rage over what you think is a terrible slight that my Kladt will gloat about and even an injustice if you had that quality in your kind to appreciate. So yes, Kladt will be typically cruel. Deal with it. Kladt will make it so you never have your admittance to my presence denied. You will pass without hindrance to tell me everything you know, suspect, or even ideate upon. Is this clear enough for you, demon?"

"Yes," Saind said without any further emotion in his heart or voice.

"Good," said the Minister. "Now, tell me where the banker, Salyette, is. Tell me she lives humbly, and the frugality of her life is a torment. Tell me you have had her delivered to the fate I decreed."

"I have had her driven to her hotel in Northampton. I took pity on the heaviness of the curses she now bears, even though she deceived me."

"You can trust that I will never deceive you, Saind," said the Minister. "I will never make the promise to free you. You are mine."

Saind said nothing. He maintained the air of being a nothing, for it seemed his fate; both at the moment and into the future.

"I did not give you orders to give her pity. I grant you this one time to have taken leeway with my wishes. You realize you have disobeyed. You couldn't leave her even after she threw you away?" The Minister lounged back with pursed lips and a falsely discreet expression of raised eyebrows. "Were you intimate?"

"Yes, Master."

"Then you will relate to me the tales of your exploits, as I desire them."

Demons were incapable of blushing, but the demeaning subservience of the answer he must give wounded him to the depths of which he had not felt in ages, lifetimes. He realized he had fallen as far, if not further, than Salyette.

"Yes, Master."

The Minister stabbed him with an accusation, "You don't know what she is doing as we speak, do you?"

"No, Master, I left her to collect the detritus of the life she lived."

"She," now the Minister's voice was silky and dangerous. "She," he said again, "She has been online, making inquiries to sell some of those things which I denied her. She has told many secrets that she should have well forgotten, but now are freely circulated. For this, she will now be killed. I have dispatched those necessary. Your deceitful human whore will be killed."

"I cannot say I care, and even more, I relish the irony in this. Yet," he strove for the deeply pensive look, his demon hair ablaze. "Yet, there is a better punishment I might suggest, Sire."

"I do not need your suggestions, and I will ask when I do desire them, however, since you are new to my stable, I humor you. Perhaps you can amuse me further."

"I would be allowed to consume her, possess her and as I watch from her eyes, and feel the pleasant terror in her heart, I could bring the very one she sought, for which she deceived you, and allow her to be present for the destruction of that one. She will be aware of the power you will gain from this First Borne's death and rue her duplicity."

"Hmm," said the Minister.

Saind continued, "I will enjoy the agony of her final moments, for I could step out of her, into any of those willing in the hall, and then, allow her to be a small part of the Bone Fire. Her death can yet serve you."

"You would gain from this, I know. I would know how beyond the revenge."

"Minister, I foolishly allowed that serpent to twist my beliefs into some hope of freedom. I know of no other demon in existence or history that has ever been freed. I was wrong and the shame of that betrayal and false hope will be part of my existence. If I have to ponder this for all time, I would request that this disgrace be tempered with taste of vengeance."

"Hmmm," the Minister continued to think. He did not say anything again for hours. But then, he spoke. "You wish to know the human's thoughts, don't you? You can know the host's thoughts and memories, can't you? You, I believe, would like to know you were loved. I am right, no?"

"I see that my Master has a deep understanding of all things, including dark demon hearts. I am learning of your grandness, assuredly this is why you are first among those who rule."

Even the Minister could not resist indulging in that vanity. He said, "Take her. Present her to the Bone Fire tonight."

Saind did not smile the smile he so tremendously wanted. Instead, he put on a fierce scowl, bowed low with a flourish and said, "As you wish."

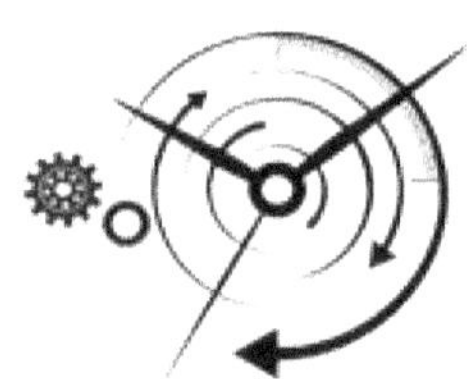

48 - Ascend to Power

Monte was dropped off in the back alley behind the bakery. It was locked and the windows were dark. Monte called a rideshare and waited for the ride, which came shortly.

Monte was barely aware of the passage of time, and soon, he was dropped off at the church. He went down the side steps, coded himself into the ante chamber and stood there in front of the camera. The inner passage opened, and he brushed past the young novice who tried to challenge him. Monte went to the same room he had previously used, and the other meekly followed. Inside, Monte instructed without turning, "Bring me a meal, any sort, and coffee. Bring me clean clothes. Be gone now."

Monte found clean clothing laid out on the bed after his shower. He thought about trimming his beard as he looked at himself while dressing. But then he thought, *No, go for the slightly wild, disheveled look of a frantic, but fruitful search, the look of passionate madness to a cause.*

His food arrived during his appraisal of himself. Monte came out and stood quietly while a meal was laid out. The server did not stop, talk, or even acknowledge Monte. It was the studied subservience of the server that helped convince Monte he was in the right role to speak to the Council this night.

"Novice," Monte began, "thank you for the meal. You bring honor to the church."

"Thank you, Your Grace."

"I want you to do something for me. Go to the tech office and get me a computer." Monte wrote on a notepad sitting on the dresser. He handed the paper to the young server and said, "Tell the on-duty operator to send this to the Boston Nuncio."

The novice saw one word on the note. He turned on his heel and left.

Monte barely finished the light meal before the knock on the door revealed the same novice, bearing an opened laptop as if it were holy. Monte took it to the table and sat it before himself. The Nuncio was already on the screen. Monte made a ceremonious head bow.

"You have the attention of the Synod Montissio Favero. The Convocation has adjourned for the night, and they are most interested in hearing from you. Your name has drawn much attention and I might add, concern."

"There is much that the Conclave must know," Monte said, "and how to fit all what I have found into all that we know is the state of the world, and further suspect, within a short period of time, I believe, the church must act."

The screen dimmed and flickered as a new member of the Conclave joined. For a few moments, the flickering became static as the number of those most high within the hierarchy of the church became part of the virtual gathering. Then it settled to a soft glow. A face appeared. Monte had no idea who this was, but surmised it was a mere officialdom of the ruling body. A mere bailiff to announce the court. The face on the screen asked Monte to identify himself and swear to truthfulness. That being done, he asked Monte his role, title, and his time spent in service to the church. Monte began to recite his credentials.

One of the voices from the virtual inquisition abruptly changed the subject, demanding attention and answers in the tone of voice that told of authority. "Narrate the events, start where this is pertinent. I care little of your life's details and your summation of the experiential opinions. Speak."

There was a moment as Monte gathered his breath, focus and composure. He fell into the role he once thought was his own persona: haughty, arrogant, sophisticatedly superior. He began to speak.

"When returning from La Guardia, Sisker bade me go to Northampton instead of checking in to the Diocese. I—"

He was cut off by the voice again. "Why did he want to go there?"

"I do not know, he asked that I pick him up and during the ride back to Massachusetts he was mainly silent. He was reading, I did not disturb him, but answered his few questions."

"What was he reading?"

"I do not know what it was."

The angry voice exploded from the screen, "Then, please do explain what you might have observed about what the Suffragan Sischtre read."

"I am sorry, Your Grace. The document was loose leaf pages, the paper old and well thumbed through. A packet of photos and business correspondence was at his side and often, he would refer to the photos, turning them various ways. Eyeing them from different angles. He would find a landmark and mark the photo with his pen. He would read and refer to the statements, circle numbers, and then read again. Somewhere near the Connecticut Mass state line, above Hartford, he found some satisfaction in his investigation, and then gave the driver an address in Easthampton. We got off the interstate before he spoke with me."

"About what?" came a voice from the unseen assemblage.

"What did he say?" asked another.

"What was he going to do?" and the barrage of questions from the faceless voices rose to a fevered, chaotic interrogation.

Monte realized his power and opportunity in this exchange. He held all the details they wanted. He wanted to parley this advantage to a higher role than was his current station in life. He began more mysteriously, for here was the opening gambit that might lead to him assuming Sisker's role.

"He was very excited, but contained, restrained, elegantly anxious, you know how Sisker was."

"We all know," the first commanding voice returned. "Spare me your reminiscing. I want facts, actionable information about the situation that you, and only you, have." He spat the next words, "Since you alone have miraculously survived."

Monte bowed his head, as if chastised. "Apologies, well, we drove to a small mill town on the outskirts, called Easthampton."

Someone off screen guffawed and was shushed.

"We drove to a converted old mill, now trendy condos. Sisker gave me an apartment number to go and surveil. I went up and let myself in." That caused a snort from one of the nameless ones reaching out through the computer. Monte paused, but nothing more was forthcoming from that accusing disbelief of one of the Most High. He assumed a humbler pose, but forced, hoping those he now spoke with, the Ones Who Know Truth, would get the subtlety of his aspirations to Sisker's now open appointment.

Monte's smile was tight as he waited to be goaded into speech. If they had to ask, then the value of what Monte held for them was proven, yet, he could not be arrogant and allow them to lose face at his fault, so just as he was about to speak, one of them said, "Did you find anything there that indicated why Sisker would peruse through another's life surreptitiously? Why do you suspect he wanted you to look?"

"I met another person there, but he was not the man Sisker bade me inquire of. I—" he was interrupted.

"How do you know? Did you ask what his motive was for him to be there?"

"I spoke with this strange person. He said he was there to kill the man I had been asked to learn about. I knew he was there to lay in wait. He said as much."

"Bah, you believed the lying creature who was probably the intended target of the inquiry. Did that occur to you?"

A slight mental sidestep of that loaded question made Monte reply, "No, Highest, I gave my allegiance to the Suffragan Sisker. I acted as he instructed. Those instructions were that the abode should be gone over and the intended one's personal life dissected, but unmolested, that it, the site, might be more useful if undisturbed and unsuspected. The one who laid in wait was crude, unsophisticated, yet," he paused again, as if pondering, then seemed to come to some conclusion, "yet he had a force of intellect about himself. A very purposeful sort."

"Did Sisker trust you with a gem?" another asked.

It shook Monte's composure. He was far into the narration he filtered through his mind; his thoughts ran far ahead of the questions he hoped to answer with an adequately convincing truth. "Why, yes, My Lord, he did invite me into the first circle of his aspirants. I graciously took that and did feel closer to him than any others, for he told me I was the only one he invited personally, other leaders and elders sent the rest."

"He says that, or, said that to all sycophants that lust after his chair. Now, what did the jewel tell you?"

"The gem glowed, My Lord. It glowed green."

"Did it reach out to anything, or to that supposed murderer?"

"The gem glowed and pulsed, but I thought the randomness of the pulses were because of the closeness of the wealth of artifacts of this one's life. I felt little but static in the predator's purposeful thought. He had personal power, a station in life far from ordinary, but still too raw and primal to be the one I investigated. I have been with Sisker for almost a decade now, and I have hunted through other's possessions long enough under his tutelage to know what he finds interest in, and that which he doesn't. There was a novelty of finding this man there, preceding me. That he also hunted this one, though with a far more intense emotion and a much shallower appreciation for the one he hunted. I could—" He was cut off by a question from the Council.

"Explain what you were hunting for."

Another interjected before Monte could begin to answer the first question. The second, overriding question stopped Monte's mind again, but not because the story needed to be arranged, but because this answer was the key to his plan to rise in the order. He again pondered, his brow furrowed, not in theatrics, in genuine wonder at the opportunity.

He began, "My Lords, Your Grace, Highest Synod, I am going to lay bare my heart and mind to you. I believe Sisker gave me knowledge that I think, perhaps others of my peers, most others actually, do not have the privilege of being trusted to have. Sisker explained many things of our investigations and inquiries. He came to trust me with knowledge that would prepare me to continue his work."

"You are brash," said the voice which had asked the last question. "Are you actually doling out information as if to curry favors? Is this what you dare?" The words were loud, menacing, and had a tonal quality that was not from the sound system, but reached across space to assault his id.

"No," Monte answered hurriedly. "I am a servant of this order, no matter at what station I find my life. The point I make, Your Grace, is that I will tell you all I know about what transpired, from the point of view I have and the understanding of the events from the knowledge Sisker shared with me, and so, with all that, I hope I am not considered a fool, for I do know there are some who doubt the theories of Sisker. That Sisker never has found proof, he believed all the evidence pointed to an answer which some belittle and decry a heresy. And so, I throw myself at your feet, in service to this mission, this inquest, which I have come to also believe in, and trust there are answers to be found."

"Yes, yes, yes," said another voice, "Please, give us a narrative of the events, and limit your summaries lest we ask. Enough of the intellectual ass kissing. I am convinced you are guarding the truth, for what reason we shall soon find out, but nonetheless, do start talking."

Monte bowed his head deeply, hoping to seem chagrinned. He began to speak before he lifted his head.

"The man I encountered in the apartment I searched said his name was Leonard. He allowed me to know that revenge motivated his intended murder. He told me the one I investigated had killed his son. He called the one he sought, 'Grigori'."

"Grigori, Leonard?" asked one of the Council. "You said he seemed above the laic station in life?"

The screen dimmed as the Highest of the Conclave withdrew. Monte sat and waited till the electronic presence returned.

"Did the man seem out of time? Was he odd in any way that betrayed him not just as an interloper into that condo, but also into this era, this society, this, ah, age?"

"Yes," Monte answered. "Leonard seemed disheveled and unkempt, but not filthy, just dressed as one of our indigent homeless, in various clothing, nothing matching, but still the garments were decent. When we got to the casket facility, I gave him new clothes and sent a younger brother to run a bath."

"You took him with you? He came willingly? Where is he now?"

Monte realized at that moment his ascension to the position Sisker held was almost assured. The interest from the council members was palpable.

"I spoke with him and invited him to come to meet Sisker. He was hypervigilant, but he at last came to understand our objectives were different, but the focus the same. And I apparently convinced him he could find answers with us rather than sitting in an empty condo for a once in a lifetime occurrence, if that."

The screen was still a matte black, but shadows oscillated across as the voices spoke. The screen became illuminated, and then, a face appeared. A hawk nosed ascetic peered at him. It said, "Monte, pull your chair closer to us. I want to see your eyes as we talk about my next question."

Monte did move the heavy wooden chair up close. He seated himself, and the other on the screen likewise moved closer, the face filled the screen.

"Monte," it was said like a lash of words, "What do you know about what Sisker was searching for?"

"I had Sisker's company many times for weeks. I was his eyes, ears, and often his hands in any situation were mine. So, many times he would talk to me about those we sought knowledge of. He told me they were long lived humans, or incarnate spirits, which defy the rules of normality. He called them First Bornes. First Borne as in those first borne up from the beasts in the image of the creator. He told me the First Bornes had genetic material far closer to the original than humans are now. He felt these beings lived among us and influenced the turn of events. He told me how he had painstakingly compiled inventories of other inquiries. He had referenced and cross-referenced payments from trusts, to holdings, to deep corporate line items and the brokers and attorneys who processed all of this. He told me he had found a similarity in land holdings and a trust fund lawyer in Northampton. We were on our way there, to try and evaluate the depth of this lawyer's involvement. But the person, ah, Leonard, was convinced to come with us, stipulating that he was allowed a destination. Sisker agreed and the man, Leonard I mean, gave us an address to the very attorney's office we were scheduled to review. We drove to the bank, saying little. At the bank, Leonard just stared at the darkened building. Sisker convinced Leonard there were answers, but the cost would be that he, Leonard, had to answer Sisker's questions. I believe a mutual agreement was struck. We retired to the casket factory and tended to food and sleep."

A voice asked from behind the Minister, "What have you learned from the one you call Leonard?" the Minister turned toward the voice, away from the camera, and silenced the one who had spoken. "I am more interested in the timeline at the moment, my fellows. So," he said to Monte, "What was that fateful day of the explosion like?"

"I think everyone slept late that morning, and when I finished my morning devotionals, I did not find Sisker, but I did have Leonard ask for me. We ate a light lunch, and the escorts were requested to have Leonard attend Sisker's meeting. I was pointedly not invited. I returned to my room, read, and did some internet searches on some of the names and places that were mentioned in the slight bits of conversation I was privy to. It wasn't until evening fell that I became needed. Sisker had delivered a message via the escorts, to retrieve his valise from the car. We had left it in the trunk last night. I have trouble remembering coherently for a length of time now, my memories are not solid. I got to the church and—"

"You are leaving out many details, let's go back to the trunk of the car. What was in that valise?"

Monte said, "I was under the impression when I picked up Sisker at the hangar, that his purpose was to evaluate the attorney and that must mean the valise had files and photos and the usual evidentiary materials. I did not even wonder, and he did not offer to inform me, he rarely did. Your Grace, as I have attended Sisker for decades. I simply obeyed this enlightened one. I served him."

"Yes, yes, of course. Continue."

"The explosion is etched in slow motion into my memories. I was walking down the stairs from the loading dock. I was looking at the car, parked a way away from the building. The blast hit me first, knocking me to the pavement. The sound shockwave hurt my ears, and then the building erupted and I was flung about and pelted with debris. I remember getting to my feet and trying to run away but my ears didn't work, and the earth tilted crazily, though now I realize it was the inner ear trauma."

Monte was again stopped.

"Are you alright? Curiously, you seem fine tonight, a mere two days ago you were flung about on the blacktop, and deaf, or close to it. You were in a massive explosion. Now you hear just fine, and you have nary an abrasion on you. I find this interesting."

There was a pause, and it held the expectation of an answer. The pause forced Monte to be subservient, and explain, for the lack of explanation would destroy the trust he has thus far established.

"After cleaning up, resting, and being fed at the sanctuary, I do admit that the recovery and the lack of serious damage do seem remarkable. I thanked our Lord for saving me from that blast. I can only think that it was divine intervention when I fell to the ground, I was protected from most of the force by the stout foundation. That building is over 100 years old, and the stonework it rests on goes deep into the earth. The frost line there is eight feet or more, so the blast was mostly funneled upward, I can imagine Your Grace because the basements in this climate are dug deep."

"Yes," a voice said with scornful disbelief. "Yes, miraculous indeed. You seem to have more than your share of incredible coincidences and astounding occurrences."

Monte said nothing to that point.

"You left off at the explosion and then picked back up at the sanctuary. What are you editing out here, Monte?"

"There is a troubling lack of clear memories for this short time after the blast. I have regained some fleeting memories of walking past the hospital, and then down past the college. I remember that familiar landmark was comforting to my confused mind. My hearing started to quiet. It is strange, that the deafness wasn't silence but a massive roaring in my head that drowned out all sound. It quieted and my presence of mind returned as I came to the church. I was let in, found a way to report to you, the council was in session, so I cleaned myself up, ate and rested. The food and hot shower helped immensely. As I waited for my council with you, I could not sleep the whole day away. Though I was sore, the events of the past day swirled in my mind, and I could not rest. I had to find answers. I knew that the Synod would be unable to break to the outside world until this night, so I pursued more inquest, as I hope will honor my mentor Sisker's memory."

"How do you know he is dead?" another asked.

"I do not know that for sure. I surmised that none survived, but if there were survivors, did Leonard survive?"

"The questions are ours to ask," intoned a deep voice. "However, it is a good question, and I will need an answer to it. Did the one called Leonard survive?"

"I am not sure if he is alive, Your Grace."

"Tell me that he did not walk away from that explosion with you."

"He did not walk away from that explosion with me."

"Humph," was the only answer Monte got.

"Where is the valise of Sisker's, did you retrieve that?"

"No, the building exploded before I got to the car. Has the car been impounded from the site? Has the church reclaimed the vehicle?"

"The car has been retrieved from impound, though not from the casket factory. The vehicle was towed from an apartment building, and an old factory converted into condos, the same one you searched the night before. Our sources say a man tried to retrieve the car and was turned away by the officer posted to maintain the access to the site."

"Site of what?" asked Monte.

"A massive police action to try to apprehend a subject of the bombing, I am told. There were government agents arriving at the casket factory just as it exploded. They did not stay but regrouped and went to the condos. There they were stymied also; my informant tells me. They have been searching ever since. You made the list of people of interest out and about during this manhunt. Pray tell why you were going to the hill towns?"

"Yes," said another voice, "the report from the steward at the sanctuary said you wanted to go to your quarters and rest. He said you stated you knew where your car was and were going to get it. Is this true?"

"Yes, but at the same time, no. I did not know where my car was, I was having the embarrassing moments of forgetfulness and I did not want the one I had to impress to get cooperation from seeing me now as doddering. I told him that to save face, My Lord. I suppose that was being guilty of vanity, and I ask forgiveness."

"Whatever," said the Councilor. "Where did you go?"

"I called for a car and driver from the motor pool. I wanted to see a friend in Shelbourne Falls. He has a bookshop there, and it is his guilty pleasure and tax write off, I believe, to be seen as a struggling bookshop owner, but the titles he stocks, and reads, are not high-volume sales items: books on the mind and religion. But he is a neurochemist, and doctor of psychiatry. He is also a practicing hypnotist. I sought out his company to try to help me put the past day's events into perspective. I do not make a great deal out of our friendship, as his shop also entertains tourists and locals with crystals, alternative religion paraphernalia and the like. I do not have trouble with my faith, Your Grace, but while he is so accomplished, I keep my relationship with him less public as my station in the church demands. Yet he has given me keen insight at times, and he—"

The other cut in, demanding. "What is your relationship with him, intimate?"

"No, god, no. We are merely fellow seekers, though he takes a different path, he has provided me with key insights on occasion. I keep the sobriety of appearances that dictates that I do not entice others to believe I am less than a committed soul. The times I have stopped at his shop, and there were others present, I did get weird looks, as his shop deals in candles and tarot. I visit there infrequently."

"So how did you get to Brattleboro? When the checkpoint reported you and then turned you back, how did that transpire to bring you to Brattleboro?"

"I was escorted down 116 to the interstate. The escort abandoned us to join a chase which I surmised was still a continuation of the search for the bomber. My curiosity and my allegiance to Sisker made me bold, enough that I, too, rejoined the chase. Though I was not after the man, Leonard, I was still after answers.

"I thought I would seek council with any of those that can help me put these past days into order. I sought out my friend, a confidant I have known since childhood. I am not having a crisis of faith, for I give all affirmation to the Church. But this is an excitement of a new self-discovery laced with the emotional trauma of the events. For I feel I am at the cusp of great change of grand design. That is how I see the events as I have likewise searched for this Order and Synod. I did maneuver around some of the instructions I was given, but now that you know I brought this discovery directly to you, you can tell what I feel is the church's rightful place. That is, as Sisker has taught me, the church's rightful place is to be foremost in the heart and mind of the human body, the entire race, and to the generations that are to come."

Monte bowed low; he kept his head down in supplication.

There was a low murmuring in the background of the digital assemblage that did not even deign to hide the frank discussion.

Then one of the Council spoke. "Montissio, you are to assume the duties and responsibilities that once fell on Sisker, in addition to your obligations. This will include security clearance commensurate to Sisker's. All your inquests, findings, facts, and suppositions; in short, anything that makes you ponder, the life you lead, and the emotions that drive it are all dedicated to the church, which, for the purpose of clarity, is this Council. I, personally, am your mentor and the one to which you will answer. That is the obligation you take in this station. What say you?"

"The life I lead shall glorify the Church. Sisker will be honored by my continued pursuit, as I endeavor to find that which he sought. I am grateful for your continued mentorship. I am humbled by the gift of your time that you give. Thank you." Monte moved from his chair to kneel and again bowed his head. He said, "I accept the burden, in hopes that this life I dedicate is found in favor of the Lord."

"Then here is your task: what Sisker sought was not a what, but a who. A person who defies age and allegiance to any. That person is one of very few, which we; the church, and many others that serve humanity from high places call a First Borne. These First Borne, they are, we believe, genetically closer to the original, or if you will, have the purest DNA. That

DNA is without the multitude of mutations to those encoded threads of a human's subsequent… soul."

Monte returned to the chair and waited, holding back the impatient questions that now raged, armed with more details about the last few days. He must have been leaning closer to the screen, because it suddenly seemed more glaring, the white light had an almost burst of ultraviolet momentarily. It was a brightness that was off the scale of human perception, yet the sapience of the mind, the part that interprets events through the pineal gland sensed the harshness. He felt the light slam out at him, through his eyes, up against Monte's well-trained mind. He rebuffed the psychic invasion, and became defensive, tinged with paranoia. But the lancing probe was withdrawn almost instantaneously. It left no trace in his thoughts. Monte was surprised, unsure if he had even experienced that momentary mental dissection and assessment. His affect betrayed him to those watching.

The screen was once again, the same hue and brightness. A face coalesced. It had an age about it that was either premature or ancient, that didn't sit naturally on him. Borrowed, time delayed, artificially 'healthified.' Fortified. Made to work, forced to function. These thoughts raced through Monte's first assessment of the One Most High. As Monte pondered the reflexive thoughts about the Minister, the eyes of the image on the screen blazed a darkness, as if the pupils grew to an abysm, and revealed an inner blackness that spilled out, excessive for the body that contained it. That, too, damped so quickly that Monte again questioned his senses. If not for the previous days, he would have questioned his sanity at this event. But now he knew.

The dark ones have insinuated themselves at the highest reaches of his religion, he realized. The keepers of humanity's collective mental constructs of belief in eternity, creation, and the Creator, he realized, those keepers had betrayed the light of the world. Monte had to compose himself. He did so visibly, smoothing his vestments and then removing his glasses and rubbing his eyes. He took a deep breath, replaced his glasses, and sat up straighter.

"This is overwhelming, your Eminence," Monte inclined his head.

The face likewise inclined ever so slightly and replied, "More than you can suppose at the moment, I think." There was a sarcasm about that comment, as if an accusatory acknowledgement of duplicity that couldn't be proven. "I do not care, at the moment, what you don't know or understand. What I, and We of the Synod want to know is what you do know, and what of Sisker's tutelage has given you comprehension of these events."

"Sisker was guarded about all he sought, yet, yes, you are correct. I have discerned much and Sisker had deigned on many occasions to correct my erroneous conclusions. What I know is this: Sisker's pursuit was to find the trail of those who lived anonymous lives, with the ability to avoid even the deepest reaches of the bureaucracy, functioning outside the system, and even having knowledge that has not been collated by the church. Sisker mostly followed money, as far as I could tell, yet he asked for very odd assignments in his quest."

"Odd, how?" asked one of the Council.

"Places not connected with financial information, for instance, the Monestareo de Piedras. He took me to a ceremony at Xpu-ha in Mexico, which observed ancient Mayan rituals. He contacted me once from Tibet to send him information. I thought he was decompressing, unplugging from the world and yet couldn't disengage. I thought he should be resting if he was seeking out respite."

"And now, what do you make of this?"

"I was granted the opportunity to attend a lecture with him. The person speaking had a belief in, what he called, 'Thin Places.' Places where the overlay of reality on the universal construct was, as he put it, more transparent, thinner, more easily transgressed. I came to understand that some of our search was to discover these sites as foci of, maybe, possibly…" he stopped, and stumbled, not on his words, but on the concepts that were mere intuitions. Information without context that was hard to put to order. "I cannot explain, Your Grace."

"That is fine, I know that Sisker had a proclivity to search, and this was his to choose. Do tell us though, what had Sisker revealed about the relevance of the information he sought to the concern of our beliefs."

"Sisker a few times revealed he thought there were certain cabals, at the highest levels of all human endeavors, which controlled occurrences and extrapolation of the approved understanding of societal events to the masses. He thought there were those that controlled, and those that stymied. He thought there were those that urged humanity higher and those that pulled the baser instincts of man to the forefront, so humanity will fall. He stated he knew there were dark ones among us, and fervently searched for the one, he thought, was a being of the light, the ones he couldn't prove, the ones that left little evidence of their passing. He was, at times, maniacal about his research."

"And you, Monte, what do you feel about these secret regimes, these dark ones. Are they a concern to the church?"

"I learned to doubt less as I spent more time with Sisker. I learned to examine the impossible and find plausibility in the sometimes outrageously twisted plerophory of people and cultures. I might be so bold to think that the Most High has an interest in the devotion of Sisker's inquest. One such as my esteemed mentor, which professes a learned interest and concern in the particular thread of incongruity to the meaning of how we understand life, well, that inquiry should be satisfied, and the answer presented to Your Grace, with finality. I did not believe, but the untimely death of Sisker, does make me question whether an answer Sisker found was too dangerous to be known as a truth to those who rule the world, and he was eliminated."

"Who was targeted to be eliminated, Sisker, or the man he brought back to the offices?"

"I do not know, but feel it was deliberate. I was meant to be silenced also, or at least unconcerned that I would be collateral damage, and only by the Grace am I here. That reasoning emboldens me to ask to be allowed to continue to pry."

"Are you vindictive? Is this search a path to revenge?"

"I know that would be wrong, and that I have enough commitment to the teachings that I would resist that urge, but as a flawed creature, yes, that emotion resides in my heart. But vastly more emphatic is the drive to serve the Council, and ensure the teachings are accurately understood, and the people hear the message that this conclave finds is the true path."

"Good answer," said one of the lesser voices. Others murmured agreement. Monte knew he had played the hand convincingly.

A face momentarily escaped the bland background of the screen and the eyes twinkled darkly. Then it melded into the electronic landscape and was gone from the connection. Several others appeared, inspected him and a few asked a rhetorical question. Monte answered none of them until one voice said, "You are so guarded in your answers and your mind. Why?"

Monte had known this question, laced with distrust, was coming, yet it still shook him as he answered, as close to his heart as he could reveal.

"Council," Monte started with an air of humility, but tried to sound assuredly ambitious. "Your Grace, Your Assembled Eminence, if I aspire to high honors among you, then I cannot afford to be found a fool. I carefully weigh my thoughts because they become words and deed. I am a careful man with my thoughts, and beliefs, but the past few days have shaken those emotional and rational constructs to the very center of my being. I am also trying to find out what it all means, but I still look at these events from the learned teachings of those such as yourself. That is why, despite this confusion in my mind, and the fierce headache of my brain, I do submit to you," he paused, took a deep breath and then finished taking the chance of a lifetime.

He rose from the chair, bowed, and then kneeled. He said, "I do humbly request I be given the position of the Suffragan. Such a role as in which my mentor, Sisker, this Council, and serve humanity. My heart in these matters has always been clear, dedicated to the Church and this Council. I am in the position to continue Sisker's work and continue to serve you. The opportunity to find answers for you will assuage my soul also, for with your blessing, and to your honor, I will seek the answers with passion, and continue to be and grow, in my servitude to this Grand Council." He rose and stood expectantly, listening to the sudden onslaught of questions and background discussions.

There was a demanding, but muted tone that played and the once multitude of voices were now silent. The screen dimmed and went out. There was no presence in the room except for Monte. He continued to stand. The minutes stretched into muscle aching hours. He resisted all urges to leave or sit. He heard small noises in the hall, though thick walls and heavy doors hid most of the noises of the world beyond this room. He fantasized that he had been discovered and he would be taken away to one of those places he had witnessed in the casket factory and knew that doubtlessly, there must be more. He looked for holes in the story he had told so far but found none in his synopsis. He tried hard not to plan on what he might do should his request be honored. He tried hard not to give away what more he knew about the demons and the leaders who had succumbed to the dark allure of power. His memories were overpowering, and he found himself weeping quietly, his exhausted mind didn't even register that he had let his heart cry until the tears dripped to his cheek. He reached up and touched them and wiped them away. He started to think about what he would say to the empty room as he walked away, having started to consider a limit to his reverence for those he knew had him watched.

The entire Council was talking about him, he knew. He thought about announcing his thanks that the Council had heard him, and would respectfully await their decision, then walk to the door, but before his mind put that into action, the screen came back to life.

"Montissio Favero, we want more time to discuss who is best to fill the seat and role that was once Sisker's. However, while time passes, there is great deviousness afoot in the world. We, this Synod, want to know what this evil is that the souls of mankind now face. We, the Synod, are granting you the consideration to assume this position. You are not expected to be Sisker, but Monte, doing what Sisker did for us. The title is not yet yours. The opportunity to exercise the responsible power of this position is," he emphasized that word, "yours, temporarily. You will not only search as was Sisker's mandate, but you will also represent that office as a functionary of this Conclave. You will attend to Sisker's duties both with the intellectual curiosity required, and in person as the office requires you attend as a dignitary. Such invites will be forwarded to you as necessary."

Monte visibly sagged as the enormity of the words struck him. His mind became feverish with thoughts of how to answer, but he was spellbound by the awesomeness of what he did, and now could do. "Your Grace," he somehow how got out, then bowed his head. He sat.

The voices on the screen quieted to one. "Montissio Favero, you are at this moment granted the provisional privileges and authorization to use the title of Suffragan. You are dismissed now, go and rest, we will assign your duties later."

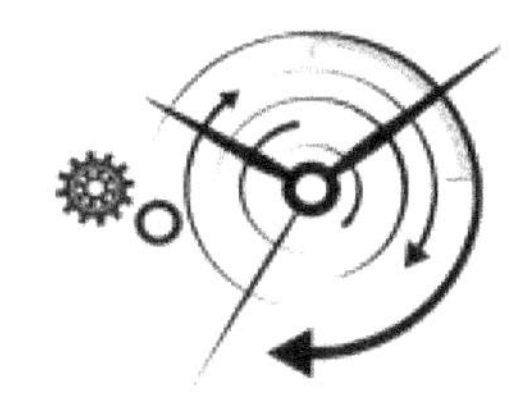

49 - Warned

The knock on his door was quiet. He answered and a meal was rolled in on a trolley. It was dished out to the side table for him, and then the servant merely stood waiting. Monte went to the table and a chair was pulled out for him, and he was seated. He studied the server in the mirror. He was older than any of the pages and initiates could possibly have been. The man was weathered and tan, not at all 'cleric-looking.'

"Who are you, my friend?" Monte asked quietly, sensing how the servant had a studied surreptitiousness about his presence.

The man went about with his attention to the task of serving the meal, noisily removing roaster covers, clattering silverware, and putting a portion on a plate for Monte. All the while, he spoke in a low voice.

"I am trusted by the First Secretary to the Council member, Gavreen. I am to tell you this; and you must listen while you eat, for you are being watched. They will see nothing other than a servant and a welcome repast for newly appointed Suffragan."

Monte tasted the food, and it was delicious, so he had no problem consuming the meal while he listened.

"You understand now, the infestation of this world even touches the church, even at the highest levels, Sisker's level, and most probably beyond. These dark ones are planning the ultimate betrayal of the Masters. There is a most horrific Rite planned. It will be revolting to the nature of mankind and an abomination to the Ones Who Dwell in Eternity. All across this world there will be celebrations of the darkness of human nature, fueled by depravity.

"The demons are going to usurp the ceremony at the time of opening from the owners of this world, we believe. The demons have convinced the ones who rule to open a portal; a *Syne*, into the flow of time, but in reality, they, the demons, will rend a vicious ragged hole in the fabric of the universe, deliberately with damage and destruction fueling their attempt to move demon-kind into eternity.

"By now, you know there are those like Sisker, who have tasted the power of, and fallen in league with the dark forces. So surely you cannot imagine you are the first or only one to suspect or even have proof. I am one of those people. It is also necessary to remember that at all times, the dark ones either know, or suspect, any and everyone of working against them. You are a suspect now. You must remain ever vigilant that you are not exposed, for that you will be killed. Or worse."

Monte cut his food carefully, taking time to say in a low voice, "I know well that they can conjure fates worth than death. I saw the demons, and I saw the angel and met the prophet, so I have not a doubt in my soul. I am glad to find there are other skeptics. Like me."

" I have a friend, a baker, from Brattleboro that is of the same ilk," said Monte.

He was surprised when the man servant asked, "Elias?"

"Why yes, you know him?"

"Yes, the friends you met are ready to accept what you have told them. They have been active for some time now, but aimless. You will change that."

The man removed dishes, served dessert and coffee, and said, sotto voice, "This late evening, Sisker was to be escorted to a ceremony where those that rule will crack open time and send an agent back. We fear that if they are allowed to send this one back, the amount of change to the social fabric and course of events will be irreparable, and the humans, us, our kind will be lost forever to the yoke of servitude to the ones that have bargained with the darkness. The ceremony is tonight. Sisker had an invitation, and now, the ones who test you expect you to go in his stead. I know there is great danger there; you must not attend. Excuse yourself in any way you find possible. If you attend, you will be killed."

He cleared the table and left a single fresh napkin. It had numbers written on it, but I knew not to pick it up, question it, or even acknowledge it. I sat back as he prepared to leave. He backed out of the door, pulling the trolly and making long eye contact with me. 'Be careful' he mouthed and was gone. The door closed gently behind him.

Monte lay resting and was woken by a quiet rap on the door. The page handed him a computer case, and said, "This was returned to you by Father Samuel early this morning. He left it in my hands to get to you, no one else, he said."

"Thank you, I did sign for it, and I may have had to pay for it should I lose it. Father Samuel is most kind, ask him in."

The page said, "Father Samuel left just after trusting it to me."

"Then thank you just the same." Monte took the case, and theatrically stifled an epic yawn. The page retreated after taking the hint.

He opened the case, thinking to erase everything on it, but was surprised to find it was not the church's computer he signed out. It was sleek, new, and a light blinked insistently. He opened the laptop.

Elias's face stared out. "Hello, friend. We have decided to accept what you say and provide what support we may."

Monte's smile came back to Elias in high definition. "Wonderful. Stay away from events. There is an unimaginable amount of evil I have discovered. Stay close to families my friend. I have been warned to ignore at all costs an invite for which it was insinuated I was ordered to attend. I think that I will avoid any encounters for a while."

"Thank you for passing it on. I will have everyone share it in every media there is available. What will those that rule say about you ignoring a summons?"

"I will continue to convalesce and shall inadvertently sleep right through the day into the night. And for you and your, our friends, stay obscure. Tell everyone to believe."

"Believe in what Monte?"

"Spinoza's God."

50 - Gathering

The drums could be felt throughout the canyon. The glass in the elegant, modern building shook at a crescendo. A horn sounded, a single note, a drawn-out primal sound. Then the guests were allowed to pass the armed guards replete with sabers, very functional looking three-foot blades. The guests made a raucous, but orderly procession down the carefully laid stone path that led to a huge pavilion before the edifice that blended into the stone and juniper-strewn desert. The building was magnificent in the high rock walls that literally ended inside the glass. The spacious architecture merely framed an entrance to a cavern, which lead down into the earth.

The building was down low in the canyon end, where the foothills started up to the sheer cliffs. The roof of the building resembled the desert from the air. It was curiously designed, with great gaping openings at the eaves. Sunset colored the sky brilliant pastels, but none of the procession saw the spectacle. The line of beings followed the twisting channels deep into the earth. At one particular grotto, the line stopped. The hush fell over the crowd as the air was suddenly rent with screeching and twisting flapping bats. Millions of them. They darkened the tunnel and boiled out of the openings in the building's eaves. The crowd screamed in delight. As the last of the creatures fled the dark recesses of the cavern, the throngs replaced them, and continued downward.

51 - Gathering

In a remote Swiss village, the assembled crowds in the streets and small inns were intense, reserved, yet very sensually driven. Drunk on their elite positions in society, drunk with power, knowledge, and drunk on the vast amounts of alcohol of the finest years. They were the elites of science who knew of the machine deep below the roots of the mountain.

Carved out of solid granite was the chamber for the smallest, and still the most powerful, cyclotron ever built. The atom smasher was going to fire tonight. It had been charging for days as the speed had been gradually brought up to accelerate particles to near light speed. The charging of the apparatus always attracted the neuronauts: people who explored thought, and the limits of the mind, and hoped to discern its creation. The machine's energy charged the ground on which the village stood.

People came when they knew the machine would be online, just for the physical experience of the energy that escaped, or maybe the cosmic forces that were drawn into the earth and atmosphere of the tiny town. They said it was a physical sensation. It was said to be a sensual experience, hence the hedonists among the elite would be found here at this time too. And the mystics, who claimed the machine caused the 'god-force' that flowed through their minds. Yet they were all of the same ilk. Dark soul fires raged in the throng. Alcohol made the voices raucous and bold. Psychotropics lowered inhibitions.

The crowds packed the streets, people spilling in and out of the cafes, bars, and inns were vibrantly alive as they moved almost as a single organism. There came a drum noise at the cavern entrance. Only those closest heard it, but the silence flowed back over the masses of people in a wave. They quieted but did not calm. They shuffled, swayed, and entangled with each other as they moved towards the carved granite portal. People came out of the buildings and joined the crush of bodies. The throngs filed into the adit, blasted out of the imposing craigs. The multitudes filed down into the tunnel, into the great recess deep below the earth. It took hours for the passage to the depths. The deep bass drums pulled them along, their steps fell in time. Inexorably, the tunnel was filled, yet the procession continued. There was no place to really go, so the movement packed bodies tighter and tighter against one another.

Hearts began to beat in unison to the drum. The first drum was joined by several others, and then a stringed instrument sang a deep-noted summons. The crush of people began to flow down the ramp that curved down, into the rock. The man-made cavern was a gallery open to the target end of the machine. The immense room was soon full, then packed to a condensed mass of flesh, then to a solid mass of enraptured humanity, undulating to the weird music of circuits and precision machinery.

52 - Gathering

A yacht came gliding to a mooring, alongside several others. Small motorboats ferried people to the quay at the mouth of the cave. The occupants disembarked and followed a path carved into the side of the cliff. The stone path wove along the blue ponds that were sheltered from the waves. The water was placid, the lights were crude torches set into the iron wall sconces. The path wound deep into the earth. The flaming torches grew fewer and farther between. Splotches of darkness grew. The dimly lit passage flared dark demon fires from within the procession. A throbbing grew, but so low it was like an immense stone ram, hung on a timber frame, being swung at the rock walls. It was such a powerful vibration, it caused ripples on the surface of the alkaline pools. Crystals knocked off the walls reflected the flickering torchlight that only described more shadows. Fires began to smoke more; the haze was hallucinogenic. Clothes were discarded as the heat and the pressure in the depths grew. The smashing of stone on stone seemed to draw out a rhythm which the myriad of voices joined in a low song. Primal. The chanting line continued down into the depths.

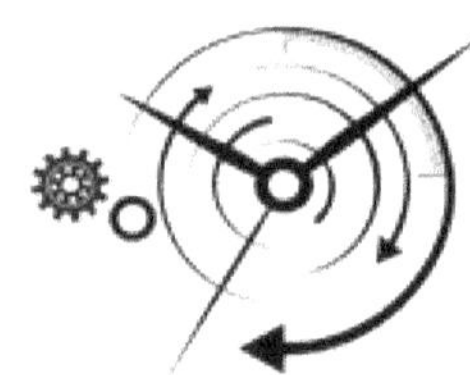

53 - The Procession

The darkened skyscraper was a needle that pierced the moonless sky. A line of limos off-loaded people in formal, bejeweled attire. They weren't interested in the dizzying heights or the grand view from the tallest floors of the tower. They were single-mindedly passionate about the basement, then the sub-basement, and then below that to the floors that held all the mechanicals of the huge edifice. The trek downward continued below the level of the footings of the huge building.

A propped open iron door revealed a steep set of stairs carved into the rock. The landing of those stairs opened onto a vast cavern, where a thunderous crowd was partying. There was a lava vent that superheated the air. The closely gathered bodies were slick with sweat and the elegant clothes were soon drenched, then shed.

There was a dais at the far end of the chamber, behind the lava vent. A channel from the vent to the center of the dais was carved into the basalt. A flood gate of dark stone kept the liquid rock from flowing up to the stage and into the pit in front of the lectern and the few rows of seats, likewise carved into the living stone of the world. One of the beings in a robe and hood gave a mere annoyed flicker of a hand motion and the stone gate was wrenched free. Lava slowly, inexorably filled the channel and emptied into the basin. The light from the pool of molten rock was a deep incandescent red. It highlighted the craggy brows and furrowed eyes of Minister Sheer, who sat directly in front of the scorching lava, seemingly unaffected. He looked out to the throng gathered for the Procession.

The scene was not as much a party, but rather felt like fervent worship. Music blared, and laser strobes flickered at varying rates and colors. Voices rose and fell in crescendos of ecstasy and orgasm. A large, skin envelope was thrown onto the open lava. The package of herbs and volatile oils exploded into a fierce flare; that singular clap of sound cut through all the laughter, screams, moans, and song. The people became more frenzied, but quieter. The music, the lasers, and the voices all synchronized into a low, solemn chant.

The edge of the crowd coalesced into a line of gyrating bodies that made their way along the far wall. The Procession had begun.

The potions thrown into the lava created a haze in the air. The line of supplicants climbed the stairs, paid honors and obescience to those few that sat. The gifts each of them brought were thrown into the lava pit.

The gifts they all brought were the bones of the innocent. They had stolen the lives and futures of the innocents, the bodies, organs, and genes of the innocents, and now they stole their souls, their last vestiges of a being sacrificed to the Bone Fire. The accumulated skeletons soon ignited to burn with unholy, sooty flames. The Bone Fire.

The Bone Fire in the pit would receive the sacrifices and fuel the spell that would allow Transveho. The Syne thus created would open to a time gone past, and one of the agents of the Rulers of the World would get into the Syne, or more accurately, jump off our time into time's wake. None would ever know him or her ever again, for as soon as the agent stepped through the Syne, they ceased to exist except in the past.

The Bone Fire raged and seemed to excite the lava in the pit. Heated globules of molten stone and ash belched occasionally. All those that had been in the Procession shrank back and gyrated off the dais. The sinuous movement of limbs and swaying, an undulating parade of bodies that once again became a mass on the huge cavern floor.

Lasers flashed faster and faster, the music reached a screeching, howling quality; primal, anguished and impotently arrogant about their mortality. It was a wallowing in the sensual and the abdication of reason and enlightenment. It was a frightful loss of rationality and a descent into the atheist's hell of the basest expression of the frantic need to experience the pleasures of a fleeting corporeal existence, believing this being their sole incarnation. There was the guilty hubris of daring to believe that one could deny mortality. It was a lucid psychosis, an intellect aware that it was a creation, and yet, with insolent gestalt denied that fact, reached out to claim godhood.

An indent was created at the extreme far edge of the crowd. The indentation grew to a path that opened in the mass of flesh and demons. The parting continued as a lone figure led a small entourage bearing a crude litter through the crowd. The bodies closed in behind and spread away in front, as if peristalsis. It was a gruesome birth canal, pulsing through the near maniacal assemblage of people that had pushed their minds and bodies right to the edge of sanity and exhaustion. The eruption thrust the group right up to the dais. The bodies closed in behind again. Salyette stood at the foot of the stairs that led to the dais, and humbly bowed to the Minister, the Highest of those who owned the world.

The Minister rose and spread his arms wide and high. The music vanished; the lights blinked out. The cavern was pitch black except for the glow of the lava. The red light silhouetted the Minister. He pointed one finger at Salyette. A vicious laser strobe highlighted Salyette alone, the rest of the crowd lost to shadows.

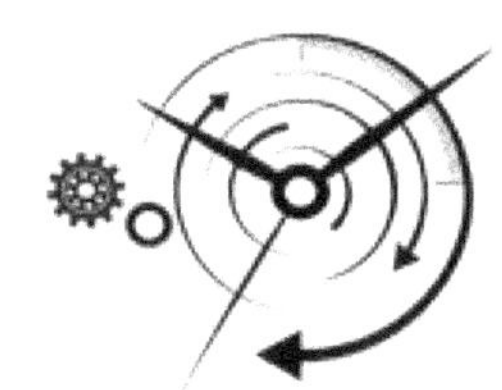

54 - Leonard

I was brought in by stretcher, rough boards, and leather plaits with which I was tied by the wrist and ankles. The bearers were gyrating, undulating unconsciously to the music, the chants, and the effects of psychotropic haze from the potions thrown on the Bone Fire. I was propped against a stone outcropping, painfully close to the blazing heat of the lava pit and the Bone Fire, still secured to the litter. The Bone Fire snapped and popped as marrow melted, and bones of the innocents shattered and turned to ash.

At a signal from the Minister, acolytes, male and female, nude and adorned with hieroglyphic tattoos and deliberately carved scars formed a line to dance a fantastic choreography of depravity around the Bone Fire. It was as if all were a single organism, an entity united. It was not the expansion of the mind and soul that achieves connectedness, for it focused on not a higher ideal or standard of being, but rather an arrogant climb up out of nothing and to claim a right, a place in the eternity.

The Bone Fire now screeched with heat and the anguish and mortal sin of the lives stolen and squandered.

Their screeching chants were taken up by the throng on the dais, and then, by every voice in the massive hall.

The dancers writhed and at times fell prostrate to be trampled upon by the others till they managed to rise again. The cavern grew brighter as the Bone Fire responded to their urgings. The Bone Fire gave off a fierce mineral glare that made it hard to look directly into the flames. Tongues of the phlogiston emerged from the Bone Fire, elemental, a chaotic rainbow focused just in front of the lava pit. It was fed by the Bone Fire.

The Minister intoned arcane words, his voice interrupting the near universal chanting of the multitude in the chamber. He raised his arms high, urging the Bone Fire even brighter, harsher, and now hungrier. He pulled a long dagger from a sash about his robe and stepped up to the line of dancers.

He spoke the ritual of the opening of the Syne, and then stabbed the random dancer who happened to cross his path at that moment. He shoved the still bleeding body into the Bone Fire. The mineral brilliance of the conflagration exploded and seared everyone's eyes. That light left an ultraviolet negative image in every mind present. The Syne was now a fluctuating locus that twisted time and space in front of the Bone Fire.

The Minister handed the bloody dagger to the next convoluting dancer that passed him, who immediately thrust it into another's chest. The person fell to the stone floor and the others rushed to retrieve the dagger. The one who first gained control of it slashed themselves, while the others shoved and kicked the fallen one into the pit. Others crowded about the knife wielder, to be slashed, stabbed, and mutilated. The fallen ones were thrown unceremoniously into the Bone Fire. The devouring flame elementals fueled the fervor of the assemblage and the intensity of the Syne.

A ripping noise unlike anything heard in the natural world cut across all ears, rendering the music moot, the now hoarse voices unheeded. Tongues of flame from the pit bent towards the Syne, forcing themselves into the center of the disturbance in the fabric of time. More bodies fell into the pit. The ferocity of the slashing knife intensified. The savagery spilled over to the masses. Cruel, razor-sharp blades were distributed to the ones that were closest to the low dais. The intensity of the madness, the cruelness and the utter barbarity rose to a crescendo. The virulence of the depravity swept through the crowd. Naked, bleeding people swarmed to the stage, and threw themselves into the now roaring Bone Fire.

The Syne ripped open the flow of time. Iridescent layers and waves of the past years, ages and eras were a torrent of events I could not focus on in the brittle light bending inward to the Syne. The effluence of lives and words, speeches, laughter, anguished cries were a cacophony that assailed my ears. I felt myself losing any sense of reality, purpose, or sense of time as I stared horrified into that morass of the detritus of the souls that had gone before into the past.

Saind stood nearby. I saw that, though he, or it, was in a different body, this time female. I saw the mannerisms, the petulant way he wore the flesh he had no doubt stolen, down to the eyes. Not expressionless, but the depth of the emptiness behind the pupils. He cast those eyes upon me a moment as I was studying him, and he probed into my mind when he caught my gaze. He smiled and sneered. His satisfaction oozed as he realized who I was. With a saunter that spoke of a realized opportunity for a coerced atonement of a hated, personal transgression, a nemesis, he came to me, undulating to the music wearing the banker's body. She was lascivious to me as the music throbbed and screamed, the lights pulsed, and the gestalt ebbed and flowed to ever higher heights of ecstasy and orgy.

Saind came to stand close, provocatively, but enticing only with malice. I could see in him that the only question was how he would enjoy my death. She spoke into my ear, head to my cheek, neck in sinuous contact with mine.

"Hello, King Leonard. I did not till now, recognize you. I think your surprise appearance will only fuel my departure. I have told them, and they listened, that the honor might be mine, if they allowed, but the power to be gained from your death in the Bone Fire could be theirs. The hatred they have for you stupefies them, for they traded all for nothing. You will see. The last moments of your life will be the beginning of mine. I will tip this altar right into the fire in a few turns of the glass; an hour, at most, in terms you understand. Then, oh my." She closed her eyes and anticipated the coming events with a lustful shiver of desire. "Oh," she said again, "oh you will go to the flames knowing that with your death, I will ask the demons of this world to revolt. Your kind will not even exist in the subservience the Masters of this World have planned for your race. No, you will be extinguished painfully, you are soon to be extinct in this universe."

"What of the one who loaned you this body, the one who is your earthly love? Will that one survive?" I asked.

"I do not know," said the Saind portion of the dichotomous being, and the subjugated Salyette rebelled, realizing what Saind had just said. The Saind/Salyette creature before me trembled, seized, and with a throaty roar shook itself like an animal. The face that came to prominence had the expressions of Saind's personae.

The Saind/Salyette creature spoke to the air, spoke to himself, to the now divided selves. "I have been betrayed by many, and this time I do as I will, thanks to the angel that showed me that power. I do claim that right, as that one who would not share his name said I may. I lay claim to choose, and I have chosen to leave, and I have chosen to not care about humanity's existence. I have taken many lives, and to take all the rest is a mere degree in my culpability for your demise."

The Saind personae continued in control, but now spoke to me. "However, the one who is with me is going to take that same leap of faith, or a lover's fate, if you will. I chose to try to be free, no matter the cost to me, or even to her. She," the face morphed into Saylette's, complete with her voice, "and I choose to follow, at my peril, wanting nothing more than to free him."

Salyette's features stayed, but the voice was Saind. "Now, if you will excuse me." She reached out to caress my face. I moved away with disgust. She pointed a single digit's nail at me, then raked a slash across my cheek, across my lower lip. The laughter that came from the thing's throat was garbled by many, long dead voices, and a strange bi-genderness to the actual, corporal body. She danced to the hellish music in a manner that seemed she was trying on the body, sensually. She went and knelt at the Minister's feet.

"Minister, as the newest member of your subserviants, I humbly request to be your instrument of opening the Syne. I would hurl the First Borne into the Bone Fire as you incantate. I will watch from my deceitful lover's eyes the glory of your agent's Transveho, at least I will watch that one's departure into the past. I sense the magnitude of the adjustment you will bring about, and I will swear—"

Saind was cut off, silenced with a wave of the old one's hand. "Silence, owned one. You will throw that one into the Bone Fire for me, as I would have had you do anyway, but after I have you take his heart from his chest. You will kill him for me."

"But Sire, Master, Minister," Saind actually stammered. "The power of the Bone Fire is best at the recalescence. The life of this one will open the Syne far back, farther than you hoped for. Your consignee will effect great changes that will so enhance you. To kill him first, I do not understand."

"I want this one dead. Dead before my eyes, dead that I no longer have to be concerned with this pathetic spark of genetics. Dead, Dead, DEAD! I demand it of you!"

"As you will it, so be it," said Saind.

"Go stand ready, I shall open the Syne. This is the seventeenth Syne I have opened. It is a prime year. Here, take my knife," the Minister said and handed it to Saind, blade first. Saind took it and had to struggle to take if from grasp of the Minister. Blood leaked from Saind's closed fist as he pulled. The Minister sneered and released the hilt. Then forced Saind's eyes down in subservience and turned his back to the creature.

Saind held the knife in his bloodied hand high. Turning to the crowd he bellowed, "*Quam celerrime!*" An open-ended phrase purposely left unfinished. It meant '*as soon as…*' The Minister spun about, and Saind, mockingly humble, bent to a knee, spread his arms wide and bowed his head.

The assemblage roared. Demons in usurped bodies intoxicated by the anticipated carnage.

The Minister felt these were his accolades coming from the thousands of human and demon throats. The Minister raised his arms high, and the lights intensified to searing, and the music assailed the mind. The pulsing sound was visceral, it demanded the heart syncopate. There were now dead among the crowd: exhaustion and murder. The masses were oblivious to any conscious thought other than the sensuality of the heat, noise, light, and friction of the contact between so many nude bodies.

I felt the madness and the insanity grow to a fevered pitch and then beyond.

The Minister pointed to the Bone Fire, said strange words in a long-forgotten tongue. His acolytes came forward with the largest offering of the innocents for the Bone Fire. They were unceremonious about dumping the contents of the rude skin sacks into the roaring Bone Fire.

He turned to the crowd, gathered his shoulders, and thrust his open palms to the sky and spoke again. Somewhere, in a large metropolitan center high above the cavern, an extremely large bomb went off at the packed stadium of a sporting event. The carnage was instantaneous and immense.

He gestured again, more sacks were emptied onto the Bone Fire, and he voiced another arcane command.

A war deliberately erupted on a long-disputed border between purposefully diametrically opposed religious cultures. The embers of terror and hate that had been carefully banked were now fanned into a holocaust.

More bones, more demonic words and plagues became startlingly more virulent, and the dead fell as they walked. The stench spread rapidly, on planes, ships, in cities and along the tendrils of the highways. Water became unpotable and food rotted.

The Minister laughed and spoke rapidly, opening the Syne. The death and destruction of the war, the hatred of the foes, and those who were now afraid of every other being as being unclean with the sickness, cast a dark shadow over the world. Not the blocking of the light, but of a dark, malevolent presence acquiring permanence. The fear grew, death rained down like the cruel munitions in the war. The music in the cavern pulsed ever more gruesomely and the twisted adulation towards the Minister was universal in that cavern, and in so many other caverns and grottos where the dark Rites had built the same Bone Fires and spoke the same rituals. The web of evil spread out beneath the planet's surface, connecting these unholy Rites along the ley lines of power.

The Minister bellowed a single word. It reverberated, palpably off my heart, around, and ever again echoing against the rock walls. The sound solidified at the edge of the now massive conflagration of the Bone Fire. The Bone Fire was hotter than the lava that kindled it. I could feel the odd twisting of space at the Syne forming near me in the inferno of the Bone Fire. The eye of the raging firestorm slowed its ephemeral cycling to attain permanence.

The Syne had been opened.

The Minister's surrogate past-self stepped up, waiting for the customary ceremony and I believe, gathering his will to do this self-mortification that another might solely reap the rewards.

Suddenly, curiously, the air began to grow colder, thicker. Saind and Salyette, as one, moved toward the Syne, trying for their opportunity to be the sole being allowed Transveho.

The Minister moved to take a ceremonial kiss from his surrogate. The Syne was a bright solid hole made of light. A hole that led to the past, through the fabric of time. The aperture's periodicity flashed through the spectrum and gained a white and then an invisible outpouring of access to a past reality, it seemed. The Syne was opened, the agent of hell would Transveho. I leaned forward against my bonds, caught up in the drama of this fight over eternity.

Saind stepped up to me, said *"Nunc aut numquam*; now or never,"* then plunged the knife into my chest. Demons erupted murderously in the crowd; the usurpation had begun. Masses of dark creatures left the bodies they wore, and either began killing those of the human race, or simply leaving the borrowed body to wither in place, the husk soon trampled in the frenzy.

The undulations of the masses became slowed and languid, and the voices and the music slowed to a deep garble. The blazing Bone Fire grew cold, while the flames—though still raging—became blue and translucent. The atmosphere in the cavern turned to the consistency of honey. Strobes flickered at longer intervals of on and off.

Saind/Salyette leaped towards the Syne. The Minister saw the movement, realized the betrayal, and bellowed a long slow, deep, "NO!" then moved to intercept Saind/Salyette, who was off the floor, in mid-leap. Time grew icy cold, deep absolute zero cold and stopped.

Parys stepped into being in the cavern, just as if I might enter a room. "Hello, Leonard," the being I now knew was an angel said. "Why are you tied to that frame still?" In that instant, I wasn't. As I crumpled, he caught me. I smiled because I knew I could have misbelieved that freedom for myself long ago, but I had trusted him to go along with this death-defying act of being the bait.

"Do not believe you are dying, Leonard. Misbelieve that blade in your chest has killed you. You do not have to believe their version of your life."

I misbelieved and the knife fell and shattered on the stone floor. I had felt the curious pull of ineffective death, and marveled that I now stood strong in his grasp. I have been overwhelmed and had begun to succumb to the pull of mortality again. Doubt had been allowed consideration, but now that Parys had arrived, I felt an anxious anticipation of what would happen next on this cosmic, theological stage.

Parys said, "Leonard, now is the one thing I must ask, that you trust me, without an explanation. You must step into the Syne ahead of any of these creatures. You must be the one that saves humanity at this point. There are no words that can be said about why I ask you to be the instrument of those who dwell in Eternity. Do this now, while I hold us out of the time stream. Please do hurry though, this is not an infinite pause I create. I tell you; this is a struggle I cannot maintain for long."

"Will I ever see you again?" I asked.

He said, "No." Then added with a slight smile, "But there will be others, if you look for them, and listen."

I set my mind and set firm features on my face. "I have been granted among the rarest of miracles, to have met you. I cannot say how grand I feel that I know the surety of the Deities, of God, and of Christ, of Buddha, of Allah, all those messengers. I do not know how to express what you, or they are."

"Then tell everyone that we are, the ones who beckon you toward eternity are real. The invitation is sincere. Simply tell people to allow the belief that we wish to have your race join us in eternity."

I nodded, humbled by this onus. I stepped to the Syne, and as I took that final step, I felt his hand on my shoulder. I felt his calm power ease my heart and mind. I fell into an exact moment, that, in another time, I just became startlingly awake.

Time blurred into motion again, just as Leonard disappeared into the Syne. Saind/Salyette continued their mid-air leap, only to be tackled unceremoniously to the rough cavern floor near the edge of the Bone Fire.

The Syne slammed closed behind Leonard. The percussion was merciless. It pulverized bodies and knocked stalagmites from the cavern vault. The lava that was held back from the vent by the will of the dark ones bugled against the ruined spell cast by the minions of the owners of the world.

The Minister and Saind/Salyette fought. Earthquakes tipped the floor wildly. Saind/Salyette and the Minister fell again in a tangle, and slid towards the Bone Fire, which was now raging out of control; plasma hot, melting the edges of the containment pit and starting to liquify the rock dais.

The angel Parys put his hands right into the Bone Fire. He reached and probed and gathered, then removed one hand, and reached to the heavens with it. He spoke and lifted his face skyward, through the layers of rock and soil. His countenance told that his mind reached the sky, then to the space beyond and then past that boundary, to eternity. There was an exodus, a flood of tortured souls released from the hell of the Bone Fire, through him. The outward flow of rescued souls wreaked carnage on the evil cast by the Bone Fire, still raging, but consuming only itself, hate consuming hate. The demonic reality in the cavern began to crumble. The vile control lost permanence. The spasms shook the cavern.

Parys stood easily apart from the grand mal seizure of this reality. He smiled, extended his arms, and stretched. He crossed his arms and slid his hands down each arm, reveling for the last few moments of his incarnation. The light emanating from him began to dim, as if the source of the light was so very far away and moving ever further. As he dimmed to nothingness, and just before he winked out of existence, he gave the wrestling, struggling Saind/Salyette and the Minister a shove over the edge of the pit into the Bone Fire. And then, he was gone.

The Bone Fire exploded as the two fell in. All control of that evil chaos was shattered. The vent of lava ruptured and flooded the cavern. The sudden release triggered another spasm of the earth, and the volcano belched a great underground lava flume. The cavern filled with lava, accompanied by the screams of those who were immolated.

Caverns around the world filled as volcanoes spewed lava. Eruptions caused deep caverns to collapse and bury those humans and demons alike under untold, and unknowable tons of rock and earth. The eruptions triggered tidal waves that flooded the caverns entered by the sea. The death of that great mass of evil was palpable.

The Earth shook.

Around the world, almost as one, people stood still. Almost to the one, except for possibly a babe that cried, people were silent as they felt the great weight lifted from their hearts and minds. The darkness vanished as if chased by the mad rumbles of the world. The sun shone clear and bright as it broke over the horizon.

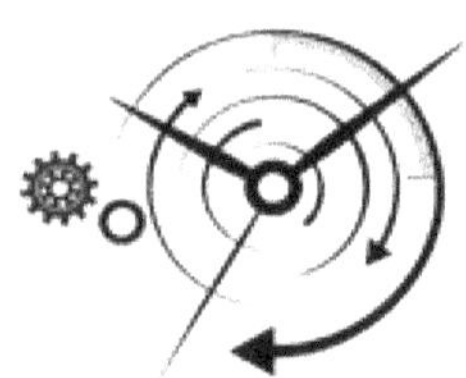

55 - Rebeginning

In my dream, I was falling from an incredible, even undefinable height, or distance, with no sense of orientation. My body was infinitely heavy, and infinitesimally small. Seconds were momentarily terrifying centuries. And then I awoke with a start, a jerk of my anatomical body pulling my ephemeral soul back in, or as if me, as a sentient soul, deliberately but unconsciously coalesced a body for myself.

I sprang out of the bed. Paced and went around and sat on the bed next to my wife. I stroked her hand and face and woke her. I said, "I have just had the most fantastic dream, or I lived another life this past night, and I brought back some memories that are not yet made. I must tell you, and I will tell you all, I will answer your every question, but for now, you must act, as I need to thwart a betrayal. I need you to be safe, my love."

A knock sounded, and the guard spoke. "Sir, Grand Advisor Grigori requests to enter."

I turned to Deborah and said, "No time to dress in more than your robe. Go to General Mattakat. Tell his officer on duty to present you to the general at once, on my order. Tell the general one word: 'Axis.' Understand, 'Axis.' Then gather our sons. Go to the safe room. His men will escort you. Open for no one besides the general or me."

The knock again sounded, more insistently. The guard questioned softly, "Sir?"

"Allow the Grand Advisor entrance," I said to the guard, then kissed my wife and told her, "Go."

Grigori came in as she was swirling a robe about her body. He realized he was staring as he felt the weight of my stare.

There was a brazen, momentary riposte challenging me, and then the personae of the obsequious Grand Advisor was back.

He bowed his head and studied the carpet as my wife walked past.

His subservience oozed from him, but now, armed with the knowledge from my dream, his servility seemed parasitic. I studied him anew.

"A beautiful woman, no?" I asked him deliberately, hoping his conundrum would buy me time. I pondered and desperately planned my next hour. I held my fate in my hands.

"I am not worthy of answering, my Sire. I, I, I—" he stammered and I interrupted him.

"You interrupted. A time to…?" Again, an emotionally baited ploy for more time.

His glance at me was both curious and betrayed an understanding of the gambit I played. His head rose and he said, unctuously, "I can delay the event. My men can wait. Or, Sire, I can cancel the event, even though the people flock along the way of your arrival."

As he played on my baser emotions of vanity and pride, I responded in kind, but now felt a kind of knife edge to the throat, awareness of the impending threat.

"No, Grigori, I am enjoying my family too much these days. I have so appreciated that you have taken the mundane tasks of governing upon yourself to give me this time, but now, once again, you are right. I do need to attend to my duties of being present and seen by the people. I am going to miss my family for half a day at most," I turned to him and asked as earnestly as possible, "This won't take all day, will it?"

"No, no, my Sire, I will make your day out as short as possible. I have an elite group for your outing today. It is a small team, but the country is safer than ever under your reign, and my team are well trained for the outing today."

"Are they enough that I might take my son with me?" I asked, hoping to not have overestimated my arrogant gullibility's role in convincing him.

Instead, he beamed at the idea. He thought for a mere few seconds before agreeing.

"Splendid, My Lord. Yes, yes, but I can bring more if you want reassurance, yet, to travel fast…" he trailed off, letting me finish the thought.

"No, then we will make this a wonderful day for my son. David will be thrilled. I have another idea, no, I have an order.

"Assemble all palace guards in the square and give me and my son a royal send-off. Full regalia." I acted again more a doting father than a ruler. I turned to my valet and began barking orders, hoping to emote a simpleness to my enthusiasm.

"Get my full military review uniform. Side arm and sword." I stomped about, trying for the enthusiasm of one in gleeful simple-mindedness. "The band shall play for my son, summon them." I marched about the room as if leading the imaginary marching band. "A banquet for the evening. Tell the Chief of Chefs that I want a banquet. And commission a PR event out of this. Pay the price of those who rob us for the media. I want my son made ready for this adventure…" and I stopped, seeming to become suddenly aware of Grigori standing there.

"Are my plans for my son's present being made ready?"

"No," Grigori said, "I merely wait for the remainder of your wishes to be known to me, and I will gladly make them occur."

"You need not stand here while I bathe and dress. You have interrupted once this morning, I have my own boundaries. You need not do more for me than express my governance, remember, I chose you for your ability to let me have this time with my family. I do not have a similarly fond place in my heart for you. My family is grateful to your holding the affairs in order but stay well a far from being perceived as inveigling into my sovereignty."

"Yes, yes, My Lord," he said almost peevishly. A dark glint in his eyes told me he knew there was a distrust in me, but I knew he vastly underestimated how I loathed him. And how, in these past few minutes, I had committed to kill him for his yet-to-occur act of treachery.

He turned and left.

As soon as the door shut, I spoke to the valet. "You will do none of those things I just told you. Here is what I want." I briefed him on the plan I had conceived just since awakening. "I want sturdy boots and stout clothes, as if I am going hunting. I want Kevlar under my clothes. I want a loaded side arm and my father's sword. I want you to leave here and order the guards outside this door to stand at attention and loudly challenge any and all who come to my door. Tell them my orders are to admit no one. Tell them they will escort me to the plaza major. Insinuate that this will be a great honor. Go now and do so without telling a soul the words I just spoke. General Mattakat is the only one you will trust. Go summon him."

He laid out the garb for me. He checked the arms and then stepped out the door. I heard him giving the orders to the guards as the door closed. I scratched at the suddenly itching scar on my cheek.

56 - Duplicity

Debbie came to the command central and told the sentries that King Leonard ordered that she must see General Mattakat and give him the King's directive. The sentries brought her into the inner offices, and one hurried off to summon the general, who arrived minutes later.

"My Lady, what is the urgency this morning?" he asked. He went to the counter to pour himself a cup of coffee.

"Axis, my husband bade me tell you nothing but the word 'Axis.'"

The general stiffened momentarily, turned slowly from the counter, the pot still pouring the hot liquid, but now onto the floor. "Axis?" he asked, "He gave the word, Axis?"

"Yes, he said say nothing else but that one word to you. Then he said for me to take our sons to the safe room and stay there and admit no one save for him or you."

The general merely dropped the pot to shatter on the floor. His boots crunched through the shards of glass and splattered the liquid puddle as he strode to the door. He gave terse orders to his lieutenants.

"Silent alert to all the alpha and bravo company soldiers. All will be in full battle gear. Armed, ready to move out on my command but to remain in the garrison. Complete operational silence. Not a single soldier is to breathe a word of the preparations. Other than my command, no one is to know we stand ready."

He thought for a few moments, then pointed at several of his men. "You, you, you. Each bring five of your best. Armed and able to move fast. Come with me."

The small squad was assembled. Light, silenced weapons were passed out and checked. Bolts clicked and magazines were slammed home. In minutes, a hard hitting and fast-moving force was assembled.

The general spoke, "The King has given me the alert that he fears for his life, his family, and his reign. I do not yet know who his enemy is, so at this point anyone not in this group potentially *is* that danger. You are authorized the use of deadly force at this point until I personally tell you to stand down. There is no exception, to any extent, to any person or group of persons who impede these orders. Enforce this to the utmost, including to terminate any that are deemed a threat, without hesitation. We escort the lady to her son's chambers, collect the boys and move to the west wing via the third-floor hall. The lady will always be protected. You gave an oath and now is the time to pay for your words, possibly with your life. Form up and move out."

The advance guards slipped out the door and secured the hall. The main body exited and moved through the empty halls with deadly efficiency. The few early morning servants ducked back into the doors and rooms from which they exited when they saw the grim faces, the raised weapons of the party that rapidly passed through the halls.

The squad came up to the floor reserved for the royal family. They were immediately challenged by the palace guards at the entrance.

The palace guards were hand-picked by the Grand Advisor, the general knew, and also knew their loyalty was to the Advisor, and not in his chain of command.

"Halt, what is your business here?" a gaudy uniformed one spoke while stepping in to bar their path. "General Mattakat, you have no authority in this residence." His tone was snide and demeaning.

The Queen stepped through the phalanx of soldiers and spoke, "I am coming to see my son." The moment the guard turned toward her, the first of the general's squad kicked him square in the chest, and soft sounds of silenced rounds were heard. The guard fell dead, bleeding from several shots to center mass. The remaining palace guards tried to bring their weapons up, but the element of surprise was against them. They all joined the first on the stone floor.

"Secure the stairs," the general ordered. "No one passes."

They swept into the chambers, barred the door, and took up positions. The child's sitter screamed at the intrusion. Weapons were pointed at her, but the Queen intervened by stepping in front of the old woman.

"No, she is trusted."

The general kept all but two of his men in the chambers. The royal family with the nurse maid were moved to the interior of the chambers, to a special area, specifically designed to be near impossible to breach.

General Mattakat and his two men came to the Royal's chambers. They were loudly challenged, both verbally and with weapons drawn. There was no element of surprise. The King opened the door from within. The general nodded that he had accomplished his mission. Leonard spoke to his palace guards.

"Admit the general. The rest remain here, at my door. Do not leave this post. You will escort me to the parade."

The door shut behind them and Leonard motioned for the general to follow him out to the terrace.

Leonard turned and asked one question, "My family?"

"Safe. Secure. A full squad of my men, armed to the teeth, Sire. And the safe room is well stocked. They are safe, at this time."

"I thank you again, Victor," I said, addressing him as an equal, a friend and well-loved brother.

"The Axis, Sire, what axis tilts away from your will in the world of the Sovereignty?"

"I am going to sound insane when I am able to tell you the reasons, I will ask what you must do. *Must*," I emphasized the fierceness of that single word. "I am going to tell you that there is a treasonous one and today there is a plan to murder me on the outing. None of your men escort me today, do they?"

"No, the escorts are all handpicked of the Loyal House Guards. Handpicked by Grigori, They…" The general's voice tapered off as he realized the threat.

The General strode to the door while bellowing, "Guards," and then in a soft voice sounding committedly deadly, he muttered, "I will arrest them all. I will…"

The door opened and a palace guard put their head in, "Sir," he said while maintaining a secure stance behind the door and probing the area for any threat. There was a commotion of the general's men and the remaining palace guards behind the entrance.

"STOP," I spoke loudly, firmly, and stood expectantly until all the talking silenced and the postures became attentive.

"You, my palace guard, will escort me, you, I grant the honor of preceding me into the square, clearing the halls and doorways of anyone. In the square, I want you to take me directly to the dais. I am not going to mingle and be known as a peer. Today, I rule.

"You will loudly and grandly announce me once we step out of that door. I want all in the vicinity to hear you laud me."

I squarely faced the general.

"General," I was staring into his eyes. He could see the fury in mine, and I could tell by his. "Your men will be rear guard. The palace guard has more regal bearing and I want the pomp and ceremony that they bring."

"Guards," I ordered, not looking away from the intense eyes of the general but trying to be enthusiastically grand about my personae. The general saw through it the instant I winked the eye turned away from the door. "Return to your post," I ordered the soldiers and guards.

The general cautiously eyed me and nodded slowly and cautiously to the soldiers.

The door barely closed, and he hissed, "What the fuck?" with not a hint of decorum.

"I must talk," I said, holding up a finger to silence him.

"Support me. I am about to sentence and execute the Grand Advisor. I have discovered a treason he is about to commit. I do not trust any of his guards. I must find out who he plans to escort me on this day's outing. At his urging, I have accepted plans for an open motorcade. I will be attacked and pronounced dead, my son killed, and Grigori will assume control as the guardian of the throne. He aims to usurp the state today, and if I do sentence him to immediate death, without knowing who else plots and is loyal to him enough to murder me, then I merely drive the snakes into hiding. And they will emerge again, perhaps threaten my son's reign, so today, I will cut the head off this snake, you will stand by while I do this. You will order your men to disarm the guard, with extreme conviction and if I ask, immediately carry out the sentence of death to anyone I shall so adjudicate. Do you give your word, to trust the explanation I promise to give after we have carried out this reckoning? You must go in advance, surround the square and fill every balcony with your men. Armed. Prepared to defend the crown today, with their lives. I think it will not come to that, but it is a day to deal out death. Generous doses may to spill to both sides if we do not act as if we are unaware of the treachery. I want your men ready to act. I can trust them to have my back, yes?"

"Assuredly."

"I am assured by you, my friend. Thank you," I said, grasping his forearm and clapping it tightly with my other hand. I pulled him hard to me, shoulder to shoulder and said, "Today we spill blood, again."

He pounded his fist into my back twice. His conviction was not in question. I could sense in him the urge to kill, as a warrior approached a battle, or as a judge about to pronounce the death sentence on a despicable one.

"Go now. Make these plans ready."

"Yes, sir," he said.

He flung the door open, and brusquely shoved the palace guard aside, physically opining to his men. They got the message. The general gave brief, terse orders, pointedly ignoring the palace guard, addressing his men.

"You are the rear guard. You are armed and ready at all times, and have full discretion of the use of force, to include deadly force. Am I clear?"

Two 'yes, sir's followed him as he turned away, with obvious disdain for the gaudy palace guard.

The General ignored the palace guard that had come to attention and walked away down the hall.

I opened the door and stepped out.

The general's men immediately went into threat awareness posture, firearms raised and safeties off.

The palace guard became stiff and formal. Useless grandiosity in conflict, but the flourish of their entrance would establish legitimacy to what I planned to do.

"Announce me," I ordered. "Take me to the square."

They looked up and down the empty stone halls, puzzled.

"Sire," said one, trying to maintain the rigid posture and still speak to me. "The Grand Advisor gave us orders we were to time your entrance to the honors he has prepared. I do not know if the ceremony is yet in place to receive you."

"I will leave now. You are ordered. Question me again and you will be relieved of this post and this duty. Do you understand?"

"Yes, sir," he said.

"I want the world to know I approach!" I shouted at them.

Their voices thundered out anthems of my greatness, voiced my title like a trumpet blare.

I moved down the hall at a brisk pace. They hurriedly pressed ahead, using most of their breath to laud me. They would tire quickly.

I let them get a few paces ahead, oblivious to all but their officiousness and, while still walking, turned to the general's men. I gave a snarl, my eyes in the direction of the palace guards and drew my hand across my throat with the slightest furtive gesture. They nodded. I knew those men would obey. Those guards were already sentenced. These men would carry it out.

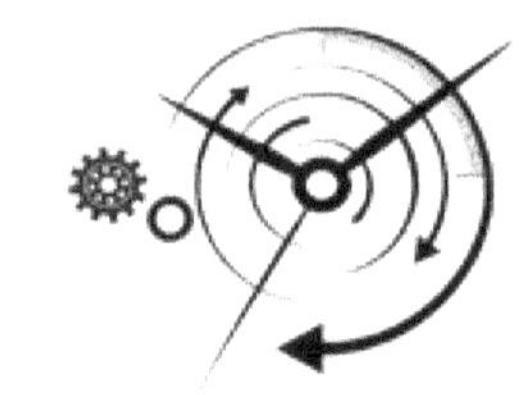

57 - My Curse

I entered the courtyard that was swarming with flags, pennants, common folk, and a formation of palace guards in splendid uniforms. The weapons they bore were likewise gleaming and ceremonial, but still lethal.

The two palace guards escorting me were working to breathe. Gasping bellows that tried hard to be the awe-inspiring announcement of my presence. We climbed the stairs to the dais. I told the two palace guards, "You are to continue on duty. You will not let anyone onto this dais except General Mattakat, his men or my family. No one!"

One looked troubled and said, "Um, ah, your pardon Sire?" The inflection raised the end of last word and hung in the air.

I turned to him, and he asked, "The Grand Advisor, Grigori, sir, shall he pass?"

"Of course, of course," I said.

The guard seemed to regard me anew, a sneaking suspicion was about to form. I asked, "Have you served in any command situation?"

The odd question threw the slight worry to the side. "I have, my liege. I—"

I cut him off. "You are now in command of this perimeter on this stage. Tell them."

"Also, I want the Adjutant officer in charge at this moment." An officer stepped forward. Saluted and presented himself.

"Major General, you know we are going on a motorcade tour to the towns. I want you to put all the guards that will be on this detail today, to be in the first two ranks. I want the lieutenants of those squads to be front and center, ahead of their men. Here is what I plan, Grigori is going to get a surprise presentation from me. I am personally administering this honor—*but I thought the honor would be mine, not his* . Make this happen, rearrange the formation."

He leapt off the stage, which I found impressive for his advanced age. There was a general grumble as the men rearranged themselves. The palace guards were still not formed when Grigori was announced with a boom of some light explosive. He was escorted up the stairs of the stage. He held his men there and came up the stairs alone. He paused at the top, before he set foot on the stage. He frowned; his order was not right. The King was already on the edge by the crowd. Grigori looked about. There was no Prince with the King. There were two military men standing at attention, but no others. He judged it not a threat, but the anomalies still bothered him.

"Sire," Grigori said, bowing, all the while still sweeping his eyes about the tableau that was unfolding unexpectedly. "King, your son is not yet ready, are the servants slow in attending to your wishes? I shall go check on your son's detail. There will be hell to pay."

"No, No, NO," I said. "My son will be along. Come, I have a special honor for you and your men, especially those that will be my guard today. Adjutant, give the order to those to step forward."

The officer of the palace guard looked at a loss on how to proceed. Between the glare of Grigori, and the steely tone of the King, he struggled. Grigori solved it for him. Through clenched teeth he said, "Give the order, King Leonard has spoken."

The guards for today's excursion were now in rows, in front of the review stand. There was that unease of a highly established ritual tainted by a novel variant in the scenario being discovered while in the midst of that situation. In that silence, a background noise emerged that was the tramp of heavy boots striding in unison. The squad of Alpha escorted the general to the same stage. The palace guard made way after the first few were shoved off the walkway unceremoniously. The well-trained and seasoned soldiers' marching tread shook the stairs as the unit ascended.

They parted at the top and fanned out. General Mattakat emerged from the phalanx, paid the briefest homage to the Advisor, then went to the King.

"General Mattakat! What a wonderful surprise, you made it to see us off today."

"I wasn't invited," he stared into Grigori's eyes, which seemed to be black with hate for a moment.

"A mere graciousness extended to you, General," said Grigori. "I thought that you would relish a day off duty. After all, the land is the most peaceful it has been in decades. Your men and you deserve the day off."

"And you are sure you wouldn't take an extra squad? After all, we are here now."

I saw the general was enjoying this little charade that cloaked the antagonism to his foe, and I worried he would carry the act too far, stretch plausibility too thin and spoil my justice.

I interrupted the general's guilty pleasure of antagonizing Grigori. "I, too, think the General and his men should be granted a well-earned day off." I turned to the crowd, paused, lifted my arms, and bowed my head. When I felt all eyes on me, I raised my face to the assembled masses and said, "Today is a day you witness a great honor. I am going to make a proclamation in the role as the Titular Head of State, the Sovereign for this body public, which I do serve, ALL OF YOU." I swept my hand grandly above the crowd and they loved it. "I will exercise the power of the state vested in me, and I will have you General, be a witness and a signatory to the proclamation I will make real today."

I turned to the crowd. The raucous noise of thousands of conversations gradually stilled while I waited. The palace guard had finally settled ranks and were at stiff attention. Pennants flapping in the breeze and the occasional child's voice were soon the only background noise. All eyes were on me. I held up my arms wide, in a gesture that took in the whole tableau of the citizens, the guards, the courtyard with its stacked terraces which lead back into the palace and then I turned to the assemblage on the stage with me.

"People, I am the one humbled here today. This office I hold is at the will of the people of this land. You are the folk that hold title to this land.

I am honored to govern. I take this responsibility seriously, as seriously as my father and his father before him, and the ones that begat him. Their blood flows down through the years to me. As does the onus to rule justly and provide the laws and governance that make this land free and great. I feel I have allowed that heavy burden to slip off my shoulders lately, and I have stepped back into the ease of being a husband and father without the worries of being head of state. I have left that burden with Grigori. I have left my people unattended while Grand Advisor Grigori has taken much, if not most of the duties and obligations I have as King. He has undertaken much in my name, and today, I will reward him for all he has done, and that which he yet intends to do. General Mattakat, escort Grand Advisor Grigori to join me here in front of the people of this land."

Grigori's eyes were puzzled, worried, angry, and haughtily expectant of an honor all at the same time. Emotions chased themselves across his features as he approached me. He stared at me, trying to divine the tack this situation was taking. I saw the dark light in his eyes and the naked ambition as he approached, with the general, armed, at his side. I pulled the sword of my father and held it casually displayed to him, and all on the stage and spoke. "Grigori, this weapon has been held by three kings before me, all with the same blood. This sword has been the scepter that has represented the will of the people for generations. This sword will once again exercise the will of the sovereign today. Today, in full audience of the people of this land, with full notice to the royals of this court and that the might of the military will know this is my edict, this sword again proclaims my will. Grigori, kneel before the people of the land."

He stood for many long moments, staring at me. His face was carefully composed but his eyes gave him away. Those dark eyes darted to the men of the palace guard I had moved to the front. He saw that it was both an honored position and placed all of his accomplices in direct supervision of the Alpha squad of soldiers standing at attention above them on the dais. The confusion as to how the situation was evolving and the vexation at the loss of control of today's events were evident in his stiff posture and icy composure. I could see he began to suspect this turn of events was not favorable to his machinations. Still, after studying my carefully neutral expression as I tried hard to emote a regal benevolence, he acquiesced. He knelt before me. He did not bow his head but challenged me with his stare. Dark, cold eyes that dared me. Eyes that were dead and empty of goodness, eyes that held only naked ambition.

I put the point of my sword to his throat. The realization came to his eyes in that moment. The veil fell from his countenance as he felt the tip bite his skin.

"General," I said. "Take command."

The general whistled and every terrace and all space around the immense courtyard was flooded with armed soldiers, weapons drawn, loaded, and held at ready. People in the courtyard screamed and there was an uproar of movement and loss of discipline in the ranks of the guard. The palace guard on the dais were momentarily stunned, but they were already covered by the weapons of the general's escort. Those at the bottom of the stairs started forward but halted as they faced up the stairs into weapons aimed down at them.

"Disarm the palace guard," ordered the general, prodding the adjutant officer with his rifle barrel.

The palace guard officer gave the order, and the assembled ranks of the guard carefully laid the ceremonial weapons on the paving stones of the courtyard.

"Grigori," I said, "the honor of this proclamation today goes to me. It goes to my father and his father's fathers. The honor goes to my son, who will ascend to rule, from whom you would steal his reign." I punctuated my words with the tip of the sword. He fell back slightly, away from the point, realizing how much of his duplicity had become revealed.

"I proclaim today that a treason has been averted, a traitor will be executed, and a son will be saved to ascend the throne and rightly continue to rule. You are hereby sentenced for the attempted murder of the king today."

"But I have done nothing other than provide you with respite from the duties of the state. What crime do I stand accused of?"

"I was to be murdered today. You would kill my son and you would take my kingdom. You have arranged a coup today that will not happen."

"I have done nothing other than arrange an outing. You accuse me of something which has not yet, nor ever would have happened except in your mind."

"General Mattakat," Grigori turned, unmindful of the blade which now drew a thin line of blood across his throat to his ear. "General, I submit that this is evidence of the King not being in his right mind. He fabricates enemies where there are none and as much as any madman would, threatens my life instead of a judicial process that would be required by law to allow me to prove my innocence. General, your obligation is clear here, you are the next in command to assume authority in the moment of the sovereign being incapacitated and myself under duress. End this and take this to the court of law."

"Yes, you are correct in the order of ascension for the rule of this land in those circumstances. I shall act. Are these men loyal to you?" he asked, indicating the escort that was tasked with today's security detail.

"Yes, hand-picked by me. Loyal? Why, of course, they would give their lives to carry out any order I gave."

The general assumed a pensive look. I saw that he continued the charade. I began to enjoy his enjoyment. I found a moment to cherish, watching a friend act with intent on loyalty. I caught his eye and nodded my head, deeply, as was my gratitude for his trust. He turned back to his soldiers guarding the palace guard that was to escort me today. "Kill them," he ordered. Weapons cracked out and the palace guards that would have escorted me fell.

Grigori cried out, "Nooooo." His anguish an assault on our souls like hatred. As if a personal hatred for every individual was revealed in all its truth.

The fallen guards gave off a noxious odor, and dark smokey wraiths that were torn apart and dispersed by the breeze which suddenly sprang up. There was a painful cacophony of high-pitched screams lost on the air of the bright sunny day. The remainder of the guard and the assembled people shrank back.

Grigori started to laugh. An evil, deprecating laugh, scornful of the danger that the moment still held for him. The general clubbed him across the head with the butt of his weapon, but aside from falling forward, it made little impact on the crazed response from the advisor.

The revulsion of seeing a tick, long undiscovered, and now gorged with one's own blood washed over me a million million times in a few seconds. I stood and fought for dispassionate self-control. But it was not to assume or remain as a neutral thought but was a vengeful urge to carry out the sentence I had imposed. But there was still a vindictive curiosity yet to be satisfied.

"Fiend, Traitor, tell me your real name so I can at least enter it into history that today was the day that word of your death was announced. Share your foul name."

"I have many names, stupid king. I would spend too much of your simple, short life just to tell you the ones by which I have been most often summoned."

The general clubbed Grigori again at the insult. The crunch of bone and torn scalp were evidence now to the general's ferocity. We both enjoyed the moment.

Blood dripped down the lank hair which hung over his face. It made a dark stain on the marble floor. Grigori raised his head and with his bloody hair across his eyes and face, he began to speak.

"I am known more by what I do, than by what title I have claimed and what meaningless name I have stolen."

"Answer King Leonard," the general thumped Grigori between the shoulder blades. He fell prone. My father's father's sword followed Grigori to the ground. Grigori still chuckled but gurgled and faltered with the ability to make speech. Grigori seemed to age and wither as he madly laughed. He rose to a kneeling posture, threw his hair back, wildly spraying blood and sweat and body odor.

"I am Grigori, and yet not. I have been known as many, but Saind is as close as you get to me. I am sure you will be cursed for knowing this name. So, we will see each other again. You and your son…"

Before he could utter another word, especially before the name of my beautiful son came from his foul mouth, I swung the sword through his neck. His head fell to the dais. Still laughing, but silently now. His body convulsed, and then some life force gathered itself to its abdomen then belched a great cloud of dark evil: stolen souls, deliberate pain and an intense hatred for those incarnate. Even the innocent. Such as we are. The evil spirit, now known as Saind, rose into the air and coalesced into a demon shape, but just the bust of head, shoulders, and arms. The wind suddenly whipped, and the sun seemed a thousand times brighter. The huge demon shape shielded itself from the blazing pure light, as the cold, clean wind out of the north shredded its form. An arm reached through from whatever side the demon was being pulled into. The arm made a finger extend, pointed at my son.

"General," I screamed, pointing at the evil approaching my son.

The general blew a whistle, all soldiers turned, saw the general point. The general said, "Defend the Prince. Intercept that demon."

The soldiers threw themselves around the prince. One snatched the lad from the arms of the old nurse maid. Weapons fired at the apparition, with little effect, but the bright sun and the wind did more damage, and finally it extinguished to a dark puff of evil spirit that sank into the fallen nurse maid, who appeared to have broken her skull when she fell after being shoved aside.

I ran to the soldiers, and the general was right behind me, barking orders. I waded through the men assembling an area of protection. I stood next to the dead nurse maid and hugged my son. I told him how much I loved him and how afraid I felt only to think about him not in my life. The emotions wanted to burst out of my chest, the fierceness enveloped me. I bellowed incomprehensible words that could only be made up to express the depth and height of that experience of loving someone so well and being close to losing them.

The general turned to me, and a horrified look crossed his features as we exchanged eye contact. I spun to look over my shoulder as the general lunged. The horrid form of the trampled maid with the broken skull had reanimated. It tottered up behind me as I turned away and crouched over my son to protect him. As I moved to shield him, the general's sword sliced her in two. The half of the now possessed nursemaid with the arm stabbed my son in the heart. He died as I shielded him. He died in my arms, his blood pouring on me. His eyes looked far away, and then he was gone. In that inkling, he was gone.

I fell to my knees, the anguish pouring out as the love I had mere moments ago. I sobbed his name, "David, David, David." I cried out, I cursed the creature, "Demon, Saind, hateful, vile, evil one. I will not rest until I have killed you. I will not forget your name, your name shall be taken out of history, and I will be the one to say it the last time anyone ever will. I will say it as I kill you. I will follow you into eternity to take your life if I must." I began to both sob and scream at the same time, "I WILL NEVER REST UNTIL YOU DIE AT MY HAND!"

I cried and screamed and fell across my blood-covered child. I hurt so terribly that my heart exploded in my chest. I screamed so hard my mind grew blank and formless except for the gray sorrow. The world spun. The lightening stroke flashed inside my head. I fell, aware of being infinitely tiny in an unfathomable universe. I lost all sense of where and when I was. The only salient point of my being was the grief and fierce violence within. I knew I would never have rest. I fell into a coma for my body, and amnesia for my brain. But it was only because my soul had escaped the trappings of the body. I felt the scalding pain of hate, and at the same time, the life-ending cold of my death. I fell into the miasma, the vortex of all the terrible emotions, focused only on following the murderous fiend, even to hell. I swore with what was left of my heart, my consciousness, and my soul, that I would follow that demon to hell if that was necessary. I said curses that ripped me free of that lifetime. I now existed only as a sentient purpose to exact revenge. I fell, hateful, into the time stream, again.